MOONRISING

MOONRISING

A NOVEL

CLAIRE BARNER

DIVERSION
BOOKS

Diversion Books
A division of Diversion Publishing Corp.
www.diversionbooks.com

Copyright © 2025 by Claire Barner

All rights reserved, including the right to reproduce this book
or portions thereof in any form whatsoever. No part of this
publication may be reproduced or transmitted in any form or by
any means, electronic or mechanical, including photocopying,
recording, or any other information storage and retrieval,
without the written permission of the publisher.

Diversion Books and colophon are registered trademarks
of Diversion Publishing Corp.

For more information, email info@diversionbooks.com

First Diversion Books Edition: July 2025
Trade Paperback ISBN: 979-8-89515-036-8
e-ISBN: 979-8-89515-035-1

Design by Neuwirth & Associates, Inc.
Cover design by Michel Vrana

Printed in the United States of America
1 3 5 7 9 10 8 6 4 2

Diversion books are available at special discounts for bulk purchases
in the US by corporations, institutions, and other organizations.

For more information, please contact admin@diversionbooks.com

The publisher does not have any control over and does not assume any
responsibility for author or third-party websites or their content.

To my parents, Craig and Debby.
Thank you for encouraging me to shoot for the stars.

MOONRISING

1

ALEX

DR. ALEX COLE'S STRATEGY FOR HANDLING A MOB OF ANGRY protestors was simple: don't stop for any reason, avoid getting sucked into arguments, and never look anyone in the eye.

The compact autocab rocked alarmingly from side to side as it crawled forward through the shouting crowd, but Alex kept her eyes trained straight ahead. She should have stretched her budget and hired a human driver instead of renting a cheap self-driving car barely large enough for her and her luggage—at least then she wouldn't be alone in here with only the slimmest protection between her and the angry mass. Then again, she was used to being alone.

Muffled chanting penetrated the glass. "Hey, hey, ho, ho, mutant food has got to go!"

How original, Alex thought. You'd think that after five years, the environmental extremists that harassed her every move would mix it up. Ahead, she could see the automatic glass doors of her destination. She calculated the distance. Only twenty feet, perhaps.

She could do this.

Gripping her bag, Alex took one deep, fortifying breath and opened the autocab door.

"Grandma killer!" a woman screamed in her face.

"Excuse me," Alex said through gritted teeth, stepping past her and wiping spittle from her cheek. *Ew.*

"Mutant food is an abomination," a looming man shouted at her side, wielding a sign that looked heavy enough to crack her skull. The small crowd cheered. *Don't engage*, Alex reminded herself. She kept her eyes on the doorway.

A young man stepped directly in front of her, close enough for Alex to smell his stale breath. "You should be ashamed! How can you live with yourself?"

"I am ashamed of nothing," Alex snapped. "Let me pass." The man's fists clenched at his sides. Alex looked him straight in the eyes, breaking her third rule, and leaned forward, the pulse jumping in her throat. "Let. Me. Pass."

Averting his gaze, the man stepped aside, leaving Alex with a straight path to the main doors of the NKI Company's headquarters. Sweat prickled under her arms. She half-expected someone to follow her, but no, the doors slid open to admit her and abruptly cut off the yells and jeers of the protesters.

In the silence, Alex lifted her chin and walked briskly through the marble lobby, her shoes echoing in the large open space. "What the hell was that about?" she demanded at the security desk.

The bored security guard looked up in surprise. "Excuse me, ma'am?"

"You knew I was coming. Why wasn't security waiting outside to escort me? Why the hell would you allow the Eco Liberation Society on NKI's property?"

"Mr. Hill believes in the importance of peaceful protest in a civil society, ma'am," the guard said blandly. He handed her a badge. "The Board is expecting you, Dr. Cole. Fourth floor, on the right."

MOONRISING

Alex took the badge with a clenched jaw.

As she waited for the elevator, Alex checked her appearance in the mirrored doors. Two spots of color splashed brightly on her pale face, but at least the encounter hadn't disarranged her close-cropped brown hair. She smoothed down her suit jacket and gave her reflection a nod of encouragement.

She could do this.

Stepping into the elevator, Alex glanced up at the live feed. News items scrolled across the screen.

WINTER STORMS CUT POWER FOR MILLIONS IN SOUTHWEST

BILLIE EILISH ANNOUNCES RETIREMENT TOUR

UNITED ARAB EMIRATES INVESTS 1 BIL IN MOON COLONY

The last item jolted her out of her fury. News from the colony always made her stomach flip. She couldn't remember the last time she had spoken to her father. The elevator chimed, and she stepped into the C-suite offices of NKI.

With a Board meeting in session, the floor was hushed, empty except for a smartly dressed receptionist who didn't look up from her tablet at Alex's entrance. Alex perched on a dark leather chair to wait. Her wool jacket grew increasingly hot and sweat trickled down her face. She hoped it wasn't smearing her makeup. Why did the Board make her get dressed up and fly out here every year just to inform her they were renewing her funding?

Finally, the receptionist lifted her gaze. "The Board will see you now."

Alex straightened her suit jacket and stepped into the boardroom. In the dark paneled room, a dozen people sat around an expansive table, their faces cast in gray light from the large windows overlooking the wintry, landscaped grounds.

"Dr. Cole, thank you for flying in from Chicago," Board President Thomas Hill said, rising to greet Alex.

3

As Hill shook her hand, Alex looked around for her only ally in the sea of bland, corporate smiles, but Victor Beard was not among those seated around the table. Her heart sank a little. *First the mob, and now this.* She had never faced NKI's Board of Directors without him.

"Dr. Cole," Hill said, returning to his seat at the head of the table. "NKI has provided funding for the Institute for Sustainable Agriculture for the last three years."

"I am grateful for NKI's support." Alex took the only empty seat at the foot of the long table. "We have made significant strides in the development of mutagenetic food with your investment."

"You are aware, of course, that mutagenetic food is prohibited from conventional grocery stores by the FDA?"

"As the foremost expert in my field, I am aware of that fact, yes," Alex replied evenly. Every year, they went through this little power play. The price for another year of funding.

Hill's lips thinned. "And that the grocery co-ops where farmers are permitted to sell mutagenic produce are frequently cited for local code violations?"

"Those are trumped-up violations." Alex was unable to keep an edge from creeping into her voice. "Local politicians are being pressured by fear and ignorance."

"Nevertheless." Hill spread his hands.

Alex leaned forward on the table, hands clasped, trying to appear calm and in control. "Mutagenetic produce sold at a co-op costs five times less than organic produce," she said patiently. "It has a higher nutrient density. Without co-ops, over 70 percent of Americans couldn't afford to introduce fresh fruits and vegetables into their weekly diet."

Hill shrugged. "We have tried, Dr. Cole, but the political environment and public opinion are against mutagenetic food. Today, we witnessed protesters gathered outside this very building. The NKI Company can no longer sponsor the Institute."

Alex thought she had prepared herself for this possibility, but Hill's words hit her like a blow to her chest. As he continued, she tried to listen through the roaring in her ears.

"We will fund you through the end of February to allow you a chance to seek alternative sources of revenue. You may wish to consider if the University of Chicago is interested in a direct investment in the lab. The details of the wind-down are all here." He slid a yellow envelope toward her. Without looking in her direction, several Board members helped the envelope travel down the long table.

When it reached her, Alex took the envelope numbly. The university paid her salary, but the facility, equipment, and staff were all funded by grants, a full 80 percent from NKI. The University of Chicago enjoyed having a lightning rod young scientist on their staff, but they did not have a strategic interest in investing in mutagenetic food. She would need to look elsewhere for funding.

Alex looked around at the circle of cold faces. *Where the hell is Victor?*

"You're making a mistake," she said with rising desperation. "The way we're living—it's unsustainable. Already the life expectancy gap between the wealthy and the poor is approaching twenty years. Without access to fresh food, the gap is widening." The Board members' faces were like stone, not even a flicker of life. They knew the situation was worsening. Did maximizing shareholder profits really matter more than saving the country from disaster?

"Dr. Cole—" Hill began, but Alex cut him off.

"The United States must adapt to the realities of climate change," she snapped, her voice breaking. "Mutagenetic food can feed our country and make us healthier. It can—it can conserve our water. And our land. Please. These are the facts. You can't let the mindless prejudice against it control your decisions."

Silence greeted her. The woman to her left checked a message on her intelliwatch.

"Thank you, Dr. Cole," Hill said, rising from his seat. "Your passion for your work is appreciated, but we have already voted on this motion. Our decision is final. We wish you a safe flight home." He extended his hand for a final shake.

Alex swallowed her rage, grabbed the yellow envelope, and headed to the door, ignoring the proffered hand. She was done playing by their bullshit corporate rules. In the hallway, she attempted to stop her hands from shaking. She glanced back at the closed door. Should she run back in? Try, one last time, to persuade them? These were facts. This was science. If she could just go over the numbers with them again—

From the waiting area, she heard the receptionist's voice rise. "Mr. Beard. We weren't expecting you today."

Alex marched back to the receptionist's desk. There, disheveled and out of breath, stood Victor Beard, her friend, benefactor, and pain in the ass.

Alex scowled at him and thrust the envelope with the wind-down timeline at his chest. "How could you have let me walk in there unprepared?"

"147 miles!" Victor exclaimed in response. His eyes were wide behind his glasses, and his blond hair stuck up in odd directions.

Alex resisted a powerful urge to shake him. "Victor, for once in your goddamn life, focus. NKI just cut off my funding."

"What?"

"You didn't know? What was the point of selling out to Big Ag? I thought your brilliant plan when you allowed your company to be acquired by NKI was to gain the influence to keep the Board on my side."

Victor glanced at the receptionist, who wasn't bothering to disguise her interest in their conversation. He grunted and gestured Alex into an unoccupied conference room. Shutting the door behind them, he said bluntly, "My plan failed. You were right about the agricultural industry. It's too risk-averse and too in bed with

MOONRISING

Washington to make the hard choices. I'm resigning from the Board at the end of the month."

Alex crossed her arms, feeling some of her anger drain out. "You are?"

"This isn't the first time they've voted on your funding." Victor perched his skinny frame on a conference room chair. "I've discovered to my chagrin that my influence over the Board has a direct relationship with the timing of my most recent media interview," he said rapidly. "It peaked when Future Tech called me the Architect of Tomorrow, resulting in a vote of twelve to four in favor of Institute funding. When I made the list of Jitter's Fifty Greatest Inventors of the Year, the vote was ten to five with one abstention. The variance—"

"I get it," Alex interrupted. She'd known Victor since her first year as a doctoral student at Cornell, and after six years of friendship, she knew how to deal with him.

Waving a hand in acknowledgment, Victor asked, "What time did they tell you to be here?"

"11 a.m." Alex indulged him with an answer, knowing Victor's non sequiturs always had a reason. "Time enough to catch a red eye and rent a self-driving autocab at JFK."

Victor glanced at his intelliwatch. "And they called you in around noon?"

Alex nodded.

"At 10:05 a.m., Hill's EA reached out to ask if I would still be attending today's Board meeting," said Victor. "Hill knew I was the keynote at the Philadelphia Charity Ball last night. He came to the logical conclusion that I would sleep in my own bed, 147 miles from NKI headquarters. And he kept today's Board meeting off my calendar. He timed everything to keep my voice out of the meeting until the resolution was passed." He scowled. "I don't like being manipulated."

7

"They wouldn't let you join remotely?" Alex asked skeptically.

"No, Hill is too paranoid for that. Board meetings are in-person only. No chance for synthetic impersonation."

Alex scrutinized Victor. He was wearing rumpled sweatpants and a hoodie, his glasses were smudged, and his hair was a mess. She wanted to stay angry at him, but the story made sense.

Except that Victor had never been outmaneuvered in all the years she had known him.

In the silence, Victor pulled a pad out of his pocket and scribbled down what looked like a physics diagram. Alex watched over his shoulder.

"What are you doing?"

"Trying to match the opposing velocities between thrust and exhaust," he said absently.

Alex thought about asking him what the hell that had to do with her current predicament, but realized she could not handle an esoteric Victor Beard lecture today.

"Fine," Alex said with a groan. She'd lost. That was that. "Well, here's what I'm going to do, then. I'm going to go home, spend the weekend overexercising, get very drunk, and make some questionable sexual choices."

Glancing up from his notes, Victor said, "Have a safe flight." A moment later he shook himself and gave her a sharp look. "You're not still seeing that graduate student, are you? The fringe environmental activist?"

"Navin isn't involved with the Eco Liberation Society anymore," Alex protested.

Victor put down his stylus. "Change your flight and come to Philly. I'll ask Harper to pick the perfect place for dinner. You know she's good at that sort of thing."

"Victor, your wife despises me. I'm not spending the whole weekend in her home."

MOONRISING

Shrugging, Victor said, "Do me one favor. Do not tell your graduate student about any of this. I don't trust him not to run directly to the ELS with the scoop."

"I do have some sense of self-preservation. I never tell Navin about my work." Alex sighed. She felt a headache starting to pound behind her eyes. "I didn't think it would end like this."

Victor grimaced. "I would make a personal investment if I could, but I'm working on a new project. All my capital is tied up."

"Another AgTech startup?" Alex asked.

"Something bigger. I can't talk about it, not yet. But I will do everything I can for you, Alex. Your work is important."

"If you wanted to do everything you could, you would have anticipated Hill's move. I thought half this Board were your allies." Yes, Victor had explained. Still, something was not adding up.

"I have to get into that meeting," Victor said, eyes shifting to the door. "I wish you solace with your weekend of debauchery."

On Monday morning, Alex's career was still on the brink of ruin, and a man who despised her life's work was snoring in her bed.

At 1 a.m., Navin had smelled intoxicating and exciting, and they had been arguing long enough for Alex to kiss him to shut him up. At 6 a.m., he smelled like a bad decision. One she kept making. Alex pressed the heel of her hand against her pounding forehead and forced herself out of bed. The aroma of cigarettes, alcohol, and sweat followed her.

As Alex brushed her teeth, she caught a glimpse of her gaunt, pale face in the mirror. She fished out a seldom-used makeup brush from the back of her cabinet. She did not need her staff to see her looking so haggard.

Not today.

Navin had flipped onto his back when she returned to the bedroom. His eyes squinted open at the sound of the door. "Hey." He stretched and gave out a loud yawn. "Alright if I stay here a bit longer?"

"I don't mind," she lied. The last time he had stayed over she had come home to a rumpled bed, dirty dishes, and the toilet seat up.

He put a skinny arm behind his head and grinned at her. "That was fun. Last night."

An unwilling smile tugged at her lips. "Yeah, it was." That at least was not a lie. She had enjoyed forgetting about her problems for a night to debate *Nicomachean Ethics* at a seedy Hyde Park bar and have drunken sex on clean sheets. "I'll be late. Make sure to lock up this time."

She did not kiss him goodbye.

Alex grabbed a mason jar of prepared matcha from her collection in the fridge and let herself out. She walked down the hall to the elevator bank, gulping the cold tea in an attempt to fully wake up. Smothering a yawn, she tapped the concierge screen with her intelliwatch and typed in her parking spot code.

"Thank you, Dr. Cole," said a crisp automated voice. "Your vehicle will be ready in approximately two minutes. Enjoy your day."

By the time the elevator opened into the sleek lobby of her building, her self-driving car was waiting under the orange glow of the electric heat lamps, fully charged and already toasty warm.

"Take me to work," she said, and her SDC moved smoothly away from her building and into traffic. The commute to her laboratory was a quiet ride from 50th to 63rd along Lake Park Avenue. Alex used the time to scroll through her messages. Nothing was urgent, and she might actually get some real work done this morning. If she tried hard enough, she could avoid talking to her lab manager for a while. Hours, maybe.

In the parking lot, Alex stared up at the Institute for Sustainable Agriculture, ignoring her pounding head and the sharp biting

MOONRISING

air. Three years ago, she had used her seed funding to build the free-standing structure made of projectile-resistant glass at the edge of the University of Chicago's campus. The front housed a laboratory and several offices, keeping the bulk of the structure reserved for the five thousand-square-foot experimental greenhouse.

How could she lose this?

Alex shivered in the dangerously cold air, remembering abruptly that Chicago was on the third day of a polar vortex, and she was in danger of frostbite if she lingered any longer. Alex tapped her ID against the scanner and entered the twelve-digit passcode followed by the facial recognition scan. The doors to the Institute hissed open into a dark, quiet, and mercifully warm entryway.

Pulling the yellow envelope out of her bag, Alex placed it on her desk before heading to the lab. The lights switched on automatically. The lab was a windowless room, full of all manner of equipment: grow lights, beakers, Petri dishes, and microscopes. Alex washed her hands vigorously at the side sink and put on a lab coat. She located the one hundred bioengineered tomato seeds she had left soaking over the weekend and brought the container to her workspace.

Alex held a pair of tweezers with one hand and fished out a seed. She placed it on its side under a microscope, turning it flat. With her other hand, Alex made a shallow cut with a scalpel. Slowly, painstakingly, she peeled back the seed coat to expose the embryo. Picking up the embryo with her tweezers, she eased it into a gelatinous Petri dish, then closed the lid, taped it shut, and marked it with a code indicating the date and contents. Alex gave out a tiny sigh and did it all again. It was painstaking work. Despite her exhaustion, stress, and nasty hangover, Alex found it meditative. Her hands were steady as she moved through the familiar motions.

By the time she had finished, students and postdocs had filtered in, bringing with them a low hum of activity. Alex took her container of samples and walked them to an incubator. They would spend the next ten days in the dark at twenty-five degrees Celsius.

Ten days.

Where would her lab be in ten days?

Unable to put it off any longer, Alex caught the eye of her lab manager, Finn, and gestured for him to step out. It was quiet in her office once she shut the door, the sounds of the postdoc chatter and metallic clink of instruments gone. Alex went to her desk, opened the yellow envelope, and pulled out the one-page cover letter. "It's bad news," she said, handing it to Finn.

"Shit," Finn muttered after reading it over. "I thought Victor said we were good for it."

"Victor has decided to resign from the Board. He said he's giving up on Big Ag." Victor had always come through for her, and she had not thought to develop a decent backup plan.

Alex should have known better than to trust her life's work to one man. *I'm a fool.*

"Victor's hiding something," Alex told Finn. "I know it. He was way too cagey when I saw him."

Finn's lips twitched. "You're suspicious of everyone. Do you even like people?"

Alex gave him a look. "I've dedicated my life to feeding the world. What further proof do you want?"

"But is there anyone you actually trust?"

"I trust you."

Finn raised his eyebrows. "Glad to hear it. Anyone else?"

Alex shrugged. "My plants."

Finn chuckled. Then, he looked out the glass office wall toward the greenhouse, smile fading. "What happens now?"

Alex rubbed her face. "Lease some of the greenhouse rooms. See if I can get you and the others placements in another lab on campus. I'm sorry, Finn. I know I asked you to come here."

"Don't be an idiot," he said. "I'm not going anywhere."

MOONRISING

"I can't pay you. You know that."

"We'll figure it out. I could crash here in the lab for a while. All I need is my air mattress and rice cooker. I'll shower at the gym and do my laundry at your place. The night custodians love me. They'll look the other way in exchange for a box of produce."

"You're serious?"

"Of course, I'm serious, Alex. This has been the chance of a lifetime. I won't quit on you just because we've gotten into a bit of money trouble."

Alex felt tears prick her eyes. She blinked them away. Female scientists could not afford to cry. "We have a month and a half. Maybe one of the long-shot grants will come through."

"Sure." Finn gave her a tight-lipped smile. But she could tell he didn't believe it. Well, neither did she.

She left Finn in her office and stepped into the Semiarid Continental Greenhouse, breathing in the thick, warm air filled with the smell of vegetables and soil. The greenhouse was the only place in the world where she felt at home. She thought about what Victor had said in New York. He was working on something big. Something that had sucked up all his capital. It wasn't like Victor to have nothing liquid. She had always thought he would come through, one way or another, even if it was out of his own vast pockets.

One funder. One corporate champion. She should have tried harder to diversify her support. The stakes were too high for her to fail.

The air in the greenhouse was alive with growing things. She could smell the tomato plants overlaid with the spicy peppers. Stalks of water-thrifty maize sprouted on platforms ten feet above her head. Blight-resistant cucumbers covered the ceiling. It was so lovely. She gave one short, shuddering sob.

Impatiently, Alex wiped tears from her cheeks. She could see a broken butternut squash at her feet. Against one wall, twenty feet up, black rot–impervious squash grew from a bed of soil five feet deep. Several more squash looked precarious. Hard squash was proving resistant to her vertical gardening methods and could hardly be put on the co-op market if it had the potential to brain unsuspecting farmers. She only had six weeks to work out a solution. She needed to get to work.

An hour later, Alex was balanced on a lift twenty feet in the air, wrestling with a vegetable brace she had just gotten from her supplier when she heard the doors hiss open.

"Alex," Finn shouted up at her. "There's some admin here to see you."

Alex frowned, placing the brace carefully on the platform. "I didn't have an appointment today. Are they from the university?"

"No idea. He just said he was an admin."

Alex looked down to see a man entering the greenhouse door unescorted. She swore softly. They had security protocols in place for a reason, and no one was supposed to enter her workspace without permission. In her line of work, eco-terrorist sabotage was an ever-present risk. She clicked a button on the lift to return her to the ground.

Alex smoothed down her short hair and stepped off the lift, uncomfortably aware that she was sweaty and caked with dirt. The man in front of her was nondescript, in his fifties, and graying at the temples.

She knew him.

"Not *an* administrator, Finn," she said with wry humor. "*The* Administrator. Of NASA."

"Very good, Dr. Cole." The man put out his hand, and Alex took it automatically. "I wasn't sure you would remember me."

Then it hit her, why he was here. Alex felt like she was seeing everything from far away. She swallowed. "It's my father, isn't it?

MOONRISING

Is he—alright?" Visions of an accident swam through her mind. It was easy to imagine: a depressurized spacesuit, an unexpected comet, a close-quarters fire.

"Goodness, no! Your father is just fine. Forgive me for dropping by unannounced. The matter is of some urgency."

The world came back into focus. Alex sent Finn away with a tilt of her head and led Administrator Anderson to a nearby workstation. It was covered in crushed blackberries and remnants of fertilizer.

"You look like him, you know. Your father." The man removed a few berries from a metal stool and sat down. "If you don't mind me saying."

Now that she knew her father was okay, annoyance was taking over. He had no idea how much he had scared her. As she sat down across from him, she found herself hoping her unexpected guest would leave with berry stains on his suit. Still, she kept her tone professional.

"What can I do for you, Mr. Anderson? I am working against a deadline."

A permanent deadline.

He looked around the greenhouse and took his time answering. "You're wasted here, you know. One full-time lab manager and three postdoctoral researchers? You should be supervising a staff of hundreds."

Alex pursed her lips. Directing a lab at one of the country's most prestigious research institutions before the age of thirty was hardly a waste. "The university fully supports my work."

"Do they? My understanding is that you have lost your primary funding source."

Word was traveling fast. Alex crossed her arms. She was liking this man less and less. "What do you want, Mr. Anderson?"

"I'm here to offer you an opportunity." He slid a bound, thick document toward her. Alex took it gingerly; it had picked up a berry. She flicked it off. "We have encountered a situation at Peary Station."

Alex's stomach swooped.

"Our hydroponic greenhouse on the Moon colony is failing to thrive. We need a new approach."

Alex frowned. Hostility, she was used to. Anderson's air of professional courtesy had to be hiding something. What was this man really after? "Surely NASA employs an army of botanists, chemists, and biologists to deal with this sort of problem."

He indicated the bound document. "Research abstracts are included." Anderson leaned back in his chair. "To be frank, Dr. Cole, you weren't my first choice. I know how controversial your research is, and I'd just as soon not deal with the political fallout. However, you come highly recommended by someone with a great deal of influence over this project, and I've become convinced that you are the right person for the job."

Alex knew of only one person stationed in the colony. Her father only called on major holidays and her birthday. They usually talked about the weather, which wasn't even a proper conversation to have with someone who lived in a hermetically sealed environment. She was absurdly pleased with the thought that not only was he following her work, but he was recommending her to NASA.

"What are you asking me to do?" she asked, feeling herself relax just a little.

"We want to hire you to spearhead the initiative to develop self-sustaining food production at Peary Station. An offer letter is enclosed. We will provide you with a competitive salary, generous budget and resources, and private accommodations on the colony. Not to mention a chance to experience space travel."

Alex stared at him in shock. "My father trained for three years to become an astronaut and waited another eighteen months for his first assignment."

MOONRISING

"Times have changed. Space travel is as safe as air travel now, and considerably safer than travel by human-operated cars. Modern astronauts aren't expected to handle emergency scenarios or operate robotics. You'll experience microgravity for a twenty-four-hour period during transit, of course, but we will provide you with training to be successful in a weightless environment."

"How long is the training?" Alex found herself asking, even though she had no interest in going to the Moon. The thought had never even occurred to her.

"Two weeks in New Mexico."

"Two weeks," she repeated weakly.

"A pair of highly qualified and experienced pilots will transport you to the colony. Life there requires little training; it's not so different from life on any other isolated research station. Residents have private rooms. You'll need to adopt a daily weighted cardio regime to combat the effect of reduced gravity, but . . ." He shrugged, his lips curving up in a small smile. "Residents often report being in the best shape of their lives during their time on the colony. The main drawback, I'm told, is the lack of fresh food—a deficiency we're hoping you will remedy."

"How many people live in the colony?" Alex asked.

"Nearly a hundred, at the moment, and growing. Additional permanent housing is currently under construction, as well as a hotel that will initially host a dozen space tourists at a time."

Alex was fascinated in spite of herself. The living conditions weren't a turn-off at all—for a scientist engrossed in a challenging project, the lack of amenities and comfort would fade into background noise. But—she had a purpose here. A mission.

"I'm flattered to be under consideration, but I can't just uproot my life. We're doing essential research here." She meant it. She could not consider leaving. Especially now, when everything was in jeopardy.

17

"We agree." The Administrator leaned back and tented his fingers. "We plan to fully fund your laboratory."

Alex froze. Did he just say what she thought he said?

"I'm sorry," she said. "Could you . . . repeat that?"

"We'd put the Institute on retainer as a resource to you during your initial twelve-month on-site commitment to us, and for the next nine years. We would provide the operational funding for you to run the lab and retain your current employees, as well as a capital improvement grant to purchase new equipment related to agricultural research under lunar conditions."

A lifeline. He was offering her a lifeline.

"Effective when?" Her voice came out squeaky.

"As soon as you sign the contract."

Her heart pounded, hard. This was too good to be true. "I wasn't aware that NASA was in a position to make a ten-year financial commitment."

"This project is financed through a public-private partnership." There was that tiny smile again. "We're not operating within the typical constraints of a government agency."

Alex swallowed. She tried to think of a lab with ten years of guaranteed funding. In her experience, the very best grant cycles were five years with arduous RFP processes and stiff competition. How much influence did her father have over the NASA budgeting process? He was a military commander, not a bureaucrat.

"When would I leave?" she asked.

"A ship is scheduled to depart in thirty-one days. We'd like you to be on it." Anderson reached into his breast pocket, pulled out an electronic business card, and tapped her intelliwatch with it. "Here's my contact information. Read the reports and think it over. Give me a call by Friday."

Alex was in a haze as she watched the Administrator leave. Despite working for the University of Chicago for the past several years, she had never shaken the feeling that she was living on the edge. She knew, even if she tried not to admit it, that the university cared more about the shock value of her unpopular viewpoint than her research contributions. The administration certainly couldn't be relied upon to keep her lab afloat in the face of funding cuts. This offer was a chance for Finn and her postdocs to finish their experiments uninterrupted. They wouldn't have to stop providing seeds to Midwest farmers or fresh fruits and vegetables to South Side co-ops. Her heart lumped in her chest, and her hands were shaking. What agricultural techniques could she invent with ten years of guaranteed funding? What leaps could she take if she didn't have to spend so much time writing reports to on-the-fence investors, trying to convince them the food she grew was safe?

Absently, Alex pulled a crate from a corner of the greenhouse. She moved wide green leaves to the side and twisted off a dozen fully grown zucchini, nestling them into the box. At the rows of tomato plants, she located ripe San Marzanos and Brandywines. She topped the crate off with kale and collard greens.

"What was that about?" Finn asked as she left the greenhouse with the crate on her hip. "Was that really the head of NASA?"

"I'll tell you later," Alex said, not slowing down. She was still too amped up to process everything, much less share the news. "I need to clear my head. I'm going to make a run to the shelter."

Finn gave her an easygoing wave in response.

Alex would normally walk the four blocks south to the shelter, but the frigid weather would freeze the produce. In minutes, Alex's car pulled into the lot of the Woodlawn Center for Climate Refuge. The front of the building was usually teeming with children riding scooters and adults chatting. Today, it was quiet and still. The orange tents that dotted the shelter grounds were frosted with ice.

"Ms. Ciara," Alex said warmly when she entered the shelter's lobby. "How are you holding up in this weather?"

The shelter coordinator's typical effusive welcome was missing. "Dr. Cole," she said formally.

Alex winced. She had been down this road before and knew what was coming. "I brought a box of veggies."

Ciara made no move to take the crate. "I'm sorry, Dr. Cole. The ELS has been papering the place with flyers all week. My manager says we can't accept your food anymore." She gestured to a bright red paper tacked to the lobby bulletin board with the headline THE TRUTH ABOUT MUTANT FOOD.

Alex clenched her hand on the crate. "Okay. But . . . would you like anything? To take home for yourself?"

"No," Ciara said quickly. "I appreciate the offer, but I wouldn't want to impose."

Alex's throat constricted and, for one horrible moment, she was afraid she might cry. "You've been eating my food for the last two years. How can you believe these lies?"

Ciara opened the door, and a blast of cold air hit Alex in the face. "My manager said it would be best if you stopped coming by."

Alex managed to make it back to her car before hot, angry tears fell down her face. When she arrived back at the Institute a few minutes later, she wiped her face and carried the crate back inside the building and left it near the entrance. Without greeting her staff, Alex returned to sit at the greenhouse table. She picked up the bound document and began to read.

By the time she had gotten through the first set of materials, she had stopped thinking about her corporate funder or Ciara's rejection. After a few hours, she wandered out, grabbed a hemp bar and a notebook, and sat down at her desk. She shoved the yellow envelope to one side as she continued reading.

It was only when her colleagues started saying good night that she realized the entire day had passed. She looked down at her notebook. There was a list of supplies next to the scribbled note *Shipping constraints*, a diagram of a detailed parallel study for the colony and the Institute to perform in tandem, and a two-page to-do list with items like *Rent condo?* and *Set up mtg with dept*

MOONRISING

chair. Alex leaned back in her chair, feeling rather stunned. At some point that afternoon, she realized, she had made a decision. Alex messaged Navin on her intelliwatch: *Jimmy's at 8? I have something to tell you.*

"I don't get it. You're just leaving?" Navin's knee began shaking up and down under the table. Even in the dimly lit bar, she could see his jaw clenching. Despite being a Monday night with a wind chill projected to drop to −25 degrees Fahrenheit, the place was packed. They had snagged their favorite table by the window, close to the exit to accommodate Navin's smoking habit, which even a polar vortex could not deter. "What about your lab?" Navin continued. "Your research?"

There was another question, lying unspoken. *What about us?* Alex hoped he would not give voice to it.

She leaned forward with her elbows on the table. "Funding for *ten years*, Navin, can you imagine? No one gets funding for that long. This will save my lab. My *work.*"

She would not have thought that anything short of a pipe bomb could take her away from the Institute, but the promise of ten years of funding was too irresistible. She wondered again how such a thing was possible in the current atmosphere of tightening purse strings and skepticism toward mutagenetic food, and then pushed the question away. If NASA wanted to entice her with what she needed most, who cared how they came up with the money?

"What are you talking about?" He waved a hand dismissively. "Your lab isn't in trouble. The university loves you. You're famous."

She snorted. "I'm not famous." Navin had never understood the pressures she faced.

"You're the face of the mutant food movement," said Navin.

"Yeah—according to the Eco Liberation Society," said Alex, not bothering to keep the sarcasm from her tone. Famous among

21

terrorists wasn't exactly a plus in her book. "And it's not mutant food, Navin. Muta*genetic*. Please."

"All I'm saying is, Riley Emerson devoted a whole article to you in last month's 'zine. Did you read it?" He grinned. "She thinks you're going to start the next Potato Plague."

Maybe he thought he was being amusing, but Alex didn't find it funny. She pictured the red flyer on the shelter bulletin board and glared at him. "The ELS is run by ignorant, dangerous buffoons with too much money and influence at their disposal. I can't believe you're still reading their 'zine. And I can't believe you're still hanging out with that unhinged zealot Riley." Oh, she was definitely going to leave here with a headache. Why, oh, why did she think it was a good idea to keep sleeping with someone so fundamentally opposed to her career?

Navin crossed his arms. "Lay off, Alex. Riley's a good person. She's fighting for a better world—just like you! Right? She's a little intense, sure, but I like intense women." He waggled his eyebrows at her. "And I'm not going to apologize for caring about the environment."

Her adrenaline was up. It was always up when she and Navin started bickering. "No, but you should apologize for forgetting you're a scholar. Everything they publish is based on faulty studies and a poor understanding of how to interpret data. How many times do I have to spell out to you and Riley and all your ignorant friends that the Potato Plague was caused by a poorly run corporation that did not test its new potato variety for levels of toxic alkaloids before putting it on the market? That does *not* make all mutagenetic food toxic." She was out of breath by the time she spewed all that out. And frustrated with herself for even bothering. Why was she wasting her energy? They had repeated this argument too many times. Alex took a sip of beer before she got any angrier. She couldn't wait to leave behind the ugly business of American agricultural politics for an entire year.

MOONRISING

Navin dug in his pocket for his tin of loose tobacco. Putting it on the table, he said, "I don't want to fight. Not tonight."

"No," she said in a low voice. "I don't either." She was so tired of fighting. With Navin. With the American public. For funding. For respect. What would it be like to not have to struggle to protect her lab's right to exist?

He refilled her glass from the pitcher on the table; it was a peace offering. "Do they have beer in space?"

"I have no idea." She took a gulp and winced. "If they do, I hope the quality is better than the crap you insist on buying."

"This stuff is great. Stop being an elitist." Navin opened his tin and pulled out tobacco paper.

"Says the philosophy graduate student at this rarified institution," Alex shot back.

Navin pressed a fist against his heart as if driving in an invisible dagger. "Touché." He tipped loose tobacco into the thin paper and lined it. "But seriously, it's hard to get more rarified than the Moon colony. An elite cadre of scientists, selected arbitrarily without a clear application process. A so-called 'international venture,' that is in fact under the exclusive control of the American government."

He drummed his fingers on the sticky table, warming to his theme. "This administration doesn't lift a finger as the famine in Sierra Leone spreads to Guinea—but they're happy to funnel billions to keep a hundred people alive. Congress does nothing but give performative floor speeches when a sixty-five-year-old train filled with working people derails in Jersey but authorizes heavy investments in a new Space Industrial Complex to launch faster rocket ships for the rich." He took a sip of beer. "The socialist revolution in the new republic of Bolivia gets a chilly reception in the UN because their new leader wasn't democratically elected, while the fate of an entire planet rests with a few white men."

"Astronomical body," Alex interrupted.

"What?"

"The Moon. It's not a planet. By definition."

Navin gestured with the cigarette tin. "I was making a point. I had this whole parallel structure thing going."

Alex stifled a laugh. She was never quite sure when Navin was serious. "You were grandstanding."

Navin opened his mouth to argue and then closed it again. When he finally spoke, it was quieter. "You're really going, aren't you? I'm going to miss you calling me out. Nobody else does that."

"I am going," she said, her confidence surprising her. "I don't care what you think about the politics of the colony. It's *space*. Can you imagine?"

"The final frontier." He finished rolling his neglected cigarette and licked the paper to close it. "Who am I kidding? I'd kill to go with you."

Her lips reluctantly tugged up in a smile. "How could you finish your dissertation without access to the Reg?"

"Fuck my dissertation." He leaned over the table and kissed her hard, one hand behind her neck. "I mean it. Fuck my dissertation. I'd come with you if I could."

When he spent the night, Alex found herself not minding. She snuggled closer and inhaled his scent. No one would smell like cigarettes in space.

2

MANSOOR

DESPITE YEARS OF ENDURING ABU DHABI'S TREACHEROUS TRAFFIC, where death by taxi was always moments away, Mansoor found driving in Boston infuriating. He watched the tan Toyota in front of him slow down at a yellow light and fought the urge to lay on his horn. He did not have time for timid drivers that morning.

His hair was still damp, his dark locks curling around his face. At least he had managed to match his suit and tie. The night before he had carefully laid out his outfit and gone to bed early. He had spent half the night tossing and turning, and, just when he had finally fallen asleep in the early morning, he had been jarred awake by a loud pounding on his front door.

His thoughts were interrupted by his car's automated voice. "Faster route found, Mans Or. Would you like to take it?"

"Yes, please." He could not shake off his manners even when speaking to a machine. It grated on him, the way his car pronounced his name. Silicon Valley programmers had never bothered to ensure their AI-generated voice technology pronounced Arabic names correctly.

"In eight hundred feet, turn left onto State Street."

Mansoor complied, narrowly missing a swarm of bike commuters. He muttered a curse. He hated the self-driving feature on his Audi, but perhaps he should have activated it. An accident would really ruin his day.

Not for the first time that morning, Mansoor pictured himself as a young man in Abu Dhabi tapping his foot while his father sat in his villa finishing his tea and chatting with Mansoor's eldest brother. "They wait upon my pleasure, *Waladi*," his father would say, unperturbed by Mansoor's impatience. "You must understand this if you are to be a man in this family."

It had been true then, and it was all the more true now. Picturing the administrator of NASA and the chair of the Senate Subcommittee on Space and Science chatting over increasingly cold coffee while they masked their impatience made his jaw hurt.

Finally, he reached the front of his office building. MacKenzie was already waiting out front, a slight frown on her face. He jumped out and tossed her the keys. "Thanks, Mac, you are a lifesaver. Are they angry up there?"

"Hard to tell with that crowd. I distracted them with baseball talk." She made a face. "You owe me one. Anderson is a Yankees fan."

"Please curb your impulse to put a Red Sox sticker on my car," Mansoor shot back as the doors slid open.

MacKenzie responded with a rude British gesture she must have picked up from him.

He was still grinning when he stepped off the elevator, but hurriedly smoothed out his expression before entering the conference room and apologizing profusely to the gathered collection of NASA bureaucrats, politicians, and political aides. As he had expected, there was no indication he had inconvenienced any of them.

"Please convey my respects to your esteemed father," Senator Garcia said as they all sat down. Mansoor attempted a smile that came out as a grimace. Such statements were a staple in his life.

The meeting began smoothly enough. Ballooning budgets and overextended timelines were routine to him. He heard the senator swallow when Mansoor responded to a thirty-million-dollar budget increase with nothing more than a nod.

When they turned to staffing, the conversation got heated.

"I am going. This is not negotiable." Mansoor delivered the lie effortlessly. His father was content to see the deal closed and the investment secured. He would not want his son stooping to an on-site logistics role. "Our company has made a considerable investment in the emerging field of space tourism and must ensure we provide the appropriate guest experience. We have a luxury brand to protect. I cannot entrust this work to another."

"We need a systems engineer to complete the hotel build-out, not a real estate executive," the NASA administrator objected.

Mansoor leaned forward, elbows propped on the table. "I have a team of Emirati engineers at my disposal. They are already successfully collaborating remotely with the colony's chief engineer. We have the technical expertise in place. What we are missing is an authority on hospitality."

Garcia laid a hand on Anderson's shoulder. "Mr. Al Kaabi is well within his rights to ask for this small favor after all he has done for the American space program."

"He doesn't have the training," Anderson hissed. His already ruddy complexion was on its way to purple.

"Didn't you just recruit an agronomist with a similar lack of training?" Garcia asked.

Anderson gave out a huff of exasperation. "At his request," he said, gesturing at Mansoor. "I didn't think that favor would bite me in the ass so quickly."

Mansoor said nothing. He knew that he did not have to remind Anderson about the many ways Mansoor had helped him over the years, including backdoor lobbying on behalf of NASA's interests and financing of NASA-friendly political candidates. Two decades into his tenure, John Anderson knew how to swallow his pride. It was part of the reason NASA had grown its power and influence under his leadership.

Anderson stuck out his hand and plastered on a smile. "Mr. Al Kaabi, welcome aboard. The ship leaves in twenty-six days."

It was snowing on his drive home, the heavy flakes clinging to his window. Mansoor loved the rare snow in Boston when it settled thick on the old buildings, looking like it belonged. All too often the winter weather was marked by cold, sleeting rain. He maneuvered his Audi into his tight reserved parking spot and stepped outside, pausing for a moment to take in the way the soft white flakes made the world still and peaceful, before bounding up his steps and opening the front door.

Mansoor's brother lay sprawled on the couch in last night's clothes. A full glass of water and two aspirin lay untouched next to an open can of Coors Light. Mansoor wondered idly where the beer had come from—it was certainly not the sort of brand he kept in stock.

"Lights on," Mansoor said, and the room was bathed in a soft ambient light.

"Ugh, brother, are you trying to kill me?" Rashid groaned in his flat American accent.

"You are doing a fine job of that all on your own." Mansoor took off his wool overcoat, and hung it in the front closet. As he sat down in a nearby black leather chair, he caught a whiff of his brother. "You smell like a sewer."

Rashid waved one hand without opening his eyes. "How was your meeting? I seem to recall a lot of shouting about it."

"Fine." Mansoor regretted bringing it up at 5:30 a.m. that morning; he had been much more honest than normal. If he had

MOONRISING

not been quarreling with his brother, he would have made his meeting on time.

Rashid finally opened his eyes. Squinting at Mansoor, he groped for his beer. "Well?"

"I am going." Despite his best intentions, Mansoor felt a warm sensation well up inside of him.

He was going.

"Father's going to have you murdered in your sleep."

"I dealt with Father this afternoon. He will not stand in my way now that he has gotten what he wants from me." Mansoor knew how to handle his powerful father, but the arrangement they had finalized today made him queasy whenever he thought about it. He resolved to stop thinking about it.

"And what, pray tell, does our dear, domineering father want from you that he hasn't already been getting from his favorite—and most sycophantic—son?"

Mansoor tried not to give Rashid the satisfaction of a reaction. Mansoor hadn't even told Victor about the conversation with his father. If he wasn't talking to his closest ally, he certainly wouldn't be taking his charming, handsome, aimless little brother into his confidence. Rashid had no notion of familial sacrifice and brushed aside his father's onerous expectations with an elegant nonchalance that Mansoor both resented and envied. To Rashid, he simply said, "I am not talking to a wanker like you about it."

"Fine. Keep your secrets." Rashid took a swig of beer and put it back on the table with exaggerated caution. "You've been in the States eight years. Are you ever going to lose that ridiculous accent?"

"*Enta lessa bete'arf tetkallem 'arabi?*"

"Of course I can still speak Arabic," Rashid replied irritably in English. "I just never have the occasion for it since . . ."

29

"I know." Mansoor regretted saying anything. He could still picture the scene at Leena's bedside, the last time Rashid had been to Abu Dhabi.

"You probably keep it so that the lovely people of Boston think of you as a Brit, not an Arab. What do you even see in this shitty, racist town, anyway? Your sidewalk is all cracked."

"Cobblestone streets are charming."

Rashid made a scoffing noise and threw an arm over his eyes. "I tripped on them getting to your door."

"The sidewalk is not to blame," Mansoor replied. "What were you doing last night?"

Rashid turned his head and gave him a wicked smile. "College girls love me."

Mansoor doubted it had been the girls Rashid had been after, but he played along. "You are disgusting."

"I feel disgusting." He groaned. "I forgot how much college girls like tequila shots."

Despite himself, Mansoor laughed. "Is that why you are here? To buy drinks for twenty-year-old women?"

"I'm here to see you, elder brother. I just got sidetracked. I needed a little liquid courage."

"I am honored," Mansoor said dryly. "Is this a social call?"

"No." Rashid was squinting at him again. For the first time since showing up at Mansoor's doorstep in the early morning drunk and stinking, he looked embarrassed. "I want to work for you."

Mansoor's response was instinctive. "No, absolutely not."

Rashid struggled to sit up. "I'm serious. What you're doing with NASA is exciting, and I want to be more involved. I want to protect the family's interests—without going back to Abu Dhabi."

"Do you need money? I can get you money."

"We share a financial advisor. You know I don't need money."

"*Akhi*, you have no skills."

MOONRISING

"I have a degree from Harvard. That's got to count for something."

"That was a decade ago. And you studied poetry." Rashid was looking at him with a pitiful expression. "Rashid, your poetry is good. I read it. Go. Be a poet. You do not want to work for me."

"It isn't enough," Rashid said, rubbing his face. "I'm thirty years old, and I've never done anything useful in my life. I thought, maybe, with this new project there would finally be a place for me."

Mansoor eyed his younger brother. Rashid was looking particularly pathetic at the moment, his skin pale and his eyes bloodshot. "Father has asked me to come home for a few weeks. Come with me." Mansoor regretted the words as soon as they came out of his mouth.

"Abu Dhabi isn't my home."

Mansoor understood why Rashid did not miss Abu Dhabi. There was a lot to love about America. He didn't have to watch his every move and follow the detailed, burdensome, unwritten customs of being a member of an Emirati ruling family, even if he was only a younger son of the Emir's brother.

Mansoor did not regret his choice to live in America, but he missed home with an ache that never went away. He was sorry his visit would not line up with Ramadan. He had not observed that year. The Sunni population in Boston was mostly Lebanese, Egyptian, and Syrian, but they would have welcomed him. The truth was, Ramadan in the West made him lonely. He missed the lively *Iftar* in Abu Dhabi. The feasting after sundown was a raucous affair; the whole city turned out night after night. Muslims in Boston did not serve *harees* or *fareed*. Fish in Boston was delicious, if a bit bland, but no one was grilling *madrooba*.

The first years he was in England, he had observed Ramadan with care. But by the time he had moved to America, he was more half-hearted. It was difficult to fast all day surrounded by food, and he had never been disciplined about alcohol. When he was home, it was easier to conform to his father's expectations.

He looked at Rashid again. He had teased his brother for never speaking Arabic, but he really did seem like an American. His voice, his mannerisms, even his worldview were much more American than Emirati. Rashid was as charismatic as their father, in his own way, and had a way of disarming people. How would American politicians respond to someone like Rashid pushing Mansoor's agenda?

"Alright. I have a job for you, in the Boston office," Mansoor said finally. "But you need to visit Father with me to understand."

Rashid didn't say anything for so long that Mansoor wondered if he had fallen asleep. "Fine." Rashid's voice was so low Mansoor had to strain to hear him. "I'll go with you."

For most of the flight to Abu Dhabi, Rashid was in a better mood than Mansoor had expected. He flirted with the pretty, young students sitting behind them, with the female flight attendants, and with the glamorous middle-aged businesswoman across the aisle. Meanwhile, Mansoor, in the window seat, worked and slept. He made the trip several times a year and knew how to maximize productivity on the twelve-hour flight.

It wasn't until the captain announced they were over Saudi airspace that Rashid began to deflate. There was a mass exodus of women to the restroom. Even First Class had a line. Rashid watched glumly as the flirtatious students returned to their seats wearing *hijabs* and long flowing skirts.

"How can you stand it?" Rashid hissed to Mansoor as the flight attendant scooped up his half-full bottle of beer.

Mansoor shrugged and continued sipping his coffee. The airline prepared it the Saudi way with hints of cardamom, cinnamon, and cloves. *Delicious.* "They are navigating two worlds with respect and dignity. Not everyone wishes to reject their home as you do."

MOONRISING

"Is it so much to expect that home evolves?"

Mansoor raised his eyebrows and said mildly, "You have joined a mission to launch passenger ships from the Arabian Desert to a colony on the Moon. You do not think we are evolving?"

"You know what I mean. In New York, I can do whatever I like, and no one bats an eye. Here, there's nothing but rules. Hell, you can't even swear! I never understood how you could come back here so often."

Mansoor did not have an answer for Rashid that he could put into words, but when he stepped into the terminal, he couldn't keep the grin off his face. Even the airport felt like home. The architecture was stunning, with dramatic and massive arched white ceilings that filtered bright sunlight onto the indoor palm trees. Everything was pristine, polished, and gleaming. In classic Abu Dhabi fashion, the ostentatious surroundings clashed with the teeming masses of humanity moving through. He could hear chatter in a myriad of languages coming from travelers in a dizzying assortment of dress styles. A call to prayer blared over the loudspeakers. Two women in flowing black *abayas* rushed past them, leaving behind a lingering scent of frankincense. A group of white men in suits debated loudly about the results of the Euro Cup. As they made their way toward the exit, Mansoor could smell *shawarma* that made his mouth water.

At customs, an agent recognized Mansoor on sight and with a cry of "*Sayyd* Mansoor!" ushered them past the line. On the other side, Mansoor said to Rashid, "Come on. The car is waiting."

Rashid tugged on his collar uncomfortably. "I'll take a cab. I have a reservation at Emirates Palace."

"The reservation can wait. Your family needs to see you."

Mansoor set off without looking back. He could hear Rashid behind him swearing and wrestling with his two suitcases. He looked like an American tourist, not the son of Mohammed bin Khalifa Al Kaabi returned home from a long absence. Mansoor

33

always packed light for these trips; he had a wardrobe waiting for him in his suite at his father's villa. Locating the driver without incident, Mansoor ushered Rashid through a blast of dry heat and into a silent town car.

Mansoor leaned back on the cool leather and closed his eyes. When he opened them, he saw Rashid hunched forward in his seat, arms hugging himself. He looked miserable.

"Are you thinking about Leena?" Mansoor asked.

Rashid did not respond immediately. Finally, he said, "I miss her."

"So do I."

"It's not the same."

Leena may have raised Mansoor since he was three, but she was not his mother. "You're right. I do not remember my own mother well enough to miss her." His tone was harsh. He was tired of Rashid's melodrama. "Maybe that is why I don't judge the family I have left and find them wanting."

Rashid straightened up. "That's not what I'm doing. I just . . ." He deflated. "She had this way of seeing the best in Abu Dhabi. She saw beyond all this"—he gestured to the window as they passed an indoor skiing and snowboarding amusement park—"to a vision of a society that was truly equal for women and for immigrants. Everywhere we went, it seemed like people tried to be their best selves for her. When Father was with her, he was always so . . . animated. And energetic."

"I remember." Leena's death had been a serious blow to their father. Mansoor didn't think he had ever recovered. There was only so much heartbreak one man could take.

"She knew she was sick when she insisted that I study in America. She must have known I had no place in Abu Dhabi without her. In America, I don't have to pretend to be something I'm not." Rashid ran a hand through his hair. He never talked to Mansoor about his mother.

MOONRISING

"Rashid, I understand. More than you realize. I do."

Rashid made a scoffing noise. "Father wishes I were like you. He sees no value in me."

Mansoor clapped his brother's shoulder. "Then we must change his mind."

When they arrived at the family villa, they were all there—his two older brothers, Hamden and Saqr, their wives, and children, his sisters, Haya with baby in arms, and Latifa with her sober teenage sons. Rashid hesitated on the threshold, but when Latifa threw her arms around him, Mansoor could see the tension leave his brother's body.

His father greeted them both with a kiss on each cheek and brought them to sit at a low table. Course after course of rich dishes arrived. They dined in the Bedouin fashion, barefoot and seated on cushions, eating with their fingers by wadding greasy lamb that tasted of cinnamon and turmeric with saffron rice. The dining area was open air, comfortable now that the sun had set, surrounded by tall palm trees that swayed in the breeze.

It was unusual for men and women to dine together and even more unusual for the children to attend. Mohammed bin Khalifa Al Kaabi was a traditionalist only when it suited him. That mild January night, surrounded by all of his children, he was in a fine mood. Mansoor watched his father's imposing form relax as the conversation flowed freely through politics, culture, and the children's latest antics. Business could wait.

As the night went on, Haya and Latifa convinced Rashid to recite a poem. Mansoor expected him to decline and was surprised and delighted when Rashid launched into a crisp recital of beautiful, rhythmic verse. The New York influences were obvious in both the subject matter—a story of lost love in Central Park—and the pulsing beat. Everyone but Mansoor was crying when Rashid finished, even Latifa's serious boys. Emirati men were not afraid to show emotion, but Mansoor had lost the trick of it.

When Rashid finally announced he was leaving, Saqr's youngest let out a wail. Rashid had ended up being the center of the evening.

Mansoor walked his brother to the door. In the vestibule, he leaned forward and hissed in Rashid's ear, "Be careful."

Rashid swatted him away. "I'm fine."

"They remember your name here. I know you pass very well as an American, but you have an Emirati passport. Do not put alcohol on your room tab. You know it is *haram*. Pay cash."

"Cash!" Rashid scoffed. No one used cash in America.

"Yes, you *hmar*. Leena is still remembered. Some will know your face."

Mansoor resisted saying more as Rashid shrugged Mansoor's hand off his shoulder and headed to the door. Mansoor wished he had given his brother a stronger warning. Ordering alcohol at a tourist bar would upset the hardliners, but it would not be the first time the son of a sheikh was caught skirting religious sobriety expectations. But if Rashid was discovered in bed with another man, the scandal would rock the foundation of Abu Dhabi. Mansoor would have a difficult time getting Rashid out of the country without being arrested.

He hoped Rashid knew it. There was no way to warn him more directly without revealing he knew Rashid's secret. With trepidation, he watched his brother walk off into the night and returned to the rest of his family.

It was another two days before Mohammed was ready to talk business with his two youngest sons. Meeting early to avoid the worst of the traffic, his father's chauffeur drove them past Yas Island and Masdar City into an area that had been nothing but desert a decade before. Now, the tall hotels glittered in the bright sun. They passed a barrage of billboards advertising their destination: Space World Abu Dhabi.

MOONRISING

The resort hotels included exclusive restaurants, high-class casinos, and opulent shaded rooftop pools, all joined by enclosed pedestrian skyways to avoid the oppressive desert heat. Mansoor's greatest achievement was the Mars Experience, an authentic simulation of the living conditions of the Martian settlement. It had launched three years prior, only six months after the real Mars astronauts had landed. The Experience was booked a year out. Those unable to get a reservation to spend a night inside the pods still flocked to view them and to imagine that the barren desert of Abu Dhabi was the surface of Mars.

The remarkable success of the product had launched Mansoor to an elevated position of authority in the company and in the eyes of his father. It had justified his continued presence in America, where he had gained access to NASA scientists, American politicians, and private space entrepreneurs.

When they exited the town car, they were some distance from the existing resort at a lively construction site that was preparing the launch complex. Mansoor took in the busy scene—men in bright orange jumpsuits and yellow hard hats laboring under the blazing sun. Despite himself, he felt queasy watching men sweating in the heat for his family's ambitions. All of it funded by oil money. *Blood money.* It was a phrase he only spoke in his own mind. Uttering it in front of his father would, of course, be impossible. But he felt it inside him like a painful knot between his ribs in moments like this, when he saw before his own eyes the cost of his father's dreams—and his own. He took a breath of the hot desert air, trying to calm his stomach.

Rashid eyed the cranes and steel pillars doubtfully. "Are you sure this will be ready in time?" he asked in halting Arabic.

"Of course it will," said their father. "We have laborers working day and night."

"With hourly water breaks," Mansoor put in. "And air-conditioned meal breaks."

37

"Yes, yes." His father waved a hand in dismissal at Mansoor's interjection. "Rashid, my son, you are thinking like an American. Anything can be done in Abu Dhabi."

Rashid looked like an American today. In his dark-washed jeans, he was sweating in the hot sun. It was only twenty degrees Celsius that winter morning, but the sun was particularly intense. Dressed in a white *kandura* and *ghutra*, Mansoor didn't mind the dust and heat. It made him feel at home.

Although he had supported his brother the Emir's regime of nearly continuous change and modernization and invested heavily in space tourism, in his heart Mohammed bin Khalifa Al Kaabi was a traditionalist who yearned for a return to Bedouin customs. He liked seeing his sons in traditional dress. Mansoor, for his part, was happy to comply. It was only a few weeks a year, and it truly was more comfortable in the desert heat. The morning before, Mansoor and his father had gone hunting with falcons in Al Rub' al Khali. Rashid had declined to join. Mansoor suspected he had spent the day by the pool.

Mohammed eyed Mansoor. "You truly wish to be living on the American colony in a small, crude room? Space World Abu Dhabi will be the glory of the Arabian Desert, and you will miss its unveiling."

Mansoor had been dealing with dry, cutting remarks about his initiative from his father since their arrival. He said mildly, "And the lunar hotel will be our greatest achievement."

His father grunted. "As long as you remember where your duty lies."

As if Mansoor could forget the arrangement he had come to with his father and the sacrifice it entailed. He pushed down another wave of nausea.

Mohammed turned to Rashid. "You have seen the site. Let us continue this conversation over *shisha*."

MOONRISING

"I saw a place just up the road," Rashid replied. "Let's walk." Rashid knew perfectly well that no one walked in Abu Dhabi, even in the relatively cooler winter months.

His father merely raised his dark heavy eyebrows at Rashid and gestured to his driver. It was a two-minute drive to the *shisha* café. As they exited the town car, Mansoor could see Rashid roll his eyes.

Mansoor walked a pace behind his father as he entered the dim and smoky café. An old AC system rattled loudly over the whining music. Half a dozen pairs of male eyes turned to them, and the conversation ceased as they took in Mohammed bin Khalifa Al Kaabi's formidable presence. Mansoor found himself wishing he had his father's effortless ability to command a room's full attention.

The proprietor hurried up. His father gave a curt order, and they were immediately escorted to a back room. A young Indian man brought them mint tea, filled the pipe, and departed, bowing.

When they had settled, Mohammed took a puff of smoke and turned his full, imposing attention on Rashid. "So, you finally wish to be a member of this family."

"I do, sir." Rashid's Arabic made Mansoor cringe. He sounded clunky and awkward. Mansoor wondered what had possessed him to stick his neck out for his brother.

"Does he understand our situation?" Mohammed asked.

Mansoor wordlessly shook his head. He filled his lungs with sweet smoke. It tasted like rose petals.

"Explain it to him."

Mansoor let the smoke trail out of his mouth as he gathered his thoughts. "The bottom has fallen out of the global oil market," Mansoor said to his brother. *Finally.* "Energy still accounts for a quarter of Abu Dhabi's GDP. Without that revenue, the Emir faces a substantial crisis. Worse than a recession. And we are ill-prepared. Two months ago, Sharjah missed payroll for government employees. That's eighty percent of the Emiratis in that city. There was a riot. We cannot let that happen here. Abu Dhabi's continued stability depends on our wealth. We will see a rise in extremism, unrest, and perhaps even civil war." He shivered. Even though he was keenly aware that the source of his family's prosperity had caused irreparable harm to the environment, he shared his father's sense of duty to provide for their people. Mansoor could not change the past. Only look to the future.

"My brother knows we must continue to diversify," his father added. "We have made substantial progress. In 2009, 85 percent of our economy was based on oil, and we knew even then this arrangement was unsustainable. We began investing in manufacturing and financial services. But we have moved too slowly and without the oil revenue, we will flounder. Our people are accustomed to a certain lifestyle. They would adjust poorly to a lack of government subsidies, and we cannot afford instability."

"I don't understand," said Rashid. "If the UAE is so worried about money, why did we just give a billion dollars to the American space program?"

"A billion dollars bought us an exclusive contract to operate all recreation and entertainment ventures on the lunar colony for the next fifty years," Mansoor replied. A billion dollars of oil money, invested in humanity's future. Not enough, not nearly enough, but it was a start.

"Right," Rashid said uncertainly. "The hotel."

Mohammed shook his head. "You must think bigger, my son."

"Bigger? There aren't enough people up there to make any money."

"For now," his father said quietly.

"The English first established Jamestown in 1620 with a hundred men," Mansoor said. "By 1700, the American colonial population had reached two hundred and fifty thousand. By 1780, it

MOONRISING

was approaching three million. Colonies grow exponentially. All this colony needs is a kick-start." He didn't say more in front of his father. Mansoor wanted his father to believe Mansoor's plans for the colony were motivated by profit. His father would put a stop to it if he understood Mansoor's true motivations. Mansoor could trust Victor to bring Rashid along with their larger plans.

"And that is where you come in, my son," Mohammed continued.

"Father, brother, I apologize for my behavior." Rashid refilled their tea cups. He was doing it wrong, of course, serving with his left hand and tilting the handle awkwardly. Still, Mansoor was touched by the gesture. "I'm ready to listen. I want to do everything I can to help."

"Good," said his father. "Mansoor needs you." He clapped his hand on Mansoor's shoulder, turning his hawk-like gaze on him. "My son, you have given me much hope. Abu Dhabi's space program will be the envy of the world. We are depending on you."

Mansoor felt the weight of that responsibility settling in on his shoulders. He couldn't let his family down.

3

VICTOR

VICTOR'S APPRECIATION FOR AEROSPACE ENGINEERING SEEMED to increase in proportion to the time he spent studying it.

He'd come to the field late in life after wasting a decade attempting to disrupt the agricultural industry. When he'd made a small fortune selling several successful ventures to Big Ag and worked his way up the corporate ladder, he'd thought, for a time, that he'd gained a measure of influence as well. But soon, it became all too clear that the type of sideways thinking he excelled at was not appreciated by the risk-averse corporate executives in the agricultural industry.

Aerospace engineering was different.

His only limitation was the laws of physics, and the more he worked at it, the more he learned that even that barrier could be overcome. Teaching himself the discipline had its advantages. He had no preexisting prejudices passed down generationally from professor to student stopping him from attempting the impossible.

Just last week, when he'd announced to his team that their ship design would achieve a propulsive efficiency of 99.9 percent, he

MOONRISING

could tell there were skeptics, but they had learned by now not to doubt their eccentric leader. It was theoretically possible. All he needed to do was make the exhaust velocity vary so that at each instant it was equal and opposite to the vehicle velocity. The only catch was the quantity of propellant required.

After barely sleeping for three days, he was close to solving it. The formulas had been running through his mind all morning as he tried to concentrate on the meetings in front of him.

It was not until his assistant ushered in his 11 o'clock appointment that he perked up. Victor scrutinized the man sitting in front of him. He was as polished and handsome as his brother. But could he truly replace Mansoor? *Impossible.* Victor had never found anyone who challenged him, pushed him, and encouraged him quite like Mansoor. But with Mansoor headed to the colony, they needed Rashid. Could he do it?

"Who are you?" Victor mused aloud.

"Rashid Al Kaabi," he said warmly, rising to shake Victor's hand. "It is an honor to meet the great Victor Beard. I was told you know my brother."

"Not your name. Of course I know your name; you're in my calendar. But who are you? Why should I care about you?"

Rashid opened his mouth and closed it several times. "I'm not sure actually." He made a half-hearted attempt to stand. "Should I go?"

Victor suppressed a grin. "Sit down. You flew out here. I even carved out a full hour. No one gets a full hour. Forty-two minute meetings are my signature move."

"Forty-two minute meetings are your signature move?" Rashid repeated doubtfully.

Much less repressed than Mansoor, Victor thought delightedly. He continued, "One minute of pleasantries. Forty minutes of content. One minute goodbye. Three minutes to reflect. Then onto the next meeting. I'm writing a book. *The 42-Minute Life.*"

43

Rashid made a face. "Are you sure that's a good idea? When do you piss?"

"Once every three meetings. And I shit from 6:30 a.m. to 6:35 a.m. every morning."

"Is that in the book too?"

"I'm not serious about the book." Maybe. It was not a bad idea. The cult of personality he was developing came with a fair share of inconveniences but on balance had been useful. He held up one finger and said into his intelliwatch, "Book. *The 42-Minute Life.* Target completion date—" He looked up at Rashid. "How long does it take to write a book?"

Rashid looked bewildered. "How should I know?"

Fifteen chapters. Six hours per day. One chapter per five days. Allow for ten days of writer's block. One day to interview editors. Two months for the editor to get back to him. Everyone said they were slow bastards. Another fifteen days for rewrites. At least fifty hours for a book tour—it would not do to skimp on the publicity. He added it up. "Nine hundred productive hours."

"What?" said Rashid.

"Cancel book," he told his intelliwatch. To Rashid, he said, "You're right. Terrible idea."

"Ah, okay, I think I'll just go then." Rashid stood up and started edging toward the door.

"You are going to need to do a lot better than that to be a successful lobbyist."

Rashid froze. "Who said anything about being a lobbyist?"

Direct hit.

"Your brother, of course. Rashid, stop looking like a frightened rabbit and sit back down. We're on the same side."

Rashid sat down at the very edge of his chair.

"So, Mansoor, the lucky bastard, has managed to bully, beg, and bribe his way onto the next ship headed to the Moon and is leaving his woefully underprepared younger brother behind to pick

MOONRISING

up the pieces. And if I want to secure an exclusive shuttle contract with Abu Dhabi, I need to find a way to make you politically savvy in enough time to pass the Homestead Act. Taami berry?"

"What?"

"Try it. Trust me."

Rashid popped the berry in his mouth and made a face at the taste. "Mansoor said the Homestead Act won't pass this year. He told me our goal is a vote on the record so we would know who to target at the midterms."

"Mansoor lacks imagination. He puts too much stock in the power of money." Rashid snorted in agreement. He was listening. Victor continued, "We pass the Homestead Act by making it worthwhile. We're pairing half the country's childhood astronaut fantasy with a logistically workable plan backed by cold, hard science. Well, you are. I can't be seen anywhere near the thing. Conflict of interest and all that. I want a U.S. government contract at the end of all this. Lemon?"

Rashid looked blank. "Why would I want a piece of lemon?"

"Trust me, you want this lemon in your mouth."

Rashid sucked on the lemon. "It's sweet," he said in wonderment.

"By itself, a lemon is sour, but in combination with the berry, it tastes sweet. The glycoprotein molecules from the berry bind proteins and activate your tongue's sweet receptors."

"Something sour turning sweet because of biochemistry? Is this supposed to be a metaphor?"

"No, I just think they're fascinating."

"You are completely unhinged," Rashid said, making no move to get up. He had a small, reluctant smile on his face. "But I'm listening."

Rashid was listening. And asking good questions. And pushing back on Victor's ideas in a way that refined them. Victor threw his forty-two-minute philosophy out the window and canceled his next

45

two meetings. By the time Rashid departed, Victor had concluded Rashid just might be the right man for the job. And he had not thought about propulsive efficiency for hours.

The loft was dark when Victor let himself into his Philly condo using the palm lock. He looked at the digital reader on the front door security system: 9:05 p.m.

Harper must be out with her colleagues, at a charity auction, or one of the other numerous engagements with which she filled her evenings while Victor stayed late at the office or on the factory floor.

Victor opened the refrigerator and found it nearly empty. There was a collection of condiments on the shelves, a few boxes of smart water, and cans of energy drinks. He found a redi-meal in the freezer and popped it in the e-oven to cook.

He ate mechanically standing at the counter, scribbling down the ideas that had occurred to him on the hour-long drive from his factory outside West Chester on the digital pad he kept on the side of the fridge. He knew he was close to solving the drag issue, but some piece of it eluded him.

A call came in on his intelliwatch, and he flicked it to the kitchen screen on the wall. A handsome bald man appeared on the screen. "Victor Beard, there you are. My people could not reach you today."

Victor gave a wave of acknowledgment and continued chewing, his brain still on his equations.

"Mansoor Al Kaabi is on his way to the American colony," Malik Al Naifeh said. "He has a great deal of confidence in your rocket ship. Have you gotten her to fly yet?"

"Close, very close. What can I do for you, Ambassador?" He looked down at his pad and realized he had lost the thread of his idea. Damn.

MOONRISING

"I want to know why you are sniffing around the Homestead Act."

Victor looked up sharply. "I don't know what you mean."

"You may have the Americans duped into thinking you are an endearing, hapless, socially awkward inventor with no political agenda, but you cannot fool me. The Homestead Act will fundamentally shift the balance of power in space. You have no business collaborating with Emirati nationals to advance an American bill."

Victor frowned at the Emirati ambassador. He thought Malik was a mouthpiece for the Al Kaabi royals, not a key player. "My understanding is that Mohammed Al Kaabi is in full support of his son's actions."

"Sheikh Mohammed is thinking about the near-term profits of his investment in the colony, not the longer-term implications. He has never been to America. He has no conception of how Americans take and take with no plans to share. My responsibility is to the future of my country, not the investment portfolio of the Emir's younger brother."

"And what is the future of your country?"

"An independent Emirati Moon colony is only a decade off. Soon, we will not need to ride American coattails to fulfill our space-faring ambitions. It is not in our interest to be so far behind the Americans when we are ready to plant our own flag on the Moon."

Victor stared at the hard, handsome face of Ambassador Al Naifah. He did not like being drawn in the middle of an internal Emirati dispute. He was not opposed to an Emirati colony, in theory. It could only speed up the timeline for the human transition to space. But the UAE was a country of twelve million. They needed the Americans to kick-start the transition. "I have to go."

"Victor, stay away from the Homestead Act." Malik's tone had turned serious. "I'll be watching."

Victor cut the connection. He leaned back against the fridge, the remnants of his meal forgotten. Did Ambassador Al Naifeh have enough sway to thwart Victor's plans? He wasted a few precious minutes mulling over the problem. When he could not come up with an answer, he filed the question away in the back of his mind with the many other questions beyond his scope. He had to compartmentalize, or his brain would overload.

As it was, he felt too wired. His mind was still racing to solve his propulsion problem, spinning in circles. He walked through the loft to the bathroom to find a sleeping pill.

The medicine cabinet was nearly as empty as the fridge. His anxiety prescription and the impressive collection of over-the-counter and prescription-strength sleeping aids were there. But missing were Harper's vitamins and face masks. He opened the side drawer to find that her full collection of makeup was cleared out. The glass shower only held his shampoo.

The adjacent walk-in closet was similarly decimated. There was the slinky red dress Harper had worn to the Pharma Industry Awards and the blue ballgown she had donned for the London Tech Week Gala. But he did not see her row of practical, professional work outfits, all lined up in neat dry-cleaning bags. Her shoe rack was half empty, only the most strappy of dress shoes and some grungy sneakers remained. She had left the lacy black lingerie Victor's AI lifestyle algorithm had purchased for her birthday.

He stepped into the bedroom and sank to the ottoman at the foot of his bed. "Call Harper," he told his intelliwatch.

It did not take long for her face to appear on the bedroom screen. She was out. Her hair was swept up in a chignon and silver earrings sparkled on her ears. In the background, plates and glasses clinked, and Victor could hear the murmur of conversation. Behind her, a cityscape sparkled, more sophisticated than Philly.

"You're home," she said gravely. "Finally."

MOONRISING

Victor looked past her face to the buildings around her. "What floor are you on?"

"Victor . . ." Harper sighed. "30th."

Victor was silent for a moment, calculating. "You're in New York. Manhattan. Lower East Side."

Her lips turned up in a sad smile. "I am."

"Work trip, is it? I'm sure you told me. A new client?"

"Victor, I moved out four days ago."

Victor knew this feeling well. There was something important he was supposed to be grasping, but it was slipping through his fingers like sand. "Moved out," he repeated.

"You haven't been home in a week. Did you notice? You haven't contacted me at all. I couldn't do it anymore. I'm tired of being your lowest priority."

"You aren't my lowest priority. That's not true. It's just that my work takes a lot out of me. You knew what I was when you married me."

"Yes, I suppose I did. I was naive and starry-eyed. I didn't think it through."

"Just give me until I get a rocket launched. Then I'll have more time. I'll be more available."

"Unmanned or manned?" she asked wryly.

"I— Well, manned, I suppose. No one gets a government contract with an unmanned prototype anymore. Though I'm developing a promising relationship with an Emirati company that seems more flexible. I'm so close, Harper. I just need to figure a few things out. The propulsive efficiency. And the contract with the Emiratis. And the passage of the Homestead Act, of course. I need to focus right now. I won't be this way forever."

"Yes," Harper said gently. "You will. Victor, I knew I was marrying a genius. I thought I understood what that meant, but I had no idea. I can't spend my life waiting for you to come home, waiting for you to call, waiting for you to pick up your head and notice me."

"I'm saving the future of humanity. I'm saving the future of our planet."

"I know, Victor, I know. But you care more about humanity in the abstract than you do about any one of us as individuals. I've had enough."

"I just need a little more time." He was begging, he realized dimly. That was not like him.

"More time," she echoed.

"Fifteen months, perhaps eighteen depending on how quickly I can solve for the friction between the exhaust pipe and the outer plating. And then there's the unbalanced weight of the anterior side." He stopped talking. What if the drag from the unbalanced weight was causing the exhaust pipe to pivot one or two degrees? He needed to return to his calculations. He stood up from the ottoman, ready to walk back downstairs.

Harper's voice startled him. He had forgotten she was there. "You've made another breakthrough, haven't you?"

"I'm sorry, Harper. I need to go. Can I call you later?"

"Don't bother. I'll send someone to pack up the rest of my things. You'll be hearing from my attorney. We have a pre-nup. I won't make things difficult. I know you don't need any distractions."

"Attorney, right," Victor said vaguely, walking down the stairs to his home office. "I have to go."

Later, after he had solved the drag issue to his satisfaction and was lying down in bed, he realized their conversation had been a test, of sorts. And he had failed. Just like he had failed in every aspect of his marriage. But then the sleeping pill took over, and he faded into the peace of oblivion.

4

ALEX

A WHIRLWIND MONTH OF FERVID PLANNING WITH HER INSTITUTE team, and a physically taxing NASA training course, were not adequate preparation for Alex's first sight of the tall, vertical ship emerging out of the desert's flat expanse.

She had been shown images of the Boeing CST-520 Starliner as a pearly white capsule moving through the blackness of space. Pressed up against the back window of the NASA town car, Alex saw instead a utilitarian orange and white booster reaching up into the blue New Mexico sky. Directly next to it towered a crane-like steel structure with a protruding walkway that led to the very top of the booster, where the Starliner rested. From her vantage point, it looked too minuscule to make a successful journey into space.

How could a spacecraft that required a booster five times its size just to get off the ground ever be trusted to reach its destination?

As they got closer, a large sign came into view, stretching over the four-lane highway, SPACEPORT NEW MEXICO spelled out in garish neon block lettering at the top and cartoon rocket ships decorating the posts. It should have detracted from the gravity of the moment, but Alex was too terrified to laugh. She wished for a moment that Navin was there with some sardonic commentary. She could imagine his choice words on how the rise of consumerism in the American populace had enabled the corporate takeover of public institutions. It was hard not to hear Navin complaining about capitalist profiteering as they drove past a silver roller coaster named for a soda brand and a whirling ride featuring a lime green space alien from a movie franchise.

It was a mild late afternoon, and the amusement park was packed with families preparing to witness the launch. As they drove through the park, children tugged on their parents' arms and pointed at the town car, noticing, no doubt, the NASA logo on the side. Alex remembered her own launch viewings as a child when her father had a mission. Her mother had always been outwardly calm but had clutched Alex's hand too tightly.

After crossing the park, the driver went through a checkpoint and pulled up to a sleek glass building flanked by security guards. He pulled to a stop and opened Alex's door. "Good luck today, Dr. Cole," the driver said as Alex stepped out of the car. Her mouth was too dry to respond.

The lobby of Spaceport New Mexico's Mission Control was an architectural ode to Stanley Kubrick, with a stark white tiled floor and low-slung bright red chairs. Its kitschy interior did nothing to ease her anxiety. Quality scientists, in her experience, cared little for appearances. The building's aesthetics were geared toward tourists, not NASA scientists and engineers.

Administrator Anderson was waiting for her, perched on the edge of one of the uncomfortable-looking red chairs. "Dr. Cole, welcome." He stepped toward her. "How are you today?"

Alex swallowed and clasped her hands together to stop the shaking. "Fine." Her voice came out in a whisper. She needed to get a hold of herself.

"First time's always the hardest," Anderson said kindly as he ushered her through a series of heavy, keyless, locked doors that grew more and more practical in appearance and finally spat them out into a beige corridor. "Of course, my first time included two weeks of quarantine, twenty-four hours of fasting, and the threat of a weather-related cancellation looming over our heads." He chuckled. "The experience is much more appealing now."

Alex remembered. On several occasions when she was a child, she had been woken before dawn to attend launches only for them to be postponed due to mild wind or rain. Her father had borne the changes stoically from behind the quarantine shield, and her mother usually managed to hide her tears until they were out of his sight. Saul Cole had always been dispassionate and taciturn. When Alex had messaged her father about her planned arrival on the colony, all she had received in response was a curt *I see you on the flight manifest.*

Anderson pointed toward another beige corridor. "Mission control for this launch is located down that hall. There will be dozens of highly trained and experienced flight controllers and ground control officers managing today's trip." He pushed open the final door and said, "Here we are."

The large room was set up like a trauma center, with a row of beds, medical machines, and curtains. Med techs in white coats hovered over three men and one woman sitting on examination chairs. Alex studied them, wondering what circumstances had brought them to be traveling in the Starliner that day.

Anderson escorted her to one of the remaining chairs. "The exam is just a precaution, Dr. Cole," he assured her solicitously. He hadn't left her side. She wasn't sure why he was there at all. Shouldn't the head of NASA have better things to do than make sure her blood was drawn properly?

Alex gritted her teeth as a med tech stuck a needle into her arm. "I understand." She did, actually. Though an agronomist by training, Alex had enough of a general biology background to know the devastating consequences of a deadly virus on a small, isolated community. She stuck her other arm out to have her blood pressure taken and looked around. The others in the room gave her friendly nods.

Anderson followed her gaze. "Andrew Salti and José Guevara, the co-pilots. Sandra Flanders, Communications. Drake Douglass, on special assignment."

"Is this the whole group?" Alex asked. She knew from her training that the CST-520 Starliner was an older supply vessel with limited passenger capacity.

"We're expecting one more." Anderson frowned and looked at his watch. He didn't elaborate.

Alex finished her checkup and introduced herself to the others. She braced for any reaction to her name, but no one seemed to recognize her. She learned Andrew and José were part of a group of regular pilots on their sixteenth trip to the colony. Sandra was returning from a three-month vacation. Drake, like Alex, was new to space travel.

"Are you nervous?" she asked him, trying for a nonchalant tone in spite of the anxiety clawing at her gut.

Drake shrugged, his face impassive. "I've been in more dangerous situations." His dark hair was cropped in a sharply lined buzz cut, and his posture was a bit too perfect. *Ex-military*, Alex couldn't help but think. What did special assignment mean, anyway? Was he working for her father?

Anderson was checking his watch again when the side door banged open and an elegant man in an impeccably tailored suit entered. "Apologies for my tardiness, John. I seem to be making a habit of it." His voice sounded British with an underlying accent Alex couldn't place. "Last-minute instructions from my father took up more time than anticipated."

"Not a problem. Not a problem at all." The administrator hurried to his side. "Mr. Al Kaabi, may I introduce you to the rest of the crew?"

MOONRISING

The newcomer shook hands all around. He took her hand last. "Dr. Cole, it is a pleasure." Anderson hadn't used her honorific when he'd introduced her. This man knew who she was.

"It's Alex," she said, steeling herself for some sort of sardonic comment about her work or probing question about why someone like her would be allowed onto the Moon colony.

"Mansoor," was all the man said. His hand was calloused and firm.

The administrator cleared his throat. "If it's not too much trouble, Mr. Al Kaabi, we'd like to give you a brief medical examination before you depart." Anderson led him to one of the examination tables.

"He's the money," Sandra said in a low voice after they had walked away. "Comes from a family of billionaire oil men from Saudi Arabia or something."

"United Arab Emirates," José chimed in.

"Why is he coming with us?" Alex asked tentatively, not wanting to reveal the depths of her ignorance about the colony. "I didn't think the colony was ready for tourists."

Sandra shrugged. "He's not a tourist; he's an investor. He's probably coming to kick our asses into gear. We could use it, frankly." She gave Alex and Drake a friendly smile. "I hope you know what you're getting into."

Her father may have quarantined for days before a launch, but it was only an hour later when Alex was flat on her back with her knees raised, strapped down in a seat with an oxygen mask near at hand, shaking uncontrollably. When she had accepted the offer, she'd of course envisioned life on the colony—but she hadn't thought about what it would be like to actually travel to the Moon. She'd been to five astronaut funerals as a child. Her rational brain knew that the odds of dying in a fiery blaze were minute now, but it was hard to think rationally in a horizontal position with a harness across her chest.

55

Next to her, she heard Mansoor's composed and level voice. "The Boeing CST-520 Starliner has a perfect flight record. Never had an accident. It is why they are still in rotation despite advancements in speed and comfort." He was so close it sounded like he was whispering in her ear.

She could only manage to respond with a grunt.

"We are in very good hands."

With difficulty, she turned her head to the right to look at him. "You've never done this before either, right?" she gasped.

Mansoor gave her a reassuring smile. His face was so close to hers, and his teeth were very white. "This is my first time traveling via space shuttle, but it is not so different from piloting a helicopter. Much of the same safety principles apply."

"You fly helicopters?"

He gave an aborted shrug, hindered by the straps. "When I can find the time."

"You're awfully young to be a billionaire," she blurted out and immediately regretted it. Rich people were always so touchy about their money. To her surprise, Mansoor gave a warm, full-throated laugh in response.

On the loudspeaker came Andrew's voice. "Alright folks, prepare for liftoff."

Mansoor murmured something in Arabic. Was it a prayer? She couldn't think clearly enough to pray. Her mind felt blank. She looked around at her companions. The bulk of the Starliner's capacity was reserved for crates and crates of supplies located at the rear, behind the passenger cabin. The four passengers were crammed into a small space behind the two pilots. Turning her head to the left, she could see Sandra and Drake strapped down across the aisle. Drake looked impassive, but Sandra was beaming.

"Get ready," she said, looking at Alex with sparkling, almost manic eyes. "Your life's about to change."

MOONRISING

The ship lurched forward. For a moment, takeoff felt familiar. There was a swoop in her stomach as they lifted from the ground. Then, the vibrations started. Her teeth rattled inside her head, and her body rammed into the back of her seat. Next to her, she heard more fervent Arabic. Mansoor wasn't as unruffled as he wanted her to think.

On instinct, she reached out awkwardly, constrained by the safety belt, and gripped Mansoor's hand. He gripped back.

A loud boom came from outside the ship, followed by an abrupt and eerie silence. Suddenly—jarringly—the only sounds were her companions' ragged breathing and faint radio chatter from the cockpit.

Something hit her face. A piece of gum she had tucked in her pocket that morning was floating a few inches from her nose. She noticed a few other items hovering around her: a screw, an M&M, and a pencil stub. She took a deep breath and realized she had a raging headache.

"We've cleared the atmosphere, folks." Andrew's voice returned to the loudspeaker. "Nothing but smooth sailing for the next twenty-four hours. It is now safe to remove your restraining devices, but please exercise caution when moving about the cabin."

Sandra already had her harness off. "There's nothing like zero-g. Enjoy it while it lasts. You won't be getting this on the colony." She did a flip in the air and gave a delighted whoop.

Alex realized with surprise that she was still holding Mansoor's hand and disengaged her fingers quickly without meeting his eyes. She gingerly unbuckled her straps and pushed herself up. The feeling of weightlessness overwhelmed her at first. Her hair floated in a halo overhead. Already, she had a minor backache. She knew from her brief training this meant the vertebrae in her spine were spreading apart.

Carefully, she pushed herself to the small circular window. Mansoor had also unbuckled and was staring out, one hand

57

pressed against the windowpane. Earth appeared as a collection of snow-white clouds floating over a deep sapphire expanse, framed in utter blackness. No stars were visible. Mansoor was crying as he looked at the view, his tears clinging under his eyes without gravity to pull them down. Alex turned away, pretending not to notice. When he wiped his eyes and flicked the liquid away, a few droplets of his tears landed on her face.

"It's like nothing else," Alex heard Sandra say to Drake from where they hovered near the second starboard window. "I never get tired of the view."

Alex was struck for a moment by the enormity of what she had done. She'd left behind her home and research for this opportunity and had no idea what to expect next. She was an astronaut now. The word did not hold the same gravitas it used to, but it was still a title held by fewer than one percent of Americans. She wondered if her mother would have been proud or horrified to discover that she was following in her father's footsteps after all.

Alex shook her head to snap those thoughts closed, and immediately regretted how the movement exacerbated her headache. Nearby, Sandra was teaching Drake about navigating zero-g. "My favorite is the back flips. Could never do them on Earth, not even as a kid."

"I used to be pretty good," Alex mused.

Sandra grinned. "Try it, try it!"

Alex pushed off from the wall, moved herself to the center aisle, and flipped over. She found herself laughing. Using her momentum, she went for a double flip. For one exhilarating moment she thought she'd done it, before she realized she hadn't stopped. With panic, she felt herself losing control and flipping three times. Belatedly, she remembered all the warnings in her training about vomit in zero-g.

"Steady, steady." Mansoor reached out and held her shoulders, stopping the spinning.

She took a deep breath and looked up at him as he floated a few inches above her. "Thanks." The pressure of his touch lingered when he removed his hands.

"Sorry!" Sandra was still grinning. "I forgot for a second you're all newbies."

Drake did a flip of his own. He looked totally comfortable and in control, like he'd been in zero-g plenty of times. He never cracked a smile.

Alex tried a few more experimental moves around the cabin. She was done flipping, though. When she returned to the window, the view outside had changed. The sun appeared to be setting, plunging toward the western horizon. The underside of the clouds glowed pink and orange as they reflected the rays of the sun.

Mansoor floated beside her, one hand resting on the side of the ship. "I was looking for a glimpse of home. I must have missed it."

"Do you think you'd be able to locate home from up here?"

He grinned. "They say that the highway from Abu Dhabi to Dubai shines so brightly it is visible from space. I was hoping to see it."

The view was changing again. The colors were shrinking. Only one thin arc of indigo remained. It faded to black. Without the sun to block the view, Alex could see a multitude of stars, some appearing farther away than others. A shooting star flashed across the expanse.

"Did you see that?"

Mansoor nodded. "Incredible." His voice was hushed and reverent.

They floated in silence, drinking in the view. The stars were not twinkling; they were fixed points of color in the black sky.

"This is the entire space tourism experience right now," Mansoor said after a while. "Thirty minutes of weightlessness and a chance to view the Earth from space. It is quite popular—the ships are booked years in advance."

"I could see it being hard to return to Earth," Alex said. "After experiencing all of this." Her problems were receding as they moved farther and farther from the planet. What would it be like to go to work without having to brace herself for an encounter with a protestor? She thought she would miss her lab fiercely, but instead it was as if she'd set down a heavy burden.

"We will be offering something very different," Mansoor said. "A weeklong stay on the colony with off-site tours on the lunar surface. The pre- and post-launch experience in Abu Dhabi will outshine what you just witnessed in New Mexico."

"Is that why you're here?" Alex found herself asking. "Sandra said you were an investor coming to kick the colony's ass into gear." She couldn't figure him out—but she kind of wanted to. Alex knew next to nothing about this man, but the sense of power radiating off him made her wonder if she should be more wary. It's not that she was intimidated by powerful men. She'd had enough early exposure to her father's friends to know power was a relative thing. But she tended to avoid powerful men in her own life. Certainly, she almost never found herself intrigued by them.

"I suppose I am. I'm here to ensure we are ready for the first space tourists."

He changed the subject with the practiced ease of a diplomat, asking her innocuous questions about her own life. He was easy and pleasant to talk to.

She had expected the flight to feel like a long, uncomfortable airplane ride. Instead, it seemed almost short. Andrew took her by surprise when he announced from the cockpit that the scheduled sleep cycle was about to begin. Sandra helped them into sleeping bags that Velcroed to the cabin walls, and then passed out earplugs and facemasks. José came to join them for a shorter sleeping shift. He explained he would trade with Andrew after four hours so they both could get some rest during the trip.

MOONRISING

Alex fell into a surreal doze. She missed the weight of a blanket and the press of a pillow. Just when she thought she would never achieve a deep sleep, she was startled into wakefulness by Sandra removing herself from her own sleeping bag. Nearly eight hours had passed.

When they all were fully awake and had navigated using the bathroom and cleaning their teeth in zero-g, Drake perched in the cockpit, interrogating the pilots, and Sandra cajoled Mansoor and Alex into a game of zero-g dodgeball that left the three of them breathless with laughter. Later they dined on pouches of dull, over-processed freeze-dried shrimp curry reconstituted with hot water and flavorless thermostabilized mangos and strawberries. Sandra explained to them that the food tasted so bland because their heads were congested from the weightless environment.

"I wish we were so lucky on the colony. Our sense of taste isn't affected there. We get to fully experience just how disgusting the redi-meals taste," Sandra said, her nose wrinkling.

Alex frowned. Was there literally no fresh food up there? Surely the colony residents weren't eating redi-meals every day?

She spent most of the flight looking out the window, watching Earth grow smaller and smaller in her view. When José announced they were half an hour from landing, Alex was almost disappointed by how quickly the time had passed.

The ride down was not nearly as bumpy as the one up. Sandra, still in teacher-mode, shouted at them across the cabin that the lower gravity of the Moon meant that launches and landings required much less energy than on Earth.

Straining her neck, Alex caught her first glimpse of the colony. She'd seen so many pictures, but it looked smaller in person—much smaller. From her training, she knew the colony was perched on Peary crater near the lunar north pole at an altitude high enough to provide the colony with nearly continuous sunlight. The crater's massive circular formation dwarfed the man-made structures. As they drew closer, the large dome—the colony's signature architectural detail—came into clearer view. Tiny figures were moving under the translucent panes of glass. Alex wondered if her father was among them.

One of the structures jutting out of the dome opened from the ceiling. The view disappeared from the window as the ship coasted to a landing. A loud noise reverberated throughout the ship as the hatch closed once more. They waited another fifteen minutes for the docking bay to repressurize before José's voice came back on, letting them know it was safe to depart.

Sandra and Drake exited first. Alex looked at Mansoor and gave him a tiny smile. Her nerves were coming back in full force. "Here we go."

She unbuckled her belt and slowly rose. As she stepped down the stairs, she almost stumbled and grabbed the railing for support. Even the Moon's lower gravity felt heavy after the experience of weightlessness. Straightening, Alex forced herself to push through the discomfort and go down the rest of the steps so that Mansoor could exit behind her.

When she stepped off the spacecraft, she found herself in a hangar with cement floors. Several smaller ships were parked nearby. Two techs had already approached the ship, checking for damage and unloading the cargo.

A man came forward to meet their group. He was pale and thin, wearing a formal navy-blue uniform jacket with silver buttons down the side lapel. *Dad*, Alex realized suddenly. With his gaunt frame and receding hairline, she hadn't recognized him. She wished he would look at her and acknowledge her presence, but all his attention was on Mansoor.

Duty first, like always.

"Mr. Al Kaabi, a pleasure." Her father extended his hand, and Mansoor shook it. "Welcome to Peary Station. I am Space Force

Major General Saul Cole, colony commander. Administrator Anderson has told me about everything you've done to keep this place well-funded. Please let me know what we can do to make your time with us more comfortable."

"It is an honor to be here," Mansoor replied politely and formally.

The commander turned to Drake next and clapped him on the shoulder. "Douglass! It's good to see you. Or should I say Inspector Douglass?"

Drake appeared to relax for the first time. "Sir."

"We'll talk further soon, I'm sure." He turned to the veteran staff and greeted them affectionately. Finally, his eyes rested on her. "You all must be tired after your journey. We have your room assignments. One of my people would be happy to escort you."

Alex waited while the others left, twisting her hands in front of her. "Hi, Dad."

Her father touched her arm briefly. "How was your trip, Alexandra?"

"Good." She cleared her throat, trying to make her smile warm. "It's good to see you." She wondered if she should thank him for pulling the strings to get her this placement, but she didn't want to embarrass him in front of the remaining tech unloading supplies.

Saul made a noncommittal noise. "Mitch," he called, and the remaining tech hurried up. "Please escort Alexandra to her room."

Alex wished he would hug her. He'd shown more emotion greeting Drake Douglass than he had his own daughter. Couldn't he be a normal father just this once? But no—he was already turning to walk down the hall, frowning at a tablet.

"Ready?" the tech asked. He grabbed her personal case and led the way.

✦

In her tiny quarters, the narrow bed beckoned. If she sat down, she knew she would fall straight into an exhausted sleep. Maybe in the morning, she would care less about her father's aloofness. She shouldn't have expected anything else from the gruff and humorless seasoned military commander. But if she was honest with herself? She'd hoped for a warmer greeting. Why else would he have leveraged his relationship with John Anderson to extend her the invitation? *Stupid.* You shouldn't expect people to change. Not really.

She looked at her intelliwatch. It was strange to see no data flitting across the screen. During her New Mexico training, Alex had been warned that the colony's radiation shielding and thermal insulation blocked most wireless signals. She manually adjusted the time to correspond to the Eastern time zone the colony ran on. It was only 7 p.m., too early for bed if she was going to adjust quickly to life aboard the colony.

Mustering the last of her energy, Alex opened her personal case and pulled out her toiletry bag. Her bathroom was simple, with a narrow shower, sink, and toilet, but she appreciated that it was hers alone. A sign on the wall explained the water rationing system. Shower usage was limited to three minutes every twenty-four hours.

Stripping off her clothes, Alex took a hurried shower. The water was lukewarm with inconsistent water pressure and smelled faintly metallic. After a twenty-four-hour spaceflight, it felt heavenly. She was pretty sure she'd kept it under three minutes as she toweled off and slipped on comfortable yoga pants and a T-shirt.

She surveyed her tiny room. A narrow, high window of warped translucent material let in light from the continuous lunar day of Peary Crater, but only offered a distorted view of the outside. A twin-size bed, a small bedside shelf with a built-in lamp, and a narrow closet took up most of the space. Alex enjoyed solitude, but how much time could she spend in the claustrophobic room without losing it?

MOONRISING

A knock at her door startled her. Opening it, she saw Mansoor, wearing a tentative smile. "Can I interest you in a nightcap?" The bottle he held up looked like whiskey. Alex didn't recognize the label. He slid inside and took a seat uninvited on her bed.

She looked again around her tiny room and, seeing no extra chair appear, settled next to him on the narrow bed. "I'm not sure I have any cups."

Mansoor produced two small rocks glasses with a cut diamond pattern out of a pocket. He'd removed the suit jacket and tie he'd worn all the way here and rolled up his shirt sleeves. Despite that, he still looked put together, not like someone who had just been through a long space flight. Alex realized belatedly that she wasn't wearing a bra.

"I hope you take it neat." Mansoor poured the glass a quarter full and handed it to her. "Ice appears hard to come by."

She took a sip. The whiskey burned pleasantly down her throat. *What kind of person brings crystal into space?*

"I was unable to quiet my mind, and I thought I should avoid drinking alone. Seemed like a poor precedent." He stared at his drink in silence for a moment before continuing. "I have traveled all over the globe, and I spend most of my time between Boston and Abu Dhabi—two cities that could not be more different. But I do not think I have ever fully understood what it means to be human until now." He frowned at his whiskey, then gave himself a little shake. "Apologies. I am being melodramatic."

Alex wondered why he was confiding in her of all people. She was used to people who wanted to argue with her. She even enjoyed a good debate. She was less familiar with people opening up to her.

"You aren't being melodramatic," she said slowly. "You know, I've been fighting against what we've done to our planet my entire career, but I never saw how vulnerable Earth is until today. We're so fragile and space is so vast." She shivered despite herself, picturing the way the planet had hung in the blackness, getting tinier the farther away they traveled. With the exception of the several hundred people spread among the colony, the ISS, and the research missions to Mars, all of humanity was on that paltry sphere.

In a low voice, Mansoor said, "I expected today to feel like climbing a difficult cliff face, or perhaps completing a black diamond ski slope."

Alex eyed him. Cliff faces and black diamond slopes? Was this guy for real?

"I enjoy the rush of adrenaline," Mansoor continued. "Usually. Today, I felt completely out of control."

"You like to be in control," Alex said. She could understand that feeling. Relate to it, even.

"I suppose I do. Foolish to expect control in space, I expect." His voice was almost a whisper.

"I've never felt in control," she admitted. "The problems I'm trying to solve are too impossible. And most Americans will do anything they can to avoid even admitting there's a problem." She cut herself off before she said anything else. He had said he lived in Boston. Surely, he'd picked up on the deep aversion to mutagenetic food there. Although, she thought bitterly, perhaps he was so rich he didn't even notice the inflated prices of the organic produce he consumed.

"Good practice for the colony, I suspect."

Alex shook her head. "I'm not sure. I suppose I'll find out in the morning."

"I can tell you what you will find tomorrow. Deprioritized experiments and a lack of interest in the greenhouse from the other scientists. The colony has had no champion for fresh food. Until now."

"You've thought a lot about my role here," Alex said warily.

Mansoor inclined his head. "I have. I need the colony producing its own food. My tourists will expect it—and they will pay for

MOONRISING

it, too. These scientists will tolerate any number of discomforts as long as their work is not distracted. How many of the researchers living here subsisted on packages of ramen and energy bars during graduate school? The redi-meals offered here are not so different. NASA has not made fresh food a priority."

Alex recoiled. "I'm here to feed billionaire tourists?" she spouted. "That's not how Anderson presented this to me. I thought NASA had been working for years to crack the code on food production." She could hear how forcefully she was coming across, but she didn't appreciate being duped. She felt herself tense in preparation for what would come next: Mansoor would either get defensive or snippy, or—even worse—try to calm her down.

But his quiet, even tone didn't change. "You read the research reports, I take it? I did as well." He tilted his head. "What stood out to me is what the reports left out. They're sending lunar-grown lettuce to a Florida research base to compare with lettuce grown on Earth in double-blind experiments. A waste of resources. I have followed your career. You write more how-to guides for farmers and home gardeners than you publish in journals."

"And?" she challenged. Wait—he had followed her career?

His lips lifted in a small smile. "And this is good, in my opinion. The colony needs someone practical and results-oriented. In my view, we can study the properties of lettuce in a decade. First, we need to grow the lettuce in abundance, store it, and distribute it. You are perfect for this role."

"How do you know so much about my work?" Alex asked, still not willing to relax. She had a reputation, of course, but surely her mutagenetic greenhouse was insignificant to a wealthy Emirati businessman.

"I studied biology at Oxford, before my father insisted I learn economics and go into the family business. It is enough of a background to follow your research." Mansoor reached for the bottle where it was perched on the bedside shelf and poured himself another drink. Alex found herself noticing the way his muscles moved under his dress shirt and abruptly remembered they were in a bedroom. "I first learned of you at the UN climate conference in '69." His eyes found hers as he paused to sip his whiskey. "I was a guest of Victor Beard. The lecture you delivered on the promise of mutagenetic produce was inspired."

Of *course* Victor knew Mansoor; he loved courting influential billionaires. Anything to advance his latest project.

"That lecture was not well received," Alex said brusquely. It was an understatement. Protesters had gathered just for her, some of them bussing into D.C. from New York and Boston. Their posters were still burned in her memory: *Mutant Food Will Kill Us All*; *My Grandparents Won't Live Through Another Potato Plague*; and the ELS slogan *One Earth, One Fight*. She had held her ground and refused to be booed off the stage, but she could barely get a sentence out before she was interrupted again. Finally, conference security had intervened.

Mansoor smiled. "You're being modest. I remember it well. I had flown in from Abu Dhabi the night before and was still jet-lagged, but your keynote woke me up. You were fearless on that stage. You gained quite a following that day."

Alex shrugged. It was an uncomfortable feeling that he knew her, but that she didn't know him.

"It's why the University of Chicago recruited me," she said. "They love being provocative. But their support doesn't come with unlimited resources." A sudden realization came over her. It was blazingly obvious. "Wait—you brought me here, didn't you?" All this time, Alex had assumed it was her father. How foolish of her. When had her father ever made the time to pay attention before?

Mansoor paused with his drink halfway to his lips. "What makes you say that?"

"Come on." Alex laughed. "The offer of funding a few days after I learn that my main grant has dried up? It's too good to be

MOONRISING

true." Victor had known, Alex realized. He had seen Thomas Hill poised to cut NKI's sponsorship, and he had let it happen. Damn him and his strategies. Why not level with Alex?

Mansoor said nothing for a moment. He wasn't looking at her. "NASA brought you here."

"And how did NASA come up with ten years of funding for my lab? The Mars project isn't even fully funded. Victor told you how I could be recruited. That bastard." Victor hadn't even had the courtesy to call her himself. He knew her too well. Why not be straight with her? Because of course Victor would have known that growing food for rich tourists would have been a hard no from Alex. *Hard* no. He had expertly manipulated her, and now she was stuck on the Moon with a signed twelve-month contract and no independent means of transportation.

"Victor and I share a passion for making this little Moon experiment work," said Mansoor. "He persuaded me that you might come to share this passion." His tone was light, too light. It made Alex wonder what he was hiding.

Despite herself, she muttered, "I'm going to murder that evil genius the next time I see him."

Mansoor let out an abrupt bark of laughter. "Evil genius, how apt. Very well. It is true. I did bring you here." His handsome face invited her to take part in the laughter, but she was far too angry at the moment.

"And what exactly is Victor's involvement in"—she gestured around the tiny room, to the distorted view from the window—"all of this? All he bothered to tell me about his new project was that it was bigger than another AgTech venture."

"No, he is not focusing on agro this time. Victor has turned his considerable intellect to aerospace engineering." There was that small smile again. "He is building me a rocket ship."

Alex nearly choked on her drink. "A rocket ship?" Victor's main priority had always been climate change. What was he doing in an unfamiliar industry working with an Emirati billionaire? Alex made a face. "And this is all for the tourists? If you claim to know me, to have followed my career, you know that my priority has never been the rich."

Mansoor shrugged in an effortlessly nonchalant way that Alex found infuriating. His left hand was braced on the headboard, and Alex could see the way his tendons stood out against his forearm. He hadn't shaved that evening. Stubble traveled down his throat. Alex wondered what it would feel like under her tongue.

She jumped up. "It's getting late. We should get some sleep."

"Indeed." Mansoor finished his drink in one smooth motion. Alex watched his throat move. Her mouth turned dry.

"Thank you for the company," Mansoor said as he left. "I look forward to seeing your work up close."

5

MANSOOR

IN A SEALED LUNAR VEHICLE, WITH THE COLONY'S CHIEF
engineer at his side, Mansoor got his first look at the hotel. He
had spent years positioning himself for this moment, increasing
his authority in his family business and building relationships with
American politicians and bureaucrats. For the last twelve months,
while contract negotiations dragged on, he advanced detailed
architectural, mechanical, and structural blueprints, balancing the
soaring vision of his Emirati architects with the practical realities
of building on the Moon. And then, finally, a contract had been
signed, and he had pledged a billion dollars of his family's wealth
to this investment in their future. In humanity's future.

The hotel was . . . ugly.

It was a one-story gray lump of Refabricator-printed interlocking tiles that faded into the lunar surface. Orange robots crawled
around it, giving it the appearance of an oversized ant hill.

Mansoor realized with a touch of nausea that John Anderson
had been right. He shouldn't be here. Not yet. The time for
Mansoor's eye for the details of luxury hospitality had not arrived.
He should have funded a team of systems engineers to support

Herb Fischer, the overworked chief engineer, instead of indulging in his own vanity trip.

"It's really something, isn't it?" Herb said beside him, his voice muffled through his helmet. "Hard to believe we've only had eight weeks to put blueprints into action."

Right, it was early days. Yes. This was just the beginning. He had six months before the tourists were scheduled to arrive. Six months was an eternity when building in Abu Dhabi. The same would be true on the Moon. The nausea subsided.

Looking at the construction site, Mansoor tried to picture the remarkable design his Emirati architects envisioned. The hotel was to be two 150-meter-high needle-like towers jutting into the bright sky. Each of the private suites would feature an elevated 360-degree view. Unlike the main colony, which was a warren of haphazardly constructed one-story wings that sprouted from the dome as the population grew, the hotel would be seamless and elegant.

The hotel wasn't ready today, but that did not mean he wouldn't achieve the vision.

Herb drove them into the bay of the hotel, and the hydraulic doors shut behind them. He opened the vehicle hatch, and they both stepped into the transition chamber. Herb pressed a switch, and the walls flipped to powerful magnets. Mansoor watched with interest as the dust covering his suit flew to the walls. They stepped through another hermetically sealed door, and Herb lifted the face shield on his helmet. "The air seal is intact on this level, and the filters keep out about 98 percent of the moon dust," Herb said in a gravelly voice.

"Are we on schedule?" Mansoor asked.

Herb hesitated. "Depends on how long it takes us to solve this setback with synthesizing window materials."

Mansoor grimaced. Herb had shown him a sample window before they had left the hangar bay. It was distorted and dark. Nothing like the stunning renderings. "*Can* it be solved?"

MOONRISING

"If your brainy engineers have anything to say about it. They could give the NASA eggheads a run for their money. You'll see. The entire hotel will be habitable before you know it. I've been working fourteen-hour days to make this happen. It'll be nice to finally have an extra pair of human hands."

Mansoor gingerly opened his own face shield. Something was taking his mind back to Abu Dhabi as he stared at the rough, uninviting space. Even under construction, the hotel was nothing like a building site in Abu Dhabi. There was no beastly hot sun beating down, heavy vibrations from the never-ceasing machinery, or body odor wafting through the air. It was the dust, he realized abruptly. The fine gray moon dust might be the wrong color, but the way it had clung to his suit felt familiar.

He looked around the drab vestibule and tried to bring himself back into the vision of the hotel. The lower level was already constructed. It included a recreational room for experimenting with low-g sports and a laboratory for tourists who wished to dabble in scientific exploration during their visits. The next floor would be a dining room and bar with a stunning view of the surface—if they could fabricate the appropriate material.

They had a windowpane issue to solve.

"Alright." Mansoor reached out to touch the coarse wall with his thickly gloved hand. "Show me everything. Time to get to work."

That evening, he felt his face warm when he ran into Alex Cole in the cafeteria. Had he really invited himself into her bedroom the night before? She was reading the labels on the prepackaged meals stacked in boxes on the side counter with a look of distaste on her face.

"I can't live like this," she said to him by way of greeting. "In what world is this steak, potatoes, and green beans? It's made

73

entirely of soybeans, yeast extract, and maltodextrin." She leaned toward him to show the redi-meal's label, and he felt her warm breath on the side of his neck. Even after eight years living in Boston, Mansoor could still be caught off guard by American women's lack of boundaries. He remembered the feel of her hand gripping his during that terrifying ascent into space.

"There is no food growing in the greenhouse, I take it?" It was what he had expected, but he took no pleasure in being right. His anticipation for dinner after a long day on-site soured along with his appetite.

"You were right, unfortunately. None of the biologists are even trying. They had the lights blasting twenty-four hours a day, plus the continual sunlight streaming through. The plants were burning up."

Mansoor made a sympathetic noise.

"*Biologists*," she muttered, like a curse. She looked so angry and fierce saying it that Mansoor smothered a laugh. Wasn't agronomy an adjacent field to biology?

"I fixed the sunlight oversaturation today, that was my first mission, but it's too late for most of the plants. And I think we're dealing with a fungus called botrytis. I've seen it before. I may need to start the whole greenhouse over to eradicate it. Natalia of the Russian contingent didn't seem to like that idea." She opened one of the crates stacked against the wall and shut it abruptly after seeing its contents. More redi-meals. "She didn't like any of my ideas." Alex scratched the back of her head. "I—uh—I may have mentioned diverting power from her experiments to the greenhouse."

Mansoor found a box of protein bars and another with multivitamins sitting on the counter. Was that preferable to freeze-dried soy-steak? "Ah. Perhaps not what you should lead with on day one."

Alex shrugged. She opened the skinny refrigerator. Mansoor could see it was empty except for several plastic containers with a clear liquid inside labeled in a handwritten scrawl *The Moon's*

MOONRISING

Legendary Moonshine. He thought about the two lonely bottles of whiskey in his quarters and wondered if he would ever be desperate enough to drink moonshine. Perhaps here he could find the discipline to abstain from alcohol. And even sex. He could live in truth the *halal* lifestyle he affected when he visited Abu Dhabi.

Alex was still glaring at the empty fridge, the white light bulb reflecting on her flushed face and emphasizing the curve of her collarbone. He remembered the way her eyes had traveled over his body the night before.

Perhaps not.

"Natalia needed to hear it," Alex said unapologetically. "They were putting zero effort into listening to the plants themselves. Everyone in the lab has their head bent over a chemistry set when they should be in the greenhouse."

"And you will be in the greenhouse? Listening to the plants?" He smiled a little. Victor had been right to persuade him to recruit Alex. "The greenhouse will be producing food in no time."

She picked up another redi-meal pouch with a look of disgust. "I have excellent motivation."

Between them, a red-headed woman reached for her own packet. She was scowling, and Mansoor wondered how much of the conversation she had overheard.

"You'll get used to it," said the woman in a thick Russian accent.

"Doubt it," Alex muttered.

The woman frowned. "I didn't have the time to run the greenhouse properly."

It sounded to Mansoor like she was picking up the thread of a conversation from earlier in the day.

The woman planted her stocky frame and crossed her arms. "I am only here for a limited time. An entire team of researchers at the Central Clinical Hospital in Moscow is depending on me to complete our research on therapeutic stem cells. Lives will be saved. I don't have the luxury of worrying about what I'm eating."

"You must be Natalia," Mansoor said smoothly. He put out a hand. "I am sure you are relieved to know the greenhouse is no longer your burden to bear. Alex has been brought on board to focus exclusively on growing food for the colony, leaving you free to pursue your own research."

Natalia did not take his hand. "I know who you are," she said, lip curling. "I am not here to make the brief vanity visits of the rich more comfortable. I am here to pack in as many experiments as I can before my time is up. So stay out of my way." She glared at both of them and stormed off with her redi-meal in hand.

Alex scowled at her retreating back. "I've been dealing with some version of that all day." She grabbed a redi-meal, seemingly at random, and pulled the warmer tab to heat it up. "Feels just like home."

"You look terrible," Zaynab, one of the younger Emirati engineers, told Mansoor bluntly. "What is all over your face?"

Mansoor squinted at himself on the video screen. "Mask lines," he said. "Moon dust is creeping into the interior of the hotel, even with the air seal."

Across the conference room table, Herb chuckled. "Lunar regolith is a bitch."

Mansoor had spent most of his time in the first weeks on the colony in a haze of sweat and dust, feverishly trying to solve their window problem. Before he had arrived, the original plan had been to construct the windows from a polycarbonate material, but it had become quickly apparent that the material could not produce optical properties sufficient to create the clear views essential for the hotel's design. Instead of finalizing a build out from the comfort of a conference room, he had needed to take on a laborious physical role. Mansoor considered the work penance for using his family's wealth to muscle his way onto the colony instead of

MOONRISING

allowing someone more qualified to take his place and put in as much time as he could squeeze out of every day.

Ten days ago, the engineers hit on the idea to extract quartz from the lunar regolith. The sample material the Refabricator had printed when fed quartz was perfect. It was strong enough to withstand the flying particles caused by the daily meteor crashes on the Moon's surface. And, most important to Mansoor and his architects, it produced a clear, transparent view.

Harvesting the quartz, however, was a struggle.

The commands to extract quartz could be sent to the robots directly by the Emirati engineering team, but Mansoor needed to manually clean off the loose, fine, and jagged moon dust interfering with the quartz extraction. It was one of the most physically taxing things he had ever done. The spacesuit was hot and cumbersome, and the moon dust got everywhere, even wearing down the joints of the suit. It smelled like gunpowder and left a metallic taste in his mouth. The machines were constantly breaking down and Mansoor, constrained by his suit's enormous gloves, wanted to scream in frustration every time he had to do a tedious and delicate hard reboot.

"You said you had good news?" Mansoor begged the assembled Emirati engineers.

Zaynab nodded. "We think we have found a way to keep the dust from interfering with the quartz extraction." She held up a lunar robot equipped with four long spires on each corner. She pressed a button, and the spires began to hum. Zaynab sprinkled sand over the robot, and it hovered above the spires and dissipated. "It's an electrodynamic dust shield. We printed the materials on our Refabricator, and we think the mining bots can be retrofitted fairly painlessly once we perform tests to confirm the effectiveness."

Herb moved closer to the screen to study the dust shields, asking technical questions of the engineers.

Mansoor laid his head down on the table in pure exhaustion. It was not that he was afraid of physical labor. He led a privileged life, yes, but his family worked hard for their country. They played even harder. Rock climbing on sheer cliffs and navigating steep ski slopes required mental and physical discipline. Those skills were transferable to maneuvering in a spacesuit, even if laboring in a suit lacked the dopamine rush of an extreme sport. But the daily physical demands on his body had been relentless.

Finally, Herb turned back to him. "Get some sleep, Mansoor. And a shower, please, man. I can smell you from here. I can do the testing tonight."

Mansoor stumbled back to his room, stripped off his clothes, and stepped into the shower, letting the lukewarm metallic water rush over him. When the beep sounded, ending his water ration, Mansoor realized he had not started washing his body. At least the worst of the dust had swirled down the drain.

Mansoor pitched onto his bed and slept the sleep of pure exhaustion.

A week later, Mansoor felt much more like himself. Quartz extraction was moving at a clipped pace, with only the occasional on-site intervention needed. The Refabricator was producing small windowpanes at a rate of ten per hour. Mansoor could finally leverage his years of experience into designing the interior rooms and the guest experience.

Drake Douglass found him late one afternoon in the ground vehicle garage, as he was returning from a stimulating trip to the site to finalize the bar and restaurant buildout. Drake waited patiently in an at-ease position as Mansoor pulled off his gear and carefully hung it in a designated locker.

Mansoor tried to ignore the sudden knot of tension in his gut as he said to the inspector, "You have been avoiding me."

Drake grunted. "I have a duty to provide Congress with an independent report."

"Of course." Mansoor kept his tone calm and confident. "Have you decided what your report will say?"

Drake crossed his arms. "The food situation is a disaster. You were right to invest there. I was initially surprised by your choice. Dr. Cole's research is controversial, and it raises ethical questions to hire Commander Cole's daughter. You need to keep ahead of the narrative with that one. I noticed the media didn't cover our launch. Your doing?"

Mansoor nodded. "John agreed it was the best course of action."

"John appears to be doing backflips for you. Did he really fly to Chicago in the middle of January to do you a favor?"

Mansoor shrugged. Although he considered Drake to be an ally, the former Marine had too rigid a sense of honor for Mansoor to trust him completely. It would not do for Drake to think he had too much power over NASA. "John and I thought in-person recruitment would be more successful."

"Seems you were right. I spoke at length with Alex Cole, and she is currently focused on producing enough food to feed one hundred residents and a dozen tourists. You should give her a more complete briefing. She seems to be very good at what she does."

"She does, doesn't she? Victor recommended her."

"Victor." Drake gave a little shudder. "He keeps trying to contact me. Get him off my back, will you?"

Mansoor laughed despite himself. "I do not control Victor. Nobody controls Victor."

"The man has no sense of normal human behavior."

Mansoor did not disagree, but he did not want to waste precious moments with Drake discussing Victor. "What else?"

Drake shrugged. "The technical capacity to build additional rooms using lunar materials is compelling. I can easily recommend an increase in the number of scientists on-site."

Mansoor's heart sank. "Scientists?"

"Look around you," Drake said, gesturing to the open hangar bay. "Does this look like a place for children? I'm not so sure it isn't a violation of the UN Declaration of the Rights of the Child. Minors can't consent to live in this box."

"The colony is safer than many situations where children live. We can make this place its own village where everyone feels responsible for the children, like the small towns of the past. I know you will come to see it that way too." He could hear his words getting too flowery and tried to stop himself. Drake would not appreciate being manipulated. He switched tactics. "Surely Congress believes families belong together. Certainly, Americans are well acquainted with the devastating impact of family separation."

His eyes narrowed. "You may have recommended me for this gig and paid for my ticket, but you have not bought *me*."

Mansoor made a placating gesture. "Of course. I would never ask you to compromise your independence."

Drake snorted. "No, just use my relationships in Washington to push your agenda."

"My agenda will benefit your country first. The Homestead Act will reestablish America on the global stage and position the United States as the undisputed leader of the next era in space."

"Save your proselytizing, Mansoor. I'm already here, aren't I?"

"You are," Mansoor said, backing off. "And I am grateful for it. Especially at a time when your star is rising. I heard a rumor that if President Fairchild wins a second term you are on the short list for secretary of defense."

For one fleeting moment, Drake's bland face looked embarrassed. "I'm too young. I'm not qualified."

Mansoor smiled. At last, he was gaining the upper hand in their conversation. "Top of your class at the Naval Academy, decorated Marine honorably discharged with the rank of colonel,

MOONRISING

hero of the Sierra Leone Hostage Crisis, and now Peary Station inspector set to testify before Congress on the most consequential legislation of this session. You may be young, but you have an impressive résumé."

Drake rubbed the back of his neck with one large hand. "I can't make a mistake here."

"I trust you to do what is right. You are more than qualified, and you are one of the most honorable men I know."

"Have you ever been around kids?"

"My elder brothers and sisters all have children."

"But you don't babysit, do you?" Drake asked. "I do. My sister will drop my niece off with me for days at a time. I know seven different hairstyles for mixed-race toddler girls. I know how to clean a boo-boo, be a tickle monster, and say no to bedtime negotiations. Do you know what I see when I look around this place?" He let out a breath. "I see sharp objects, poison, and choking hazards. I see no fresh air or trees. I see no open spaces to run. I see no teachers or daycare providers. I don't think we're ready."

"What would change your mind?" Mansoor asked steadily.

"I'm not sure. When you and Victor asked me to put my hat in for this role, we agreed that my testimony before Congress would be my own. I need the breathing room to come to my own conclusions."

Mansoor knew when to retreat. "Then that is what you shall have."

When the second floor of the hotel was finally constructed, and the robots were scurrying around building the upper bedroom floors, Mansoor and his Emirati team were ready to think about furniture. For the restaurant, the team had designed curving wave chairs printed in the Refabricator from a single piece of material. They were a dappled, silvery color and glittered in the sunlight.

Mansoor was unloading a stack of chairs from a robotic cart when Alex stepped into the dining room. She was the first resident besides Herb to have come into the hotel, and Mansoor had a hard time containing his delight at seeing her in his domain. "You're here," Mansoor said, a bit stupidly.

"I hope that's okay. Herb directed me to try out your new passage," Alex replied. Her cheeks were flushed.

In the Moon's vacuum, it had taken the robots a mere 72 hours to construct the 1 km air-sealed passage wide enough for four people. *72 hours.* The potential speed of lunar innovation was astounding.

If the human capacity could keep up.

All the remote programming in the world did not matter if there were insufficient personnel on the Moon for maintenance. Now that Mansoor was here, it was increasingly clear: everything depended on the Homestead Act. There would be spouses looking for work. Potential colonists willing to take any job for a chance to live on the Moon. Perhaps, eventually, tuning up robots could be a teenage summer job. But without the Homestead Act, exponential scale would not be feasible.

Alex looked around the nearly finished dining room. "These windows are striking. I forget sometimes that Peary Station experiences continuous daylight. I didn't realize how narrow and dark the rest of the colony appears until seeing this view."

"The station was built on one of the crater's *pics de lumière éternelle*," Mansoor replied, stepping next to her to share the view. On the craggy surface, the communications array reached into the sky, its giant satellite pointed toward Earth. "'Peaks of Eternal Light.' French astronomer Camille Flammarion named them nearly two hundred years ago. Rather poetic, don't you think?"

Alex gave a little snort, but he could tell she was intrigued. He wanted to impress her, he realized. He had a soft spot for capturing the imagination of practical, data-driven scientists.

MOONRISING

"I have a team in Abu Dhabi that helped me create these window-panes. The hotel would not have the same impact without this view. Victor is after me to patent the technique."

"Victor is obsessed with patents." Alex grinned up at him. "He has never understood why I don't apply for patents for my seeds." She looked at the view again. Her eyes were shining. "You can't limit this. What a gift these windows will be to future wings of the colony. And I'll need your secrets when I'm ready to build a second greenhouse."

He gave her a little bow. "My secrets are yours."

Alex blushed. Mansoor took a closer look at her. She was nervous, he realized. Her lips were chapped and bitten, and tendrils of her hair had escaped her ponytail in wisps around her face.

"Actually . . . I came here because I need your help." Alex was fidgeting, practically bouncing in the Moon's low gravity. Mansoor wanted to reach out and steady her as he had done on the ship. "It's important."

"You have my attention." He pulled one of the new restaurant chairs over and sat, concealing a sigh of relief. It felt good to get off his feet.

"My mandate, as I understand it, is to develop a sustainable food production system for the colony, yes?" He noticed the flush continued on her neck, and he wondered idly how far down it went.

He thought about Drake's advice to brief Alex on his true ambitions for the colony. It was too early, he decided, and made an encouraging noise for her to continue.

"A plant-based diet is going to be a challenge," Alex said. "Even once I finally eradicate this damn fungus, the pure caloric daily output will be insufficient for the population. The amount of legumes we can produce won't generate enough protein. And fats from olives or walnuts, well . . . that's a long way off." She paused her fidgeting and twisted her hands together. In a quieter, hesitant voice, she said, "I brought chickens to the colony."

"Chickens," he repeated, rather stunned. What had Victor gotten him into?

"Chicken eggs. I'm keeping them warm in an inflatable incubator I brought with me. They're about to hatch."

"Chickens," he said again. "Without informing NASA?" He braced himself to hear the answer he knew was coming.

"The administrator found out today when Natalia filed a complaint. I've never seen Anderson in a temper before. He got all—" She grimaced. "Purply." Mansoor tried not to laugh at her rueful expression. Alex continued in a hesitant tone, "He wants to terminate, immediately. He's afraid of avian flu."

"Is that a legitimate concern? Could they be carrying diseases?"

"Of course not. They're mutagenetic. This breed of chickens has done more to combat the famine in West Africa than the entire USAID organic food program. And these particular eggs were bred from isolated chickens in my lab, personally supervised by me." She jabbed her thumbs into her chest.

Mansoor was getting over his initial shock and found himself suddenly captivated by the possibilities. "How will they live?"

"Herb taught me how to program the Refabricator, and I'm halfway through building a coop in the brood room. This breed is designed for communities experiencing food shortages. The chickens can live fully on vegetable waste, like dead leaves and strawberry stems. Each chicken produces as many as four eggs per day, once they're fully mature. We can feed the entire colony a meal's worth of protein on this stock. Every day. *And* their waste makes excellent compost."

Mansoor could see why Anderson was upset, but he was also beginning to understand why Victor had pushed so hard to get Alex on this project. Mansoor and Victor had known for a long time that if they wanted the colony to grow exponentially, they could not move at NASA's pace. But he also could not afford to alienate every other ally. "Are you accountable to anyone?" he asked. "At the university?"

MOONRISING

Alex crossed her arms defensively. "Not for my research methods. That was my most critical condition when I negotiated the contract. Most schools wouldn't give me that option. Not every institution values free speech and intellectual autonomy as much as the University of Chicago."

"Well, you are part of a chain of command now. You cannot make these decisions on your own. You need to build up the political capital. Anderson did not want to hire you, you know." He tried to say it gently.

"I got that sense," Alex admitted. "I don't think anyone wanted NASA to hire me. The colony scientists have made that clear enough."

"I wanted NASA to hire you. In fact, I insisted," he said. His tone came out fiercer than he had intended. Had the other colony residents been making her feel unwelcome? He should have noticed. He had a responsibility to her. The long, grueling hours at the hotel had distracted him. "I have a great deal of political capital with Anderson. It is not just the funding I bring to the relationship. Anderson trusts my judgment. I earned that trust over years of delivering results for him. I chose to advocate for you because Victor persuaded me that you are a unique talent."

Alex did not look pleased. "I didn't ask you to do any of that. Victor—someone I like to consider a close friend—never even mentioned you. I came here to save my lab."

Mansoor shook his head. "I don't think so. If you were just here for the funding, you would be keeping your head down. You would not be picking fights with the Russians because they bungled the greenhouse. And you would not be bringing unauthorized livestock into a tightly controlled space colony."

Alex took a deep breath as if reining in what she wanted to say to him. She pulled out a chair and sat down, facing him, leaning forward to look him straight in the eye. "I can do this if I have enough room to maneuver. I can feed everyone on this station, even your fancy tourists. But I need the leeway. I need you to fight for me." Alex was looking at him with an intensity that went straight to his groin. Mansoor felt a desperate overwhelming desire to do everything she asked of him.

"Very well," he said. "I will fight for your chickens."

MacKenzie was not pleased.

"Mutagenetic chickens?" Even through the screen, Mansoor could feel her disgust. "I thought those were illegal."

"Not illegal, just not widely distributed in the States. In many countries, mutagenetic meat is the norm. Americans are the ones afraid of agricultural advancements."

"For good reason." MacKenzie frowned at him. "I don't think you understand. You weren't in the States at the time. Mutagenetic potatoes, Mansoor, that's what caused the outbreak. We're Irish. We used to eat potatoes at least once a day. My entire family was sick for weeks. I'll never forget the sight of my father convulsing on our kitchen floor in the middle of dinner. Mutagenetic potatoes put my grandmother in a coma, and she was partially paralyzed for the rest of her life. I wouldn't eat a mutant potato if you force-fed me."

"I am sorry for the suffering your family endured," he said uncomfortably. Anderson had warned Mansoor he did not fully grasp the American aversion to mutagenetic food—but MacKenzie was giving him a picture.

"Mutagenetic food makes me taste bile. I have a visceral reaction to it. You didn't live through the Potato Plague. You don't understand."

MacKenzie wasn't given to dramatic embellishments, and he wanted to take her concerns seriously. But she was right, he couldn't understand her reaction. The infected potatoes' supply chain was US domestic, and the outbreak was confined to the continental United States. He knew one in three Americans were

MOONRISING

sick enough to stay home from work or school, and the death toll had reached one hundred thousand, hitting the young and the elderly especially hard. It had caused the USDA to impose severe restrictions on mutagenetic food while the rest of the world was learning to embrace it as a counterweight to the threat of famine caused by climate change.

"You knew we were bringing Alex Cole to the colony," said Mansoor.

"I did. I didn't like it, but I support you, Mansoor. I trust you. And I'm not going upside, so it doesn't impact my health personally."

"Anderson said something similar. I got him to approve the mutagenetic chickens, but he is worried about the rumor of their existence getting out." He sighed and rubbed his face. Perhaps this challenge was larger than he realized. "We need to get out ahead of the press."

"Fine," MacKenzie said in reluctant agreement. "You know I always have your back. Let's make a plan."

When they had finished the outlines of a media strategy, Mansoor updated MacKenzie on his conversation with Drake.

MacKenzie frowned. "He's thinking about his niece? I don't think that's where we want his head to be at." She looked aside. "Rashid will be with Senator Garcia next Tuesday at a fundraiser in D.C. We could beef up the education and childcare plans by then, and commission some renderings of an indoor playground. I would pay good money to hear Rashid pitch a playground on the Moon."

"You would?" Mansoor asked with some surprise.

"Your brother—he's good," MacKenzie said. "Garcia brought Senator Lin to our office when they were in town to support the Teamsters strike, and I got to see him in action. I swear, Rashid made Lin feel like he was the most fascinating and important person in the world. These senators love to talk, but with Rashid it's like they go to a deeper level. The way he listens with his whole body without saying a word. It's a gift."

"Huh," was all Mansoor could think to say.

"You're acting like you're surprised." She laughed. "Well, he is your baby brother. He's probably different with you."

Mansoor shook himself out of his stupor. "Senator Lin? Garcia is reaching with Lin."

MacKenzie smirked. "I wouldn't be so sure." She cut the comm.

6

ALEX

ALEX SNIFFED AT THE FUZZY GRAY SPORES COVERING A CHERRY tomato leaf. The mold infection was back.

Again.

At least the Swiss chard in the next tray looked healthy, the plants' vivid red stems contrasting with their vibrant green leaves. Chard could handle almost anything, in Alex's experience, and it was comforting to see that remained true even under the harshest of conditions.

Bending down, she examined the radishes in the lowest shelf. The leafy tops were yellow and shriveled. She scowled at the high-pressure sodium lamps. The wattage was too strong, she was sure of it, but she had not yet hit on the right light balance.

All around her, the continuous sunlight shone through the warped translucent windows, letting in the sun's energy while blocking harmful radiation. When she first arrived, she had theorized the windows provided sufficient sunlight for the plants growing on the top shelves to thrive without grow lights, and she had been rewarded with snow peas shooting up so fast she had needed to string twine to the ceiling window supports to give the plants something to climb.

The week she'd arrived on the colony, Alex had ruthlessly eliminated trays blighted with botrytis, sterilized them, and replaced them with her own mutagenetic seeds for hydroponic friendly plants. At least 70 percent of the seeds she had brought with her would be useless without some sort of soil or a passable imitation, but she could at least start growing with seeds she trusted, using the best practices for hydroponic gardening her biologist colleagues hadn't bothered learning.

The greenhouse was well laid out, Alex admitted. The NASA scientists on Earth who had designed the room had maximized every square foot of the ten by twelve space. The floor-to-ceiling shelving held polyurethane trays of plants with their roots immersed in chemically enhanced water. Each type of plant grew in its own system that contained its own reservoir, pump, aerator, and water heater. Plants should have been thriving in such an environment, not covered with mold spores.

Alex took a moment to debate how she wanted to spend her day. Should she eliminate the latest mold outbreak or attempt to resolve the underlying cause? It was still strange not to have access to eager postdocs ready to jump at her instructions.

She was alone.

She had not expected to feel so isolated on a colony of a hundred people. The majority of the residents were scientists, frantically focused on maximizing their time on Peary Station to squeeze in as many experiments as possible. They didn't trust her. Alex could sense it immediately, even before Natalia had unleashed on her. Her reputation had preceded her, and she could feel herself being iced out before she had gotten the chance to prove herself.

Stepping into the hallway outside the greenhouse, Alex frowned up at the air duct. She needed to do something about the airflow. It was not only to eliminate the mold blight. She suspected the room had built up an excess of ethylene without the presence of natural wind to carry the colorless gas away. It would explain the stunted growth of many of the plants, especially on the lower shelves farthest from the vents.

Alex walked a short distance down the hall to the nearest laboratory and addressed the room at large. "I need a ladder and a screwdriver. Where are they?"

Three biochemists had their heads bent together over a lab table, goggles covering their eyes. They looked up in unison. "You got an orientation tour, didn't you?" one of them said in annoyance.

Alex responded with raised eyebrows. "Natalia must have neglected to mention it."

"Supply closet, end of the hallway," another biochemist said, and returned to her bubbling experiment.

Alex located the items she needed and carried the lightweight ladder back to the greenhouse. She climbed up and wrestled with an access hatch on the duct with the screwdriver. Once she managed to get it open, she pulled her torso inside to get a better look. It was a large shaft and sturdy enough to accommodate her full weight, if necessary. She peered at the internal rotating fan and adjusted the settings from low to maximum. She would need something more sophisticated in the long term. Maybe Finn could run some experiments at the Institute.

By the time she had gotten the hatch back in place and the supplies returned, the greenhouse already felt different. The plants waved in a friendly manner, enjoying the breeze. The humid air felt less heavy and stale. She stretched her arms up and did a few side bends.

Time to tackle the blighted tomatoes.

Alex tentatively knocked on the colony commander's open office door. Saul looked up from his console.

"I brought you a salad," Alex said as she stepped into the room, uncertain of her welcome. Her father had barely made any time for her since she had arrived on the colony.

Saul took the compostable plate from her. "Ah, thank you."

"I can't imagine all of these processed redi-meals are good for your cholesterol."

Saul took a bite and made a face. "What is this?"

"Chard," Alex said, perching uninvited on the side chair across from his desk. "And a mix of herbs. There isn't much producing yet in the greenhouse. We used to grow chard in the yard, do you remember?"

"Hm." Saul took another bite and winced. "I don't recall it tasting quite so bitter."

"It's better cooked. Remember, Mom used to sauté it with white wine, garlic, and lemon juice? Topped with Parmesan cheese." Her mother had taught Alex how to sow Swiss chard seeds in mid-summer to overwinter outdoors and produce early harvests in the spring. Her mom had always known how to make the most of an abundance of greens.

Saul looked away at the mention of her mother. Pushing down the familiar ache, Alex said, "We'll have garlic here within the year, I hope, and maybe lemon trees in the next three."

Saul didn't respond. His attention was caught by something popping up on his console. Alex debated her options. Crying never worked. Or shouting. Or begging. Not that Alex wanted to do any of those. She decided to channel her mother's serene patience and wait him out.

After a moment, Saul looked back at her as if surprised to see her still there. "Lemon trees?" he repeated. "I hardly think the colony needs lemon trees. We are first and foremost a military base."

"And a scientific research station," Alex said, keeping her voice calm despite the sting of his casual rejection of her work. "I was thinking of the hotel, actually. Have you had a chance to see the

MOONRISING

dining room space yet? Mansoor's bots built a splendid bar. I'd like to keep it stocked with a steady supply of citrus."

"To mix with imported top shelf alcohol?" Saul took another bite of the salad. "Maybe I shouldn't say this, but I'm dreading the day we have high-net-worth tourists wandering around the dome acting entitled." He shuddered. "Security nightmare."

"You don't want tourists on the station?" Even though Alex hadn't been thrilled about catering to tourists either, she found herself bristling. "You seemed pleased to see Mansoor the night we arrived."

Saul shrugged. "We appreciate the investment. The colony must continue to modernize. U.S. military capabilities must never stand still. To be honest, the environment I'm operating in is changing. When we conceived of a permanent moon base, it was as a Space Force military outpost with a few scientists. Now, the scientists outnumber my people, ten to one. I am obligated to keep Peary Station secure, but my resources are dwindling."

"Do you need more Space Force personnel on the station?" Alex asked, curious.

"I won't go over anything classified," her father said, tapping one finger on his desk. "I'll just say that the best way to keep the peace is deterrence. I don't like how small my force has become."

He finished the chard and rose to drop the plate and fork in the composter outside his office. Alex followed him. It had been a long conversation, for her father, and she was willing to be dismissed.

"Thank you for the salad," Saul said. He hesitated, as if he wanted to say more but could not find the words.

Alex gave him a nod and left him to his work.

"I need your brain," Alex told Victor when he answered her late-night call. She was making use of one of the public phone

93

booths in the central dome. He stood in his kitchen, and, behind him, Alex could see that his refrigerator was covered in equations.

"That's what they all say." Victor ate a forkful of a redi-meal and turned his back to her, scribbling on the fridge.

"You're going to give Harper a heart attack," Alex teased.

Victor said nothing for a moment as he finished writing. Then, he turned to face her and put his marker on the countertop. "Harper is divorcing me."

"That's an extreme reaction for some appliance graffiti," Alex said flippantly, then abruptly shut her mouth when she saw Victor's vulnerable expression. *Oh*. He wasn't joking.

Victor fiddled with the marker. "You always said I would be unable to satisfy her. It seems you understood my wife better than I did. She didn't last two years married to me."

"I didn't say that. I said that she was trying to *mold* you. Which, by the way, anyone who knows you should realize is impossible." She tried to make her face compassionate despite the fact that she'd seen it coming. "I'm sorry, Victor—it's on Harper that she couldn't accept you as you are."

"And what am I, Alex? I failed in AgTech."

"You sold three patents for multimillions," Alex objected.

Victor blew out his breath. "For what? I was tinkering around the edges. Americans still reject mutagenetic food. I didn't make any substantive change in the agricultural industry at scale."

"You're awfully maudlin tonight. Is it Harper?"

"No, not Harper. We haven't started launch tests. It's nearly April. I promised Mansoor I'd have a ship ready for him this summer. I *promised*. I can't figure it out." Victor leaned against the counter and clutched his blond hair. "I'm so close."

Alex had been friends with Victor a long time, and she knew how to shake him out of a funk. "Are you saying a PhD in biological and environmental engineering didn't prepare you to be a rocket scientist? I'm shocked. I could have told you this would happen if you'd bothered to take me into your confidence at any point."

Victor glared at her. "You said you needed my help? This must be important. We haven't spoken since you berated me for securing you a decade of lab funding and the career opportunity of a lifetime."

"You mean since you let NKI cut off my funding and lied to me about it? Since you got the administrator of NASA to personally recruit me?"

A grin crossed Victor's face. "That wasn't me. Mansoor is the one with the political connections. It was a good move, though, wasn't it?"

Alex's lips tugged up in a reluctant smile. "Yes, Victor, it was a very effective manipulation tactic. Ten out of ten." She tried to picture her idiosyncratic friend in cahoots with the elegant, reserved Mansoor. It was hard to fathom.

"So, what do you want with my brain, Dr. Cole?"

Alex explained to him about the mold fungus. "I've set the vent fan to high, but the ethylene volume is still over ten parts per million. I need the Institute to design something that can be constructed with lunar materials."

Victor nodded absently and frowned at his tablet. Alex waited him out, looking through the clear glass of the phone booth to watch Mitch, one of the Space Force personnel, bend over a console in the quiet command dome. She wished the heavy radiation shielding in the residential areas didn't force calls to be confined to the hardwired phone booths and conference rooms of the dome. She would have liked to be taking the call from the comfort of her bed.

Victor suddenly shouted, "Rutile!"

Alex turned her attention back to him. "Rutile?"

"TiO_2. It's been found in minor phases in lunar sample mineralogy."

"And how will that help my plants?"

"It's a natural formation of titanium dioxide. Coat a tube in titanium dioxide to convert the ethylene to water and carbon dioxide."

"Photocatalytic conversion," Alex said with excitement. "Yes, I think that will work."

"Good," Victor said. "Have Finn call me if your team gets stuck."

"I will." Alex could see Victor already drifting back to the equations on his refrigerator. "And Victor? I'm sorry about Harper."

Victor gave her a crooked smile. "No, you aren't. But thanks for saying it."

"Are you watching the segment about the colony tonight?" Sandra asked Alex at dinner the next night, sitting down across from her at the edge of the communal table in the cafeteria. Alex looked up at her in surprise. She had gotten used to taking most of her meals alone after her few attempts at conversation were met with either coldness or outright rudeness. "I think part of it might be about you?" Sandra said. "I overheard Mansoor filming earlier today. Did he fill you in?"

Alex stiffened in shock. She had a terrible feeling this was about the chickens. Mansoor had told her he would defend her chickens to NASA, but—was he planning on doing it publicly? She pushed away her half-eaten redi-meal and looked uneasily at the other residents milling around the cafeteria.

As a communications officer, Sandra was in her father's chain of command and didn't appear to share the same suspicion of Alex that the scientists did. She would have expected scientists to know better than the general population, but nope. To many of them, the Potato Plague represented the failure of science to live up to its promise. To Alex, the failure belonged to corrupt and self-serving American corporations, not science.

MOONRISING

"I don't like publicity," Alex said to Sandra. "Nothing good ever comes of it."

"You've got nothing to worry about," Sandra reassured her. "We don't do interviews without preconditions here, and the coverage is always positive. Nothing captures the public imagination quite like the Moon."

"The segment is about to air," called Carson, one of the American geologists. Alex rose reluctantly with Sandra and moved to the lounge adjacent to the cafeteria. She wrung her hands together. Her palms were already sweaty.

At least twenty people had packed into the space, squeezing onto the couch and pulling in chairs from the cafeteria. Alex hung near the door. With the lack of connection in her bedroom, this was the only way she could hear what Mansoor was going to say about her—and even though part of her just wanted to go hide under her covers, it was important for her to know, in case she had to do damage control after the fact. She looked around for him, expecting him to be there, but Mansoor was not in the crowd.

The digital version of Mansoor appeared on the screen, in a prerecorded interview with a media personality she vaguely recognized. He began by describing the fabulous lunar hotel under construction. As he spoke, beautiful renderings flashed across the screen. Alex had been to the hotel site not long ago and was confident it looked nothing like the fantasy art on display. At least not yet.

Alex tensed when Mansoor said, "We are excited to partner with world-renowned University of Chicago scientist Dr. Alexandra Cole to provide our guests with chef-created meals grown right here on the Moon." Mansoor looked as handsome and polished as ever, the phone booth background displaying the dome command center. "While our guests can expect to consume a vegetarian diet in their week with us, they will not need to be fully vegan thanks to Dr. Cole's remarkable West African chickens, suited to a low-water environment." An image appeared on the screen of a happy free-range chicken that looked nothing like the hairless baby chicks currently sleeping in their colony brood.

Every eye in the room swiveled to Alex. Julien, a French astrophysicist leaning against the pool table, asked with interest, "We have chickens?"

"Chicks," Alex corrected. "They've just started to hatch."

On the screen, the host was asking Mansoor if all food provided on the colony was organic. *Here we go,* thought Alex. But Mansoor didn't flinch.

"All food grown on the Moon has been vigorously tested according to WHO standards," Mansoor said smoothly. "Our scientifically-minded guests understand that cultivating organic food is not always possible in the harsh growing conditions of the Moon, and that some light gene manipulation may be necessary to produce healthy and abundant local produce."

Alex waited for the grilling from the host, but the woman just nodded and moved on to ask about the hotel accommodations. Alex was stunned. When had a journalist ever let the issue of mutagenetic food go so easily?

Julien gave her a friendly smile, "Is there *coq au vin* in my future?"

Alex noted a few of the Americans making faces of disgust. With some irritation, she said, "Of course not. Do you have a supply of red wine and fresh mushrooms on hand?" She winced internally when Julien's face fell. In a more measured tone, she said, "What I mean to say is, it's never going to be economical to raise animals for meat here. My chickens will be used for eggs. When they're old and they stop producing, we can slaughter them for meat, but by then they'll be stringy and tough. I could see us raising goats, eventually, for dairy. Not cows. Their methane production would be too big of a challenge in a closed ecosystem."

Kayla, the head of polar ice mining operations, curled her lips. "I'll stick to redi-meals, thanks." The station doctor, Naomi, made a noise of agreement. Under her breath Kayla muttered, "*Nasty.*" Naomi laughed.

"Fine," said Alex, turning to leave before the segment finished. She'd heard what she came for. "No one is forcing you to eat the food I produce."

Alex stepped into the empty cafeteria, her anger welling quickly upward into tears of frustration. She had a sudden, overwhelming urge for her mother. She closed her eyes and pictured her mother's kitchen, with its wall of fresh herbs. When she was a child, they would harvest their dinner from the garden every night, making pesto, caprese, or gazpacho together. Alex missed her mother every day, but she was grateful she had not seen her daughter become a pariah in the scientific community.

Alex knew that she was producing safe food in the greenhouse. But what was the point if the Americans on the station refused to eat it? She had allowed herself to be pulled away from her real work in Hyde Park to grow food for scientists who mistrusted her approach and wealthy tourists who hardly needed the nutrition boost.

It may have been the administrator of NASA who had come calling with the opportunity, but she knew who was really to blame.

Without pausing to think, Alex found herself searching the directory on a side panel at the mouth of the residential hall to find the room number to Mansoor's quarters.

Mansoor answered at her pounding knock. When he saw her face, he asked, "Did it air?"

She wanted to scream at his nonchalant attitude. "Yes, it aired. And you completely misrepresented the science." She stepped into the room without waiting for an invitation. "What the hell is 'light gene manipulation'?"

He gave a shrug of his elegant shoulders. "We had to control the narrative."

"You don't understand. Every time my name is mentioned in the news, the Institute gets threats. It isn't safe for my lab manager or my postdoc researchers. The Eco Liberation Society is always looking for more content to inflame their supporters."

"Or," Mansoor said calmly. "I have just convinced every aspiring space tourist to rethink mutagenetic food. If they want a seat on our ship, they will need to support our methods. I know these types. They are much more likely to act as if they knew all along their trip would include mutagenetic food, and they are sophisticated enough to understand it will be safe."

He sat down in a chair and gestured for her to do the same. Alex dimly registered his room was slightly bigger than her own, with two chairs on either side of a tiny table. The table held a datapad, the remnants of a redi-meal, and one of Mansoor's crystal glasses.

Alex gripped the back of the other chair, glaring at him. "You and Victor did an excellent job maneuvering me into accepting this position. You must think you're very clever. But you cannot manipulate every potential tourist. No one has that much charisma."

Mansoor's lips twitched. Was he suppressing a smile? "It's not really about the tourists."

"What are you talking about? You threw ten years of funding at my lab. That wasn't for your space tourism industry?"

He spoke deliberately as if choosing his words with care, tilting his head up to meet her eyes. "What if we could live in space? Sustainably? With no monthly shipments of supplies to keep us alive."

She didn't understand. "That's what I'm working on, isn't it? That's why you defended the idea of eggs. Sustainable food production for a hundred people."

"Not a hundred," he said gently. "What about a million?" His expression was intense.

MOONRISING

"What are you talking about?"

"I believe, and Victor believes, that the colony could sustain a million people in our lifetime if given enough rope."

"A million people," Alex repeated, stunned. Surely, he realized that wasn't possible. "You think there are a million people interested in leaving their families behind to come here?"

Mansoor's eyes shone. "What if they didn't need to leave their families? What if the colony could support children as well?"

She frowned at him, "Why?"

Mansoor stood up, touching her arm to stop her agitated fidgeting. She looked up at his face, intimidated by his deadly serious expression. "We can protect the Earth if we reduce the strain on her resources. We can reverse the worst effects of climate change. Despite the switch away from fossil fuels, pollution caused by heavy industry is still the leading cause of climate change. We're already mining water and turning the elements of the lunar regolith into useful materials using the Refabricator here on the colony. What if we shifted most of the mining of resources to the Moon, to Mars, and to asteroids?" His voice rose with a passionate intensity. "The Moon is bursting with resources like aluminum, Helium-3, and rare earth metals. We could be exporting these materials to Earth in a matter of years, disrupting and perhaps closing the polluting mines on Earth. We have seen the number of climate refugees rise every year, and it is going to get worse. A billion people currently live below sea level. What if there were jobs and opportunities for those disrupted families—in space? Over time, given the right mix of incentives, the majority of the human population may choose to live in space." How could he make such an extreme statement sound so confident? "The biodiversity of Earth could be preserved. It cannot all be done in our lifetime, but fully colonizing the Moon is the first step."

Alex took a step back. Of course she cared about preserving Earth's biodiversity—and all the other things Mansoor had just lobbed at her. But this—this was too much. Absurd, even. "That's too big for you to take on," she stammered. She had thought Mansoor was an attractive, often infuriating, rich businessman playing at being an astronaut. She had not realized he harbored such grandiose visions.

"Not me alone. Victor is my partner in this. And now you know. Will you join us?" He held out one hand to her. He was looking at her steadily with his rich brown eyes.

Alex stared at him blankly. Could she be part of an effort to develop agricultural systems to feed a million people? It was hard to credit the idea. The picture Mansoor had painted seemed like the delusional fantasy of a billionaire accustomed to throwing money around to get his way.

"I—I—I have to go," she stammered, and bolted from his room.

Alex slept fitfully and woke up late, rushing to meet her appointment slot for her required treadmill workout designed to keep her bones strong in low-g. When she arrived at the gym, she stopped short. Kayla was finishing her own session. Alex remembered her look of revulsion from the night before.

Kayla stepped off the treadmill, wiping sweat on the edge of the fuchsia scarf holding back her short twists. She scrubbed the machine with a towel and dropped it into the recycler. "The Machine of Torment is all yours," she said breathlessly. "Clean it twice, will you? After you shed mutant DNA all over it." She gave Alex a wide berth, as if Alex was infected with something. Enough was enough.

"What's your problem?" Alex spouted.

Kayla spun to face her. "My problem? I don't want you here. No one wants you here. We don't want the poison you're pushing."

"Poison?" Alex sputtered. "Listen to you. You're a scientist. You know perfectly well that what I'm growing isn't poison."

MOONRISING

"I'm an engineer, not a shill for Big Ag. I don't lie to people for profit."

"Neither do I," Alex said, strapping her legs into the heavy weights connected to the treadmill. "You know nothing about me." *A shill for Big Ag.* That could not be further from the truth.

Kayla waved her hand in a dismissive gesture and made to leave. Then, she turned back, coming to face Alex at the front of the treadmill. "My granny killed my grandad. She served him funeral potatoes, and he collapsed. He went into a coma and never woke up. She was the best cook I ever knew, but after that she never cooked again."

For a second, Alex just looked at her. What did she want? An apology from Alex?

"Look, Kayla. I'm sorry for what happened to your grandfather. But it has no connection to what I'm doing in the greenhouse," Alex said.

"Seriously?" Kayla's dark brown eyes glowered at her. "That's all you have to say?"

Alex shrugged. She said the first thing that popped into her mind. "What are funeral potatoes?"

Kayla made a scoffing sound. "Aren't you a Midwesterner? How have you never had funeral potatoes? Creamy? Cheesy? Cornflakes on top? No?"

"I grew up in Bethesda."

"Bethesda," Kayla repeated with distaste. She made it sound like an insult. "Of course you grew up in Bethesda."

"But why are they called funeral potatoes?"

"It's a casserole you bring to a homegoing. But my granny used to make them every Sunday. They were my grandad's favorite." Kayla grimaced. "She never expected they would cause his own funeral."

Alex wasn't sure what else to say. She'd already said she was sorry for Kayla's loss. She hadn't personally known anyone who had died from the Potato Plague. At the time, she was growing her own strain of hearty waxy yellow potatoes in her family's garden. Her father had been sick, she remembered. He had sweated in the upstairs bedroom, cursing the fries he'd eaten in the NASA cafeteria. But a few days later, he was fine.

She felt a brief pang of envy for Mansoor's easy charisma. It would come in handy now.

"I can't grow potatoes until the compost bins build up enough soil," said Alex. "But maybe someday we could re-create funeral potatoes. They sound good."

"I don't want to eat your mutant potatoes!" Kayla practically shouted at her. "Did you hear anything I just said?" She slammed the door on her way out of the room.

Alex took a moment to breathe in the silence. So much for trying to smooth things over; somehow, she'd made things worse. She switched on the treadmill and started running. Her mind replayed the interaction with Kayla once, then twice, then a third time, her frustration mounting with each repetition. It wasn't the first time someone had shoved the death of a grandparent at Alex. She'd run out of empathy for the tactic, though maybe she could have done a better job faking it. After the workout, she showered and went to feed the chicks.

Alex scattered lettuce and kale among the chicks, watching them scamper after their breakfast on tiny legs. She could not reconcile Mansoor's vision for a million people on the colony, fed by mutagenetic food, with the barrier of Kayla's disgust—and all the other Americans she represented—looming over the effort.

She needed another perspective.

Leaving the chicks, Alex walked through the research wing to the central dome and claimed an empty phone booth.

Navin answered after a moment. He was outside on the University of Chicago campus and yellow daffodils appeared

MOONRISING

behind him. As soon as his face popped on the screen, Alex felt an unexpected wave of affection for him.

"Alex Cole, can it be? I was beginning to think you'd forgotten all about me."

"Hi, Navin," Alex said with a lopsided smile. "I should have called sooner. I'm working nonstop, and the only way to connect to video is in these tiny phone booths that have a wired connection back to the communications array."

Navin waved her excuses away. "It's nice to see your face."

"You too." Navin looked even scruffier than usual, with an unkempt beard and a black hoodie with the Eco Liberation Society logo on the chest. And—was that a shadow, or a bruise on his cheek? A shadow, she decided. To her surprise, she realized she'd missed him.

"I was hoping to get your perspective on something," Alex said. "Are you still involved with anti-mining activism?"

Navin scowled. "I rode the Amtrak to Arizona just last week to take a stand against new mining operations on indigenous land."

"With the ELS?" Alex asked, already knowing the answer. She wasn't surprised to see Navin drift back to the ELS once she was gone.

Navin shrugged in acknowledgment. "One Earth, one fight. I know you'll hate this, but I have been spending more time with Riley. Did you know she's taken on a leadership role within the ELS? Anyway, she's getting us more involved in direct action to stop polluters." He grinned, even though he did look a little shamefaced too. "It's exciting, Alex. I think the ELS is finally speaking the language American corporations understand. They'll have a harder time contaminating sacred hot springs with burnt out equipment."

Alex very deliberately did not engage on that topic. Whenever Navin's friend Riley had breezed into Chicago, she spent her time lecturing Alex on the dangers of mutagenetic food and attempting to persuade Navin to break things off with such a dangerous anti-environmentalist.

Instead of getting into it with Navin about the ELS, Alex said, "I've heard a theory that we could close Earth mines if we tapped into the resources of the Moon."

Navin snorted. "Billionaire propaganda. The elites pushing growth on the colony are totally disconnected from the realities of both climate science and the toxic impacts of neoclassical economics. Did you know that keeping a human alive in space is two thousand times the carbon footprint of someone living on Earth?" He made a familiar impassioned gesture with one hand. "And the U.S. government is considering legislation to expand the number of people on the colony. Of course they're trying to justify it with vague promises about mining. It's a distraction. Increasing the supply of precious metals by mining them on the Moon won't reduce demand for more mining on Earth. Our economic system fetishizes maximizing profit above all else."

"I feel like we're at Jimmy's," Alex said with a smile. "It still doesn't take much to get you going."

"Too much?" Navin asked ruefully.

"You're always too much," Alex said with affection.

"It just infuriates me that we'll be replicating the problems of the modern age on another planet." Navin raised scraped, reddened hands in mock surrender. "Or should I say astronomical body?"

"I think you've got the colony wrong," laughed Alex. "This is a place of science and engineering."

"Until the billionaire tourists arrive. The colony is exacerbating the wealth gap by showing social deference to the mega-rich."

Alex shook her head. "The research I'm conducting will benefit the scientists as well as the tourists. Look at it this way. If tourist dollars pay for it, hey, the more NASA can save for scientific exploration and experimentation."

MOONRISING

"Do you really believe that?" Navin scoffed. "Have you done any investigation into the corporation that stands to benefit from the colony tourists? Come on, Alex. The company is funded by oil money from this powerful family in the UAE. Open your eyes. You've spent your whole career dealing with the havoc Big Oil has wreaked on our environment. The Al Kaabi family has leveraged petroleum resources to build an untouchable dictatorship in Abu Dhabi. They've ruled unchallenged for *decades*. Not to mention, their collection of superyachts and private planes make them one of the biggest individual contributors to climate change."

"How do you know all this?" Alex asked, her stomach suddenly in knots. She thought about Mansoor's casual references to helicopters and black diamond ski slopes.

"We're keeping close tabs on the colony."

"'We' as in the ELS?" asked Alex tiredly.

"Yes," said Navin with an air of annoyance. "And we followed the money. NASA is so desperate to keep their dominance in space that they aren't scrutinizing their investors. You think the House of Kaabi gives a shit about advances in science or space exploration? All they care about is making unholy amounts of money to fund their lavish lifestyle. So, we have to ask, why would this family make such a large investment in Peary Station? What are they really after?"

If they were actually at Jimmy's, Alex would be ending their conversation with flirtation and an invitation to her apartment. But instead, they were separated by a screen with only their words and ideas. Navin felt very far away.

It's not like she didn't hear what he was saying. She'd had her doubts about Mansoor, too. But she wasn't interested in Navin judging his motivations from a distance.

"They've made an investment in me," Alex said carefully. "And the Institute. I'm benefiting from it."

107

"Then you're being played," Navin snapped. "What do billionaires want with mutant food? You should join us in stopping the growth of the colony by any means necessary, not getting in bed with Big Oil."

"You were happy for me when I got this opportunity," Alex said, unable to keep a note of sadness from creeping into her voice. Couldn't Navin just be proud of this incredible moment for her?

"What does a career matter on a dead planet?"

"Right," Alex said. She shouldn't have expected more from him—hadn't they always put their ideas first, above everything? "I have to go back to work." She cut the comm, trying not to feel like she just lost a friend.

7

VICTOR

EUREKA! VICTOR SCRAWLED ON THE HOTEL WALL, UNABLE TO KEEP the manic grin off his face. He felt the sense of bone-deep satisfaction he experienced anytime he solved a problem others might deem impossible. He rolled his neck from side to side, working out the kinks, and almost knocked over a nearby lamp when he glimpsed a figure in the doorway.

"Wondered how long it would take for you to notice me," Rashid said, tapping a hotel key card against his thigh. His eyes took in the clothes scattered around the floor, the remains of Victor's room service lunch, and the projected writing covering three walls and much of the ceiling.

"How the hell did you get in here? No—don't tell me yet." He turned back to his calculations and reduced the projection to one wall, studying the completed figures painstakingly. His work appeared flawless. If an error existed, his competent engineering team would find it; they had plenty of experience deciphering his handwriting. He turned off the projector on his intelliwatch and sent the whole thing off to Teru, his chief engineer.

When he looked up again, Rashid was sprawled across his unmade hotel bed, his arms propped behind his head, watching Victor. His feet were crossed at the ankle, revealing soft looking forest green Argyle socks. "What are you working on?"

"Increasing the speed of our rocket prototype by a factor of two. Maybe two point five."

"I've never seen someone with your power of concentration. I swear you haven't blinked for twenty minutes. No wonder you weren't returning my calls."

Victor looked at his watch again. Five calls and twelve messages. Most from Rashid. He winced. "I do that sometimes."

"I know." Rashid's lips twitched. "That's why I was forced to take matters into my own hands."

Victor looked at him again, truly registering Rashid's presence for the first time. "You're here! In my locked hotel room! How did you pull that off?"

"Called the front desk." In a passable imitation of Victor's rapid-fire speech, he said, "This is Victor Beard. I'm expecting a young man in my hotel room shortly. Give him a key and show him every courtesy. I know I can rely on your discretion."

It took a moment for Victor to process the implication. "A prostitute. My hotel thinks I ordered a prostitute."

"A high-end prostitute," Rashid said with a smirk.

Unwillingly, Victor burst out laughing. "Next time, I'll answer your call. The first time."

"Good. Now get yourself in the shower and put on something decent, preferably clean and wrinkle free. We have a meeting in half an hour."

"It's 7:30? Already? We'll never get there in Manhattan traffic."

"This is the third time we've done this. I have you figured out. We're on my home turf, and I refuse to be late for this meeting. I've already conspired with your assistant, and we're only going down the block."

MOONRISING

Victor got ready in record time. On the way out the lobby door, Rashid gave the clerk a wink, and Victor could feel himself blushing scarlet. Victor never blushed.

They met the powerful New York senator in a private room at the back of a trendy root-to-stem restaurant. Victor knew Senator Jones was skeptical of Rashid, but he had been willing to take the meeting in exchange for Victor's promise to film a thirty-second promo for his reelection campaign, and, perhaps, if the meeting went well, make an appearance on stage with him at an upcoming rally or two. Politicians had always liked the idea of surrounding themselves with innovators willing to push the envelope, even if they never seemed to enjoy Victor's company when face to face. Tonight, Victor allowed Rashid to take the lead, trying to recede into the background.

It only took four minutes and thirty-two seconds for Jones to relax—Victor clocked it. After seven minutes and thirteen seconds, Jones was clapping Rashid on the shoulder and recommending a seasonal Brooklyn pale ale. At nine minutes and forty-five seconds, Rashid noticed his little experiment while Jones was perusing the menu, and gave Victor a reproving look, forcing him to turn off the stopwatch.

The first time Victor had seen Rashid in action, he was surprised to see he was a natural. He had a way with rhetoric. A permanent settlement on another world was an easy thing to sell, especially to a senator. The colony clearly fit into the idea of American exceptionalism. Rashid painted a picture of a colony founded on the ideals of America's founding fathers—liberty, egalitarianism, and individualism. Victor had no idea if Rashid believed what he was selling, but the words drew Victor in regardless.

Jones basked in Rashid's attention. In spite of everything Rashid had gotten across, Victor observed that Rashid was actually letting the senator do most of the talking. And yet, somehow, the conversation was moving in the precise direction Rashid wanted it to go.

"My duty, my responsibility is to the American people," Jones told Rashid earnestly. "Giving American families a path to live on the Moon would be one hell of a legacy."

At the end of dinner, Rashid handled the bill with Victor barely noticing the transaction. They left with Jones eagerly promising Rashid a meeting with the other two senators that made up their cadre of powerful centrists known as the Gang of Three.

When they parted ways from the senator, Rashid let out a long breath. "How do you think that went?" For the first time that evening, he sounded young and uncertain.

"It seemed to go well, but I can never tell with senators," Victor said. "They're too experienced telling everyone exactly what they want to hear. You'll have a better idea when you meet with the two sycophants he flanks himself with."

"I suppose. C'mon, it's early yet."

Victor hesitated.

"You aren't going back to your room to do more math, are you?"

"Physics," Victor corrected automatically.

"I do beg your pardon. *Physics*. Come with me." Rashid took his arm and led him down the street in the opposite direction of the hotel. Rashid kept a hold of his arm as they walked. His body felt warm against Victor's, and Victor could feel the pressure of Rashid's fingers curled around his bicep. It was almost too soon when they reached a tiny salsa club, and Rashid let go of his arm to push his way inside.

The club was classic Manhattan: small, crowded, and loud. By the time Victor had squeezed through the door, Rashid was already at the bar, commanding the bartender's full attention. Victor stood awkwardly in the crowd trying to avoid getting hit by a gesticulating hand from the conversations around him.

When Rashid returned, Victor began, "This isn't really my scene."

Rashid ignored his comment and handed him a drink. "It's a Paloma," he said in his ear. "Cheers."

Victor automatically clinked his glass against Rashid's and took a tentative sip. "It's good," Victor shouted, half in surprise.

Rashid downed his drink, slammed it on the table, and said, "Come on."

He stepped in front of two women sitting on stools at the bar, eyeing the dance floor. To the prettier one, he said, "Care to dance?"

The woman eyed him up and down. "Yeah, alright."

Victor, clutching his drink, watched them walk away. Rashid had a hand low on the woman's hip.

"Aren't you going to ask me to dance?" the remaining woman asked.

"Sure." Victor tried to finish his drink in one go, and promptly spilled ice down his front. The woman gave him a doubtful look.

"Come on then," he said, pushing his glasses into place and taking her hand. It was a disaster, of course. He had never been much of a dancer and in the crowded club he kept stepping on the woman's feet. When the song ended, he bought her an apology drink and made himself scarce. He hoped she had not recognized him. He was much less inept while reading a teleprompter or in an interview setting.

He was leaning against the wall, contemplating leaving when Rashid found him again. "I can't believe I let you talk me into this," Victor complained. "I hate dancing. It's too loud. I don't know how to salsa."

Rashid grabbed his hand, pulling him back to the dance floor. "I'll teach you."

"What?"

"Don't worry, I'll lead."

Feeling horribly self-conscious, Victor allowed himself to be led back onto the dance floor. Rashid put his hands on Victor's hips. "Relax. Feel the rhythm of the music." He moved Victor's hips from side to side. "Now move your feet. Front. And back. And front. And back. Good."

"It's not good. I just stepped on your foot."

"My feet can take it. These are sturdy shoes."

Victor began to relax. He wasn't sure he was getting any better, but he stopped worrying so much about it. Rashid spun him once. Then twice. A new song started, and Rashid did not let him go. They danced for five songs before Victor finally begged to stop, saying he was tired.

"Come on," Rashid said in his ear. "I'll walk you home."

The outside air was chilly and refreshing. It cleared his head. He took a deep breath and immediately regretted it. "Why does this city always smell like garbage?"

"Don't say that too loud. A New Yorker might beat you up."

"You're a New Yorker. You don't seem like much of a fighter."

"My older brothers taught Mansoor and me to wrestle. Dirty. It wouldn't be pretty. You may end up with a sprained finger or sand in your eyes." He grinned to himself.

Victor wasn't great at reading people, but he was beginning to understand Rashid. "You miss him, don't you? Mansoor?"

Rashid ran a hand through his hair in a gesture Victor had often seen from Mansoor. "Sometimes. I just don't want to screw this up. It's his dream."

"You're better at this than Mansoor."

Rashid snorted.

"I mean it. Don't get me wrong, I think your brother is brilliant. I trust him with my life. I upended my Agro career for him. But when he's wooing politicians, he always keeps things too formal and transactional. The way your family spends money like it's meaningless makes everything feel like a bribe. Tonight, you made Jones feel like he was with a friend. You disarmed him completely."

Rashid was silent for so long that Victor was afraid he'd offended him. Finally, he burst out, "Mansoor is my father's golden boy. My father would have made him his heir, if he thought he could get away with it. Above everything, my father values innovation and creative thinking. My older brothers, they're good men, but they aren't exactly changing the world."

"Has it occurred to you that you're an innovator too?"

"Hardly."

"How did you know what Jones wanted to hear? How did you know to frame it as a high school civics lesson wrapped up in an adolescent outer space wet dream?"

Rashid shrugged.

"You have a gift for reaching people. It's valuable."

They'd reached Victor's hotel. The doorman gave them a single polite nod and then studiously avoided looking at them again.

Victor felt at a loss for words. Finally, he said, "Thanks for the salsa lesson."

Rashid was looking at him with an expression Victor could not decipher. "Good night, Victor."

With Victor's breakthrough in propulsive efficiency, his team was finally on a path to finish the rocket. They worked around the clock, often sleeping in the office to save time. A table was kept stocked with catered food, chips, protein bars, fruit, energy drinks, and pain killers. Everyone was unshaven, unclean, and humming with a haggard, manic energy.

Victor loved every second of it.

And then, one day in early May, the ground trials were complete, and the ship was ready to fly.

Victor's test pilot Camila hopped from foot to foot as Victor clumsily popped a bottle of champagne on the factory floor. His chief engineer Teru passed out red Solo cups.

"Can I fly it? Today?" Camila asked him with glee as she held out her cup for champagne.

Victor and Teru exchanged a glance. "I'll inform the FAA," Teru said.

"Pull her out," Victor called, and the eager team gulped their drinks hastily and hurried to obey.

There was no fanfare. No reporters or spectators. Just Victor, his team, and his pilot. They set the rocket in place using a crane and wheeled over the scaffolding so that Camila could scamper into the pilot's chair. Victor had designed a ship that needed no Mission Control. Much of the ship's commands were automated, and the rest were fully controlled by the pilot. His ships would change the nature of spaceflight, making launches and landings easier, faster, and cheaper.

After confirming Camila was safely strapped in, Victor walked back into the warehouse. Instead of a packed flight control center, there was only Teru, sitting at a console inside, observing the run of the AI-powered final risk check. They flashed Victor a wide, eager grin. Victor stood behind Teru's chair, watching the console confirm the ship was clear for launch.

"Do it," Victor said, clapping Teru on the arm.

They nodded and pressed a countdown button on the console.

"Sixty, fifty-nine, fifty-eight," Victor called as he hurried back outside. His team joined him in the countdown, all of them shouting themselves hoarse. With a loud crack, the rocket ship shot into the sky. The boosters broke away and flew, controlled, back to Earth, landing undamaged in the field outside the launch pad. Victor watched his ship fade into a tiny pinprick and then return, slowing in speed as it came to land smoothly on the designated landing pad.

MOONRISING

The stairs lowered, and Camila descended, beaming. The team rushed her, screaming, laughing, and crying all at once.

Teru stepped out of the warehouse, joining Victor, and the two of them watched a pair of engineers carry Camila in on their shoulders. "You did it, Victor," Teru said. "You've reinvented spaceflight."

Victor gave them a sidelong look. "Not without you, I didn't. Will you clean up here? I think I'm going to pass out if I don't go home and get some decent rest."

Teru nodded. "Go, I've got this."

Victor drove in a stupor. At home, he showered and collapsed on his bed. He didn't move until mid-afternoon the next day.

When he finally dragged himself into his office, it was quiet and peaceful. Teru had given most of the team the day off.

Victor's assistant breathed a sigh of relief at his appearance. "You're here, good. The ambassador to the United Arab Emirates has called me five times. Personally."

Victor rubbed his forehead. Too much sleep had given him a headache. "What does Malik want now?"

"He's asked you to come to an event he's hosting tonight in D.C. There's a car waiting."

"What, now? That's a two-hour drive."

"I know. I tried to head him off, but he kept calling. I packed you a bag."

Victor closed his eyes. The ambassador was powerful and had a direct line to the Emir. He couldn't risk his still-unsigned contract. "What would I do without you?" he said to his assistant, grabbing the duffel.

Victor slept deeply on the cool leather seat of the ambassador's town car. He awoke to the driver clearing his throat. "Sir, the Four Seasons."

Victor mumbled his gratitude and walked into the classic brick hotel. A bellhop whisked away his bag as he stepped into the lobby. It had a timeless feel with fresh flowers and framed artwork. Victor tapped his intelliwatch at the reception kiosk and was escorted to the rear event space.

The room was beginning to fill with a well-dressed crowd. He looked down at his wrinkled Beard Enterprises polo shirt and wondered if his assistant had packed a suit.

One especially elegant man in a black pinstriped suit stepped up to him. "Mr. Beard, you made it."

"Ambassador, hello."

"If you'll come with me?" Malik Al Naifeh gestured with an air of easy confidence. "I have business to discuss with you."

Victor allowed himself to be led to a side room with large wingback chairs and an actual woodburning fire in the stone hearth. To Victor's surprise, Rashid was seated on one of the chairs, looking tense and unhappy.

"Sit, sit," Malik said, turning to a nearby bar cart and pouring a measure of brown liquid for Victor. "Cognac?" Victor took the snifter automatically and put it next to him on a side table. Malik handed Rashid a glass of Perrier with a lemon and took another for himself.

Victor's brain started calculating the energy units in joules consumed per hour by a woodburning fireplace and comparing it to the energy consumed by rocket fuel. He missed the thread of polite conversation until Rashid, seated next to Victor, snaked his long leg to the side and rested his foot briefly on top of Victor's. Victor abruptly sat up and started paying attention.

"The problem, my friend, is that you're too persuasive," Malik was saying smoothly to Rashid. "The Emir does not intend for the Americans to pass the Homestead Act this session. The UAE needs time to build up local infrastructure." Malik gave a nod to Victor. "Mr. Beard will have some competition from Emirati aerospace startups."

"My father has made a significant investment in the American colony," Rashid said. "A larger population will support more tourism. The UAE will profit from the Homestead Act."

MOONRISING

"How long do you think the Americans will honor your contract to operate all entertainment businesses on the colony once aspiring entrepreneurs move in? Don't be naive. The Americans look out for their own." Malik leaned back in his armchair and took a sip of his drink. "Let me tell you a story. Seventy years ago, when the UAE was still a young country on the world stage, we attempted to make an investment that would give us the concession to run six major shipping ports in the United States. Do you know what the Americans said? 'Why not turn control directly to Al Qaeda?' Hillary Clinton called it a surrender of American ports to a foreign government, conveniently ignoring that these ports were already run by a British company. The 9/11 families called the United Arab Emirates a rogue state. The Americans could not see the distinction between Emirati businessmen and terrorists.

"And in the end, we capitulated to the pressure. We sold our stake in the ports. And we vowed that we would never again endure that kind of humiliation.

"We have worked hard to be seen as a trusted American ally. They sell us arms, and they sign security agreements with us. They have helped us become the most powerful military in the Arab world. But never forget, the Americans could turn on us on a whim. They could lump us together once again with extremists. The only way to ensure our continued power and stability is with independence."

"Seventy years is a long time," Rashid said levelly. "Today, American politicians see the UAE as an ally, not as an adversary."

"They see you as an ally, certainly. You may have an Emirati passport, Rashid, but you are American through and through. I wonder if your father would be so quick to trust you if he knew about your extracurricular activities?" Malik smiled, but the smile didn't reach his eyes. "Would he think you were an appropriate mouthpiece for Emirati interests and values?"

119

Rashid's only reaction to Malik's words was a slow blink. To Victor's surprise, however, he realized he could read Rashid perfectly. Rashid's face and posture were calm, and yet Victor could tell he was seething.

Rashid said coolly, "Thank you, Ambassador, you have made yourself perfectly clear. Victor had not seen fit to explain the situation to me before. I will desist in my efforts." Rashid grabbed Victor's untouched glass of cognac, downed the drink, and rose smoothly. "If you don't mind, I don't want to miss the concert."

Victor nodded awkwardly at Malik and stumbled to his feet, following Rashid out.

"What—" Victor started as soon as they had left.

"Not here," Rashid hissed back. "We mingle—no politicians. We go to the concert. We look like we're having fun."

When they reentered the ballroom, attendance had swelled. Rashid glanced around, quickly sizing up the crowd, and approached an older woman in a flowing white evening gown. "Maggie, lovely to see you. You must know Victor Beard."

Maggie peered at him over her glasses. "Victor, when will we get you to sit down for a *Post* profile?"

As Victor stammered something inane, Rashid interjected smoothly, "Maggie, how would you like an exclusive first look at the UAE's investment in Beard Enterprise's shuttle program? A warehouse tour and an interview with both of us?"

Maggie gave Victor's arm a squeeze. "I've heard rumors about what you're up to in the boonies of Pennsylvania, Victor Beard. Your staff are very closed-mouthed." She looked at Rashid pointedly. "An exclusive, you said? I'm in."

"Good, good," Rashid said. "We'll call you."

An announcement from the stage indicated that the concert was about to start, and the crowd murmured in excitement. The artist's name meant nothing to Victor. He would have left if not for Rashid's presence keeping him rooted to the spot.

MOONRISING

The music was loud, and Victor's head began to hurt again. He tried to look alert, knowing the ambassador's people might be watching him. He felt a hand on the small of his back as Rashid leaned into his ear. "I've got to get back tonight, and I need to talk to you. I know it's a long way, but will you come with me?"

Victor drew his eyebrows together in a frown. "To New York? Now?"

"The ambassador's wife is flying out tonight and offered to give me a lift in her helijet."

Victor thought about the punishing sprint he had just put his team through and his lonely condo in Philly a two-hour drive away. "I could do that. When?"

Rashid nodded to a man in the corner who could only be a bodyguard. "Pretty much now."

They followed the bodyguard down the halls of the Four Seasons. Victor noticed Rashid's head turn to look at several of the paintings lining the halls, but he did not stop to linger. A bellhop followed in their wake, carrying Victor's and Rashid's bags. They crossed M Street to a small jet pad with a sleek helijet waiting for them, stairs descended.

Victor immediately began examining the curve of the wings. It was an H452 or perhaps an H455. He had not seen one before, but he had studied the schematics. He wondered if the pilot would allow him access to the engine before departure. The newer helijets were supposed to be the smoothest ascension technology yet, and he wondered if there were applications for his shuttle that he had not considered. Had he been so focused on increasing the propulsion that he had forgotten to account for the implication of lift-off impact on passenger comfort?

"Sir?" said the bellhop timidly. His hands were empty. "Madame Al Naifeh is waiting."

Victor looked at him blankly for a moment and then shook himself and ascended the stairs.

Sena Al Naifeh was sitting in a white suede chair on the airplane, Rashid in the seat to her right, and a young woman Victor assumed was a personal assistant to her left. Sena gave him a warm smile. "Victor! It has been too long. Rashid was just filling me in on the latest timeline on the Abu Dhabi lunar project. How exciting!"

"It is," Victor agreed, buckling himself into one of the remaining seats. He launched into an explanation of his design's propulsive efficiency. She listened for longer than he expected and asked several technical follow-up questions. Rashid had taken out a paper notebook and was scribbling furiously. Belatedly, Victor realized he was not taking notes on Victor's lecture but writing what looked like a poem.

After a while, Sena said with an air of finality, "Well! That was certainly an education. You must keep me apprised of your launch date, Rashid. Malik and I will surely want to be in attendance."

Rashid put his notebook down on his lap. "It won't be long now."

"I am so glad to see you back in the fold, Rashid. I wasn't sure you would be returning to us."

Rashid gave a little uncomfortable shrug.

"You know Leena was a dear friend of mine."

Rashid looked up sharply. "I didn't—" He cleared his throat. "I didn't know."

Sena smiled. "Your mother enchanted every room she walked into. She shone with such a bright light. You have that quality too. People are drawn to you. I think she would be very proud of you."

Rashid swallowed. "I hope so."

They landed on the rooftop of the Ritz-Carlton, overlooking Central Park. The city twinkled in the darkness. Sena gave them another warm smile as they separated. "I'll see you again soon in Abu Dhabi. We wouldn't miss it."

Rashid was quiet in the town car. Victor felt wide awake and aware of Rashid's mood in a way he had never experienced before.

MOONRISING

He had never cared to notice, he realized. It wasn't that he didn't know how to read people. It was that his brain could only process so many things at once, and he'd never prioritized another person's feelings before.

It was a revelation.

Rashid's SoHo apartment was nothing like Victor had expected. While Mansoor's Boston brownstone favored grays and whites, leather and glass, Rashid's style was downright bohemian. Colorful portraits covered every wall, eclectic sculptures adorned every surface, and even the furniture looked handcrafted and striking. As he neared the balcony, Victor was drawn to a portrait of a beautiful laughing woman with dark eyes and white teeth.

"She looks familiar."

Rashid came up beside him. "Leena."

"Your mother." Victor squinted at the signature in the right corner. "Did you do this?"

"I did."

Victor looked at him in astonishment. "You never told me you were a painter. In all these months we've known each other, you never mentioned it." He looked around the room again, recognizing the same colorful, bold style in many of the paintings. An open door revealed a glimpse of an easel and a speckled drop cloth.

"It's just a hobby. I don't exhibit."

"Why not? You're good enough."

Rashid shrugged. "I'm not going to self-fund some vanity project to stroke my own ego."

Victor opened his mouth to disagree and realized he could tell Rashid did not want to discuss it. He closed his mouth and leaned in to examine the portrait. "She looks happy, your mother."

"It's how I want to remember her. She wasn't happy often, in the end. She didn't laugh much—it hurt her chest. And her hair had all fallen out from chemo. But this is what she was like when

I was a child." He cleared his throat and said impatiently, "I need some air."

Rashid slid open the thick glass doors and stepped out to the balcony. Victor followed. It was a mild night, and the lights of Manhattan glittered around them. For a while, neither of them spoke. Victor could lose himself in Rashid's silences. His mind was typically calculating and processing, but with Rashid, his mind could rest. It was an odd sensation.

"We need to do something about Malik," Rashid said finally, his hands touching the balcony railings and his gaze distant. "I don't think I understand the full picture. I expected him to think Mansoor's methods were foolish, operating out of his tiny Boston office and surrounding himself with a small staff driven by personal loyalty, not politics. I expected him to tell us we should be employing the old UAE lobbying machine—make substantial donations to Washington think tanks for sponsored research, court political reporters, and hire the best lobbying firms stocked with former congressmen and insider strategists. But it's not that he wants us to do things his way. It's that he doesn't want us to try at all."

Victor grunted, leaning against the balcony's wrought iron railing in order to watch Rashid's profile.

"I think Mansoor's strategy is brilliant. I knew my brother was capable, but I didn't see how shrewd and subtle he was being until I was close to this. On the surface, he's got his legitimate investment business that has an appropriate amount of influence on NASA's decisions. There's a reasonable amount of media buzz about the first space tourists headed to the Moon. And everything else is completely in the shadows.

"No registered lobbyists, no traceable money trail, no relationship with UAE's American consulate, and no ties to the UAE government beyond blood. The people he does bring in are wholly unconventional. He pulls you in—and you're not a Washington insider on paper no matter how well known you might be. He handpicks the inspector in charge of reporting back to Congress. Politicians know him, and they know that their opponents receive massive boosts in donations if they oppose him. But they don't talk about it, not even amongst themselves. And so, no journalist, no watchdog group, and no regulator has a whiff of this."

"Yes," Victor agreed quietly.

"Mansoor is off the beaten path, isn't he? The UAE lobbies for OPEC, for Saudi Arabia's Gulf interests, for favorable trading agreements. They don't lobby for the Americans to authorize a family-based permanent settlement on the Moon. It's so far outside of UAE's traditional interests that I'm not sure it even makes sense as a strategy. I'm not even sure Mansoor's growth projections hold any weight."

"They're my projections," Victor put in. He felt an absurd need to take the credit. *He* wanted to be the one Rashid called brilliant. "There are a number of assumptions in the model that could be false. But if constraints are removed, the colony will grow exponentially. It's inevitable."

"Constraints like water and oxygen?" Rashid asked. Was there a teasing note in his voice?

"Water and oxygen are the easy part. It's the bureaucracy that really gets in the way. Every new innovation is currently tested in lab conditions on Earth and studied for half a decade before being implemented. NASA's funding moves up or down with each new Congress, making it difficult to plan long-term. We need the Homestead Act passed to cut through the bureaucracy. To make a permanent settlement a reality."

Rashid turned his head and looked at him. Really looked, like he was seeing him for the first time. "I'm not lobbying on behalf of the UAE, am I? Whose idea was it?" he asked. "To write this bill? To grow the population on the Moon?"

Victor shrugged evasively. "Ours. Both of us. Over the course of years of conversations and planning. This is bigger than tourist dollars. This is how we save humanity."

"Save humanity?" Rashid asked skeptically.

"If we learn to sustain—truly sustain—human life from birth to death on the Moon, we can replicate it on Mars. And then someday interstellar migration where generations live and die on a vessel in space, traveling to a new planet that can be developed to host human life. It's not a fantasy. We need to do this to ensure humanity's survival. And the only way to make it happen is to make it work financially."

"And does it?"

"Of course it does," Victor said patiently. "The reason Mansoor persuaded your father to invest in the Homestead Act is simple—there's more profit to be had. NASA gave your family the rights to operate every tourist and entertainment venture that springs up on the colony for fifty years for the low, low price of a billion dollars. Without the Homestead Act, your family's company will double their investment in ten years. With the Act, it will only take five, easily."

Rashid frowned. "But Mansoor understands your underlying purpose?"

"He shares it. Despite what Malik says, your lobbying efforts haven't gone against the interests of your country. But your true scope includes the interests of the whole world. Malik and the Emir can plan an Emirati Moon colony with my wholehearted endorsement. The more the merrier. The Americans are simply the furthest along, so we're pushing them—but we want the rest of the world to follow."

"So what do we do?"

"You mean, do we let Malik Al Naifeh bully us out of a real shot to alter the course of humanity's future?"

Rashid grinned. "Well, when you put it like that . . ."

MOONRISING

"Rashid . . ." Victor took his hand. He had never noticed the specks of paint under Rashid's fingernails. "Sena was right. When you walk into a room you shine. You're good—the best I've seen. We can't stop now. Not when we're this close."

Rashid put his hand on top of Victor's. "Okay." He squeezed. "Okay, we finish what we've started."

"Good. My wife would be angry with me if I put her through all this misery for nothing."

Rashid abruptly dropped his hand. His face shuttered. "Are you hungry? I'm starving. Let's get a slice."

"Alright," Victor agreed, noticing Rashid's change in tone, noticing his closed face, noticing the way his shoulders had a slight hunch they had not had moments before. They grabbed their coats and left Rashid's loft, riding down the elevator and out into the bustling Manhattan streets.

They grabbed their pizza and a few beers at a tiny joint one block over and sat down at a counter overlooking the street. Victor folded his slice in half and took a bite, the sauce squirting down his chin.

"You never told me you were married," Rashid said abruptly.

Victor took his time swallowing, savoring the chewy crust. It was impossible to find bad pizza in New York. "Not for much longer. The lawyers are dragging it out. My assets are all tied up in Beard Enterprise investments, not cash. She could own half the company and make a killing once we go public, but her lawyers don't trust me or the company."

"You're getting divorced," Rashid breathed. The tension left his body in a shudder.

"So they tell me." Victor took a long swallow of cold beer. "She left me on a Sunday, but it took me until Thursday to notice."

Rashid snorted. "I'm sorry." He laughed out loud. "I know that's not funny to you, but . . . that's really funny."

Victor found himself smiling unwillingly. "I thought she was on a business trip. She's a PR consultant, always traveling. And

I'm a terrible listener. I didn't want to call her and admit I didn't remember what city she was in. But then, it hit me."

"On Thursday."

"Thursday." He hadn't made any brain space for Harper since she'd left. He thought back to that night, to the call he'd handled so poorly. "I couldn't make her happy. I never make anyone happy. I forget to notice people when I'm working. I miss what's right in front of me. They get tired of me, and they leave. I thought Harper understood that. I thought she had such a fulfilling life of her own that she wouldn't need my undivided attention. But she needed *something* from me I obviously didn't give her. I think I'm broken. My brain isn't wired for relationships."

"Maybe you just weren't with the right person," Rashid mused.

He looked at Rashid and realized he could see quite a lot. Rashid had let go of the tension he had been holding when Victor had mentioned his wife. He was still keyed up about the encounter with the ambassador but comfortable letting it go for the evening. Rashid was nothing like Harper, who had always kept her feelings in a box Victor did not have the key to open. He was nothing like any of the people Victor had failed to connect with in his string of disastrous relationships.

"Maybe you're right," Victor said quietly. "Maybe you're right."

8

MANSOOR

IT WAS AFTER DINNER ON A NIGHT IN EARLY MAY WHEN MANSOOR heard a knock on his door. Drake waited in the hall wearing his customary stoic expression. "May I come in?"

With knots in his stomach, Mansoor gestured Drake inside. Mansoor had been expecting this conversation with a mix of anticipation and dread. Surely, Drake was here to let him down gently, as a professional courtesy.

"I'm leaving tomorrow," said Drake. "My ninety days of observation are complete."

"I am aware," Mansoor said neutrally.

"I wanted you to hear it from me, before I left, that my report will support families emigrating to the colony."

Mansoor blew out his breath, suddenly dizzy with relief. "Sit down, please. I believe this conversation calls for the last of my supply." Mansoor found the nearly empty remaining bottle of eighteen-year single malt Scotch whiskey and poured the final ounces between two glasses.

Drake settled on the chair and took a sip. "I haven't tasted anything this good in three months." He closed his eyes in satisfaction.

When he'd taken a moment to enjoy the whiskey, he opened his eyes again and cleared his throat. "I'm proposing a tiered approach. To start, I recommend immediate approval for qualified spouses and partners of existing colony residents and an equitable application process for adult couples and solo aspirational colonists." He gestured with one finger." In the first year, the objective will be to build the healthcare infrastructure with a focus on obstetrics, gynecology, and pediatrics to allow for healthy infants to be born on the Moon." Drake held up a second finger. "In the second year, the objective will be to build the childcare infrastructure to allow both parents to work full time. After two years of growth, I recommend a follow-up assessment to determine if the colony is ready to support the emigration of families with children."

Mansoor nodded. "I follow your logic."

"We must ensure that minors raised on Peary Station receive the basic rights entitled to all children. Clean water and air are provided in abundance. Fresh, healthy food seems to be progressing at an appropriate pace. The family apartment prototype Herb constructed demonstrates the colony's ability to provide appropriate shelter. Other rights aren't yet in place. I've reviewed Senator Garcia's compelling future plans for childcare, education, and play, but the colony needs a suitable runway to ramp up these activities."

"When will you submit your report?"

"It's finished. I'm scheduled to testify before the Senate Subcommittee on Space and Science in ten days."

"Ten days," Mansoor repeated, his mind racing. Could Garcia get the bill out of committee in time for a floor vote before the August recess? He tried not to get his hopes up. The Homestead Act had little chance of passing with the current Senate. The bill was facing attacks from all sides. The cost was astronomical. The left argued the money would be better spent on poverty alleviation; the right argued for increased defense spending. Conservative religious leaders declared that God did not intend for children to be born in space. Environmental activists opposed the measure on the grounds that an increase in rocket fuel consumption would add carbon to the atmosphere. Lukewarm support from an unpopular president had done little to sway the Senate in either direction.

Still, it would be close—closer than he had dared hope. He would be well set up for the next senate, after the election cycle. He was funneling a fortune in Super PAC contributions to a half dozen potential senate races poised to be more favorable to the Act. But now that he was on the colony, he felt the sting of waiting another eighteen months to try again. The colony was ready for growth now, and the waiting galled him.

"I'm grateful that I was the one trusted with this opportunity," Drake said. "This station is safe, organized, and well-run. It's a testament to human ingenuity."

"I am glad you have come to see it that way," Mansoor said. He lifted his glass. "To the future of Peary Station."

Drake clinked his glass against Mansoor's. "To the colony."

The next morning, Mansoor felt his sense of optimism radiating onto everyone he met. At breakfast, he sat with Julien, who soon had him shaking with laughter at a story of the astrophysicists' first attempt at distilling alcohol on the colony.

He noticed Alex the moment she entered the cafeteria. Julien observed Mansoor's eyes following Alex and called, "Dr. Cole, join us."

Alex stepped over with a mug of tea in her hand. "I'm on my way to the greenhouse. But, Mansoor, there's something I need to ask you. Can you stop by when you're done here?"

Alex had been keeping her distance since he'd described his vision for a million people on the colony, and he was eager to reconnect. "It would be my pleasure."

When Alex had departed, Julien wagged his eyebrows at Mansoor. "Are you two . . .?"

"We are not," Mansoor said with all the dignity he could muster.

"Not yet," Julien said.

Mansoor took a sip of coffee and said nothing.

When he arrived in the greenhouse, Alex said to him brusquely, "That took you long enough." She was bent over a plant growing in a tray and barely looked up at him. "Look at this tomato plant."

Mansoor wasn't sure what he should be looking at. "It looks . . . very green?" he hazarded. "Healthy. I see no signs of fungus."

"It only has three flowers." Alex gestured with a pair of shears, and Mansoor took a subtle step back. The shears looked very sharp. "I can't do beefsteaks in this environment."

"Is that why you wanted to see me?" Mansoor asked. He had no idea what beefsteaks meant, but he assumed she didn't mean a porterhouse. Pity.

"Come with me," she said to him and moved abruptly to the adjacent room, which housed the chickens. The unexpected organic smell made him gag. Alex went to the side wall and opened the lid of a large bin. "See?"

The bin smelled worse than the chicken coop. Mansoor peered at the black chunky mass of unrecognizable organic matter. Unperturbed, Alex took a stick and stirred it. "At this rate, the compost will take another two months to mature. I wish I had worms, but I'm reluctant to introduce an invertebrate to the colony. They're harder to control than chickens."

"And you think compost would help you grow beefsteaks?" Mansoor hazarded.

"Not on its own, of course. I need something lightweight with similar properties to peat or perlite to mix in. I've been

MOONRISING

experimenting with using the compostable redi-meal containers to create a highly permeable medium to combine with the compost and allow roots to grow. Once we have usable compost, we can grow so much here. Onions, potatoes, corn, wheat. I'm too constrained by the hydroponic greenhouse."

Despite the putrid smell of the room, Mansoor's mouth watered involuntarily at the mere suggestion of fresh food. "How can I help?"

"I need an electric composter to speed up the process. But an industrial-size composter will never meet the weight requirements to ship, even disassembled. You have a group of engineers working with you, right? The ones that helped you invent a suitable window glass for the hotel? I was hoping they could come up with a design for me that can be printed on the Refabricator. I can't figure it out on my own."

Mansoor repressed a grin. Of course Alex would have attempted to build a composter herself first. He could tell she was uncomfortable asking for help. He wondered how the eager-to-please engineers from Masdar City would receive Dr. Alex Cole. He was looking forward to finding out. "Those foods sound essential for a well-rounded vegetarian diet for the hotel. I believe I can justify expending Emirati resources on this request."

"Thank you," Alex said, sounding relieved.

Mansoor flashed back to his conversation with Drake. He had another sudden desperate hope that the Homestead Act might actually pass. The robotic ice mining in the permanently shadowed interior of Peary Crater had been functional for nearly a decade now, processing enough water and oxygen to supply the station. If they could produce enough food, they could take care of their residents. Sustainably.

"Do you have to justify it?" Alex asked. "Don't you have the power to allocate resources however you want?"

Mansoor raised his eyebrows in amusement. He faced the limits of his power every day. "I am nothing compared to my father, and even he must answer to my uncle."

Alex closed the lid of the compost bin. In a more hesitant voice, she said, "I spoke with a friend of mine who said some pretty disturbing things about your family. He said you were untouchable and above the law. I've been . . . processing that news."

"Is that why you've been avoiding me?" he asked. "I thought I had scared you off with my silly ideas for a larger colony." He said it lightly, knowing he had spooked her when he had started talking about a million residents. He needed her as an ally.

"I haven't meant to avoid you," Alex said, wiping her hands on a cloth hanging near the compost bin. "I've had a lot to think about."

"Can we talk somewhere else?" he asked, wrinkling his nose.

Alex led him back to the greenhouse and spread a blue tarp on the floor in between the tall shelves. She gestured for him to sit. "Welcome to the best room on the colony." She closed her eyes and took a deep breath, her nostrils flaring. "Do you smell the fresh herbs?"

Mansoor lowered his eye lids and sniffed cautiously. "Thyme, I think."

"It's making you crave something, isn't it?"

"*Manakeesh*," he admitted. "Flatbread with za'atar and olive oil."

Alex plucked a sprig of thyme from a plant growing on a middle shelf. She knelt and rubbed it under his nose, her fingers brushing his lips. All at once, Mansoor felt transported to his father's home, seated on low cushions in the open air. He opened his lids to find her green eyes inches from his own.

"I think herbs have a way of evoking memory," she said, taking the thyme away from him and putting a small sprig in her mouth. She closed her eyes again, her face relaxing. "Roast chicken on

MOONRISING

a bed of rainbow carrots and fingerling potatoes. With a crisp Sauvignon Blanc and a loaf of fresh baked sourdough."

"That sounds nice." He reached over, his fingers scraping hers, and rubbed the thyme leaves, inhaling the spicy, lemony scent. He wanted to kiss her among the green thriving plants. He wanted to roll her back on the thin tarp and explore her body inch by inch.

Instead, he pulled himself away from her and said, "You are wondering about my family."

"Yes."

Mansoor tried to gather his scattered wits. "My family is difficult to explain. Your friend said we are above the law. I think that is a fair assessment. In Abu Dhabi, my family has absolute control. We fund the construction projects and museums. We run the boards of all major corporations. We subsidize the cost of living for our citizens. We even control the media coverage."

"'We,'" she repeated, frowning. "Doesn't that make people angry? Aren't you afraid they'll rebel and topple your family's power?"

Mansoor drew in a shaky breath. She had hit on the crux of all his fears. He felt suddenly exhausted and drained. "Until recently, no, we were not concerned. Our citizens live comfortably. There are no taxes. Their lifestyles are financially supported by my family. But the price of oil gets lower every year. The demand is projected to zero out within the year. We need alternative streams of revenue." He ran a hand through his hair. What must he sound like to her? Complaining about the price of oil. "My father . . . he believes that space tourism will save us from ruin. In his vision, ships will launch from the spaceport in Abu Dhabi weekly. Not only will we receive revenue from the space tourists, but also from their families waiting for them below, distracting themselves at our clubs and casinos. It is a bold plan, and if it fails, we could lose everything. Our people are not restless now, but if they suddenly needed to pay the true cost of living, things would change." The words flowed out of him. He had not meant to go into so much detail.

"You sound different when you talk about it. I'm surprised to hear you say, 'our people.' You don't seem like royalty. You're just . . . you." She drew up her knees, looking at him with a troubled frown.

He shook his head. "I am the third son of the brother of the Emir. I am in no danger of ruling. But the pull of my family is rooted deep down." He touched his chest involuntarily.

"Even here, you feel that? On the Moon?"

"Yes, even here. Especially here." He picked at the edge of the tarp. "I tried to escape it, you know. When I was younger. I moved to England and studied at Oxford, and I found I could slip between worlds. It took some time to discover the trick of it. When I first arrived, I was a very good Muslim. I prayed five times a day. I never drank. Moving to England was something of a culture shock." He gave Alex a half smile. "I spoke excellent English, and I thought I understood Western society. But I was naive to think my gender-segregated English language education in Abu Dhabi was sufficient. I had no idea how to live without structure in place. In Abu Dhabi, everything is either *haram* or *halal*: prohibited or permitted. It is easy to know your place in the world. I did not know how to behave when faced with freedom. I had no boundaries, and it made me feel exposed and vulnerable. I did not know how to behave around English women. In Abu Dhabi, it is disrespectful to look directly at a woman you are not related to. It is considered an encroachment on her modesty.

"It is strange to think of now. But when I was eighteen, I felt differently. English women seemed impossibly daring and risqué. And please do not think I am being vain when I say they adored me." He pursed his lips. "I was still wearing a *ghutra* then and I must have looked very exotic to them. When we were out, my Oxford friends loved dropping into the conversation that I was

MOONRISING

a member of a royal family. The Brits do love their royalty. The son of a sheikh was a great conquest." The last sentence came out bitterly. Well, that was how he felt.

"That sounds . . . dehumanizing."

"Yes, that is the right word. I found it was easier to slip into the role of a Westerner. To wear suits and drink bourbon. I stopped praying." His stomach burned with shame at that confession. He had not meant to forget his faith so completely. "But I could never shed my responsibilities to my family."

He studied Alex. Her expression was open, and he sensed she was waiting to see if he was going to keep talking. He tried to recall if he had ever spoken so freely before, to anyone. Not to his father, certainly, who believed Mansoor was leading the same life-style in Boston he led in Abu Dhabi. He cared about MacKenzie, but he had never opened up about his culture to her. With Victor, he talked about the future, not the past. Rashid would understand, he thought. But it was difficult to confide in Rashid when his brother kept his own life so closed off.

Alex, though . . . her expression was soft. Vulnerable. It was something he had never seen on her face before. He had not meant to confess his deepest fears and greatest regrets to her.

He wished he could lose himself in her.

He wished, more than anything, that he had not told his father he would consent to an arranged marriage in exchange for his blessing on Mansoor's time living on the colony.

Alex was right to be skeptical of his family's influence on him while he was 384,400 km away. What if he told his father he was not ready? That he needed more time? Just long enough to get Alex out of his system.

To Alex, he said, "I always say more than I mean to around you. You have this way of making me want to tell you everything."

Alex's face turned red.

Without thinking, he blurted, "When your blush travels down your neck I find myself wondering what it would feel like under my mouth."

Alex's blush deepened. She was sitting very close.

With effort, Mansoor pulled back. "I apologize. I should not have said that. I will speak to my team about the electric composter. I should go."

Mansoor fled before he did something he would regret.

"Father, I need to speak with you," Mansoor said, trying to keep the urgency and emotion out of his voice.

Mohammed's eyes crinkled with happiness to see his son's face. "I am glad you called, my son. I have wonderful news. You remember my old friend Waleed bin Ahmad? We worked together on the International Petroleum Investments Corporation when we were young. He has a most suitable daughter, Aliana. She has been raised in Abu Dhabi and attended the best schools. You will be pleased to know Aliana's English is impeccable. Best of all, she is studying to be an engineer at Khalifa University. I am sure we will find a place for her on the Space World project once her degree is completed."

His father sounded like he was describing a prospective employee, not a wife. Mansoor tried to muster his original argument about needing more time, but it was slipping away.

"Waleed has kept her from the company of men," his father continued. "She is modest and traditional. Your sister paid her a visit and confirmed she is a suitable match."

Mansoor had only been with experienced confident Western women. They usually approached him from across the bar, attracted to his expensive, well-tailored suits and his orders of top shelf whiskey. He tried to picture taking a young and inexperienced Emirati woman to his bed and winced. He could be patient and gentle if he tried. He was not a monster. Unwillingly,

MOONRISING

he thought of Alex's flushed skin and her fierce expression. What would it be like to sleep with someone who actually *knew* him?

"You will come home to finalize the marriage contract, of course. As soon as the first tourist visits are successfully completed."

"Yes, Father." He could not fathom leaving the Moon now, not when he and Victor were so close to success. He would have to keep the trip to Abu Dhabi as short as possible, just long enough to satisfy his father. Mansoor moistened his lips and cleared his throat. "I look forward to meeting Aliana and her family. I am honored by your selection."

"Good, good," Mohammed bin Khalifa said with finality. "Tell me, how is the hotel progressing? I am told the Americans have been most accommodating on the engineering complications."

"We are making excellent progress. We are in debt to the American engineer on-site," Mansoor said, attempting to sound upbeat. He gave a superficial description of the latest work that appeased his father. "We are on schedule to welcome our first guests in August."

"I am pleased with what you have accomplished. It is not a simple task to work with the Americans. It was not supposed to be like this, my son, begging for scraps at America's table. We were supposed to build the first city on Mars. The City of Wisdom. We were supposed to be the ones to demonstrate to the world that human ambition has no limits."

"Yes, Father." It was not the first time they had had this conversation.

"Do you remember what I told you when you wanted to study in England? I said the Prophet Muhammad, peace be upon him, told us to go as far as China for knowledge. You have traveled a great deal farther than even China. I am proud of the work you have done. You will do great things when you return home to establish your household."

139

"I—" Mansoor's throat felt dry. "I hope to do so."

"Starting a family changes a man. It gives you a sense of balance and responsibility. Having children is terrifying and wonderful. I remember when I held your brother for the first time, it was as if the world changed for me. I viewed the problems in our world differently. He was so vulnerable, completely dependent on his mother and me for protection and guidance. You will see soon enough."

"Yes, Father." What else could he say? He felt his father's formidable love through the screen. He was his father's favorite. He had always known that. And yet, his father had let him risk himself by traveling to space. He had trusted him with one of the most critical ventures of their nation-state. He never suspected Mansoor had more grandiose plans. It was not too much for him to ask his son to marry and start a family. Not in exchange for the chance to fulfill his greatest ambitions.

When they had made the arrangement in January, when Mansoor had finally acquiesced to his father's oft-repeated request to let him find Mansoor a wife, it had seemed like a fair agreement. A sacrifice, perhaps, to his freedom, but one he could live with. But now, the sacrifice seemed so much greater. How could he leave this project unfinished, in the hands of others, when he had worked for so long to be in exactly the right position to finally influence the direction of space colonization? And Alex. He would need to cut himself off from her. The feelings he was developing were too strong.

To his father he said simply, "I will forever strive to live up to the example you set."

9

ALEX

"THANK YOU," ALEX SAID AUTOMATICALLY TO THE ROBOT WHO delivered the final printed piece of her new electric composter. She projected the schematics from her intelliwatch onto the blank wall of the room housing the chicken coop. Around her, the hens clucked and pecked at the shredded compostable material of their home. Alex examined the directions from the Emirati engineering team and carefully screwed on the top piece. When it was secure, she attached the composter to a solar power source and listened to it whir to life.

"There," she said in satisfaction to the chickens. "Now your waste will actually be good for something." One of the hens pecked her shoe in response.

"Talking to the chickens?" Herb asked from the doorway.

She smiled at him. "Got to have some form of socialization." Her voice was light, but there was a bitter truth there. Besides Mansoor, and her occasional interactions with the energetic Sandra, no one had really taken to her. Good riddance, she thought. But the days did feel long and lonely.

"I'm ready to break ground next door. Thought you'd want to see."

Alex followed Herb into the hallway. The outer walls of the colony's maze of long halls held a series of hatches that led to the Moon's vacuum, providing easy access to expand the colony when the need arose. Today, Herb would be utilizing the hatch between the hydroponic greenhouse and the chicken coop to build Alex something new. Near the hatch, the hall was packed with supplies: clear quartz windowpanes, interlocking gray tiles, and steel beams.

"Ready?" Herb entered a command on his tablet.

Alex jumped out of the way of two orange bots as they pulled a thick plastic sheet from a robotic cart. In sixty seconds, the white film fully sealed off the area, separating Alex and Herb from the hatch and materials. A squealing sound indicated the bots were opening the hatch, but the air pressure on Alex's side did not change.

"How long will it take?" Alex asked.

"Oh, about eight hours."

"*Eight hours?* To install all those windowpanes? In a thirty-by-twenty room?"

Herb chuckled. "You make sure that snazzy new composter is working on overdrive. You'll be ready to plant tomorrow."

When he left, Alex stepped into the hydroponic greenhouse. She had covered the side window with black-out curtains to prevent the continuous lunar sunlight from burning the plants. Now, she peeled it back to watch the bots at work. They had already framed out the room, the tall support beams reaching into the lunar sky. As Alex watched through the distorted glass, the vinyl flooring came together, and then the interlocking tiles that formed the side walls.

She thought about watching the Institute's construction in Hyde Park, so long ago. The permit process alone took months. The speed of construction on the Moon made her head spin.

Later, after a stilted dinner with Carson the geologist and Mitch in operations, where they kept looking askance at the side salad she had assembled to complement her redi-meal, Alex returned to the new greenhouse.

The film seal was down and the dust vacuumed. Alex opened the door and stepped inside her new soil greenhouse.

The first thing she noticed was the clarity of the windows. The sun and stars shone above, and the Moon's cragged surface stretched into the horizon. The room felt enormous after all the time Alex had spent in the cramped hydroponic greenhouse. It had four tall sets of shelves, with three spacious rows between them. Each shelf held a tray, ready to be filled with soil and seeds.

She reached out a hand and touched a shelf. She couldn't wait to get started.

Alex sat up sharply. The blaring alarm sounded in her head, bouncing off the walls of the tiny room. Involuntarily, she covered her ears and pulled her legs into her chest—but it wasn't in her head.

The colony's emergency alarm. *Right.* Exit the room. Get somewhere safe.

Stumbling out of her room with bare feet, Alex stared into the flurry of activity in the hall. *What time is it?* she wondered muzzily.

A hand clutched her arm. Kayla thrust an oxygen mask into her hands. Her eyes bored into Alex's. "A fire. Get to the end of the hallway."

Fumbling with the mask, Alex joined the crush of bodies moving to the newer wing of the residence hall.

Another hand reached out, grabbing hers. Mansoor pulled down his oxygen mask. "Are you alright?" he asked urgently, his forehead pressed to hers.

Alex swallowed and nodded silently.

Mansoor pulled her down against the wall.

Anderson's voice floated into her memory. *Two weeks in New Mexico.* Had her brief training covered fire?

Smoke rises, so move to the floor. Right, she was on the floor. They were all on the floor.

Use an emergency oxygen mask in case the recycled air is compromised. Check.

What else? Something about safety doors to contain the spread. She hoped someone else more alert handled that task.

She was on a rock without atmosphere.

Without a spacesuit, on the surface of the Moon, they would all be dead in thirty seconds.

Maybe sixty.

Around her, the only sound came from the blaring alarm and the whoosh of air moving in and out of the masks. She never wanted to let go of Mansoor's hand. It was rough and scraped and strong in hers.

What would kill them first? Smoke. It was always smoke that was the deadliest in a fire. Did it hurt? To die from smoke inhalation?

Alex breathed in. She breathed out.

With his free hand, Mansoor touched her hair. His eyes, so close to hers, were a light brown. Almost hazel. His eyebrows drew together in concern at whatever expression she blinked back at him. Alex squeezed his hand.

Sandra, upright, without a mask, came toward them through the hallway. "There was an electrical short in the kitchen," she told them in a hoarse voice. "The fire is out, but the lounge and cafeteria are completely destroyed."

Voices rose as the residents removed their masks. Kayla's voice carried above the others, frantic. Angry. "Are you saying the food supply is gone? All of it?"

"Yes." Sandra rubbed her soot-covered face. "We have potable water and whatever food you've hoarded in your rooms. That's it."

MOONRISING

Alex jumped to her feet. "That is not it. If the fire was contained to the kitchen and lounge, then the greenhouses and the chicken coop are intact. The new greenhouse hasn't had time to produce yet, but there's plenty of food in the hydroponic greenhouse."

Kayla made a face. All traces of the care she had shown Alex earlier were gone. "I'd rather starve." Next to her, Naomi nodded in agreement.

"You might get the chance," Alex snapped back, the fear of the past minutes somehow funneling into rage. "What an ignorant, narrow-minded hill to die on." She knew she wasn't being diplomatic. Screw diplomacy. This was stupidity.

"No one is starving," Sandra said in a voice of deliberate calm, gesturing for Alex to step down. "A supply ship and a forensics team are projected to reach us in 48 hours."

Mansoor squeezed her hand once more and let it go. "I'm going to shower."

Alex numbly watched the rest of the residents disperse back to their rooms or to view the destruction.

Sandra stepped toward her. In a low voice she said, "Alex . . . you have to understand that most of us have had it drilled into our heads by our government our entire adult lives that mutagenetic food is dangerous." Her expression was compassionate. "You aren't going to undo years of programming by yelling at everyone. You need to"—she spun her hands—"you know. Bring them along."

Alex shook her head and blew a breath out her nose. No amount of tact would convince the Kaylas of the world. She'd been at this too many years to believe that.

"I think we're going to need you over the next few days. Think about it." Sandra turned away and trudged toward her room.

In her own room, Alex stepped into the shower, letting the metallic water wash away her lingering terror. She remembered how Mansoor had described building trust with Administrator

Anderson with years of work. She remembered Finn asking her, *Is there anyone you actually trust?*

Was trust a two-way street? Could she earn the respect of others by giving it back to them? But people like Kayla didn't deserve her trust, and she wasn't in the mood to fake it, even if it was strategic. She had never mastered the trick of persuading people. But she didn't want it to be a trick. If they would just be *rational* about it, she wouldn't have to play games at all, and—

The shower turned itself off abruptly, and she shivered. After pulling on clean pajamas, she returned to bed. But sleep didn't come for a long time.

By later that afternoon, the situation they faced had become clear. A ship was preparing to launch at dawn the next day with food supplies, along with a full forensic team to investigate the cause of the incident. The command team had ruled out arson caused by a colony resident based on the security footage, but the possibility of remote sabotage would need to wait for the independent investigation. To hold them over until help arrived, every resident scoured their rooms for food and turned it into a single supply cache.

Each resident was given a time to report to the medical wing for a smoke inhalation screening on the AI-powered medi-scanner and to receive their portion of the available rations.

As soon as she understood the situation, Alex went to the hydroponic greenhouse and harvested a full tray of kale, peas, zucchini, yellow squash, mini-cucumbers, bell peppers, and several varieties of cherry tomatoes. She brought them to a table set up outside of the clinic where Mitch was sorting the packaged food.

He looked at her tray doubtfully. "Is that safe?"

"Of course it's safe," Alex retorted. Then she remembered Sandra's words and tried to modify her tone. "Every variety of fruits and vegetables I brought to the colony has been tested in my

MOONRISING

laboratory at the University of Chicago Institute for Sustainable Agriculture. Many varieties, I designed myself."

"If you say so," Mitch said, but his expression was still skeptical. "We're distributing one protein bar per resident as they come in for their lung scans. We don't have much. 123 protein bars, seven redi-meals, and one jar of vitamins." His upper lip curved slightly. "And everyone's candy stashes from home." He gestured to a pile of Pocky, Swedish Fish, and Lindt chocolate. "Treats for all."

Carson came up to the table, pulling something out of his pocket. "I forgot I have this." It was a bottle of Texas Pete hot sauce. He jiggled it. "Any use to you?"

Mitch laughed. "Dude, I'm not taking that. Hot sauce has almost no calories."

"It would be good on eggs," Alex offered. "My hens are starting to produce."

Carson slipped the hot sauce into his pocket. "Mutant eggs, right?"

Alex schooled her face to remain neutral. "The breed has been rigorously tested for safety. All the food I produce has been tested on lab animals and has been circulating in the Midwest co-op scene. I didn't bring anything experimental with me—just proven winners, especially strands designed for low water, limited or no soil, and reduced space." There. She was pretty sure she'd said it calmly.

Carson made a "humph" sound, his eyes straying to her box of produce.

"Did you know that many of the seeds growing in the greenhouse Alex designed herself?" Mitch offered tentatively.

"I'll think about it." Carson moved away hurriedly when he saw Julien exit the clinic. Naomi stepped out to usher Carson in. Her lip curled when she noticed the overflowing tray.

Julien came over to the table. "*Docteur* Berg gave me the all clear. No smoke inhalation for me." He grinned at the sight of

Alex's tray of vegetables. "Look at this bounty." He picked up a pepper and ate a bite of it like an apple.

Mitch turned his head away, but Alex could still see him wince.

"How much can I take?" Julien asked.

"As much as you can carry," Alex said glumly. So much for her calm demeanor winning everyone over. "I have a feeling there will be plenty to spare."

Alex knew she should leave and save herself the humiliation, but instead she stayed at the table and tried to offer produce to each person coming to the clinic. Soon, a line had begun to form for Dr. Berg and the medi-scanner. Naomi stepped out again to explain that while she and Herb had recently installed upgrades to the AI-powered health machine, it was still taking longer to perform each lung scan than anticipated.

"Feel free to leave and come back if you have work to do," Naomi said with a pointed look at Alex.

Ignoring Naomi's hint, Alex stayed and gave everyone the same explanation she'd given Carson. She figured the repetition was good practice for her. As she went through her little speech for the umpteenth time, she found her thoughts wandering to Mansoor—always so calm and diplomatic. Did it come easily to him? Or had he had to practice like Alex was doing now, stuffing down anger in the face of foolishness, pretending to be unfazed?

"Good, you're here," her father said, bypassing the crowd of people waiting for their turn at the clinic. He picked up a mini-cucumber and took a bite. Everyone stopped talking at once. Two dozen heads swirled to look at the commander. Alex's heart thundered. This was exactly what she needed. A show of support from an authority figure. Her father didn't appear to register the attention as he said, "Herb will have four hot plates and four pots ready for you by tomorrow afternoon. I told him to make it a priority after the air was scrubbed."

"Thank you," Alex said with relief.

MOONRISING

"This is good," he said, raising the cucumber. His voice carried, and Alex realized her father knew exactly the impact he was having on the other residents. "Very crunchy." He turned to the room at large. "I regret to say I have discouraging news. Wildfires in Canada, Germany, and Siberia are causing the global air quality index to be projected to stay at the Hazardous level for at least the next three days. The supply ship can't launch yet. It'll be a few more days, at least. I suggest you make your protein bar last." Then, he handed Alex a small canister of salt and lowered his voice. "Thought you could use this for your cooking. I keep it at my desk to make the redi-meals tolerable." Alex took the canister and turned it over in her hand, her throat suddenly tight with some unnamable emotion. "I know, I know," her father said, raising his hands. "I should be watching my sodium intake to lower my blood pressure." He gave her a wink like he used to do when she was a child and left.

Mitch watched him go. So did everyone else. Then, as the chatter resumed, Mitch turned to Alex. "Can I try a cucumber?"

Carson found her the next afternoon as she worked in the soil greenhouse. Ducking his large body into the room, he said, "Herb asked me to find you. He set up the hot plates in the hangar bay." He looked around the greenhouse with more curiosity than Alex would have expected. "You really design the seeds yourself? I wouldn't have a clue how to do that."

"Would you like a tour?"

Carson gave a casual shrug. "I reckon."

Alex showed him around the new greenhouse, introducing him to each variety of vegetable and fruit she had recently planted. About half of the four rows of shelving already contained new plants, in deep trays of soil. A few seedlings were starting to peek up.

"I've never owned a plant," Carson said. "I always say to my buddies, I'm a simple man. No kids, no pets, no plants. Just rocks.

Rocks don't care if you forget to feed them or wake you up at 4 a.m."

Alex's lips turned up. "I'm not a pet person either. Too many long days in the lab."

Carson snorted in sympathy. "I hear you on the long days." He scratched behind his ear. "Well . . . I should get back to my rocks. Thanks for the tour."

"Carson," Alex said hesitantly. She was suddenly filled with an overwhelming urge to try a little harder. Yesterday had been a start, but she knew she could do more to . . . how had Sandra put it? To bring people along. "Can I show you the rest of my process?"

"I suppose," Carson said slowly.

How had Mansoor handled the journalist who'd asked about her chickens? Calm. Confident. Straightforward. "Do you know what caused the Potato Plague?" Alex said as they walked to the shared laboratory across from the greenhouse.

"Everyone knows what caused the Potato Plague. Mutant, I mean, mutagenetic potatoes pushed by Big Ag into our food supply."

"Yes! You're right," she said, registering how Carson relaxed a little at her approval. "But those particular potatoes had a problem. Solanine."

"Sure, I read about that, I think," Carson said. "In college biology maybe? It's the toxin found in mutagenetic food."

"You know what's interesting?" Alex asked as they entered the lab. "It's a toxin found in all potatoes. The problem is when there's a build-up. In organic potatoes, it's always obvious when that happens. The potatoes look green under the skin. Anyone could tell they're spoiled and throw them away." She sat down on a lab stool.

"Oh . . . Right." Carson nodded and sat down opposite her. "Mutagenetic food hides toxins. I do remember that from biology."

"That was absolutely true in the '40s and '50s." Alex leaned forward. "There was a push to ensure all produce using mutagenetics looked uniform in color, texture, and size to keep pace with the standardization of processed foods. At the time, the agricultural industry was a mess. Funding cuts and deregulation had made the FDA practically useless. Companies were skimping on safety testing. And that's when the Potato Plague hit. The potatoes had been designed to look perfect, and they didn't show toxic levels of solanine. And nobody tested them before they were sent to grocery stores and processed at factories."

"Exactly. Why do you think we're all so concerned about mutagenetic food being grown on the Moon? It isn't safe." Carson leaned back on his stool, suddenly frowning. "Look, Alex, I know some folks here have been rude to you. I've seen it. But people are *scared*. First, there's this big foreign investment in the colony that appears to shift the purpose of this station from research to tourism, and the next thing we know a rogue scientist known for lax food safety standards is coming to the colony to feed us."

"A rogue scientist?" Alex pressed her lips together. *Stay calm,* she coached herself. "I suppose I've been called worse. I'm not pushing for a return to the old way of doing things. I've learned from the mistakes of the Potato Plague. I never design vegetable strains for their looks or hide their chemical composition. Everything I'm growing here has been tested on mammals—we do rodent testing at my Institute in Chicago. And then I do further testing here on every batch of food I produce. Look—I'll show you."

She gestured to Carson over to her work station and showed him how she checked each variety for levels of alkaloids, furocoumarins, and phytotoxins. Carson's brow furrowed as he studied Alex's meticulous charts of the toxicity levels of each vegetable strain growing on the colony.

Alex watched his face as he read through her data. She'd managed to keep her temper in check, but had she found a way to persuade him?

Carson looked up and met her eyes. She swallowed.

"Okay," he finally said, scratching the side of his head. "Well, you've given me a whole heck of a lot to reconsider."

Alex's throat felt suddenly tight. She'd been waiting her entire career for a moment like this. "Come on." She led Carson to the hydroponic greenhouse. He looked around the small space, lush and full of ripe vegetables.

"These golden tomatoes are my favorite. They're so sweet." Alex picked one off the vine and offered it to Carson. *Be confident*, she told herself.

Carson took it gingerly and stared at it for a long moment before putting it in his mouth. His eyes popped open. "Shit, that's good," he said. "Can I have another one?"

Alex gestured for Carson to pick his own and he did, groaning a little as he ate another.

"What are you planning to use the hot plates and pots for?" Carson asked.

"I thought I'd make vegetable soup tonight. Something simple, since we don't have a real kitchen right now," Alex said. "But I'm not sure how much to make. The demand . . . might not be high."

"Can I help?" Carson offered tentatively.

Yes! She could have skipped. Shouted. Danced. Run to Mansoor and told him everything she'd learned about communicating more diplomatically in the last twenty-four hours. Instead, she remained calm. That seemed to be working for her.

"Sure," she said, unable to keep the huge smile from her face. "That would be great."

Alex handed Carson a pair of gloves and showed him how to reach into the zucchini grow tray to find some mature squash hiding under the spiky leaves. She showed him how to twist the peppers where their stems met the branch so they would come off easily without damaging the plant. Together, they filled two bins with vegetables and carried them to the hangar bay.

MOONRISING

Herb had set them up well. Next to the hot plates were cutting boards, knives, and large pots still warm from the Refabricator.

They got to work in companionable silence, Alex chopping tomatoes and Carson dicing zucchini. A few other residents wandered into the hangar bay and did a double take. Alex knew they weren't expecting to see Carson chopping mutagenetic vegetables and smiled quietly to herself. This would speak louder than any of her words, she knew.

"You sure you want to be touching those, C?" one teased.

"Y'all need to hear this," Carson said, waving a few people over. He began to describe the safety techniques he had observed in Alex's lab, making expansive gestures with the knife. Two of them made excuses and left, but Sandra stayed, a little smile on her face when she caught Alex's eye. When Mitch's shift at the clinic ended, Sandra and Carson convinced him to join.

Julien arrived with a few other international residents in tow. "Put me to work," he said, rolling up his sleeves.

Soon there was an assembly line of laughing geologists, biologists, astrophysicists, and operations staff chopping zucchini, yellow squash, tomatoes, green beans, bell peppers, chard, basil, oregano, rosemary, and thyme.

"I'll send a few more folks over to carry chairs and tables." Alex's father said to her when he stopped by to check on the meal's progress.

By the time Mansoor arrived after wrapping up a day of work at the hotel, the comforting smell of vegetable soup wafted through the hangar. He touched the small of Alex's back briefly before going to help with setting up chairs and tables. Julien passed around a few bottles of moonshine the astrophysicists had stashed in their rooms, and Sandra piped in jazz music through the comms equipment.

Alex was just starting to relax around the table with the others when Kayla and Naomi stepped in, arm-in-arm. The conversation around the table went still.

"Would you like some soup?" Alex offered tentatively, standing and reaching for the ladle.

Naomi snorted. "Tell me, what were you doing in 2061?"

Back to the Potato Plague, thought Alex, but she forced herself to answer calmly, "Sophomore chemistry."

Naomi smiled thinly. "I was an ER doctor at Johns Hopkins. In the Pediatric Emergency Department. No, I don't want any goddamn soup."

"We'll take some moonshine, though," said Kayla, gesturing to one of the bottles.

Julien glanced guiltily at Alex before scooting over to make room and pouring them each a glass.

Sandra, who was next to Alex, pulled on her arm for her to sit back down. She whispered, "The soup is good," she said. "You should be proud of yourself."

From farther down the table, Kayla loudly asked, "Dr. Berg, does the clinic stock anti-nausea meds?"

"I'm glad you asked." Naomi stood up, holding her glass of moonshine. "I want everyone here to know, I take my vocation seriously. Do not hesitate to reach out, day or night, if you feel lightheaded or nauseous."

"Thank you, Dr. Berg," Saul said mildly, his soup spoon halfway raised. "Your devotion to your profession is admirable." He slurped.

Naomi tilted her cup in his direction and sat back down. Kayla hid her laughter into Naomi's shoulder. Alex's head was pounding. She could feel anger gathering. She had half a mind to stand up and confront their stupidity right here, right now—

"It's okay," Sandra said in a low voice, touching Alex's arm. "They're trying to bait you."

"Yeah, well. It's working," Alex muttered back.

"Try the soup," Sandra urged. "You haven't even taken a bite yet."

MOONRISING

Alex raised a spoon to her lips. It was savory and warm—and delicious. Instantly, the anger left her body. This was good—and she had made it.

She looked around the table. At least a dozen people were eating this soup made from the seeds she had designed, and brought across hundreds of thousands of miles of cold space, to the Moon. To make this meal, on this day.

Naomi and Kayla didn't seem so important after all.

"This is the best meal of my life," Alex said to Sandra, a smile breaking across her face.

Sandra's mouth quirked. "Good."

The next morning, Alex made a batch of hard-boiled eggs served with dill and diced red peppers and a strawberry mint salad. A few residents who had avoided her the night before came in silently and filled their plates with the meager breakfast without meeting her eyes.

"Any more?" Julien asked, holding out his plate with a doleful look.

Alex shook her head. "The hens only produce once a day." She leaned in, jerking her head to the new group devouring the meal with heads down. "Besides, I have a few more mouths to feed this morning."

"Tomorrow, I will cook us *des omelettes* the way we do at home. You have tarragon, yes?"

Alex grinned, her mind already turning over how to prepare omelets without butter. "I do."

After breakfast, several members of the mining team stopped by her lab. "Carson convinced us to let you give us the spiel," one of them said, her arms crossed. "I'm a scientist. I'm not afraid to change my opinion if there's new data."

155

Alex ducked her head to hide a smile. "Alright, I'll give you a tour."

By lunchtime, Alex estimated that a full third of the residents had eaten the spinach, edamame, cucumber, and basil salad Alex assembled.

On the third day, her father joined breakfast with a serious expression. He took a slightly burnt French omelet from Julien and pulled Alex to the side. "The wildfire smoke isn't dissipating. How many calories a day would you say you're providing?"

"Not enough. Fewer than a thousand per person. And there're still some holdouts who haven't eaten in days."

Saul looked around the room. "Are there more people here than yesterday?"

Alex felt a little surge of pride. "We've fed about eighty people this morning." She'd calculated that about twenty residents remained in the Kayla and Naomi camp, refusing all mutagenetic food. An eighty percent success rate. *Not bad.*

Saul took a bite of his omelet. "Good," he said. "Keep it up." Alex couldn't help but feel warm at his small words of approval.

As the days went on, Alex's hope soared each time the residents joined her meals. She was accomplishing here what she had never been able to accomplish on Earth. On a smaller scale, granted—much smaller. Still, it felt so good to remember people could change. There *was* hope. What would it look like if she could somehow replicate that level of success on earth, in America? *But how?*

Somehow, the fire had built a sense of community that not even Kayla's or Naomi's sour dispositions could damper. The residents joked about their forced foray into a healthy lifestyle. Some, unused to the reduced calories, overindulged on moonshine. Carson became a frequent visitor of the chicken coop and named all the hens after football players.

MOONRISING

When the supply ship finally arrived in the hotel hangar bay on the morning of the seventh day, Alex braced herself at lunchtime. She made a skillet ratatouille for a smaller group; there would be some, she knew, who had only eaten her food out of necessity and would likely return to the redi-meals. As it cooked, she tried to hold on to the feeling of belonging for a bit longer, before it went away again.

"What is that delicious smell?" Sandra asked over her shoulder. She leaned into the pan. "Eggplant, yes? And zucchini?"

"Do I smell basil?" asked Mitch, escorting a robotic pallet of redi-meals and ration bars into the hangar. "Save me some."

The residents ate redi-meals, of course. Even Alex knew her body desperately needed the protein. But when she looked up from inhaling her meal, she saw the skillets of ratatouille were all wiped clean.

She had not been rejected after all.

10

VICTOR

BEFORE VICTOR OPENED HIS EYES, HE COULD SEE IT.

Newton's second law.

He leapt up, grabbing his glasses from the bedside table. In the bathroom, he found an old tube of Harper's lipstick and scribbled a few ideas on the mirror as he brushed his teeth. A higher concentration of rocket fuel would cause the gas to expel at a faster rate and increase the upward thrust of the rocket. He went immediately to his desk and found a paper notepad.

Freezing liquid oxygen would allow for a greater density in the fuel tanks. Oxygen froze at 54.36 K, but it would need to turn liquid at a rapid rate when the combustion engines were ready to expel it.

Victor mapped out several approaches to the problem and bent his head to run through the calculations.

When the doorbell rang in a staccato succession, it took a moment for Victor to register the noise. He got up from his desk with stiff legs and walked to the security camera. "Rashid?" he said in surprise.

"Victor, let me in. And turn on the news."

Victor left the condo door ajar and cast a news feed to his living room screen. By the time Rashid had raced up the three flights of stairs and arrived panting in his condo, he was caught up on the basic facts of the fire on the colony. Freezing rocket fuel to increase ship propulsion was no longer at the forefront of his mind.

Rashid put a duffel bag down in the foyer and took off his shoes. He looked tired and frayed.

"They said no one was injured," Victor said. "Is Mansoor alright?"

"He's fine, physically at least. But, Victor, the Homestead Act is up for a floor vote in three weeks. Everything we've worked for is gone. I don't know what to do."

Victor touched his empty wrist. "What time is it?"

"Ten a.m. I took an early-morning bullet train from New York when it was clear you weren't answering your messages."

Victor got up and hunted for his intelliwatch. He found it sitting on the kitchen island with a dead battery and put it on its charging pad.

"You should have gone straight to D.C.," Victor said when he returned to the living room and sat beside Rashid on the sofa.

"I can't do this without you." Rashid turned his body to face Victor and pulled up his long legs.

"I'm tapped out of introductions," said Victor. "I don't have a sovereign wealth fund. And politicians seem to want less of me the more they get to know me." He grimaced. "You don't need me for this."

"I always need you." Rashid's cheeks darkened, and he ducked his head. "Flights are grounded anyway due to smoke from the Canadian wildfires." He snorted. "Fire on Earth. Fire on the Moon. *Some say the world will end in fire.*"

"Do they?" Victor frowned in thought. "The Earth's most probable fate is absorption by the Sun in 7.5 billion years. What appears to us as burning is actually nuclear fusion, not chemical combustion. I don't consider nuclear fusion to be fire."

Rashid hugged his knees into his chest. The expression on his face confounded Victor for a moment until he belatedly realized it was affection. "It's Robert Frost. 'Some say the world will end in fire. Some say in ice. From what I've tasted of desire I hold with those who favor fire.'" Rashid was blushing again. "I should stop talking."

"You should go on to the capital. You should not have gotten off the high-speed rail, but at least I'm in the right direction. What will you say to Garcia?"

Rashid ran a hand through his dark hair. Victor wondered what Rashid's hair felt like. It looked soft and curly. Would it wind around Victor's finger?

"I think frame it as a success story," Rashid said. "Mansoor has gotten me some information in the SMS bursts that have made it out. No one was injured. Not one minor injury. The alarm system worked flawlessly, and all residents were in a safe zone wearing oxygen masks in a matter of minutes. The bulkhead doors immediately activated to contain the fire to only the cafeteria and lounge. The colony's safety protocols were tested—and they held."

"Do you think that argument will work?"

Rashid leaned the side of his head against the sofa. "No. I don't think any argument will work. I think the Homestead Act is dead."

A thought stirred for Victor at his words. If a large fire was going to happen on the colony, this was a best-case scenario. At 4 a.m., most residents would be in their quarters, except for a few stationed in the 24/7 command center. The kitchen was its own short wing, easily sealed off without disrupting the airflow to the rest of the colony. And yet the kitchen was stocked with critical supplies, and their loss was a blow to the colony.

MOONRISING

The Homestead Act was scheduled for a floor vote in three weeks.

Was this a coincidence? Or an act of carefully planned sabotage designed to maximize economic pain with a reasonable certainty of no human casualties? He would need to run some scenarios.

"You have to try," Victor said to Rashid, not voicing his theory. "The Homestead Act isn't defeated yet."

When Rashid left to catch the next high-speed train to D.C., Victor returned to his desk and turned his notebook to a blank page.

A week after the fire, Teru found Victor in front of an office whiteboard. "Victor, you need to sleep."

"I figured it out," Victor said, taking his chief engineer by the arm and pointing at the board. "Look."

"What am I looking at?" they asked patiently.

"The colony's electrical grid is monitored and controlled by NASA," Victor said rapidly. "They have the capability to remotely increase and decrease wattage, shut off faulty wiring, test, and monitor. In the event of a problem, two-centimeter AI crawlers can investigate and fix most problems." Victor tapped the whiteboard. "The forensics team found pieces of cable strippers at the site."

"Cable strippers," Teru repeated. "Why is that significant?"

"They're used only by the electric crawlers. None of the other bots have cable strippers. There was no electrical work scheduled in that section of the station, and yet a crawler was there on the wires. A crawler caused the fire."

"They've ruled it an accident, I thought."

"It wasn't an accident. It was sabotage," Victor said. "And a damn sophisticated operation. I've spent the last forty-eight hours trying to hack into the colony's system. There's no way in. Not from here. You would need access to NASA's headquarters or the ability to program bots from the colony."

"Are you saying the saboteur is a NASA employee? Or even a colony resident?"

Victor flopped down on a nearby chair, suddenly exhausted. "Or a better hacker than I am. It isn't a skill I've perfected."

Teru looked over the whiteboard. "You need to take care of yourself, Victor. I can turn these notes and equations into a digestible report for NASA while you eat something." Teru, bless them, was quite comfortable translating how Victor's ideas came out on a whiteboard into legible materials.

Victor shook his head. "I'm not reporting this."

"What? Why?"

"It's too circumstantial. I've found out nothing that NASA doesn't already know. An unsubstantiated theory about an unknown boogeyman with this kind of reach would delay the first tourist launch and push the Homestead Act even further off course."

"So, what will you do?"

Victor shrugged. "Wait. Monitor. See if whoever did this slips up."

Victor sat with Rashid high in the Senate visitor gallery. Rashid's leg next to Victor's vibrated with tension as they watched the proceedings below.

"Inspector Douglass," Garcia said from the chairman's seat. "Thank you for returning to speak with us. We have only one question to put before you. Does the fire at Peary Station on June 27, 2073, cause you to revise your testimony today?"

"Senator Garcia, it does not."

There was a buzzing in the gallery at his words. Victor felt Rashid's whole body sag with relief.

"Elaborate, please, Inspector."

Drake's Medal of Honor glinted on the top of his formal military jacket as he leaned forward into the microphone. "In the weeks since the fire on Peary Station, we have witnessed a community coming together to support one another. During the seven-day period before fresh supplies could arrive, the colony residents pooled their food supplies, harvested vegetables from the colony's hydroponic greenhouse, and cooked communally. Rarely have I witnessed a close-quarters, high-stakes living environment operate with such a collective will."

"Did you put him up to this?" Victor asked in an undertone.

"Me?" Rashid gave a quiet huff. "I've never met the man. I think this is his sincere belief."

"I have studied the forensics report," Drake continued from the floor. "It is clear to me that the fire was unintentional and not the result of negligence. The colony's chief engineer has already implemented the report's recommended precautions to ensure the conditions that caused the accidental electrical fire do not occur again. The colony has shown adaptability and flexibility in the face of this disaster and is safer for it."

Victor had not told anyone but Teru about his own theory of causation. He kept quiet to Rashid now.

"While this incident demonstrates a healthy community willing to adapt in the face of setbacks, it does support my initial recommendation to proceed with caution when introducing children to the colony. Progressing at a gradual pace with frequent assessments on the living conditions of the colony will be more likely to lead to a successful outcome."

"Liar!" A shout came from the visitor gallery opposite them, on the other side of the chamber. A man stood, gripping the railing and glaring at Drake from afar. "The colony is an abomination. It's funded by blood money and is spreading mutant food. Space colonization is destroying our planet." Two Capitol Police officers grabbed the man by the arms and dragged him up the stairs. "One Earth, one fight!" he shouted before they pulled him through the doors.

"Does that kind of thing happen a lot?" Rashid asked Victor.

Victor shook his head, staring at the closed doors where the man had been. Something was slipping through his brain, just out of reach.

"Order," Garcia called, banging his gavel. "This chamber will have order."

"Senator Garcia, if I may," Drake said into the microphone. "The potential of Helium-3 mining alone is enough to justify the environmental cost of increased trips into space. Many scientists believe Helium-3 could allow us to eliminate nonrenewable sources of energy. The Homestead Act will be a net win for the environment."

"Thank you, Inspector Douglass." Garcia turned to look at the other senators arrayed around him. "My distinguished colleagues, I move that we have no further delay and continue the floor vote as planned."

"Seconded," said the senator seated at Garcia's right hand.

"All in favor?"

"Aye," said a majority of the gathered committee members.

"The motion is passed." Garcia slammed down a gavel. "This session is adjourned."

Victor bounded down the stairs to the first floor with Rashid behind him, stepping into the wide halls of Congress.

"Thank you," he said to Drake when the inspector exited the chamber.

"Beard, hello," Drake said cautiously. "My duty is to testify truthfully and to the best of my knowledge. I didn't do it for you."

"Nevertheless, thank you."

"Thank the man next to you," Drake said, nodding at Rashid. "I am not the one who fundamentally altered the political consensus around the Homestead Act." He walked away down the hall.

"I hope he's right," Rashid said in an undertone behind Victor, his mouth close to Victor's ear. "The Homestead Act may not be dead after all."

11

ALEX

"WHAT DO YOU THINK, ALEXANDRA?" HER FATHER ASKED. HE CON-
templated the new kitchen plans on display in the dome conference room.

"The island needs to be bigger." Alex touched the screen with one finger. "Longer and wider. Enough for several cooks to prep side by side plus a clean surface opposite for serving."

Herb made a note with his stylus. "Is the cold storage adequate?"

"It'll do for now. In the long term, I envision a new agricultural wing of the colony with fields of wheat and olive trees. Facilities for food preservation and storage should be housed in that wing, not the communal kitchen."

"First it was lemons, now it's wheat and olives," Saul grumbled to Herb, giving Alex a wink. "Next it'll be a cattle pasture."

"Don't be silly," Alex said to her father. "You know cattle are a major pollutant."

"What I wouldn't give for a juicy beef patty and fries fresh out of the grease," Saul lamented.

Ignoring the commander, Herb said to Alex, "How are you thinking about successfully growing trees?"

MOONRISING

Alex sat down at the table. "Shallow root, compact trees only. The type that can be cultivated in large pots on Earth. Olive trees are grown in lower-moisture soil, and we can plant them as hedges with only five feet of spacing. I think we could produce olive oil on the colony in about three years if we have the resources to develop a new wing. We have an important long-term need for local sources of lipids to cook properly."

"Olive trees," Saul said. "That would be a sight to behold. Do you have what you need from us, Herb?"

"I do." Herb stopped casting. "I'll get right to work. I'm eager to reclaim the hangar bay for ships, not hungry diners."

Alex watched Herb's retreating back.

"Do you believe the fire was an accident?" she asked her father. She'd been turning the idea over in her mind. If someone wanted to sabotage the colony, destroying their food supplies was a logical move. Though whether accident or sabotage, Alex had to admit the whole situation had turned out in her favor. Without the destruction of the colony's food supplies, residents wouldn't have been so open to trying her food. *Silver linings*. Still, the idea of someone on the colony trying to take it down from the inside was disturbing.

The commander walked to the conference room window and stood looking out at the hotel spires. "As the leader of this station, I must accept what the experts have concluded."

Alex wasn't sure he would confide in her even if he did suspect foul play, but she asked anyway, "And what about as a father speculating to his daughter?"

Saul let out a breath. "As a father, I worry it was an attack targeted toward you."

"*Me?*" Alex exclaimed. "I was nowhere near the fire when it happened."

Saul sat down opposite her at the conference room table. "Have you read Drake Douglass's report on the station?"

167

Alex shook her head. "I've heard people talking about it, but I haven't had a chance to read it yet for myself."

"He organized his evaluation of Peary Station into a series contemplating the colony's successes and gaps in providing an adequate standard of living, as defined in the Universal Declaration of Human Rights. He considered water, oxygen, housing, food, clothing, sanitation, and medical care. In the report, he described your greenhouse at length. Any reasonable reader might conclude that the colony residents were enjoying fresh food in the cafeteria on a daily basis. Mutagenetic food."

"But . . . that's not accurate at all. At least not until the fire."

"You have enemies, don't you Alexandra?"

"I do," Alex said slowly. "I've been the target of sabotage before."

"Did you know the FBI now considers the Eco Liberation Society to be a domestic terrorist organization?"

"You think the ELS was responsible for the kitchen fire?" Alex shook her head. "No. They don't have that kind of reach. What does NASA say?"

Saul raised his hands. "I have no evidence. It's not even a theory, really. More like a hunch. And I'm biased, aren't I? I don't like the idea of anyone trying to hurt my little girl."

Alex swallowed a sudden lump in her throat. He hadn't called her that since before her mom died. "I'm fine, Dad," she said, aware of the strange stiffness in her voice.

"I know. You've handled yourself well these last few weeks."

"Not well enough. Kayla, Naomi, and their little contingent still won't touch mutagenetic food."

Saul shrugged. "You won't get them all." He stood to go, touching her shoulder briefly in passing. "But it was good to see you as a leader here. Like your old man."

Alex stared at his retreating back. Did she want to be like her father? He was respected here. Beloved by his team. Alex could

MOONRISING

see how he had poured his entire self into the colony—but at the expense of his relationships on Earth. Including his relationship with his daughter.

She *was* like him, she realized, an uncomfortable feeling pressing at her chest. How many times had her sense of duty and purpose and obligation put her at odds with people? Caused her to push people away—or suspect the worst of them, sometimes even before they said a word?

She'd spent her life fighting to feed humanity, even though most people didn't seem to want her help. But something had changed. The night of that first dinner, she realized. When she sat around the table and ate soup, surrounded not by humanity in general but a dozen people, sweaty and tired and hungry, all from different backgrounds, all eating the same soup.

She thought of Mansoor, pressing his forehead against hers. She thought of Sandra, encouraging her to bring people along. Of Carson, saying folks had misjudged her. She even thought of Kayla, pushing an oxygen mask into her hand.

She didn't want to be like her father.

Of course she cared about her science. That would never change. But she'd always assumed that meant she had to be alone. For the first time, she was starting to think she was wrong.

Maybe she could have both.

Mansoor found Alex at her workbench carefully removing an onion seedling from a gelatinous bath designed for accelerated growth.

"I met your new hotel chef," Alex said, holding the tweezers and placing the seedling in a mix of compost and shredded redi-meal containers. "Charming fellow."

Mansoor ran his hand through his hair and winced. "He's rather famous in the Parisian dining scene."

"Chef Pierre was upset to discover chives are the only allium I could offer him—for now." Alex placed another onion seedling in the soil and arranged the roots.

"I hope he is worth the trouble. He has already asked me twice to postpone the first tourist visit to give him adequate time to familiarize himself with the equipment and ingredients available on the colony. He seems very used to getting his way."

"Do you feel ready?" Alex asked, pausing in her work and looking up at him.

"Yes," Mansoor said confidently. Then— "No. But I have two more weeks to get there."

"I'm glad the fire didn't derail your timeline."

He let out a puff of air. "Not at all. My clients have been waiting for this moment for years. They would let nothing stand in their way of being the first tourists on the Moon. But there is still so much to do. The ship that brought Pierre came with crates of supplies for the hotel rooms that I need to set up. And the weeklong agenda still needs to be finalized. I have recruited Carson to conduct moonwalk tours of the Taurus-Littrow site. It is a great location for geology. He wants to fit in a test run tomorrow."

"A moonwalk? That sounds exciting. Well—" Alex laughed. "Maybe not to you. I know you've spent more than enough time fixing the robots in a space suit. But it sounds thrilling to me. It's strange to think I haven't been outside in six months."

"Would you like to join us?"

Alex snorted. "I'm hardly your target demographic."

"I know." Mansoor's lips turned up in a smile. "Would you like to come anyway?"

Alex swallowed. Mansoor's intent brown eyes followed the movement of her throat. "Alright."

The next day, Alex found herself preparing to don a spacesuit for the first time after half a year living on the Moon. Mitch helped her and Carson into the enormous pant legs, carefully reminding

MOONRISING

them of the safety protocols. Mansoor, who had performed maintenance on the robots in a full suit hundreds of times, put on his own without difficulty.

"Your hands may swell," Mitch warned, fastening her gloves. Losing the serious tone, he flashed a grin. "Have fun out there."

Carson pounded Mitch's fist with his gloved hand. "Let's do this."

The tourist shuttle had arrived in several parts, transported in the same ship that had carried Pierre. It was smaller than the Starliner that had brought Alex to the Moon in February, designed for short day trips on the surface of the moon. The passenger area contained fourteen roomy, cushioned seats. The walls primarily consisted of windows, giving the passenger an unlimited view of the surface.

José, their pilot for the day, arrived with a cheery "Good morning." He was not moonwalking and wore less cumbersome clothing. As Mansoor strapped himself into the seat next to Alex, she found herself remembering her hand clamping down on his during that first terrifying launch into space so long ago.

This flight was an entirely different experience from their jarring ascent from Earth. They lifted up with barely a whisper and the ceiling of the docking station slid open to let the shuttle depart. The ship stayed close to the ground, about a hundred feet in the air, gliding smoothly away from the station.

Alex craned her head to get a full view of the colony. The dome lit up against the black sky. Alex could see the corridors leading from the center like wheel spokes. Some were short, like the passage to the hangar bay and the fledgling medical wing. The residence wing looked like a jumble of sticks, haphazardly placed. As she looked at the laboratory wing, she could see a glimpse of muted sage green from the smaller original hydroponic greenhouse and flashes of brown from the soil-based greenhouse.

The hotel's two spires reaching into the sky were a work of art. To Alex, the hotel's aesthetic seemed like a vision of what the Moon's surface would look like in a decade, as more planned construction projects launched, building on the lessons of the past.

Carson pointed out geological features to the two of them, practicing the tour he'd be giving the first lunar tourists in two weeks' time. Geology was hardly Alex's primary interest, but she found herself enthralled by Carson's words as she beheld the valleys and craters up close.

When they arrived at their destination, José moved them down smoothly onto a patch of relatively even ground. He helped Alex and Carson fasten their helmets and carefully checked their suits for leaks or damage. Finally, with José safely sealed in the cockpit, the gangway lowered.

Alex took her first step onto the surface of the Moon.

When her foot made contact, the surface's thin crust gave way. Alex lifted her head, taking in the open space around her. Without the colony to block out ambient light, the bright sun overpowered the stars. The sky was thickly black from horizon to horizon, Earth a half-lit cobalt presence in the blackness.

Her labored breathing was the only sound.

Carson's voice piped into her helmet, his tone uncharacteristically formal. "Our tour will begin with what remains of Apollo 17." He half-walked, half-bounced toward a man-made structure some fifty feet away.

Alex and Mansoor awkwardly followed. She thought she was used to the low Moon gravity, but in the cumbersome suit with no walls or ceiling she felt strange and out of touch with how her body moved. Several times, she flew too high in the air and had to catch her balance.

"Apollo 17 was the last lunar landing in the twentieth century." Carson stopped in front of the structure. "This Lunar Roving Vehicle was left here by the Apollo 17 astronauts. They

MOONRISING

used it to explore the Taurus-Littrow Valley over a three-day period. During this time, they collected sample Troctolite 76535, central to the theory that the Moon once possessed an active magnetic field."

Carson continued to explain how this sample helped scientists develop a theory for the timeline of the Moon's history. The Moon may have once contained a molten core and two billion years of active volcanoes. Alex was fascinated. She looked around the surface as Carson spoke, imagining the gray wasteland as the site of active volcanoes with bubbling lava.

When the tour concluded and they hopped back to the ship, Alex's suit was covered in sticky, fine-grained moon dust. As soon as the doors were sealed and José gave the all-clear, Alex removed her helmet and her gloves. Her knuckles and the back of her hands were raw, and her body was damp with sweat.

She had left her footprints on the surface of the Moon.

She had stood nearly alone under a bright sky, beholding the Earth.

Mansoor met her eyes, and she shivered. She remembered his tears when he had first beheld Earth from space. She could see a similar expression of awe and reverence on his face now as he looked at her.

On the ride back, Alex listened with half an ear to Mansoor and Carson discussing the tour, and how they would modify it when the guests arrived.

She was not ready to speak yet.

Once they docked, Mansoor thanked them all for the adventure and the four of them trudged back to their rooms. Alex still had not said a word. She stepped into the shower in a daze and then pulled on clean clothing. She was halfway down the hall, hair still damp, before she realized she had left her room.

When Mansoor answered her tentative knock, he didn't look surprised to see her. He stepped back and allowed her in. Alex found she still could not speak. She couldn't put into words the overwhelming feelings the experience had stirred up.

Instead, she kissed him.

Mansoor didn't hesitate. His hand tangled in her hair as he pulled her toward him. She wrapped her legs around his waist, and he carried her the few steps to his bed before gently laying her down.

For a moment, he simply looked at her, his rich brown eyes mapping out her face and body as if to memorize her. He cupped her cheek in one hand and traced his thumb down her lips and chin before settling on her throat. Alex whimpered in frustration and jerked his shirt over his head in one rough motion. Mansoor grinned at her impatience and moved his mouth to her belly, kissing his way up her skin inch by inch as he slowly pulled up her shirt. After four hours confined in a spacesuit, the feeling of his skin on hers seemed a glorious indulgence. She was hyper-attuned to the sensory contrast of the rough scrape of his stubble and the soft planes of his chest.

She made another noise and pushed his hand under the waistband of her pants. He kissed her jaw, one finger lightly circling. Alex jerked her hips, wanting more, craving release. "Slow down. I've got you," he murmured in her ear.

Alex wasn't used to surrendering in bed. She wasn't used to the tender look in Mansoor's eyes. But she'd known, since that very first night when he'd come to her room, that going to bed with Mansoor, with his powerful family and grandiose ideas, would not be anything like her usual late-night casual fuck.

Mansoor slowly removed the last of her clothing, pulled down his comforter, and laid her out naked on his sheets. There was nothing casual about the way Mansoor's eyes took in every inch of her body. Alex found herself trembling under the intimacy of his gaze, the knowing smile curving his lips.

Alex surrendered now. She let him set the pace. She let him kiss and touch every part of her until finally, *finally*, he brought his mouth in between her legs and carried her to a pleasure that climbed higher and higher before she climaxed in a drawn-out peak.

He moved up her body again, fitting himself inside her. Mansoor's self-control seemed to break as he brought her legs to wrap around his torso, moving faster and faster.

Was this what it was like to go to bed with someone who understood her? Who saw through her hard, cold exterior and didn't let her put her walls up? They'd shared the experience today of standing alone under the blackness of space. Of pushing the limits of human ingenuity. They'd shared an intimacy so unique and profound it was difficult to put into words. But their bodies knew how to express their feelings.

Mansoor spoke in short broken phrases as he came and then collapsed on top of her. He kissed her neck, her jaw, her mouth, before pulling out of her to lay on his stomach, face turned toward her and one arm wrapped protectively around her waist.

Alex stared at him, her body humming and her mind tangled with a confusing mix of desire, affection, and a little fear. She'd let him see her, the real her. And, to her surprise, he liked what he saw. He wouldn't allow her to close herself off. He wouldn't allow her to push him away.

She thought again of standing on the surface of the Moon. It should have made her feel alone and vulnerable. But instead, the memory made her feel a sense of connection. To Mansoor. To the colony. To the new chapter in human history that they were writing together.

Aloud, speaking for the first time in hours, she whispered, "I've never experienced something so extraordinary."

Mansoor gave her a slow, satisfied smile, his head pillowed on his bicep.

"I mean the trip," she clarified, blushing. Okay, she didn't just mean the trip. The sex had been on the extraordinary side, too. "Stepping on the crust of the Moon. Seeing the American flag standing there. It was like nothing else."

He lightly traced her scraped hands. "I know," he said, voice hushed.

She wondered if it was all tangled up for him, too. Intimacy, sex, the Moon. She wasn't ready to talk about the two of them, not yet. So instead, she asked, "What was it like for those last twentieth-century astronauts? To leave all that equipment, get back into your ship, and fly away, not knowing when humanity would return? They must have thought it would be a decade before the next mission to the Moon, not nearly eighty years, but even still it must've felt like a tremendous responsibility. Do you think they were scared?"

"The commander was a Navy captain during the Cold War. If he was scared, he would not have shown it."

"You're right. The old NASA guard was tough. If you showed weakness, you were less likely to make it into space. The competition was fierce. I saw it enough growing up."

"Tough, yes, but they could not help being sentimental. Do you know what Eugene Cernan said, before he became the last man on the Moon for seventy-eight years? 'And, as we leave the Moon at Taurus-Littrow, we leave as we come and, God willing, as we shall return, with peace and hope for all mankind.' You could not help but be affected by it. No matter how tough you were."

Alex let out an involuntary giggle. "You have that quote memorized?"

"It is on our promotional materials," Mansoor admitted.

"It's lovely."

And it was. *Peace and hope for all mankind.*

12

VICTOR

"IT WAS A GOOD TRY," MANSOOR'S VOICE SOUNDED WEARY, EVEN through the spotty connection. Victor kept himself off-screen, sitting in the enormous suite at the Willard InterContinental in the capital. Next to him on the sofa, Mansoor's favorite employee MacKenzie twisted her wedding ring over and over on her slim finger.

Rashid sat in a wingback chair across from the video screen, his long legs crossed at the ankle casually in front of him. Rashid was relaxed, Victor realized. It was not a front. He was genuinely relaxed. Leaning forward and locking eyes with Mansoor on screen, Rashid said, "Brother, the vote hasn't started. What do you mean 'a good try'?"

"We do not have the votes. We are three shy."

Rashid grinned. It was a lazy, confident grin that made Victor's heart speed up in a way he didn't understand. "We'll see."

The other screen in the suite was turned to C-SPAN. The procedural elements were dispensed with, and the presiding senator called the vote. In the suite, no one said a word, eyes fixed on the screen as the results came in on the electronic tally. In a matter of minutes, it was over, and the screen displayed the results.

53 to 47.

"The ayes have it," the presiding senator said into the microphone. "SB 153.21 passes."

Victor let out a slow breath. Years of work—accomplished in a matter of moments. Just like that. He looked immediately to Rashid, who had turned back to Mansoor.

Mansoor was staring at his brother in shock. "You knew?"

"Senator Jones has been spending time with me. We share a love of the Five Boroughs."

"Jones?" Mansoor looked at his own notes. "He flat-out refused me. Said space travel was a drain on his anti-poverty legislation."

"I told him the Homestead Act would bring a lucrative contract to HVAC manufacturers in Syracuse in order to supply crucial parts for the expanded colony residents."

"You did?" Mansoor did not bother keeping the surprise out of his voice.

"I may have had some coaching," Rashid admitted. He looked back at Victor and MacKenzie with another grin. MacKenzie was fumbling with the champagne on ice that Victor had thought moments before would go unopened. Victor didn't know what expression he gave Rashid in response. He wondered if he was in shock.

"And that was enough to sway him?" Mansoor asked.

Rashid shrugged. "He also liked my poetry."

"What about Mitchell and Dudley? I thought they were 'No' votes too."

"The four of us had dinner here in D.C. And tequila. Lots of tequila."

"And they liked your poetry, too?"

"They did, actually. I've got a great performance piece about the colony."

MOONRISING

Mansoor was sounding giddy. "I have been working on those three senators for years. You are telling me that all it took was some spoken word and tequila shots?"

"In fairness, I think Mitchell and Dudley's opposition was at the direction of Jones. The three of them vote in lockstep."

"Rashid, I know that." He looked closer at his brother. "But I did not expect *you* to know that."

"I'm trying. You're a hard act to follow, you know. MacKenzie thinks you can do no wrong." He looked up. "Speaking of."

MacKenzie elbowed her way onto the screen. She was beaming. "Mansoor! You did it." She handed Rashid a glass of champagne and took a long swallow of her own glass.

"We did it. *Rashid* did it," Mansoor said.

"Team effort all around." She pulled Victor over on screen, and he gave Mansoor a little salute before shoving away and returning to the sofa. He didn't want to step on Rashid's moment. Mansoor and Victor could connect later. They had always understood one another.

MacKenzie was beaming. "Mansoor, give yourself some credit. It was years in the making. I don't think the bill would have made it out of committee if not for you."

"I wish I was there to celebrate with you."

"Are you kidding?" MacKenzie gave him an exasperated look. "You're on the freakin' moon. I bet there will be a wicked party tonight."

Mansoor gave a small, private smile. "Something like that."

"Good night elder brother," Rashid said, raising his glass in a toast.

"*Tesbah 'ala khair, akhi.*"

Rashid's lips turned up. "*Wa-anta min ahl el-khair.*"

"Your accent is improving. Have you been practicing?" Without waiting for an answer, Mansoor flashed a final smile and terminated the connection.

MacKenzie went to the other side of the room, offering champagne to Mansoor's other staffers. They were all smiling like loons. Rashid turned off the screen and came to sit next to Victor, bumping their legs together.

"I knew it was mathematically possible," Victor said to him. "But I'd run a hundred simulations, and the odds of an affirmative vote were ten to one. No one in the media thought this bill would pass. I didn't think Drake's testimony after the fire would be enough."

Rashid turned his body, leaning against the arm of the sofa and stretching out his legs. His feet touched the side of Victor's thigh. "You seemed so confident."

"I always project confidence. It's the only way to inspire others to take risks. To—" He searched for the right words. "To go along with my madness."

"Like me."

"You—" Victor shook his head. "You exceeded my wildest expectations. You flipped the Gang of Three. And you brought Su, Hayworth, and Royes off the fence." Victor ticked them off on his fingers. "Six senators. That's unheard of. We're going to grow humanity's presence in space exponentially. The course of human history will change. Because of you."

Rashid shook his head, declining to take credit. "I just talked to a few people. That's all."

"No, I've been working on this for years. So has Mansoor. Hell, John Anderson has been working on this for a decade. We couldn't get it over the finish line. You accomplished what the rest of us could not do."

"And now on to Abu Dhabi? To launch tourists into space and see if these rocket ships of yours will fly?"

"My ships will fly," Victor said, a little hotly. "Politics is hard to predict, but physics is a constant."

MOONRISING

◆

Victor *was* confident in his rocket ships. But his stomach did not share that confidence. As he stood in the desert, overlooking the rocket ship he had designed and built from the ground up, his gut burned uncomfortably.

The ships he'd sold to the Emiratis were constructed with a mirrored exterior to reflect the endless blue sky of the desert. They looked sleek, elegant, and futuristic. Camila had flown a dozen manned test runs in Pennsylvania and another the week before on the Abu Dhabi launch pad. Every test launch had been a textbook success. And today was the real event.

Twelve tourists would travel to the Moon.

Next to him, in the viewing area, stood Ambassador Al Naifeh, clothed like his fellows in traditional Emirati dress. His wife Sena was gathered with the women at the end of the viewing area, her hair covered by a scarf. The Emir of Abu Dhabi himself stood with his brother Mohammed bin Khalifa, wearing identical inscrutable expressions and surrounded by men in a mix of Emirati dress and suits.

The atmosphere was clear, the air quality finally back to a reasonable level after weeks of fluctuating between Hazardous and Very Unhealthy. Even in the late afternoon, it was beastly hot. Resort staff circulated offering cool compresses and ice water as they waited on the outdoor platform.

The first Moon tourists stepped into view. They wore jumpsuits with their names embroidered on the breast and the logo of the UAESA below. Victor realized suddenly he had never bothered to pay attention to who had paid a premium to be on the first shuttle. Victor could ask Rashid later. Rashid would know their names, their children's names, and probably their hearts' deepest desires.

The tourists all knew Victor, of course, pausing as they passed him on their way to the shuttle to shake hands enthusiastically, pose for photos with the official launch photographer, and tell him what an honor it was to meet him.

As the passengers reached the shuttle doors, the lower platforms cheered, the crowds waving tiny moons on sticks. As hot as he was, Victor suspected it was hotter in the crowd below. He could see sweat dripping off their faces as they held water bottles with the Space World Abu Dhabi logo to their foreheads and handheld branded e-fans to their faces. Many sported moon sunglasses, and a few wore alien antennae headbands. Victor leaned forward to get a better look at the headbands. The crowd spotted his attention and shifted their cheers into a chant. "Victor! Victor! Victor!" He grinned at their enthusiasm and raised one jittering hand.

The passengers were entering the ship now. They would be strapping in horizontally and preparing for the final AI-powered launch sequence.

Teru and several of the other Beard Enterprise employees were down below in the mission control room with the Emirati engineers who would be responsible for supervising the routine launches. Victor's ships required a mission control staff of two and a four-person technician unit to set the ship in place next to the permanent platform the Emiratis had constructed to maximize tourist viewing. The glossy ship design might be the media's focus, but Victor knew his real innovation was the minimal ground support staff required to launch and land his ships.

Victor went to find Rashid, who stood a bit apart from the Emirati men, gripping the railing with white knuckles. When Victor went to his side, Rashid took a careful step back, more closed and wary than Victor had ever seen him.

"I thought you had more confidence in me. My ship is flawless. She'll be going Mach 25 in no time."

"It's not that." Rashid ran a hand through his hair. "I'm just on edge. I don't like being here."

Victor was about to ask him why when an enormous countdown clock began flashing down from fifty. The crowd went wild, screaming the numbers. Victor looked at the beautiful, sleek ship.

His ship.

Three.

Two.

One.

He let out an involuntary gasp when the ship rose suddenly into the air, shooting into the sky at an accelerating rate. In a matter of moments, it was a speck, and then gone.

He had done it.

The audience gave a final cheer and began dispersing. The men on the platform shook his hand as they walked past him, offering hearty congratulations. Malik gave him a reserved handshake, saying diplomatically, "This is a great day for the UAE." He eyed Rashid without commentary, his neutral face not quite concealing the anger simmering below.

One man introduced himself as Waleed bin Ahmad, telling Victor he was proud that his family would soon join the Al Kaabi family in the space tourism business. Victor cared little about the details of the Emirati business interests as long as their funding allowed Peary Station to grow. Emirati space tourism was Mansoor's department. He nodded at the man vaguely, his attention on Rashid standing next to him. Victor heard Mohammed bin Khalifa saying something emotional in Arabic and embracing his youngest son.

When the men had gone, Sena came up to both of them. "It was a true honor to bear witness to this momentous occasion. What a wonder you have brought to Abu Dhabi."

Victor liked Sena, who had followed his engineering explanations and was kind to Rashid. "I'm so glad you and Malik were able to attend," he said.

It was a sincere statement about Sena at any rate. Malik could tumble off the side railing into the desert for all Victor cared. His anger had been a damper on an otherwise triumphant day. Malik must know that the warning he gave Victor and Rashid to cease their attempts to influence Washington was now moot. Last week, President Fairchild had signed the Homestead Act with great fanfare in the Rose Garden.

Finally, it was only Victor and Rashid on the upper platform, listening to the raucous crowd below as they scattered to the relief of their cool hotel rooms and the resort's air-conditioned bars, restaurants, and casinos. Victor took some time to enjoy the relative quiet. He wondered where Rashid went when he got reserved and thoughtful. It was still a new sensation, to care about what another person was thinking.

After a few minutes, Victor asked, "What did your father say to you?"

"He said my mother would have been proud to see this day." Victor watched Rashid's throat move as he swallowed. He was blinking rapidly. "Let's go."

The stairs were enclosed and air-conditioned, comfortable after the punishing desert heat. At the landing at the bottom of the first flight of stairs, someone stood, watching them.

It was Malik.

"Did you forget something on the platform?" Victor asked stupidly.

Malik ignored the question, his attention fixed on Rashid. "I was clear. Very, very clear."

Rashid made to step around him. "I don't answer to you."

Malik followed Rashid's movement, blocking his path. "You should have listened. The Homestead Act should not have passed."

MOONRISING

"It's over now," Rashid said.

"I am not finished," Malik said. "Do you think you aren't being watched? You are a member of the House of Kaabi. While you are living in America, it is my job to keep tabs on you. Everything you do."

Rashid went pale. "I don't know what you mean."

"No? I have been cleaning up after you for years. You don't think some of the men you sleep with don't look you up and see who your family is? They come to me, with pictures, and ask for money."

"You're lying." Rashid looked around uneasily as if to see if anyone was in earshot. Victor checked around, too. They were alone. There was security below to prevent the crowd from coming up, and everyone else had departed.

"Do you want to test me?"

"Don't make a scene here, please." Rashid's voice was deadly quiet. "You know the Emir won't like the scandal."

"What scandal?" Victor asked, genuinely confused. "Who would care about your sex life?"

Well, not completely confused. *Victor* suddenly cared very much about Rashid's sex life. He remembered the way Rashid had held him when they had danced together at the tiny club in Manhattan.

Rashid gave him a stricken look. He was afraid, Victor realized. "It's illegal to be gay in the UAE."

"What?" Victor said dumbly. "In 2073?"

A more familiar exasperated expression crossed his face. "How do you not know that? Straight cis white men can be so infuriating."

"But I'm not—" Victor tried to say, but Rashid was already speaking to Malik.

"I pulled back when you asked me to. My part was already done. It was Senator Jones that flipped the other five, not me. I'd already convinced him when you found me."

185

"You could have stopped this. I know it." Malik was leaning into Rashid. He was not a large man, but the look in his eyes made him menacing.

Without thinking, Victor stepped between them. He put a hand on Malik's chest. "Back off."

Malik's eyes narrowed, but he complied.

"Show me the pictures," Victor ordered. His voice sounded harsh and strange in his ears.

Malik scowled.

With a confidence he did not feel, Victor said, "I invented the fastest rocket ship model in existence, and I am the majority shareholder of my company. After today, every spacefaring country will want a contract with Beard Enterprises. I could pull out of my contract with the UAE. I can afford to pay the penalties. I could make the UAE a laughingstock on the international stage. Show me the pictures."

His face twisted with rage, Malik pulled his intelliwatch off his wrist and handed it to Victor. The photos were tiny on the screen, but they were unmistakably Rashid. He was in his apartment, naked and covered in paint, laughing. Victor had a sudden urge to send a copy of the photos to himself and get prints framed and mounted on his bedroom wall. Instead, he deleted the photos. There were only five. Hardly the cadre of blackmailers Malik had described.

"Where are the copies?" Victor asked, without looking at Rashid.

"I did not keep copies," Malik said.

Victor leaned into Malik's face. "Where. Are. The. Copies?" he said, slowly and deliberately.

Malik grabbed the watch back, moving his fingers rapidly, and showed Victor and Rashid a folder in Arabic. He deleted it.

"Thank you. We're done here."

He wanted to grasp Rashid's hand and lead him away. He wanted to take Rashid into a dark corner and show him very thoroughly that he was *not* straight. Why did Rashid assume he was straight? But, instead, he kept a foot distance apart and walked away down the flight of stairs. Rashid, looking miserable, walked by his side.

After a while, Rashid said, "There's no way you could afford to pay a contract cancellation penalty and the divorce settlement money. You haven't turned a profit yet."

"I know, and you know," Victor said, and flashed Rashid a grin. "But Malik didn't."

13

MANSOOR

AFTER YEARS OF METICULOUS PLANNING, THE FIRST TOURIST SHIP was finally on its way.

Mansoor watched the televised launch from the newly built resident lounge, standing with his hands clenched on the back of a chair and his heart in his throat. Around him was jovial laughter as other residents joined him, juggling coffee cups and boiled eggs.

Alex slipped in right before the ship took off, drenched in sweat from her morning treadmill workout. He was grateful for her presence by his side.

The launch was flawless, of course. The mirrored ship rose into the sky, reflecting the vast blue sky and the twinkling sand of the desert. He knew that almost no one residing on the colony wanted wealthy tourists in their midst, but everyone still cheered when the ship burst into the sky, clapping him on the back and shaking his hand in congratulations.

A corner of Alex's mouth tilted up. "I need a shower," she said and stepped out of the room.

MOONRISING

He muttered vague excuses to the others and followed Alex out. When she entered her room, he stopped the door with his hand before it fully closed. She had already stripped off her shirt in preparation for a shower, and her hair was matted with sweat.

He kissed her hard, twining his hand in her hair to undo her ponytail. This was how he wanted to celebrate.

He wrenched his mouth from Alex's and spun her around, sliding her pants down in one smooth motion. Anyone passing could have heard the noise of the lightweight printed door rattling in its frame, but he did not care. He knew she liked it like this—hard and fast and a little bit rough. When they'd both finished, he collapsed on her bed, pulling her with him. The bed was so small, they needed to lie on their sides to fit. She melded into his body perfectly.

"You're in a good mood," she observed in a breathy voice.

Mansoor was panting as if he had run a race. "The ship launch was glorious."

"Shouldn't you be in the hotel frantically preparing last-minute details?"

Mansoor kissed her neck. She tasted like salt. "It is a twenty-four-hour trip. I have time to panic."

Alex pulled his arm around her waist, intertwining their fingers. "Victor told me it would take twenty-two hours. I spoke to him the other day, and he wouldn't shut up about it. He's trying to get it down to twenty. He's got a theory involving freezing rocket fuel that I couldn't quite follow."

"I hope not twenty. A 5 a.m. Eastern arrival time would be brutal week after week. My father would not be in support of morning launches Gulf Standard Time. The casino and bar revenue from the spectators is too important. Though, I suppose it will not be long before I will have staff at the hotel to greet the guests when they arrive."

"Oh?" Alex turned her head to look at him. "You hadn't told me you're bringing up more people."

Mansoor shrugged. "Nothing is official yet. But now that we got the Homestead Act passed, there will be a line of spouses and lottery applicants looking for a Moon-based occupation."

Alex sat up. "What do you mean? What do you have to do with the Homestead Act?"

He lifted his head and kissed the side of her mouth. "Everything," he said, without thinking.

She abruptly disentangled herself from his body. "I'm going to shower."

Mansoor flopped back and rubbed his eyes. He could hear the sputtering hiss of the shower jet. He was not sure what he had done to upset her.

A shower on the colony was not much of an escape. Three minutes later he heard the familiar beep as the water shut off. Alex stepped out, wrapped in a towel. She did not look at him as she rummaged for clean clothes.

"Something is bothering you," said Mansoor. "What is it?"

Without turning, she said, "You influenced the American legislative process to pass a major law entirely behind the scenes. As a foreign national. From space. You're a little bit scary."

He was always revealing too much to her. Trying to backtrack, he said, "Many Americans were advocating for this bill. Administrator Anderson, for one."

She spun around to look at him, slipping on a bra. "Who are you?"

Mansoor spread his hands in a helpless gesture. "You know who I am."

"But I don't. How does a tiny Middle Eastern nation come to have so much influence over the American space program?" She kept putting on her clothes, with abrupt, fierce movements, as if donning armor.

MOONRISING

"I do not have that much influence."

"You just told me you were responsible for the passage of the Homestead Act."

Mansoor winced. "I was exaggerating. A postcoital high."

She gave him a look of exasperation. "Please don't lie to me."

"I . . ." His voice trailed off. "Very well." He wondered what it would be like to be honest with her—fully honest. He had been lying to everyone he knew his entire adult life, in some way or another, trying to contort himself into two different people from two different worlds.

"I don't know what we're doing here. Our lives are so dissimilar," said Alex, her voice tight. "I'm still paying off my grad school debt. I have a mortgage and a car loan. Your concept of money is very different from mine. And power. I can't even influence my own industry. You have . . . power, Mansoor. So much power. And you're playing this long game I don't fully get."

Alex stepped back into the bathroom, leaving the door open. Mansoor watched her brush her wet hair into a knot on the top of her head. He did not know what to say. He had always regarded his wealth with trepidation, tracing back to the oil fields it had come from, but he had never met a woman who thought it was a problem.

"I am sorry," he offered. "I am not sure what I can do." He pulled himself up and sat naked at the edge of the bed.

Returning to the room, she said, "You've been such a strong advocate for me. You've gotten me the resources I need. You saved my chickens. You helped me build an industrial composter. You've supported my research publicly, with journalists, which is a level of support I've never received before. Not from anyone. But I don't know if this thing between us is worth jeopardizing our professional relationship." She frowned, and he could see distress in her eyes. "I'm not sure if this is just convenient sex for you."

"That's rubbish." The room was so small he was able to reach out with one hand and pull her toward him, settling her standing between his knees. "I can remember so clearly the first time I saw you at the UN conference. You were wearing a green sheath dress. Your hair was shorter. I can picture every detail perfectly. You faced down a group of hecklers without getting flustered. I thought you were splendid. And then when I finally met you in person, I could not take my eyes off you. When you took my hand during takeoff, I was so embarrassed to be weak in front of you. I had wanted to impress you now that I had finally gotten the chance to meet you. I have always wanted to impress you. You are it for me, Alex. You're the one."

Fuck.

He had not meant to say that.

He had not even meant to think it.

Clearing his throat, he said, "I mean, you are the one I want." He pulled her toward him, snaking a hand up her back under her T-shirt. He could feel her softening under his touch.

Alex brushed a lock of his hair away from his face. "I want you too," she whispered. "Since the moment I met you, when I realized you were aware of my reputation and still wanted to know *me.* Mansoor . . ."

She leaned down and kissed him gently. He sat braced on the side of the bed as she climbed on top of his naked body, her clothes rough on his bare skin and her lips soft. She only drew back to pull down her pants, and then she was sinking down on him, her green eyes locked on his. Mansoor watched those beautiful eyes flutter closed as she took her pleasure, her face unguarded. He loved seeing this side of her. Loved knowing he could bring out a sweet vulnerability she seemed so determined to hide.

In seven months, he would be in Abu Dhabi signing a marriage contract with someone he barely knew. He might never return to space. He clung to Alex and tried to hold on to everything in that moment: to his victory, to the place that was increasingly feeling

MOONRISING

like home, and to the woman with whom he was trying not to fall in love.

His time was running out.

After parting with Alex, he hurried to the hotel. She was right—he did need to spend the day ensuring all was ready for the first guests.

When he reached the dome, he paused, taking in the view from the hotel. The two glass spires rose into the air, contrasting with the black sky. Below the spires, he could see the restaurant, elegant and polished with floor-to-ceiling views.

The commander spotted him staring and stepped out of his office. Clasping Mansoor's shoulder, Saul said, "She's a beauty. Good luck today."

"I am grateful for the hospitality you have shown me," Mansoor said to him sincerely. "Without your generous sharing of resources, the hotel would not be ready in time."

"I have a duty to uphold NASA's vision of the colony. Whether or not I agree with the direction we are moving, I've been impressed with your work ethic and partnership. My people have your back."

Mansoor hoped Saul would not regret his kind words when he inevitably learned Mansoor was sleeping with his daughter. He shook Saul's hand formally. "My thanks." He collected himself and went to finalize the preparations.

Although Mansoor had walked the passageway connecting the dome to the hotel countless times, today he felt the weight of the moment. In the kitchen adjacent to the restaurant he found Pierre, the minor celebrity chef he had enticed to leave his Michelin-starred Parisian restaurant to spend a year on the colony.

"Mansoor, there you are!" Pierre exclaimed. "I am doing the prep work to create the most exquisite frittata when the guests arrive in the morning. I know you prefer local ingredients, but

I imported a wheel of Pecorino di Fossa directly from Rome. A scant tablespoon will enhance the piquancy of the frittata without distracting from the flavor of dill and parsley."

Mansoor listened with half an ear, wishing MacKenzie had dug up a more taciturn chef. As Pierre continued describing in minute detail each dish he was planning all week long, Mansoor adjusted the chairs and checked for any lingering moon dust on the tables. The restaurant looked perfect. The lunar material used to create the tables and chairs made them sparkle in the sunlight. A high bar against one wall was ready with a variety of glassware, top-shelf liquor that had taken up a considerable weight allowance to import, and small jars of cordials and simple syrups Pierre had created with strawberries, rosemary, and basil from the greenhouse.

After all this time, the view still took his breath away. The cobalt and white Earth peeked out from beyond the lunar surface, floating in the blackness. In the foreground, the dome was visible, and robots worked steadily on expanding the residential wing.

Mansoor stepped to the window, trying to let the view smooth over his impatience with Pierre's prattle. He took a deep, calming breath and then froze.

Something was wrong.

A faint whistling sound, coming from the window. Mansoor bent his head closer. The windows had been constructed in facets to mitigate the risk of damage from any one piece—and he saw the problem immediately. The pane of glass had separated by several millimeters from the titanium frame. Mansoor quickly moved to the next section of windows and heard the same high-pitched whistle.

He looked at the time on his intelliwatch. The tourists were due in fifteen hours, and his hotel was leaking air.

MOONRISING

"I have to go," he said to Pierre. He descended the ramp leading from the restaurant to the tunnel connecting the hotel to the rest of the colony. Once out of Pierre's sight, he began to run.

✦

"A whistling sound?" Zaynab repeated in crisp Arabic. "Is there a gap?"

"Not a consistent gap. More like a crack between the window and the frame leaving a vent ranging from two to four millimeters. Zaynab, it is everywhere."

The Abu Dhabi workday had ended by the time he reached his engineering team, but they all quickly turned their cars around and returned to the lab. Now, they were gathered around a large meeting table heaped with simulated lunar materials.

"An incompatibility between the caulk and the composite frame," another engineer said. "What was the material of the caulk?"

"It's a polyurethane," another responded rapidly. "Aromatic diisocyanates, toluene diisocyanate, and graft polyols."

Mansoor did not try to track the technical discussion that followed but waited for their conclusions with sick dread in his belly. The ship had already launched. Twelve of the world's richest and most powerful people would be on his doorstep the next morning.

Zaynab turned to look at Mansoor through the screen. "If it is the caulk, it will need to be removed in its entirety before a new substance is applied."

Mansoor looked at the time. Fourteen hours. He pictured the number of panes and the careful motions the robots would need to perform to scrape off the existing caulk without damaging the windows.

It was impossible.

Zaynab seemed to understand the despair in Mansoor's expression. "Can we dissolve it?" he heard her ask another engineer. The reply was lost to Mansoor as the room exploded in cross conversations.

As they spoke, Mansoor sent a short SMS to Herb explaining the situation and asking him to keep the Refabricator open for him today.

Finally, Zaynab called for silence in the room. "We have a solution, Mansoor. First, a compound of isopropyl alcohol and acetone is applied to the area where the pane meets the frame. After ten minutes, you must wipe it clean. The original caulk will dissolve. Then, a new epoxy resin is applied to the area. Finally, you must apply thermal curing to convert the resin from a liquid to a solid state."

"Do we have the materials for the full process here?"

Zaynab raised her eyebrows at him. "Who do you think you are dealing with, Mansoor?"

"Alright," Mansoor let out his breath. "Send the commands to the Refabricator and the bots, and we'll get this started."

"Ah." Zaynab winced. "There will be no robots involved."

"What do you mean?" Mansoor asked blankly.

"The procedure must be done by hand. By human hands. It is too delicate to entrust to the bots without simulations and testing first. We would risk cracking the windows, which would be a much bigger problem."

"The tourists are due in thirteen hours," Mansoor almost wailed.

"Can they double up with the other residents?" Zaynab suggested. "They are only there for a week."

Each spot on the first tourist trip had cost US $1.3 million. He could not have his inaugural guests crash on the floors of the scientists' bedrooms.

There were thousands—perhaps ten thousand—individual panes in the hotel, each the size of a car window. He could never hope to caulk them all in thirteen hours.

He would have to try.

"Send the materials to the Refabricator," he told Zaynab.

The work would have been satisfying, if not for the knot of tension in his gut. The dissolving compound bubbled as it touched the caulk and wiped away clean. The resin went on smoothly and oozed comfortingly into place covering the frame and the glass edge. Curing took the form of a heat blower that could be set and left to complete the hardening of the resin.

But there were so many windows.

After an hour's worth of work, during which he only finished ten windows, Mansoor was forced to admit he could not do this alone. He blearily thought through the math. He would need a thousand hours to accomplish the task himself.

Leaving the heat blower running, he left the hotel and went to the command center. Saul was in a staff meeting with the ten Space Force staff members. He saw Mansoor hesitating at the door and gestured him inside.

"Mansoor," the commander said. "Take a seat. You look exhausted."

Mansoor moistened his lips. "I have a favor. A large favor." He explained his predicament.

Saul listened without comment. When he was finished, he raised his eyebrows. "And you want me, all of us, to drop our critical tasks for the day to help prepare the colony for your wealthy tourists?"

"I do."

Saul exchanged a glance with Sandra, who nodded at him. "Very well. We may all be here for different reasons, but we are one community. We take care of our own."

Sandra left to corral other residents while Mansoor took the Space Force contingent to the hotel. Mansoor handed them buckets of dissolving compound and resin, explaining the process as clearly and succinctly as he could.

He had just finished when Kayla arrived. "Sandra tells me you're in a pickle. Put me to work."

From there, the colony's residents trickled in, in groups of two or three, dressed for mess, goggles already in hand. Mansoor handed them materials as quickly as Herb sent them up from the Refabricator.

Some residents he was not surprised to see. Alex, of course, came quickly, and Julien was always ready to help. Natalia, however, was unexpected. She had made it clear she had limited time and no interest in the tourists. And Kayla and Naomi, who had been so cruel to Alex about mutagenetic food, worked side-by-side without complaint.

In the end, it was the sheer number that shocked him. All one hundred and two residents packed together in the restaurant, working efficiently and cheerfully. Even his chef Pierre consented to cease his prep work for the week to help.

Saul was right. They felt like one community.

The residents worked through the night and finished with only an hour to spare, but that was enough, giving Mansoor enough time to power nap, shower, shave, and down two cups of instant coffee. Victor's optimistic flight time calculations were spot on—damn him—leaving Mansoor once again sprinting through the halls of the colony to meet the ship at 7 a.m. ET.

When the hangar bay repressurized, Mansoor stepped inside, beholding Victor's ship in all its glory. It was beautiful. The mirrored sides reflected the large room's ground ship and equipment. The front was sleek and bold. On the side, in square block lettering,

MOONRISING

the ship's name was printed: *Diana's Arrow*. When he and Victor had picked the name at the recommendation of a high-priced marketing firm, Mansoor had thought it banal and cloying. Seeing it now, emblazoned on the side of the stunning ship, gave Mansoor a lump in his throat.

The side stairs lowered, and the first passengers descended. As it happened, Mansoor knew them personally.

"Mansoor Al Kaabi," the sandy haired man said, clasping Mansoor's hand. "A pleasure to see you again."

George Williams looked much the same as Mansoor remembered. He was a bright-eyed British expat who had made Abu Dhabi his home over a decade before and was an enthusiastic supporter of Abu Dhabi's space program. "You remember my son Stewart?"

Stewart was eighteen now, Mansoor knew from the passenger bios MacKenzie had made him memorize, but he looked younger. "Mr. Al Kaabi, great to see you again. I'll never forget our climb of Mount Elbert."

"Neither will I. You were only fourteen at the time, I believe. Hard to credit. Did you really climb Kilimanjaro in May? I am impressed."

The boy flushed happily. "What can I say? I'm an adrenaline junkie, just like Pa."

Mansoor greeted each of the ten passengers in turn. George and Stewart were the only passengers he knew, but he found a personal connection with each of them. It wasn't difficult. They were all, as Stewart put it, "adrenaline junkies," looking for the ultimate adventure. Mansoor could feel their eager excitement filling the hangar bay.

"Welcome to the colony, my friends," Mansoor said to the group when the last person had descended. "The inaugural flight of Victor Beard's revolutionary ship *Diana's Arrow* was a resounding success." Raising his voice above the cheers, he continued, "Some of you were already astronauts, but now the twelve of you can call yourselves temporary residents of the Moon. We have made history today. Among us we have the first Brazilian Moon resident and the youngest Moon resident. Though, Stewart, I am afraid your title will be short-lived as the homesteaders arrive early next year." Stewart blushed and ducked his head at the attention. "You are scientists, explorers, and thrill-seekers. We aim for this week to be the most memorable of your life."

The rest of the day passed in a blur. Dozens of tiny experiments planned for the tourists launched in the laboratory. Low-g games commenced in the gym. Three exquisitely prepared meals were served in the restaurant with different resident guests invited to each. Saul tolerated a chaperoned tour of the full colony, and even the most cynical of the scientists managed to put on a welcoming front in the face of the tourists' enthusiasm, while concealing their own weariness and resin-stained hands.

Mansoor felt like he had passed through his exhaustion and come out the other side. When he finally bade the tourists good night, leaving them to a passionate discussion over cocktails in the restaurant, he felt euphoric. He and Victor had done it. They had built the infrastructure to bring humans into space and back three times per month. It was a monumental achievement for his country, for the colony, and the future of the planet.

Alex was in his room waiting for him, sitting on his bed with her datapad. Her eyes sparkled when she met his. He pulled off his clothes and slipped in beside her, finding he was not as tired as he thought.

Later, they lay drowsily together. Alex's head was nested on her arms, eyes at half-mast. "What a day," she said to him. "My whole body aches. I had no idea putting resin on windows would be so physically demanding. My back is killing me."

Mansoor moved so he was positioned over her. His hands moved down her back, kneading her muscles. "How's this?"

MOONRISING

She gave a little groan in response. "You're good at this."

"I love massages. They are great after a rock climb."

He could not see her face, but he knew her well enough by now to sense she was rolling her eyes. "A rock climb. Of course."

He kissed the top of her spine where the bone jutted out. "You should try it. It is exhilarating. I will take you to Red River Gorge someday. It is not far from Chicago."

She made a soft sound in response. He could feel the tension in her back receding. Without warning, a loud automated voice from his intelliwatch said, "Phone booth video call incoming from Aliana."

"Decline!" he said hastily. Too hastily.

Alex opened her eyes and looked up at him. "Aliana?"

"My sister. I will call her later."

"I didn't know you had a sister."

"I have two, actually." It was a matter of public record. Though neither were named Aliana. He realized he had stopped the massage. His hands were frozen on her back. With effort, he made himself resume.

"Are they in Abu Dhabi?"

"They are. Haya is the one who called. Aliana is a nickname. She has a young child. Latifa is older. She works with the Education Council." Mansoor kept talking, but Alex was no longer listening. Her eyes had drooped shut, and her breathing was evening. He removed his hands slowly and tucked a blanket around her. He lay down beside her, watching her drift to sleep, his heart pounding.

He could not believe he had been so careless. How could he have forgotten about his appointment? It was almost too late now. It would be nearly 8 a.m. in Abu Dhabi. The lack of sleep and spike of adrenaline put his head in a fog.

He waited until he was sure Alex was asleep before slipping on his clothes and shoes and stepping outside. When he reached the phone booth, he saw his reflection in the tablet screen. He looked

201

like a wreck. Aliana might be too innocent to recognize what his mussed hair implied, but he could not be sure. She was so smart. It was why his father liked her. Not to mention that he needed to keep the good opinion of Aliana's grandmother, who would be sitting quietly outside of the video screen's view, chaperoning the conversation. Hastily, he ran his fingers through his hair and made the call.

"Mansoor!" Aliana smiled affectionately at him. In lilting Arabic, she said, "I wasn't sure I'd hear from you today. I couldn't get through before." They had been speaking twice a week at a time after Mansoor's work was complete for the day and before her morning university classes began.

"I apologize. I was behind with work, and I lost track of time. Did I catch you too late?"

Aliana shook her head. Her *hijab* swayed as she moved. It was a dark green color that brought out her wide brown eyes. "I have some time. We don't have regular class this morning. I am attending a demonstration on saltwater filtration at Masdar Institute."

"Tell me about it."

She did, her voice light and cheerful. She was so young. He tried to concentrate, making all the right noises and exclamations. He said very little about his own life. How could he tell her about his day? It had been exhilarating, triumphant, terrifying, and exhausting all at once. He could not speak of it without revealing too much about his love for the colony and its people. He did not dare divulge his deep, repressed desire to stay.

At 8:30 a.m. GST, she said, "I have to go, Mansoor." She gave him another sweet smile. "I am so glad we were able to talk. I look forward to seeing you in person."

"Soon," he said. "I plan to come to Abu Dhabi for a visit in October."

"I am counting the days until you come home."

He cut the connection and laid his head on the table. *Home.* He was not sure what that meant anymore.

14

VICTOR

WHEN VICTOR STARTED DOING BUSINESS IN THE UAE, THE close-knit American expat community had embraced him as one of their own. He had already been making a name for himself at twenty-five after selling his first AgTech startup and jumping headlong into the next two ventures. The American expats had all said the same thing to him—the Emiratis are richer than you can imagine and will spend money on you without reserve if they think there is something in it for them, but they will never fully trust you. They will never invite you into their homes or confide in you about their personal lives. They won't be your friends.

Thankfully, Victor wasn't interested in making friends. The transactional nature of the Emirati business relationships suited him just fine.

Until he met Mansoor.

They kept finding each other. First, at the Global Space Congress in Abu Dhabi. And then at COP74 in Brazil. Then over and over again. At the Humans to Mars Summit in Tokyo. The World Meteorological Congress in Geneva. The UN Summit on Climate Change in D.C.

They would talk late into the night, closing out the hotel bar wherever they happened to be, and then pick up the conversation the next morning over mediocre breakfast buffets. The world was broken, they both agreed. Cities like Bangkok and Khulna had already fallen, and wealthier countries were struggling to preserve Savannah, Amsterdam, and Venice. Earth could not sustain humanity without a severe cost. Flooding, famine, and wildfires were all coming faster and faster.

It was Mansoor who was first taken by the ideas of Princeton physicist Gerard O'Neill, written over a hundred years ago. O'Neill believed it was possible to fully shift polluting industries away from Earth and into space, allowing Earth to be preserved as a biodiversity park. To accomplish this, it was necessary to leverage the matter and energy available in space to build permanent settlements, bringing the exponential growth of space colonies within reach. They were not the first to see O'Neill's ideas as the solution, but Victor realized right away that the two of them were uniquely suited to do something about it.

And so, a relationship that looked on the surface to be a typical association between an Emirati son of a wealthy sheikh and an American serial entrepreneur became the most meaningful friendship Victor had ever known. Friendship was an inadequate word for their meeting of the minds. They were partners in a plan that would outlast both their lives, a quest to preserve the Earth.

Still, the advice those expats had given him all those years ago held true. Mansoor had never taken it upon himself to extend Victor an invitation to his father's compound.

Until now.

Victor vaguely noticed that the compound was aesthetically pleasing. The high white walls concealed a beautiful villa with intricate molding and an elaborate carved wooden front door, surrounded by lush vegetation. He was warmly greeted by a housekeeper, who took him efficiently up the marble staircase and through the wide, airy hallways to Mansoor.

Mansoor's bedroom was nearly the size of Victor's entire Philadelphia condo. A dramatic four-poster bed sat at the center, and off to the side was a sitting area with large, ornate furniture, a luxurious rug, a mahogany dining table with seating for six, and French doors that led to a balcony, which stood open to the inner courtyard below. Mansoor was dozing in his bed when the housekeeper knocked and announced Victor. She bustled in and propped two pillows behind his head, helping him rise.

Though he remained in bed, Mansoor raised his arms to Victor, who leaned in awkwardly. Mansoor gave him a bone-crushing hug at odds with his weak, pale countenance. "Victor, my brother, it is good to see you in the flesh. I have missed you."

Victor felt his throat constrict. He had noticed Mansoor's absence more than he expected. To cover his unexpected emotion, he said brusquely, "We speak all the time."

Mansoor squeezed his shoulder and fell back weakly on his pillows. "It is not the same."

"How is the transition back?" Victor asked, eyeing Mansoor. He looked awful. Mansoor was one of the fittest people Victor knew, and it was a shock to see him looking so weak.

"We have a problem, I think. It appears the returning scientists have been downplaying the extent of the health issues present upon return. This is jet lag from hell."

Victor wasn't surprised that the scientists might not be fully transparent with NASA when they returned to Earth. He barely noticed physical discomfort when he was in the middle of a breakthrough. Anyone who managed to reach the pinnacle of their careers by doing research in space would not complain about having to spend a few days in bed upon their return. Especially if they wanted NASA to approve a return trip. "You've been upside for eight months. That's a fairly long tour. Have you followed all the procedures while you've been there?"

Mansoor made a face of distaste. "Of course. I have never missed a workout on the torture machine they call a treadmill. I take a cocktail of daily supplements. My diet is solid. The food got better once the greenhouse began producing. I do not think there's anything unique about my health."

"It must be the prolonged exposure to low gravity. It cannot be just the travel. Rashid tells me the tourists jump around cheering after they return and stay out until 3 a.m. doing shots. There's plenty of research on the long-term effects of low-gravity, and the treadmill workouts are designed to counter that. But I'm not aware of any research on an ideal return window to mitigate jet lag. That would be something to study."

"By you?" Mansoor asked. Someone else might have laughed at the idea that Victor could take on this problem so soon after launching the most successful Moon transportation vessel yet invented. But Mansoor knew him.

Victor shrugged. "I'll put some thought into it."

"Come on," Mansoor said to him, carefully moving his legs to the edge of the bed. "Help me into the courtyard." Mansoor grabbed Victor's arm and pulled himself to his feet.

"Are you sure?"

"I have not felt the sun on my bare face in eight months," Mansoor replied, leaning heavily on Victor as he hobbled to the door. "I have rested here long enough."

Victor helped Mansoor down the marble staircase and into an open-air inner courtyard. With a groan, Mansoor sank into a low turquoise couch under the shade of several palm trees. Victor sat on a cushion opposite him, watching Mansoor get his breathing under control.

MOONRISING

"There," Mansoor said with satisfaction. He lifted his head and closed his eyes. "I do not think of Abu Dhabi as a particularly windy place, but I can feel the air moving on my face." He opened his eyes and took in Victor's expression. "I am fine. Stop worrying."

Victor shrugged.

"We're making progress on the colony," Mansoor told him. "Now that the Homestead Act has passed, Herb has the robots on overdrive building family apartments. Anderson is recruiting a larger medical team. Alex is in the early stages of planning an agricultural wing."

"Is it enough?"

"Nothing will ever be enough, but it is a strong start. The momentum has shifted. Exponential growth, you always said. I hated to leave, even if it is just for three weeks." Mansoor paused. "You were right about Alex. I don't think Drake's report would have been so positive without a food solution in place. And I am, personally, very grateful she is in my life."

"Oh?"

"We have become quite close." Mansoor seemed to be bracing himself for Victor's reaction.

Victor thought of his own confusing mess of feelings for Mansoor's brother. He was not in a position to object to Mansoor sleeping with his friend. Lightly, he said, "Is that how it is? I shouldn't be surprised. You've mentioned her UN speech a disproportionate amount in the time I've known you. I only have a few real friends, Mansoor. Don't fuck this one up."

Mansoor winced at his words, and Victor wondered if his tone had been off. He did not usually have that issue with Mansoor, who knew him better than anyone.

"I have never done this before," Mansoor said in a low voice. "It is terrifying."

Victor raised his eyebrows. "I've seen you go back to the hotel room of more than one woman at a conference."

"Sex, yes. But I have never been in a real relationship. I have never let anyone be close enough to see who I really am. I wish I could be like you."

"Me?" Victor scoffed.

"You have never hidden who you are. You have never conformed to what others expect or been careful to do the right things or say the right things or think the right things. I can see why you and Alex get along. She is a lot like you. Uncontained. The opposite of me." Mansoor looked at the courtyard around them. "I thought once we achieved our goals, once I was able to leverage my family business and wealth to make a real change for the planet, to make amends for Abu Dhabi's role in the destruction of the environment, I would feel free. I thought I could do it all. Be a respectful son, a successful businessman, and still build the world I wanted to see. But I forgot to factor in my sense of self. I have built myself a trap, and I am walking willingly into it."

Victor was not sure how to respond. Their conversations usually looked outward, not inward. Before he could decide what to say, the housekeeper entered the courtyard, holding a tray with three glasses of bubbly water that she placed on the low table. A pretty young woman stood by her side, dressed in a bright green headscarf and sweeping colorful pants. She gave Mansoor a shy smile.

"Aliana," Mansoor said and made an aborted attempt to rise from the couch.

She said something quiet and apologetic in Arabic.

"No, no," Mansoor said, in English. "This is Victor."

Victor rose and crossed the courtyard to her, putting out a hand automatically. She gave him a friendly nod with her hands clasped behind her back, and Victor quickly put his hand down. "Pleased to meet you. Are you one of the sisters I've heard so much about?"

"No." Aliana's hands twisted in front of her. In a quiet voice, she said in English, "It's nice to meet you. Mansoor, I'm sorry. I

MOONRISING

should go. I only wanted to see you in person before the agreement on Wednesday. I should have called."

"Please," Mansoor said. "Sit."

Victor gestured for Aliana to take the cushion next to Mansoor. "I'll just go," he said.

"No!" Mansoor's eyes looked a little wild. "We need a third person."

Victor was feeling very out of his depth with this odd situation.

Aliana sat and gave Victor a look of uncertainty. "How is your recovery?" she asked Mansoor.

"Fine, fine." Mansoor gestured to his swollen legs. "They say today is the worst day and then the swelling goes down. I should be back to normal by Wednesday."

"Mansoor! That looks terrible." She reached out as if to touch him and then abruptly pulled back.

"Do not worry about me. I just wish I was in a better state to greet you. You are even lovelier in person."

Aliana blushed and ducked her head. "I hope you will not think it too forward, me coming here like this."

"No, not at all."

Victor felt his eyes glaze over as they continued conversing in this bland, pleasant fashion. They were clearly speaking English for his benefit, but the conversation was hardly worth listening to. Victor was just trying to figure out a way to tell Mansoor he could find his own damn third person, thanks, when Aliana rose.

"Thank you for seeing me, Mansoor. I am looking forward to the agreement." She gave Victor a friendly smile on her way out of the courtyard.

Mansoor waited until her footsteps had faded on the marble floor before laying his head down on the edge of the couch and groaning.

"Do you need a painkiller?" Victor asked. "I can fetch one."

"No," Mansoor said with a sigh. "I need a different life."

Not one to let jet lag stand in his way, Victor was on the factory floor the morning after his flight from Abu Dhabi. He paced around the latest prototype while his team stared at him with bated breath. They had turned his early morning idea to leverage frozen oxygen for increased thrust into a shiny black ship.

"What do you think?" Victor asked his test pilot, Camila.

"It looks pretty," Camila said, resting a hand on the side of the ship. "But I'm not flying it until the simulations have the odds of pilot heart attacks below .1 percent."

"We're close," one of the engineers broke in. "We're down to 2 percent."

Camila whirled on him. "2 percent? We're talking about my heart here. My living, beating heart."

"Victor," Teru's voice called tensely from the opening to the hangar bay. "Come here, please."

Victor stiffened at his chief engineer's tone. Gesturing for the others to remain where they were, Victor hurried to the front of the factory.

Standing in the open mouth of the hangar, arrayed around Teru in a semicircle, stood five people. On the mild October day, they were wearing light jackets open to reveal holstered weapons. Victor tried to place them. They were on the younger side, in their twenties and thirties, without the stiff posture Victor associated with a military background. The skinny man with a scruffy beard closest to Teru looked familiar to Victor.

"We aren't open to the public," Victor said mildly.

"Victor Beard?" the man asked.

Victor, who had been featured in three different prominent media profiles in the last month, did not bother to reply to the rhetorical question.

MOONRISING

"We have a message for you from the Eco Liberation Society. Stop." The man took a step toward Victor. His voice was low and intense. "Stop building rocket ships. Stop selling them to petrostates. Do not finalize your pending contract with NASA."

Victor looked back at Teru. "I thought you said the contract with NASA was confidential."

Teru winced. "NDA, Victor."

"Right . . . I can neither confirm nor deny any business relationship with NASA." That should satisfy the lawyers.

"Cut the bullshit and listen," the man growled. "You cannot colonize space at the expense of the ecology of the Earth. The last thing our planet needs is the increase in carbon from mass transit rocket ships for the wealthy."

"My ships are 2.7 times more energy efficient than our nearest competitor," Victor objected.

The man made a derisive sound. "Spare me the talking points. You know the carbon footprint of each trip is ten times that of a private jet."

Victor waved his hand from side to side. "9.4 times."

"Are you fucking serious?" Behind him, his companions laughed without humor. "We're at the most critical juncture in all of Earth's history, and you're happily pumping even more carbon into the atmosphere. We're already facing mass extinction. How many more species will be obliterated by your rocket ships?"

"You're exaggerating the influence of my ships. And underestimating the environmental impact of each permanent resettlement on the colony." He eyed the guns. He was pretty sure no one was firing them today. "Come back to my office, we'll run the numbers."

Teru cleared their throat. "Victor, you are not taking that man into our offices."

The bearded man turned on Teru. "If Victor Beard wants to collaborate with the ELS, who are you to stop him?"

"You need to go," Teru said. "We don't allow weapons on the premises."

"I don't see a sign." The man stepped closer to Teru. "Why shouldn't we be prepared to defend ourselves? Small-town Pennsylvania doesn't have a good track record of safety for brown people. I'm surprised you aren't armed yourself."

Teru's cheeks darkened. "This town has been nothing but welcoming to our diverse team."

"Navin Shah!" Victor exclaimed.

The man turned away from his standoff with Teru to look back at Victor. "What?"

"I knew I recognized you. Alex told me you weren't involved with the ELS anymore. She seems to be behind the times."

A woman with short curly red hair and cold eyes said, "You know Alex Cole? Are you also responsible for growing mutant food on the colony?"

Victor shrugged. "I may have played a role."

"Riley, we aren't here about mutant food," Navin snapped.

"I've done the analysis," Victor said, looking at the fully assembled group. "The colony is on a path to being self-sustaining. An average upper-middle-class family living on the Moon will produce at least twenty times less waste than if they lived in America." He offered his intelliwatch to Navin. "I'll send you my calculations."

Navin looked at the woman Riley, and she shrugged. He tapped his intelliwatch against Victor's, giving him his contact information.

"If you'll excuse me, my team is waiting for me on the factory floor. And oh," he turned to Teru. "We need to develop a gravity boot prototype. This week. You would not believe what the return to Earth did to Mansoor's legs."

"We're not fucking finished here, Beard," Navin growled.

"Oh—but I'm finished," Victor replied, turning his back on them and walking away. Once they saw the math, they'd understand. Teru made a helpless noise of frustration and followed Victor. "I'll send you my numbers."

15

ALEX

"I'M NOT SURE IT'S A GOOD IDEA," ALEX OBJECTED TO SANDRA. "I hate journalists."

"She's not a journalist, not exactly," Sandra said. "More like a celebrity advocate with a large following. You probably know her one song—'Glitter & Love'?"

"Even better," Alex muttered.

"Just give her a chance." Sandra crouched and opened a lower panel in the phone booth before inserting a cable into it.

"Phone booth video call incoming from Navin Shah," the automated voice of Alex's intelliwatch trilled. Alex hesitated, frowning at her watch.

"You have time," Sandra said, unwinding the cable. "I still need to set up the wired connection to the greenhouse."

"Accept," Alex said reluctantly, settling into the adjacent phone booth.

"Alex," Navin breathed. "I'm so glad I caught you." He was in a drab room with peeling flowered wallpaper and a brass headboard behind him. A motel, maybe?

"Is everything okay?"

MOONRISING

Navin twitched. "Everything is fine. I was wondering if you were attending COP78 next week?"

Alex let out an involuntary laugh. "In Tokyo?"

"I think it would be a wonderful opportunity for you. I can get you a ticket. And a hotel room."

Alex drew up her knees on the phone booth chair. "Navin, I'm on the Moon! You know I can't just jump in a rocket ship whenever I want." She paused. "What is this really about?"

Navin rubbed his unshaven face. "I'd like to see you. Next week. If not Tokyo, you should come home. Please?"

Alex scrutinized the background behind him, looking for clues as to his whereabouts and finding none. "Are you in some kind of trouble?"

"Me? Of course not. Will you come home? Next week?"

Sandra rapped on the windowpane. At her side was a beautiful woman in her early twenties with long dark hair and bright red lipstick. Gabriela Sanchez, heir to the Sanchez Hospitality hotel chain, pop star, and aspiring sustainability advocate. Alex did know her song. It was catchy.

"Hi-ya!" Gabriela squealed in a high-pitched voice, her diamond tennis bracelet sparkling as she waved.

Alex gave a short ripple of her fingers and turned back to Navin. "Now I'm worried about you. When's the last time you spoke to your therapist?"

"I'm fine, Alex. I just want to see you. Next week. Will you think about it?"

Alex looked back to where Gabriela waited. "Sure. I need to go. Can I call you later?"

"I'm kind of . . . off the grid right now. I'll call you," Navin said. "Just be careful, okay?" He cut the comm.

"I'm so excited to meet you," Gabriela gushed when Alex opened the phone booth door. She wrapped Alex's hand in her

215

soft manicured fingers. "I just can't believe I'm here, you know? What a dream come true."

Alex gave her a tight-lipped smile. As they walked to the greenhouse, Alex let Gabriela's chatter wash over her. Should she attempt to contact the university? Or figure out how to get in touch with Riley? She wasn't sure she had any right to interfere in Navin's life.

"Wow," Gabriela said when they stepped into the soil greenhouse. "This is so pretty." She plugged a tablet into the long cable Sandra had set up, pressed a button, and handed Sandra the tablet to film. "I'm coming to you live from the Moon colony," Gabriela said into the camera. She put an arm around Alex. "I'm here with the brilliant Dr. Alex Cole. Just look at these tomatoes." Gabriela held one up. "Black Brandywine?"

Alex blinked in surprise. So the pop star knew her fruits. *Shouldn't have stereotyped.* "That's right. Would you like to try one?"

Gabriela twisted a large blackish-purple tomato off the vine and held it to her face. "This smells like the earth. Like nature. Like a picnic in a meadow." She gave Alex a conspiratorial smile. "You might just inspire me to write a song, Dr. Cole."

"Thank you?" Alex hazarded.

Gabriela gave Alex her full attention. She was exceptionally beautiful. "I read that you monitor the steroidal alkaloids in your tomato plants. Can you tell us how you do that?"

Alex tried not to look flummoxed at the singer's correct pronunciation of *steroidal alkaloids.* "Um, yes, that's correct. The most common alkaloid found in tomatoes is tomatine. It has many benefits, including anti-inflammatory and anti-cancer properties, but with all mutagenetic plants we're careful to monitor the chemical composition to ensure the dosage is appropriate."

"Because a large dosage of tomatine could be toxic?"

Alex nodded. "This Brandywine variety has five milligrams of tomatine per kilogram." She held up five fingers. "When we created these seeds, we first tested the amount of tomatine in a

MOONRISING

laboratory. We then fed them to lab rats and observed the effects. When we were sure they were safe, we distributed seeds to co-op farms. And when I planted seeds here, I tested the first batch of tomatoes again to confirm the amount of tomatine."

"What amount of tomatine would be considered to be toxic to a human?" Gabriela asked.

"Oh, about ten thousand milligrams per kilogram."

"So this tomato contains .05 percent of the tomatine that would harm a human?"

Alex gaped at her and took a moment to do the math in her head. "Uh, yes, that's correct."

Gabriela blinked long fake eyelashes. "Fascinating." Turning to the camera, she bit directly into the tomato, her ruby red lips puckered on the fruit's skin. "Delicious. Dr. Cole, you sure know how to grow a tomato."

Behind the camera, Sandra grinned.

When Gabriela finally terminated the live broadcast, she grabbed the tablet back and began scrolling. "Dr. Cole, this is wonderful," she squealed. "Look at all this engagement."

Alex peered over her shoulder.

Wow, I haven't eaten a tomato in years. YUM

Sign me up for the next rocket ship.

UR beautiful Gabriela!!!

We are coming for you and your mutant greenhouse abomination. One Earth, one fight.

Alex stepped back abruptly, a sudden vision of the kitchen fire crowding her brain. The smell of smoke. The fear. "You think it went okay?"

"Fantastic," Gabriela assured her. "They love you." She laughed and showed Alex and Sandra a video mashup of Gabriela's famous single and a slow-motion close-up of her biting into the tomato. "Very sexy."

"I don't think anyone has made mutagenetic food sexy before."

Gabriela squeezed her arm. "I believe in your cause, Dr. Cole. We need to adapt to climate change, not keep trying to grow food using the same methods we used a hundred years ago. I want to help you feed the world."

Behind Gabriela's back, Sandra raised her eyebrows at Alex.

"Thank you," Alex said with a genuine smile. "I'm grateful for your support."

16

MANSOOR

"I AM GLAD TO BE HERE, MANSOOR," ALIANA SAID, HER WIDE brown eyes taking in the tall, mirrored ship, the steel scaffolding, and the tourists gathered below. "Thank you for the invitation."

Mansoor forced himself to smile at her. "I am pleased to see you again before my departure." He inclined his head at Aliana's wizened grandmother standing beside her. "Thank you for coming, *Jedda*. You honor me."

The lady crinkled her eyes at Mansoor. "Spaceships in Al Rub' Al Khali. We dreamt of this day when I was younger."

"I have been studying Victor Beard's ship design at Khalifa University," Aliana said. "All the engineering students have. His innovations in propulsive efficiency are revolutionary. Though, I must confess I do not fully understand the calculations yet."

In front of her grandmother, Aliana did not mention she had met Victor. Mansoor wondered what courage and curiosity had driven her to come to his father's villa alone. He liked Aliana. He allowed himself to see that. She was bright and inquisitive. When their families had met for the formal agreement, her thoughtful questions about the family business had made his father beam with pride and delight.

But Mansoor was not sure he could love her. He did not think his heart had the space.

Rashid, standing beside Mansoor, offered, "We'll connect you with him, the next time he's in Abu Dhabi. I'm sure he would be thrilled to explain his calculations to you. At length."

Aliana's eyes were wide and bright. "Would you?"

"Absolutely," Rashid said. "Would you excuse us? I need a private word with my brother."

"I will call you," Mansoor said to Aliana. "When I arrive." He cleared his throat. "I look forward to our wedding."

Aliana turned pink. "I do as well."

Rashid took Mansoor's arm and led him to the far side of the scaffold. "Why does Victor think you're having a passionate affair with the colony agronomist?" he asked in an undertone.

Mansoor glanced involuntarily to where Aliana stood with her grandmother. She was out of earshot. "It does not mean anything."

"That's not what Victor told me."

"That was a private conversation." Mansoor clutched the scaffolding railing and leaned forward to look out into the desert.

"What are you going to do?"

"What I must. I will break it off with Alex before the wedding and come home. I will wed Aliana in front of Father and all his guests."

"*Akhi*," Rashid said, and Mansoor smiled around the constriction in his throat at his brother's affectionate Arabic. "Is that what you want?"

"I got what I wanted. The hotel is beautiful and functional. We are generating revenue at a faster rate than projected. The Homestead Act will jump-start emigration to the Moon. Victor's ships make the travel easier and more affordable. Everything I have worked for is accomplished. I won."

MOONRISING

"Then why do you look miserable?" Rashid asked.

"I have to go. I am squeezing into the emergency seat in the cockpit, and I need to be there before the tourists' grand entrance." Mansoor reached for his brother and hugged him hard. "Thank you for your concern, little brother, but I am fine."

Mansoor raised his hand in farewell at Aliana and her grandmother and walked toward *Diana's Arrow* with his head held high.

Mansoor left the cockpit as soon as they reached weightlessness and floated into the main cabin. The tourists were clustered by the large windows, admiring the view. Mansoor remembered his first glimpse of Earth from space, with Alex by his side. He had felt overwhelmed with emotion that day.

The cabin had padded walls and rubber handlebars for navigating in weightlessness with ease. Even with his additional body, there was room for the new astronauts to maneuver. They tried backflips and spins, their laughter ringing through the ship. Mansoor remembered gripping Alex's shoulders to stop her from spinning out of control. He remembered the way she had looked at him when he removed his hands.

Mansoor tried to focus on the flight. He conversed with the passengers and answered their eager questions about the hotel. He tried to take note of areas for improvement in the ship design and the travel experience. But his mind kept returning to Alex.

It was surreal to land in the hotel's docking bay. Carson was there to greet them and gave his own enthusiastic welcome speech. In the three weeks Mansoor had been downside, Carson had been managing the hotel with grudging help from Pierre.

"Good, you're here," Mitch said as he unloaded supplies and checked the ship over for damage. "This flight transported eight crates for Alex that need to be delivered to the track. Mind taking them for me?"

Mansoor had no idea what Mitch meant by "the track," but he followed his instruction easily enough, the transporter trailing behind him. Mitch's directions led Mansoor to a room that had not existed three weeks ago. It was vast for the colony, down a recently constructed hall branching from the new family suites.

Alex was levering a wheelbarrow, dumping a pile of rich brown compost into a circular space. A wheelbarrow, Mansoor wondered. Had the colony possessed a wheelbarrow three weeks ago?

He came up behind her and put a hand on the small of her back. She turned to him, beaming. "You're back." She smelled like earth and sweat.

"I am." He indicated the transporter behind him. "I brought your delivery from the ship."

Alex lowered the wheelbarrow and stepped around him to pull the first crate off the cart and open it, revealing several sets of knee-high black boots of various sizes.

Mansoor raised an eyebrow. "New fashion trend?"

"Your request, I believe." Alex pulled a set of boots out and sat on the flooring next to the dirt pile to pull them on. "Victor has been on the phone with Herb nonstop all week."

Alex stood up in the boots, wobbling a bit, and caught Mansoor's arms to steady herself. "Gravity boots," she said. "Victor invented gravity boots in ten days." She took a few steps gingerly on the gray floor. "Wow. I feel really, really heavy."

"What are they supposed to do?" Mansoor asked.

"I'm not sure I fully understand the physics, but the general idea is that the track is magnetic, and the magnets in the boots connect with the ground to simulate Earth's gravity. It's not an original idea, but Victor came up with the idea of using grav boots on a track." She gestured at the flooring. Upon closer inspection, Mansoor could see the room was encircled by a meter-wide path enclosing a space the size of a basketball court. Piles of dirt dotted the area inside the path. "It's much more practical than trying

MOONRISING

to magnetize the full colony floor and make us march around in these all day." She looked closer at him. "Victor said your recovery downside was brutal. He's looking for a better long-term solution."

Mansoor shuddered. The swollen, itchy, tingling legs were a particular blend of torture, causing him to wake in discomfort at 3 a.m. for three days in a row. "It was. I must have looked worse than I felt to have inspired Victor to work so fast."

"You know how he is when he's running with an idea. His thought is that we can wear these boots and walk the track for an hour every day, maybe even replacing some of those horrible treadmill workouts. And I figured if we were building a track, we could build a park. I've been running the composters on their highest settings all week to produce enough soil."

Victor was not the only one who was prolific when an idea took hold, Mansoor thought.

"What is in the other crates?" he asked Alex.

"Clover to create low-water ground cover for a field. Oh, and dwarf apple trees." She sat back down and pulled the boots off with a forceful, impatient motion. "I've been thinking a lot about the children. The kids born here won't know what it feels like to be outside. I thought we could give them a little taste of that."

"That is a lovely notion," Mansoor said. Unbidden, an image came to him of a child sitting underneath a fully grown apple tree. His child. Alex's child. Here, on the Moon. He tucked the thought away. He was only torturing himself.

"I think I'm starting to understand why someone would want to be a homesteader," said Alex. "I spoke with John Anderson the other day. He's interested in my plans for an agricultural wing. We talked about potentially hiring a staff, up here, instead of solely relying on my colleagues at the Institute downside. He needs to find the funding first, of course. But isn't it exhilarating? The idea of feeding an entire community?" Her face turned wistful. "I wanted to feed the world, you know. I just didn't think it would be this little world." She turned to the unopened crates. "Starting with apples."

The crates did hold tiny trees, each a half-meter long, wrapped snugly in burlap. Mansoor helped Alex remove them carefully from the crates. He forgot his tiredness from the trip—he wanted to help Alex. Soon, he was hauling soil from the composters in the lab and raking it over the rocky drainage system she had assembled from lunar materials. Alex was adamant that the trees needed to get in the ground immediately, and she showed Mansoor how to carefully remove the burlap to reveal the root balls and plant them in a combination of compost, dead greenhouse leaves, moon rocks, and imported fertilizer. Around each tree, they laid mulch that Mansoor recognized as shredded food cartons, the nutrition labels still visible. Herb joined them to lay newly printed stepping stones, and then they spread out the clumps of clover in a systematic pattern.

Mansoor finally lay on his back, exhausted, and watched Herb run pipe in the walls to connect to a mounted faucet and hose. Alex watered each tree in turn, intently checking the water gauges embedded in the soil next to each tree as she went.

He had no idea what time it was when he and Alex stumbled back to his room, covered in dirt. They shared a cramped shower, using both their water rations to stretch the shower to a luxurious six minutes.

Mansoor discovered he had a pocket of energy left after all.

He lifted Alex easily onto his small bathroom counter, burying his face between her legs. He had missed everything about her. The way her eyes flashed when she was angry. The way her teeth shone white when he got her to laugh. And now, the way her fingers clutched his hair and her thighs tensed. He knew with an uncomfortable certainty he would always come back to her.

✦

MOONRISING

Mansoor slept like the dead and awoke groggily to find Alex gone. He lay in bed, taking his time to reorient himself to his surroundings. The bed was hard and only tolerably comfortable. He sat up, feeling the ache in his back from the wheelbarrow runs. Not, he suspected, from the journey. Victor's ship had been a smoother ride than some airplane flights he had taken and had left him with enough energy for a full day of hard labor. Remarkable.

His mind turned to Alex's comments from the day before. She was considering staying. When she mentioned children, was she picturing children with him? He had always known that children were part of his future. It was his father's clear expectation. Children with Aliana seemed unobjectionable. She would be a good mother. The cultural pressure to start a family would not begin in earnest until she had finished her degree. She would not be expected to sacrifice her career for her children, the way an Emirati woman might have in the past. He would love their children, he assumed.

But the idea of starting a family with Alex, a family on the colony, filled him with such a strange mixture of emotions he could barely identify what he was feeling. Terror, yes. And a deep well of longing. He could be a different kind of father here. There would be no nannies, perhaps no childcare of any kind for a while. He could strap the baby on his chest and bring it with him as he went about his day. He could be like one of those American fathers he sometimes watched in Boston, chasing their toddler around the playground, a stylish backpack slung on one shoulder, ready with Band-Aids and snacks.

He tried to push the image away as he rose from the bed. Alex had left a small bowl of strawberries on his table. He lifted a berry to his lips, sweet juice exploding in his mouth. He prepared to enjoy the time he had left.

225

17

ALEX

ALEX CROUCHED, INSPECTING THE WATER GAUGE OF AN APPLE TREE. The trees appeared healthier and more vibrant in the week since they were planted, their small leaves stretching open.

"Morning," Carson called to her. He grabbed a set of grav boots from a shelf near the entrance to the park and plopped down on a bench to fasten them. "How are your baby trees?"

Alex rose and joined Carson on the bench. "They seem to have survived the shock of transplant remarkably well."

Carson gave an enormous yawn. "Man, I'm wiped. I'm not cut out to be a hotel manager. Glad Mansoor is back to clean the rooms and wash the linens. Three weeks was enough of that."

Alex was startled by her intelliwatch chiming with an SMS message from Sandra. *Alex, please come to the communications center. It's urgent.*

"Sorry, I've been summoned," Alex said, rising from the bench. "Enjoy your walk."

Carson grinned as he stood, stretching out his back. "It helps if I pretend that I'm on the field with the boys drilling high knees

MOONRISING

with ankle weights." He stepped onto the track and sunk into a low squat. "Later."

As she walked toward the communications center, Alex made a mental note to warn Victor that the grav boot data collected on Carson might reflect a more vigorous workout than Victor had envisioned.

When she crossed into the command dome, Mansoor called, "Alex, there you are." He strode to her side and murmured low in her ear, "I was hoping, now that the latest batch of tourists have departed, that we could have a proper date tonight."

Alex beckoned him to walk with her. "Are you going to take me for a night on the town?" she teased.

"I was thinking a bottle of imported Italian wine and a night of stargazing."

Alex opened the closed door to the communications center and stepped inside. "It's a date. But tell me one thing—"

She stopped short in the doorway, causing Mansoor to stumble behind her. He caught himself with a hand on her waist. For a moment, her mind was completely blank.

"*Navin?*" Alex sputtered.

She took in Navin's unkempt hair, grungy beard—and the gun trained on her chest. Now her heart started beating.

"Slowly, Alex," he ordered. "Hands where I can see them. And you behind her—get in here and shut the door."

Alex raised her hands and stepped fully into the room, Mansoor's body close behind her. Her heart clamored harder and louder in her chest. She couldn't seem to wrench her eyes away from the gun. "Where's Sandra?" she asked stupidly.

"Who are you?" demanded Mansoor. She should have pushed him out the door. She should have yelled for help. *Too late.*

"Your communications officer is fine," Navin said to Alex, ignoring Mansoor's question. He gave her the barest hint of his normal self-deprecating smile. "I needed to make sure you were safe before it starts."

"Before what starts?"

Mansoor's voice behind her was calm. Even. "Who is this, Alex?"

"I know who *you* are," Navin said with a bitter laugh. "Mansoor bin Mohammed Al Kaabi." He looked at Alex, his lip curled. "Who knew you'd go for someone with so much blood and oil on his hands?"

"You're here with the ELS, aren't you?" Alex asked, her voice sounding paper-thin to her own ears. Navin could not have gotten here on his own. How many were here? What were they planning?

"One Earth, one fight."

Alex swallowed her panic. "Put the gun down, Navin." If only she could get him talking. They had always loved a good argument over cheap beer. "This isn't how you and I talk to each other."

"Talk?" Navin scoffed. "It's too late for that, don't you think? And don't start pretending you had any respect for my political beliefs."

"And a gun will make me respect you?" Her hands in the air felt unnatural. *Vulnerable.*

"Violence is the only language the American government speaks. We need aggressive action against climate change, and you and your friends are dumping carbon into our atmosphere to send fucking billionaires on vacation."

"If it's billionaires you have a problem with, take that up with me." Mansoor's voice was clear and even. He stepped forward, brushing Alex's shoulder as he moved in front of her, his body now between Alex and the gun. "Let Alex go."

"Get the fuck back!" Navin yelled, lunging forward with the gun as Mansoor and Alex backed up against the wall. "And stop

MOONRISING

pretending you care about Alex when you're about to fucking marry someone else."

Alex felt the breath leave her body. The hard wall was behind her, unyielding, keeping her upright. Her eyes met Mansoor's.

"He didn't tell you, did he?" Navin asked. "Fucking billionaires think they can use the rest of us and discard us, just like they've used up the planet."

Mansoor's eyes were grave as he met hers. *Navin wasn't lying,* Alex realized, her stomach churning.

"Why are comms still up?" a cold voice cut in from behind them. A tall brawny woman wearing dark clothing strode toward them through the door. Alex recognized her immediately. Riley Emerson. She held a gun too, with extra ammunition belted across her torso. So many bullets. How many were already dead?

Riley gave Navin a vicious shove on the shoulder. "You were supposed to be disabling outside communications, not looking for your mutant-loving girlfriend. Think you can manage that?"

Navin scowled, lowering his gun. "I have this under control, Riley."

She pointed to the console across the room. "Comms, Navin. Now."

Glowering, he walked over to the console as Riley turned to Alex, a smile on her face. Behind her, Alex could see Navin pulling out fistfuls of cables. The scent of smoke filled the air.

"Dr. Cole," Riley said with quiet menace, green eyes flashing. Her gun dangled at her side, almost casually, but Alex was not enough of a fool to think she would not use it, and fast. "So nice to see you again. It's not every day that I'm in the same room as the most dangerous anti-environmentalist in our country."

Alex, shaking, kept her mouth shut. Navin, one. Riley, two. How many more? Was the rest of the colony safe, or dead?

"Nothing to say?" Riley smirked. "I have missed the unique pleasure of your conversation, you know. But I suppose we aren't at Jimmy's now."

"What do you want with us?" asked Mansoor. *How could he be so calm?* Alex could not decide if she wanted to cling to him or slap him.

"They call us eco-terrorists," Riley drawled. "But you're the true terrorists, aren't you?" She raised her gun, waving it between Mansoor and Alex. "Space colonization is destroying our planet, and mutant food is poisoning humanity. I'm ready to do whatever it takes to stop it once and for all."

"You're going to kill us," stated Mansoor.

Riley grinned. "Maybe. But not yet." She pulled a pill bottle out of her pocket and handed it to Navin, who was walking back toward them, leaving the console a ruined mess of severed cables.

"Give them two. No—make that three," ordered Riley.

"Sleeping pills," Navin said as he unscrewed the cap. "We'll come back for you when the station is secured." He shook out pills into his hand. He offered three to Alex along with a water bottle from his pocket.

Alex shook her head and took a step back. "How do I know these are really sleeping pills?" It could be poison.

Riley pressed the barrel of her gun to Alex's forehead, and the back of Alex's head banged against the wall.

"If I wanted you dead, you would be dead. Sleeping hostage or corpse, you decide."

The gun felt cold against Alex's skin. Shaking, she took the pills and water. The pills scraped her throat going down.

"Make sure your girlfriend didn't stash them under her tongue," Riley said to Navin. "I'll check him. Open."

Alex opened her mouth in tandem with Mansoor. Navin took her chin in his hand and inspected her mouth in an awful parody

MOONRISING

of intimacy. "She swallowed." He caught her eye and his mouth turned up, inviting her to share in the double entendre. Alex tasted bile.

"Watches," said Riley, and Navin worked the intelliwatches off Alex's wrist first, then Mansoor's. Alex's hand felt numb as Navin pulled the watch off.

"Sweet dreams," said Riley.

"You cannot honestly believe you can hold this station hostage against the entire weight of the U.S. military," Alex said, finding her voice at last. "As soon as they realize what you've done, they'll come with full strength."

"Oh, don't worry," Riley said with false cheer. "By the time they get here, this place will be rubble."

The bottom fell out of Alex's stomach.

"Let's go," Riley said curtly to Navin.

"I'll come back for you," Navin promised to Alex. He shut the heavy door behind them. A loud bang reverberated through the tiny room.

Immediately, Mansoor grabbed the handle and tried to pry it open. It didn't budge. "They must have activated the emergency bulkhead door. We are sealed in."

Alex drew a deep, shaky breath. *Think, Alex. Think.* "There has to be another way." She looked around the small room. Desk, chairs, dark console, narrow window. She was barely taking anything in.

Stupid. She was so stupid. She had known Navin was back with the ELS. What had he said to her? *Come home. Next week.* She'd forgotten all about it after the success of her video with Gabriela. Why hadn't she taken Navin seriously?

Mansoor crouched next to a grate near the base of the floor. He pried it open and reached one hand in.

Alex kneeled next to him. "Anything?"

"Too small. Navin lured you to quite an isolated location on the station."

"I have excellent taste in men," Alex muttered.

"Will you let me explain?" His voice held a pleading note Alex had never heard before. His dark eyes were somber.

Alex looked away, casting her eyes up and noticing a larger vent in the ceiling. Not wanting to ask Mansoor to help, she positioned a chair in the center of the room and climbed up.

"Please, Alex, will you listen to me?"

The vent had four tiny screws holding it in place. "Is there any sort of toolkit in this room?" she asked as she attempted to twist a screw with her thumbnail. Then— "Fine. Are you getting married?"

"To a degree."

"*To a degree?*" Alex looked down incredulously at him.

Mansoor raked his hand through his hair. "I have agreed to marry a woman, yes." He opened the desk's top drawer and pulled out a pen and several paper clips.

Her heartbeat hurt in her chest, like it was stabbing her with each thump. Navin had told her the truth. "So, there's some poor woman out there, happily planning her wedding to the man she loves, unaware he's being unfaithful." Her nail cracked as she jammed it violently into the screw.

"She does not love me." His voice was flat as he handed her the pen. "She barely knows me. We have only met in person a few times."

The pen's tip was too thick for the screw's small head. Without looking at Mansoor, she asked, "When?"

"When I went home to Abu Dhabi."

Alex let the useless pen slip through her fingers. After he had told her she was the one he wanted. After he had made her feel desired and respected.

MOONRISING

Loved.

"You told me you went home to supervise the next stage of Moon tourism."

She couldn't bring herself to say the rest. *You told me I was the woman you wanted.*

"I know." Mansoor stooped and picked the pen up from the floor. "I could not bring myself to tell you. I went home to finalize the marriage contract. And to meet Aliana. Here, try the paperclip."

"So this is what, an arranged marriage?" Alex bent the paperclip.

"Our families arranged it, yes. It is still a common practice in Abu Dhabi, especially among the sheikhs. She is completing her studies, and the wedding is set for the end of the semester."

"Her studies? How old is she?" Alex asked, not sure she wanted to know the answer.

"Twenty."

"I can't do this," Alex growled in frustration. She lowered her shaking arms and stepped down from the chair. She sat heavily.

Mansoor pulled a chair next to her. He leaned toward her. "I consented to this arrangement before I met you. It was the only way my father would allow me to take charge of this project on-site. You have to understand. I did not have a choice."

Alex's slow-moving thoughts turned to the times before they had started sleeping together when he had seemed interested in her, only to pull away.

Until she had barged into his room while they were both euphoric from their moonwalk.

When his guard was down.

Had she misinterpreted the way he looked at her? Had she read adoration in his expression when it had held nothing but lust? She should have kept her walls up. Letting people in only led to disappointment.

"Don't tell me you didn't have a choice." Through her fatigue, she tried to hold on to her anger. It was better than feeling her heart shatter. "You could have kept our relationship professional. At the very least, you could have been honest with me from the beginning. I could have handled it. You didn't have to make me fall in—" She cut herself off, closing her fist as if to close off the words tumbling from her mouth. "It doesn't matter now. We have bigger problems."

Mansoor looked up at the vent and took the ruined paperclip from Alex's hand. He climbed on his chair and attempted to move the screws. "Do you think the ELS is capable of blowing up the station?"

"They've made threats against the Institute. In the past, I mean." Alex rubbed her face. "The Chicago police decided they weren't credible." What had ever possessed her to start sleeping with Navin? *Stupid.* "Did you hear about the explosion at that Santa Cruz factory, where they were making gas-powered lawn equipment? Lots of people said it was the ELS . . . but there wasn't enough evidence. And I'm convinced they firebombed the University of Texas at Austin's Center for Urban Horticulture." She lowered her head into her hands. "They're not just some disorganized group, Mansoor. I really think they have the technical expertise to blow up the station."

And not just the expertise but the ruthlessness, she thought. Perhaps she recognized it in them because she had a kind of ruthlessness, too. Except while she grew things, they destroyed them.

Mansoor lowered his hands from the vent. "This is not budging." He stepped down from the chair. "*Diana's Arrow* is in Abu Dhabi. José and Andrew are on a supply run in Cape Canaveral. We have no ships on-site capable of evacuating the residents in time."

MOONRISING

Alex felt close to vomiting. Was Navin capable of murdering one hundred people? Of course not. And yet, she wouldn't have thought him capable of holding her at gunpoint.

Alex abandoned the chair and walked around the room, as if an exit she hadn't noticed might appear. None did. Her round completed, she slid to the floor and leaned back against the wall, closing her eyes. Mansoor joined her, close without touching. For a while, they didn't speak, and Alex wondered if he had fallen asleep.

Finally, Mansoor said in a low voice, "When I agreed to let my father find me a wife in exchange for his blessing on my plan to spend a year on the colony, I thought it was a fair price to pay. I wanted to be a builder, to carry on the legacy of my great-great-grandfather. I wanted to be remembered as the man who restored the greatness of Abu Dhabi. And I was tired of fighting my father's constant pressure to marry and start a family. What is the point of establishing a legacy if you do not have children to honor you for it?" Mansoor turned to look at her. "I did not treat you with respect, and for that, I must apologize. I should have been honest with you."

"You're getting married in three months. *Three months.*" Perhaps it made no difference, with the threat of death by fiery explosion imminent, but it mattered to her.

"I know. I kept hoping that if I did not think about it too hard, it would all go away. I did not plan for any of this. I did not expect to fall in love with the Moon. With the colony. With you." Mansoor turned to her and took her hand. "I should have told you."

Alex stared down at their interlaced fingers. She closed her eyes and opened them again with difficulty. Did a wedding three months away matter if they only had hours to live?

"You love me?" she asked sleepily.

Mansoor leaned his forehead against hers. "I love you."

Alex wished her brain was not in such a fog. "You should have told me. About your engagement." *Hadn't he just said that?*

Mansoor kissed her brow. "I know."

She leaned against his shoulder and closed her eyes, then opened them again with effort. The room was small, and the consoles were dark. They were trapped. There was nothing they could do now.

Her eyes drooped shut as the pills took effect.

18

VICTOR

TERU PUSHED OPEN VICTOR'S AJAR OFFICE DOOR. "THE LATEST simulation results from the prototype are here." They tapped their intelliwatch against Victor's tablet, and a series of charts and tables popped onto the screen.

"Good, good." Victor adjusted his glasses and studied the charts. "These look excellent. This cuts the travel time to the colony to twelve hours and fourteen minutes. That's shorter than a direct flight from New York to Tokyo. We need to do a test run as soon as possible."

Teru shook their head. "Not yet. The risk of pilot heart attack is still .8 percent. It's a significant improvement over the last sim but still too high to fly."

"What if Camila took beta blockers before the test run?" Victor suggested.

"No," Teru said firmly. "We'll keep making adjustments. Let me know if the data spark any other ideas that do not involve drugging our staff."

Victor waved his hand, and Teru departed.

He was on hour two of scrutinizing the charts when he heard a soft laugh. Victor looked up to see Rashid leaning against the doorframe.

"Your power of concentration is still unmatched," Rashid said.

"Don't tell me I've been ignoring your calls again."

"No, I was in the neighborhood."

"You were in West Chester?" Victor asked skeptically.

"Wilmington. A friend had a gallery opening at the Delaware Contemporary last night. And since you and I were set to check in with Mansoor on building entertainment infrastructure for the new residents, I thought we could take the call together."

"You didn't have to take a cab to rural Pennsylvania to call your brother."

One corner of Rashid's mouth turned up. "I know."

Victor felt an unfamiliar flutter in his stomach. "Since you're here, should we have dinner, maybe? In Philly?"

And after dinner, it would be late. Too late, perhaps, for a train back to Manhattan. Could Victor invite Rashid back to his condo? Was his condo clean? He mentally re-ran the last time his cleaning service had come by and the state of his bathroom. If he invited Rashid to his place for a drink, did he even have a bottle of wine? Harper had handled stocking their liquor cabinet. He should have cleared her lingerie out of the closet.

Rashid was watching him as Victor's brain went into full panic mode. "Dinner would be lovely," he said firmly, stopping Victor's spiraling thoughts.

Victor checked the time on his intelliwatch and was relieved to see he could avoid embarrassing himself any further. "Call Mansoor Al Kaabi," he told it.

The familiar connecting sounds buzzed.

"How is the grav boot testing going?" Rashid asked Victor as he pulled a chair next to Victor's side of his desk.

MOONRISING

"Promising. 32 percent of the colony residents have agreed to participate in trials, and the initial week of data shows a comparable heart rate to the colony treadmills. It's too soon to review data on bone density or muscle mass."

The buzzing continued until, finally, Victor's display screen read, *No Answer.*

Victor sent Mansoor an SMS message and received *Incomplete Delivery* in response.

Rashid looked at Victor's intelliwatch and frowned. He sent his own message and received the same response.

"Call Alex Cole," Victor said aloud.

Rashid drummed a hand against the back of Victor's chair as they waited for the call to connect.

No Answer.

Victor tried an SMS message to Alex.

Incomplete Delivery.

Rashid's body, so near to his own, was growing increasingly tense. Victor needed more data.

"Call Drake Douglass," Victor said.

Drake's serious face appeared on the screen. His heavy dark eyebrows were creased. "What do you want, Beard?" He looked at Rashid and in a more measured tone said, "Rashid Al Kaabi, hello."

"You answered!" Victor blurted. "You never answer."

"Beard," Drake growled. "I don't have time for this."

"Because you're dealing with the crisis on the colony," Victor said authoritatively. It was one of his favorite techniques for getting more information.

"How in God's name did you know about the hostage situation?" Drake demanded.

Next to him, Rashid sat up straighter.

"As you know, I am very well connected," Victor said.

"Why do you think I took your call? It wasn't for the pleasure of this conversation, that's for sure." Drake made a frustrated huff. "The Eco Liberation Society managed to get a flight out of Spaceport New Mexico while the park was closed for annual maintenance. They held the Mission Control skeleton crew hostage and succeeded in blocking communication for over a day."

Victor absorbed this information, his brain clicking into overdrive. "Do they have demands?"

"They do," Drake said uninvitingly.

"Shut down the colony, end space tourism, and void the Homestead Act?" Victor offered.

"What do you know about it, Beard?"

"They came to my factory a few weeks ago. With guns. They threatened me with vague dire consequences if I didn't liquidate my company."

"Beard, why didn't you report this to the FBI?" Drake was nearly shouting. "They consider the ELS to be a top domestic terrorism threat."

"I thought I handled it. I sent them a spreadsheet."

Victor could see Rashid bite the inside of his cheek.

"A spreadsheet," Drake repeated flatly. "Thank you for the insight. I have to go."

"Wait!" Victor said. He could not sit by and let the colony be attacked. "What's going to happen?"

"We're in a hold and monitor situation. The president does not want to risk his reputation by attacking a group of American citizens."

The fire, Victor realized. He'd found his culprit. If the ELS set the fire remotely, and the damage did little to slow down lunar tourism or the arrival of homesteaders, of course they would try something more drastic.

MOONRISING

"I don't think we can afford to wait. The ELS is too fond of bombs."

Drake winced. "I agree."

"What if the response was unofficial? They launched one ship from New Mexico, yes? The largest ship they could have sent holds fourteen people, including the pilot. We could match their numbers. I have a new prototype ship that will get us there in half the time. And a brilliant pilot. And a launch pad. Rustle up some Marines and meet me in West Chester. We'll save the colony together." Mansoor and Alex were under attack. It was unthinkable that he would sit this one out.

"Victor." Drake's voice was almost gentle. "You can't come. You aren't trained for an operation like this. Have you ever fired a gun?"

"If you want my ship, I'm coming. I'm not a soldier, but I will earn my keep. I know the schematics of the colony inside and out. And I know the ELS. We share the same fundamental goals. I can persuade them. They just need to have the right data." Clearly, they hadn't looked at the data Victor had sent—or perhaps they hadn't understood it. But he could explain.

Drake compressed his lips. "Beard, you don't have the right skill set for a high-stakes situation like this. What we need is an experienced hostage negotiator."

"Do you know anyone?" Victor asked.

Drake's eyes slid to Rashid. "I know the person who flipped six senators to support the Homestead Act with no prior relationships."

"No way," Rashid protested.

"I have heard a great deal about your powers of persuasion," Drake said. "You would be an asset. I can get muscle. I *am* muscle. But I don't have the skill set to talk down armed terrorists."

"Neither do I," Rashid protested.

Victor turned eagerly to Rashid. "My ideas, your words. It will be exactly like the Homestead Act. We can do this."

241

Rashid looked at Victor. His brown eyes were grave. He let out a slow breath. "Alright." To Drake, he said, "I want everything you have on the ELS members on the station. Their names, backgrounds, work histories, family histories. Everything."

"Done," said Drake. "I'll be there as soon as I can."

Once Drake sent the information on the ELS personnel, Rashid sequestered himself in a spare office to prepare as best he could. Victor, meanwhile, rallied his staff to once again do the impossible.

Soon the factory floor was humming with energy as the Beard Enterprise team rushed around the ship, checking each component and removing the staging surrounding the vehicle.

Teru came to find him. "The ship isn't ready," they hissed.

"It's ready," Victor said confidently. "The last two rounds of simulations were a textbook success." The frenzied excitement from his team washed over him as they called out questions and commands to each other. The movement had not ceased since Victor had announced his plan.

"Except for the chance of a heart attack."

Victor waved his hand in dismissal. ".8 percent. This isn't the time to be risk averse."

"We haven't done a test launch." Teru grabbed his arm when Victor made to walk away. "We've done zero simulations on passenger safety. *Zero*, Victor. We don't know if the human body can stand this trip. A heart attack could be the least of our concerns. Let NASA figure this out. You don't need to go all half-cocked on some vigilante suicide mission."

Victor whirled on Teru. "This is my fault. The ELS came here to order me to stop building ships. They came armed. They threatened me. And who did I tell? No one. I thought they were all bluster, and I blew them off. Everyone is always telling me I'm a

MOONRISING

genius, and I let it get to my head. I thought I was smarter than the ELS, and if I shared my superior knowledge, they would see it my way. And now look where we are."

"Victor, listen to yourself," Teru begged. "What do you think you're doing right now?"

"I have to go." Victor gestured to the team around the ship. "I'm needed elsewhere."

By 8 p.m., the November night was freezing and very dark at the factory. Spotlights illuminated the prototype shuttle that Victor's people had moved from the warehouse to the launch pad. Teru had grudgingly wrapped up the preflight checklist when Drake's team pulled up in two black SUVs. Victor, Rashid, and Camila stepped outside to greet them.

Drake briskly shook their hands. "Are you prepared?" he asked Rashid.

Rashid hesitated. "I think so. Tell me, how sure is your intelligence that Riley Emerson is the leader?"

"We are confident she is the most senior operator. But domestic terrorist cells don't typically have a rigid chain of command."

For a moment, Rashid looked like he wanted to say more, but instead, he simply nodded.

Drake turned to Camila. "How many night flights have you done?"

"None," she admitted. "I'm a test pilot. I've flown our other model dozens of times but only for short stints and never at night. The ships returning from the colony sometimes land in the dark, but no one has performed a night launch with our ships yet."

Drake exchanged glances with the broad-shouldered Marine next to him that he had introduced as Patrick. "Perhaps we should postpone until dawn."

243

"We don't know what the ELS is capable of," Victor protested. "I'm not underestimating them again."

"It won't make a difference," Camila said. "The readouts don't require sunlight. Day launches are for the spectator experience, not for safety." Victor nodded confirmation.

"Very well," Drake gestured to the Marines milling around the SUVs. "Move out."

"There is one more thing you should know," Victor said.

"Yes?"

"This ship model has never flown—" He hesitated. He was not about to admit to Drake that the ship was untested. Drake would surely abort the mission. "The ship has never flown a long distance. It's designed to maximize thrust over comfort. It should get us there in twelve hours, but it will be uncomfortable."

Drake shrugged, already striding crisply to the ship. "These men can handle a little discomfort. We'll be fine as long as you can keep up."

Victor and Rashid followed the soldiers. Victor glanced at Rashid. He appeared calm and composed. Why was Victor positive that Rashid was petrified?

"I'm not sure I can do this," Rashid said. "I'm not sure you can either. Are we making a mistake?"

Was it a mistake? Would he be putting himself and Rashid into a situation they couldn't handle? No—if there was one thing Victor knew, it was recruiting the right person for the job. Drake had carried out a successful hostage rescue before, in Sierra Leone. And Rashid had charmed six cynical senators into passing the Homestead Act. They would pull this off. They would save the colony.

"We aren't making a mistake," said Victor confidently. "We'll fly the ship. We'll get there faster than the ELS would anticipate a response. The Marines will provide cover. You'll talk down this

MOONRISING

Riley Emerson person. We'll have the station free in twenty-four hours."

Rashid snorted.

"Trust me," Victor said.

"I trust you," Rashid said quietly. "Always."

Victor admired the efficiency of the Marines. It was not long before the ship rose into the sky, smooth and fast, more like a bullet train than a rollercoaster. Nevertheless, Victor took note of every rattle and every bump. He noticed how the seat buckle dug into his shoulders and let his brain run through a series of ideas for buckle design improvements.

When they escaped Earth's gravity, their speed did not slow. Victor felt the pressure as his body pressed into the chair. His glasses were an uncomfortable weight on the bridge of his nose.

"Do we need to stay strapped in the whole way?" Drake shouted at him from across the aisle.

"No," Victor gasped. "We're still accelerating. Once we reach uniform movement, no g-force will be applied to our bodies, and we'll be able to unbuckle. We are accelerating from the 3 g force of liftoff to 4 g and then will cease our acceleration. Let me know if you begin to feel lightheaded."

Next to him, Rashid gave him a familiar look of frustration. "Is this safe?"

"In theory," Victor said. "We capped the thrust at 4 g. Most human bodies can handle 4 g with no ill effects." He tried to decide if the pounding in his head was cause for any concern.

From the cockpit, Camila's strained voice came through the comms. "I'm getting a message from NASA."

"Patch it through," Drake growled.

A stiff voice carried through the cabin. "Unidentified vessel, you are not cleared to launch from American soil. Turn around immediately and return to Earth."

Victor craned his head around his straps and looked at Drake incredulously. "You didn't inform NASA?" Victor peered at Drake's stoic face. In a less certain voice, he said, "But the military knows, right?"

"I wanted to give the president plausible deniability," Drake said through gritted teeth.

"If the military hasn't approved this mission, how did you find these soldiers?" Victor asked.

"The colonel called. We came," offered one of the Marines seated behind Victor, as if it was a simple matter.

"This could end your careers," Victor protested. "You could be court-martialed."

"Not if we win," Drake said grimly. "Not if we're heroes. I know President Fairchild. He'll jump at a chance to take credit for this mission—*if* it's a decisive victory." With effort, Drake pressed the button on his chair to reach the cockpit. "Ignore the message," he ordered.

Victor swallowed. Drake was already a hero. He had received a Medal of Honor from the president's own hand for the daring rescue of a commercial ship that pirates had hijacked off the coast of Sierra Leone. If Drake was arrested for leading this operation and his heroic reputation was torn to shreds, Victor would be the cause.

There was a sudden silence as the acceleration stopped. "We've reached free fall," Camila said from the cockpit. "Any heart attacks back there? Did anyone pass out?"

Victor gingerly unbuckled his straps and pushed himself up.

"Pass out?" Rashid muttered for his ears alone. "Did you think to mention that?" His eyes rolled back in his head, and his face went slack.

"Rashid!" Victor cried. With shaking hands, he tried to undo Rashid's straps.

Too slow.

MOONRISING

Patrick came to Rashid's other side and undid the buckles with brisk efficiency. "What do we do?" he asked Victor.

Victor's brain wasn't working. He stared at Rashid's blank face. No ideas came. With a shaking hand, Victor reached out and touched Rashid's neck.

There was no pulse.

Drake held his shoulders and spun him so they were face-to-face in the weightless cabin. "The flight caused him to pass out. What does he need?"

"I—I—" Victor didn't know. He took Rashid's wrist.

Still no pulse.

"Victor Beard, you are the smartest man I have ever had the dubious privilege of knowing. You have invented the fastest rocket ship in existence. You know the answer. How do we help him?" Drake's voice was steady and calm.

"Blood flow," Victor gasped. "He needs blood flow to his brain." He looked at Patrick. "Spin him."

Patrick nodded and turned Rashid gently around.

"More," Victor said. "360 degrees in three dimensions."

Rashid was upside down from Victor's point of view when he opened his eyes and let out a gasp. Patrick held him steady. "Water," he barked at the watchful Marines. He helped Rashid drink from a pouch.

Rashid looked muzzily around him. Victor felt frozen in place, unable to go to him. It was Drake who said to Rashid, "The rate of acceleration made you pass out. How are you feeling?"

"Fine, I think. A bit of a headache."

Drake looked around him. "Everyone, get moving. You need to get the blood flowing to your brains again."

As the Marines moved their bodies around the cabin, Victor pressed the comm button on his chair. "Camila? Are you alright?"

She laughed. "Best adrenaline rush of my life. I want to fly this ship all the time."

Victor did not think he was ever flying this particular ship again. It could be recycled for parts on the Moon for all he cared. He went to Rashid. "I'm sorry." He could barely look at him.

"I'm okay," Rashid said.

"Your heart stopped beating. I thought I'd killed you." Victor felt an odd wetness stuck under his eyes and realized with shock he was crying. He tried wiping away his tears, but they clung to his fingers. "I should never have taken you on an untested prototype." Teru had warned him, and he hadn't listened.

"I'm not dead. I feel fine." Rashid gave his arm a squeeze and let go. "We don't know what we're facing on the colony. I'm glad we're getting there as fast as possible."

Drake had moved to a screen on the wall and pulled up the colony schematics. "Beard, I need you. There are two shuttle ports. Which do you think would make for a stealthier landing?"

"Neither." Victor wiped his wet hands on his shirt and ensured his glasses were snug against his face. As soon as he refocused on the mission, he realized his back brain had been contemplating the problem for hours. He left Rashid and pushed himself over to join Drake. "We should land here." He pointed at the far side of the hotel, behind the twin spires. "If they've cut off communications, they're blind too. Whatever they're up to, they aren't going to post lookouts in the tourist bedrooms while the hotel is in between tourist visits. As long as we avoid visuals with the dome windows, we may preserve the element of surprise."

"And land in an environment without atmosphere," Drake said, raising one eyebrow.

"There's a hatch here." He pointed to the long hallway connecting the hotel to the rest of the colony. "We squeeze into a seal film attached to the door, activate the emergency opening lever, and step right in. We'll be in the ship's emergency suits for ten minutes, no more."

Patrick looked at Victor, then at Drake. "Let's do it."

MOONRISING

✦

The ship landed on the far side of the hotel, settling on the uneven lunar surface with a jarring bump. The Marines picked up quickly on Victor's hurried instructions for properly donning space suits, and he ended up being the last one fumbling to fasten himself into a cumbersome suit.

"No chatter on the comms," Drake instructed before he put on his helmet. "We don't know who might be listening."

Camila lowered the ship's stairs, and they carefully descended onto the surface of the Moon. Victor caught his breath as he gazed at his surroundings, taking in the stunning hotel spires reaching into the sky. Beside him, Rashid reached out a gloved hand and briefly touched Victor's helmet. He looked as awed as Victor felt.

The Marines, unfazed by the surreal backdrop, were halfway to the hatch by the time Patrick waved frantically at them to move. With slow, deliberate steps, Victor followed the Marines to the hatch.

Victor awkwardly knelt next to Patrick and silently assisted him in inflating the seal film. The Marines maneuvered their five crates of weapons and supplies into the seal. When all fourteen bulky forms were inside, Victor closed the entrance, and Patrick turned the crank on the side of the door. The hatch opened with a whoosh of air, and they stepped inside one by one.

In the corridor to the hotel, the Marines efficiently stripped their suits and piled them in stacks, then opened the crates and armed themselves with a mix of rifles, handguns, stunners, and several long dart pistols with a hinged angle—and all this before Victor was out of his suit.

"We set up a perimeter at the hotel," Drake murmured. "Bring your suits and the crates. Leave no trace."

249

The corridor sloped up to a second level. It was the restaurant, Victor realized. The Marines efficiently moved tables to set up a barricade. Victor stayed out of their way. He had already reached his limit of action, and they had only just arrived.

Instead, he stared at the view illuminating the floor-to-ceiling windows. The stars were points of light in a black sky, too many to count in one night, even at Victor's pace. "Mansoor has outdone himself," Victor said, his voice coming out unexpectedly hushed.

Rashid shifted a crate of supplies into the corner and came to stand next to Victor. "I'd like to paint this, and not from memory."

"Paint is a flammable substance. It would never pass the safety tests." Victor was struck with sudden inspiration. "I'll recruit some eager chemist to invent fire-resistant paint. It's a brilliant startup idea. I'll sponsor the patent application."

Rashid gave him an exasperated look. "Not all paint is flammable. Haven't you ever heard of watercolors? Or acrylics? I wish I'd brought some with me."

"Okay, if you don't plan to paint during this visit, what about poetry?"

"Nah. Poetry about the Moon is so overdone. 'Arise fair sun and kill the envious moon, Who is already sick and pale with grief that thou, her maid, art far more fair than she.'"

Victor blinked in startlement. "That's beautiful."

Rashid looked at him skeptically. "You're serious."

"Of course I'm serious. Forget painting. Focus on your poetry. That was lovely."

"That was *Shakespeare.*"

"Shakespeare, right," Victor said vaguely. The look on Rashid's face was a startling mixture of amusement and affection. Victor wondered for a moment what it would be like to slip his hand into Rashid's. Would it be warm or cool? Soft or callused? Would it feel bigger than his own? He shook himself.

MOONRISING

"I need to tell you something," Rashid said. "If Riley Emerson is in charge here, I don't think we'll be able to negotiate. She's on the run from the FBI. Looks like she's linked to the death of two people in a factory bombing in Santa Cruz. And Victor, she *hates* Alex Cole. Her writing on mutagenetic food is full of disturbing violent fantasies. I don't think she's going to settle for anything less than destroying Peary Station."

Victor winced. He should have called the FBI as soon as the ELS had left his factory. He hadn't known Riley was a fugitive. "Why didn't you say anything before we left? You know how dangerous this is. You could have stayed behind."

Rashid took his hand. "I couldn't let you come alone."

Victor's frustratingly slow-moving brain processed that Rashid's hand was cool, but not clammy, and was slightly larger than his own.

Drake stepped up to them, a semiautomatic weapon held in one hand. "It's time."

19

MANSOOR

MANSOOR BLINKED OPEN HIS EYES AND LOOKED AROUND THE room. *Trapped. Still trapped.* Alex was warm against him, her face pressed into his chest. His back ached from the awkward sleeping position, his stomach rumbled in hunger, and his bladder was uncomfortably full.

When he touched Alex's hair, she sat up and gestured to a corner of the room. "I pulled out a desk drawer as a toilet," she said, her face reddening.

Mansoor got up to relieve his bladder and returned to sit beside her against the wall. Alex handed him half a protein bar and the remains of Navin's water bottle. He took it without comment and sat back down, pulling Alex close against him.

He pictured sitting with Victor sipping cachaça at a hotel bar in Rio, the first time they had spoken aloud their vision of a million people living on the Moon in their lifetimes. It was euphoric, connecting with someone who could conceive of ideas on the scale of millions and centuries. And when they started putting the dream into action—a heady, intoxicating bliss.

Lost. All lost.

At least Victor was safe. And Rashid. They would rebuild from the ashes.

Mansoor kissed Alex's hair. His life would end without discovering a path to merging his divided selves. He would never have the opportunity to find a balance between the man his father wanted him to be and the man he wanted to be for himself.

So much regret.

A scraping sound came from the door. Mansoor and Alex scrambled to their feet as Dr. Berg stepped into the small room. The door stayed open behind her, letting fresh recycled air into their small, stale room.

"*Alhamdulillah*," Mansoor murmured gratefully. The hallway beckoned. *Freedom.* Together, they could find a way to save the station.

"Naomi," Alex breathed. "Thank goodness you're here. The Eco Liberation Society is trying to blow up the station."

"I know," said Naomi and raised a gun.

Mansoor's brief flare of optimism died instantly. *The ELS had an inside woman.* "Dr. Berg," he said evenly. "The ground vehicles do not have the capacity to evacuate all the residents. If the ELS destroys the station, everyone will die."

"Everyone here is a collaborator," Naomi spat. "They deserve what's coming to them."

"No one deserves this death," Alex said. Her face was stark white. "Please, Naomi, I know you hate what I'm doing here, but—you don't have to do this."

"Do you know who didn't deserve their deaths?" The gun shook in Naomi's hand. "The children who came into the ER seizing from solanine poisoning. Do you know how they died? Choking on their own spittle, gasping for air, unable to draw the breath to cry for their mothers. This isn't about *me*, Dr. Cole. I will not let you start another plague. Let's go."

Mansoor obeyed, exiting the room behind Alex with leaden legs. He kept his eyes trained on Alex's back, drawing strength from her as Naomi pushed them toward the dome. They picked their way through overturned chairs and piles of debris, until Alex stopped short, her shoulders sagging.

In front of her, a body sprawled at an awkward angle, eyes staring vacantly. Brown blood crusted on the gray vinyl floor. Mansoor recognized Mitch's soft doughy face, and his stomach churned. Alex bent and put her hands on her knees, and Mansoor reached out a hand to gently rub her back.

"He was one of the first to try my food. A cucumber." Alex whispered into her knees. "And Carson—the two of them are inseparable. He's going to be devastated."

"Keep moving," Naomi barked.

Alex spun around and glared at her. "How could you do this? Mitch was nothing but kind to you. To all of us."

"I said keep moving." Naomi shoved Mansoor with her free hand, and he nearly toppled over before catching himself against Alex. "Mitch thought a desk job in Space Force operations was a match for the ELS. He was wrong."

Mansoor took Alex's shaking hand in his and led her forward. "His fiancé—" Alex turned her stricken gaze on him. "She was joining us on the first homesteader ship."

"Do you think I care about that?" Naomi growled behind them. "More carbon in the atmosphere. More people eating your disgusting mutant food. We are putting a stop to all of it. Starting with the two of you."

They had reached the center of the dome. Mansoor took in a slow breath as he tried to make sense of the scene in front of him. He needed to stay strong. For Alex.

Riley, Navin, and a dozen unfamiliar people surrounded two chairs positioned to face each other, a tablet on a tripod, and

MOONRISING

another tripod holding an LED light. A wire ran from the tablet back to a phone booth.

"Sit down," Riley ordered. She held what looked like an old-fashioned black walkie-talkie in her hand.

Mansoor sank into a chair. Alex took a seat opposite him, her hands clutching the armrests.

Navin crouched in front of Alex and tenderly pushed a wisp of hair back from her forehead. "Are you alright?"

Alex jerked back from his touch. "You betrayed me to a terrorist organization, drugged me, imprisoned me, and now you want to kill over a hundred innocent people. What do you think?"

"He's really got a hard-on for you," Riley remarked conversationally to Alex. She raised an eyebrow at Mansoor. "What is it about this bitch you both find so irresistible?"

Mansoor bit the inside of his cheek and said nothing. He took another slow breath in and out.

"Right." Riley held up the walkie-talkie. "Let's set some ground rules here, 'kay? We've set explosives throughout the station, ready to detonate when I press the trigger."

Alex drew a hiss through her teeth. Mansoor pictured the quartz glass windows on the hotel spires shattering and falling to the Moon's surface. Is this what his years of work would amount to?

"But you don't have to die," Riley continued. "We may find room on our ship—for the two of you." Her lips twisted in a smile. "Provided you do exactly as I say."

20

ALEX

ALEX'S WORLD HAD SHRUNK. THERE WAS MANSOOR, SITTING across from her, looking deceptively calm. Navin, standing behind her, vibrating with tension. And Riley, holding the detonator meant to kill them all.

"We've established a connection to Earth," Riley said. "Our comrades on the ground are ready to amplify our live broadcast." She placed the detonator carefully on a console desk and pulled her gun out of her waistband. "Alex Cole, you are going to look at that camera and renounce mutant food to the world."

Alex's heart was clanging in her chest. Of course her sense of self-preservation was screaming at her, *save yourself.* But attitudes toward mutagenetic food were finally shifting. She was not going to take them backward. The stakes were too high.

"I can't do that," she said.

"You can and you will."

Alex thought about the bleak future in America without mutagenetic food. The hungry climate refugees who had taken shelter in Woodlawn. The Wisconsin farmers who had seen the crops their fathers and grandfathers had grown for generations wither on the

MOONRISING

vine. The millions of children all over the country who had never tasted a fresh strawberry. Even if the world had rejected her, it was still worth saving. People were worth saving.

She steeled herself. "No."

The surprise on Riley's face gave way to a rapacious grin. "Fine. You want to play hardball?" She swiveled.

The gun flashed in the light.

A shot rang out.

Mansoor rocked back.

21

MANSOOR

A SHARP CRACK RENT THE AIR. MANSOOR JERKED FROM THE BLOW of a punch. Then, white-hot pain lanced through his shoulder. Something trickled down his arm, hot, liquid, and for one confused moment, he wondered if the sprinkler system had been activated.

He turned his head. Bright red blood spurted out of his shoulder, running in rivulets down the length of his arm. He reached his left hand across his body, clutching his shoulder. The blood drenched his hand.

Across from him, Alex shook her head, tears streaming down her cheeks. "Please, don't hurt him." He had never seen her cry.

I am fine, he wanted to say, but it would have been a lie. His fingers were sticky, and his head throbbed.

"Script," snarled Riley. She pulled a crumpled piece of paper from her back pocket and thrust it into Alex's shaking hand.

"Riley, please," gasped Alex. "I know our methods are different, but—"

"No more arguments." Riley grabbed Mansoor's uninjured left arm, and Mansoor felt the barrel of the gun on his head. The pain

MOONRISING

radiated from his shoulder. "You will read the fucking script, Alex, or your lover dies and you with him."

Mansoor tried to keep his wits intact as the blood dripped through his fingers. His vision blurred, but he kept his eyes on Alex.

So beautiful.

So fierce.

Mansoor was shivering now, his body betraying him with jolting shudders. He tried to keep Alex in focus, but his eyelids were heavy. Mansoor remembered the first time he saw her from a distance, so long ago at the UN conference. She had never wavered in her convictions as she stared down that group of hecklers with poise and confidence. And she was not wavering now. Strong, unbreakable Alex.

He felt a surge of love and pride. They had the same goals, the same values, he realized. Together, they shared a vision to protect humanity. To protect the Earth.

It was a cause worth dying for. And maybe he was dying. It certainly felt like it.

He left the choice to her.

22

ALEX

ALEX STARED AT MANSOOR'S ARM. THE BLOOD FLOW HAD NOT slowed. Why was no one helping him? Naomi was a doctor. She must have taken the Hippocratic Oath. Why was she standing by?

"This is too much, Riley," Navin protested from his position behind Alex. "We had an agreement. You promised me Alex's life."

"Circumstances have changed."

Navin scowled. "We aren't here to get our rocks off on death threats and torture. We should stick to the plan."

"Shut up," Riley snarled. "I'm in charge. I decide what we're here for."

Navin stepped in front of Alex. "I won't let you kill her."

Riley lifted her gun and pointed it at Navin. "Back off."

Navin wrapped both hands around his own gun but kept it trained toward the floor. "Guarantee to me that Alex lives, and I stand down."

"You're fucking pathetic!" Riley screamed at him. "She's always made you into a sniveling little coward."

Navin took another step toward Riley, and she pulled the trigger.

MOONRISING

Navin crumpled to the floor.

Alex let out an involuntary gasp. Riley's script in her hand fluttered to the ground, its corner landing in a spreading pool of blood. Navin lay on the floor, eyes open in surprise, a bullet nestled in his forehead. Turning her head, Alex heaved up the meager contents of her stomach.

"Move him," Riley ordered. Two ELS operatives scrambled to obey.

Alex wiped the back of her mouth with one hand, tasting bile. Riley grabbed the piece of paper and shoved it back into Alex's hand. "You read this, and you live. No more stalling." She gestured with her gun in the air. "Start the fucking broadcast! Now!"

Naomi fumbled with the LED light.

"Wait—" gasped Alex. She scanned the blood-spattered paper. The words swam in her eyes. *Space travel is spewing carbon into the atmosphere . . . mutagenic food is poison . . .*

The paper shook in her hands. Mansoor? Or the world?

"Now, Naomi," Riley growled.

Naomi pressed a button on the tablet. Alex could see her own ashen face reflected back at her. Her eyes were swollen, her cheeks wet with tears.

The broadcast was live.

Riley resumed her stance behind Mansoor, her gun pressed once again against his head.

"My name . . ." Alex looked up into the camera. "I'm Dr. Alex Cole—" She looked at Mansoor. He was still bleeding. His eyes were slipping closed. Riley was gesturing frantically at Alex. Right. The script. "Um . . . I am speaking to you from the Moon. I am—"

Riley's face was set, the gun still pointed at Mansoor. She would kill him. If Riley had killed her own ally so callously, she would not hesitate to kill Mansoor. Alex knew she should recant. It was just words, after all.

261

Alex raised her chin and looked into Mansoor's brown eyes. He was pale, and his eyes kept flickering closed. She didn't know how much more blood loss he could sustain.

But she did know what she had to do.

23

MANSOOR

THE WORLD WAS FUZZING OUT, BUT HE KEPT HIS GAZE FOCUSED on Alex. The gun was hard and cold against his skull. Alex's face was upturned to the camera. Her tears were coming faster now.

Mansoor trusted her. Always. And he had never loved her more.

"*La ilaha illa Allah*," he whispered and prepared to die.

24

ALEX

ALEX TOOK A DEEP BREATH. THE PAPER TREMBLED. "MY NAME IS DR. Alex Cole. I am—" She swallowed. "I am here to—"

I am here to make a confession. I have been lying to you about the safety of mutagenetic food. I have forged data to cover up my dangerous findings . . .

Her eyes slid toward Mansoor. "I'm sorry," she whispered. Mansoor smiled at her. The love and understanding in his eyes made Alex's heart ache.

Alex turned back to the camera. The LED light in her eyes was blinding. She spoke fast, but as clearly as she could. "I'm being held hostage, and they're threatening to kill the man I love. Mutagenetic food is safe. Listen to me. Please. It's our only hope to feed the world. It's—"

Riley yanked the cord out of the tablet and kicked Alex's chair, sending her toppling to the ground. "You sanctimonious lying bitch!" she screamed.

Alex caught herself sharply on her wrist and lay winded on the ground.

MOONRISING

A gunshot rang out, and Alex heard the thud of a body. Short hiccupping sobs wracked her. She could not make herself open her eyes and see Mansoor, dead.

Her choice.

Riley was swearing in a steady stream, and then there were shouts, feet pounding. Alex raised her head, her eyes blurred by tears. It took her a second to understand what she was seeing. Riley, fighting hand-to-hand with a burly black-clad figure. Another ELS member, turning on his leader? Riley knocked him to the ground. But there were more black-clad men—lots more. The scene had become a brawl, the recording equipment lying forgotten on the floor. Chaos. Riley grabbed the detonator from the workstation and pelted from the dome, away down the corridor.

Alex spotted Navin's gun, lying next to a pool of blood and vomit. Adrenaline shot through her, and with it, clarity. She would not allow anyone else she cared about to die today.

She picked up the gun and ran after Riley.

25

MANSOOR

MANSOOR FELT HIMSELF SHOVED TO THE GROUND AS A GUNSHOT rang out. His arm screamed in pain as he toppled onto it. He rolled, panting, onto his back. He was alive; he hurt too much to be dead.

Why was he alive?

He blinked open his eyes and through cloudy vision beheld the worried faces of Rashid and Victor.

"How?" he croaked.

"Hi, elder brother. You look like you could use a drink."

"You're here," Mansoor said in a daze. He struggled to raise himself to a sitting position before giving up and lying back down. "On the Moon. What are you doing here?"

"Rescuing you, of course," Rashid said with a crooked smile. "Well, us and a squad of heavily armed Marines." He looked to Victor. "What do we do?"

"Tourniquet." Victor opened a medical bag and pulled out a black cuff.

MOONRISING

Mansoor blearily turned his head from side to side as Victor fastened the tourniquet above the wound. "Where's Alex?"

Above him, Rashid and Victor exchanged a look.

"She grabbed a gun," Victor said. "And ran after Riley Emerson."

26

ALEX

AFTER RACING PAST THE EMPTY CAFETERIA, ALEX SKIDDED TO A HALT at the junction between the residence hall and the research wing. *Left or right?* She heard a bang and chose left, pelting past the lab workrooms in the direction of the sound.

The door to the soil greenhouse gaped open. Riley stood in the center row, taking big, panting breaths, surveying the room with a curled lip. In her hand, the detonator. Every muscle in Alex's body seemed to be spasming with tension as she beheld Mansoor's killer.

"Murderer," Alex spat. She raised Navin's gun.

Riley smiled, revealing a chipped tooth, and held up the detonator. Her thumb hovered over the trigger. "Put the gun down."

"You'll die," Alex gasped. "All of you will."

"I am not afraid to die for my cause. One Earth, one fight." She brandished the detonator. "Drop. The. Gun."

Alex cast around for a source of inspiration. She was out of ideas. Only her white-hot anger kept her upright. And then, her eyes fell on someone crouched in the left row behind a bed of zucchini leaves, out of Riley's sight.

Kayla.

MOONRISING

She raised bloodshot eyes to Alex's, her face dirty and drawn with exhaustion. Had she been hiding in the greenhouse the whole time?

Alex knelt and placed her borrowed gun on the ground under the shelf containing the zucchini plant. To her knees, she murmured, "She has a detonator rigged to blow up the station. Get it away from her and find help."

Alex rose and advanced slowly toward Riley, hands in the air. Her mind raced. *A distraction.* She needed to keep Riley's attention to give Kayla a chance to act.

Riley watched her movements with upturned lips. "I thought I would end this here, in your abomination. It seems poetic."

Alex reached a shaking hand out and pulled a sprig of rosemary from the middle shelf to the right of the center row. She crushed it between her fingers, releasing a woody scent. Riley wrinkled her nose in distaste. "Stop that." Riley turned her body to face Alex, her view away from Kayla.

Yes.

Alex saw Kayla crawl forward through the left row, the gun in her hand.

"Have you ever tasted roasted rosemary potatoes?" Alex kept her voice light.

"I don't eat potatoes," Riley growled.

"No, of course not. You prefer organic whey protein." Alex smiled. "I *love* potatoes."

Riley's full attention was on Alex, her face frozen in rage. Kayla had moved another foot.

"I like to use red potatoes," Alex continued. "With nothing but a good olive oil, fresh cracked pepper, and sea salt. Let the rosemary shine. If you do it right, the potatoes get crispy on the outside and stay tender on the inside."

Kayla stood and fumbled with the gun. The whir of the greenhouse fans masked the sound.

"Why are you talking about this right now?" Riley yelled at Alex in frustration. "Don't you understand you're about to die?"

"I'd like to die thinking about herbs." She met Kalya's eyes and dropped to the floor.

The pop of a gun sounded over and over. Alex looked up to see a wild spread of bullets lodged in the greenhouse window behind her.

Riley spun around to identify her assailant, and as she did, from her position on the floor, Alex swept her leg under Riley. She fell to the ground. The detonator skidded across the smooth vinyl, under the shelving. For a moment, all three women froze, eyes following the path of the detonator. It halted at Kayla's feet.

Alex held her breath.

The button did not depress.

Kalya snatched the detonator from the floor and pelted back up the corridor to the greenhouse entrance. From the ground, Riley lifted her gun and pointed it at Kayla. Past thinking about her own life, Alex grabbed Riley's bicep, pushing her arm upward. Instead of hitting Kayla, the gun went wide, spraying bullets all around the greenhouse.

Swearing, Riley pushed Alex off her and rose to her feet, fumbling with the extra ammunition strapped to her chest. Alex jumped up, ready to run.

Crack.

Alex and Riley turned their heads to see the greenhouse windows fissured in long jagged lines, peppered with embedded bullets. They were fracturing.

"We need to go," Alex said urgently.

Riley set her teeth in an ecstatic grin. "I'm not going into custody." She grabbed a tray of cucumber plants aloft. With a grunt, she flung the tray toward the nearest glass window. Leaves, soil, and tiny cucumbers spilled onto the greenhouse floor. Grabbing

MOONRISING

another tray, she ran toward the windows again and threw it as hard as she could.

Alex scrambled backward to escape the fallen glass. Air vented from the room with a sucking pull. The plants swayed.

With both arms, Riley scaled the greenhouse's shelving until she reached the ceiling. She took the butt of her gun and, with a shout, slammed it against the splintered windows.

The air whooshed around Alex. The newer small seedlings started to drag out of the soil and lift into the air, smacking against the windows.

"Stop," Alex shouted, her hair whipping around her face. "You'll kill us both!" Plants and soil sailed around her, pulled to the cracks in the ceiling.

As the cracks grew, unfiltered UV sunlight streamed through, bringing with it scorching heat. Alex felt her body pull toward the windows and grabbed a shelf leg. Keeping a two-handed grip on the shelf, she yanked herself backward toward the door one step at a time. The places where the unfiltered sunlight touched her bare skin started turning an ugly red.

Alex ignored the pain on her skin and the dirt in her eyes. She focused all her attention on the door. Each difficult step brought her closer.

Behind Alex, Riley was laughing maniacally as she pounded on the windows over and over. Then, she let out one short piercing scream and was silent.

Alex's curiosity won out, and she turned her head to look back. Riley's body, stuck to the ceiling next to widening cracks, was changing. Her red skin stretched like a balloon, her cheeks swelling and distorting. Bubbling blisters covered her arms.

"Alex!" Kayla shouted over the shrieking air. She had one hand braced on the edge of the doorframe and the other reached out into the greenhouse.

Alex turned away from the horror show that was Riley's body and returned her focus to her goal.

The door.

She took a step, fighting the suck of the vacuum. Her skin burned. The air pulled. The door was still out of reach.

She took another step. Another.

She did not want to die today.

Alex took another step and, reaching, she grazed Kayla's fingers.

Kayla grabbed her hand and pulled her through the door. Alex fell backward into Kayla's arms. Alex remained on her knees as Kayla climbed to her feet. Side-stepping the pull of suction from the open doorway, Kayla pressed the recessed emergency button, and the bulkhead door slammed shut.

Silence.

Stillness.

Alex took a deep breath. She did not think she would ever again get enough oxygen. An ugly red sunburn covered her bare arms, and her entire body trembled with shock and exhaustion.

But she had to see.

To bear witness.

Alex pressed her shaking arms to the ground and forced her body to stand. Leaning on Kayla for support, she hobbled next door to the hydroponic greenhouse. With quivering hands, Alex raised the blackout curtains she had installed so long ago on the hydroponic greenhouse's side windows. She pressed her face against the distorted glass.

In the soil greenhouse, the larger plants were now flying through the air between the cracks in the window. Each time a plant made it through the glass, it shriveled up immediately, like a time-lapse video of decay. On the surface of the Moon, dead withered plants lay scattered, surrounding Riley's hideous swollen body.

MOONRISING

"I handed off the detonator to Drake Douglass before I came back for you," Kayla said softly. "He brought a contingent of Marines to liberate the station. And I could have sworn I spotted that famous scientist Victor Beard among them. I expect the Marines will be along to collect us soon."

"Victor is here?" Alex asked blankly. If anyone could defuse the bombs safely, it would be Victor.

The final pieces of quartz glass shattered, and the remaining plants dropped to the ground as the air inside the greenhouse fully dissipated into the Moon's vacuum.

Alex stared numbly at the ruins. She had lost so much in one day.

Kayla squeezed her shoulder.

"We'll rebuild."

27

VICTOR

VICTOR TURNED OVER THE DETONATOR IN HIS HAND. NEXT TO HIM, Drake frowned. "We could evacuate the station and bring in a bomb squad in thirty-six hours."

Victor gestured to the ragged ELS members sitting on the floor of the dome, their hands zip-tied behind them. "Do they look like the kind of people that build bombs with industry-standard safety features? I can defuse them. It's just physics. All you need is a basic understanding of electrical circuits." Victor looked at Patrick. "Find me a bucket of water."

Patrick glanced at Drake, who nodded soberly.

"This trigger sends out a magnetic pulse," muttered Victor. "The pulse will force each bomb's circuit to close simultaneously and set off the detonators." Did he have enough data to calculate the pulse radius? What was the equation? The product of the mass of the charged particle, the charge, and the velocity perpendicular to the B-field. How could he determine the size of the charge?

Victor looked up with surprise when Patrick returned with a bucket and placed it at Victor's feet. "Ah, thank you." To the

MOONRISING

gathered crowd of Drake, Rashid, Mansoor, Patrick, and a couple other Marines, Victor said, "If you disrupt the magnetic field—" He dropped the detonator into the water. Around him, everyone sucked in a breath. "It will neutralize the detonator."

"Perhaps warn us next time," Mansoor said weakly. He was sitting in a chair with his wrapped arm propped on a desk.

"Trust me," Victor said.

"I do trust you," Mansoor replied fondly. "We all trust you. You saved my life today." He looked around at those assembled. "You all did."

"Well—not yet. First we have to finish the job." Victor turned to Drake. "Take me to the nearest bomb." He looked at Mansoor. "And you, stay here until you can get patched up."

Mansoor gave a weak wave of acquiescence with his left hand.

"I'm coming," Rashid said stubbornly.

The closest bomb was in the corner of a dome conference room. Victor got on his hands and knees to examine it. "It's what I expected. A simple loop of conductive material connected to a battery and a detonator. As long as the circuit remains broken, no charge carries through. If I permanently sever the link between the components, the bomb is disarmed."

Drake silently handed him a pocketknife open to a small sharp pair of shears. Victor hesitated. When had he last studied Kirchhoff's Voltage Law? Or L/R Time Constants? He had been wrong about the safety of the ship prototype. Was he wrong now?

Rashid knelt next to Victor and took Victor's hand. Victor looked up into Rashid's expressive brown eyes. He had never seen such a look of faith and affection. And something else.

Love, Victor realized. *Oh.*

"Are you sure?" Rashid asked.

He looked again at the bomb. He was not trying to measure the voltage drop or the battery's polarity. He only needed to permanently break the circuit. And kiss the man he loved.

Victor squeezed Rashid's hand. "I've never been more sure in my life."

He cut the wire.

Drake let out a slow breath. "Simple enough. Patrick, show the boys what to do and have them gather the detonators for off-site storage until they can be permanently disposed of." They departed, leaving Victor and Rashid alone.

Victor grinned at Rashid. Leaning forward on his knees, he took Rashid's beautiful face gently in both hands and kissed him.

"I wasn't sure if that's how you felt," Rashid whispered when they parted.

"It took me a while to figure it out. How long have you known?"

Rashid's lips twitched. "Since you told me to put a piece of lemon in my mouth."

Victor laughed. "That long?" He kissed him again. "You'll have to be patient with me. I'm a slow learner."

28

ALEX

KAYLA LEFT WITH SEVERAL MARINES TO HELP FREE THE RESIDENTS, leaving Alex alone in the hallway outside the ruined greenhouse. Her adrenaline rush was rapidly fading, leaving her body as withered and dead inside as the plants scattered on the surface of the Moon. All she wanted to do was lay her head down on the hard floor of the hydroponic greenhouse and let sleep bring oblivion. *Not yet.* She forced her aching body to plod back to the dome.

Mansoor was dead.

Had he known, at the end, that she'd forgiven him?

Had he known that she loved him?

At the mouth of the dome, Alex took stock of the situation. The ELS goons were lined against the wall with their hands behind their backs, disheveled and shell-shocked by the turn of events. *Good fucking riddance*, she thought bitterly. Marines moved efficiently around, cleaning up and exchanging information.

Victor shouted, "Alex!" He strode over to her with a grin on his face, holding the hand of a man who looked vaguely familiar to her. "Thank you for sending me the detonator. I neutralized it, and Drake's team is cleaning up the last of the bombs." Victor was *glowing*. There was no other word for it. Alex had never seen such a joyful expression on his face. "This is Rashid," he said possessively.

Rashid stuck out his free hand to shake hers. "Dr. Cole, it is a pleasure to finally meet you." He was smiling too. Both of them were much too happy for the terrible situation.

They didn't know. Alex shivered.

"You're Rashid Al Kaabi?" Alex hazarded. "Mansoor's brother?"

"That's me," Rashid agreed cheerily. "I'm the fun one. He's the brooder."

"I'm sorry to be the one to tell you," Alex began, twisting her hands. "Mansoor is dead. The ELS killed him."

"He better not be dead," Victor objected. "Not after all that work we did to tie off his wound. I am not a fan of blood, but I did my best. A Marine with experience as a field medic is patching him up right now."

Alex froze. "Where?" she managed to croak.

"The medical wing," Rashid said. "We were just headed that way to check on the progress. Care to join us?"

Alex took off running, racing across the dome and into the short medical wing. She banged open the door to the clinic.

Mansoor sat on the hospital cot, his arm propped on a side table while a tall man with blue medical gloves tended to his shoulder. He met her eyes, and his whole body sagged with relief.

"You're alive," Alex breathed.

Mansoor's lips twitched up. "So are you."

Alex stepped to the left side of the clinic bed and took Mansoor's hand in hers. He squeezed her fingers so tightly the bones ground together. She barely noticed the sting on her sunburned hands. "You're alive," she repeated.

Victor knocked on the open door. "Room for two more?"

"For my rescuers? Of course."

"How's our patient?" Rashid asked the Marine medic.

MOONRISING

"He's fine." The medic put down the needle and placed a bandage on Mansoor's shoulder. "I cleaned and stitched the wound. He'll need a tetanus shot and antibiotics. And then some good painkillers and a night's sleep." He rummaged in a cabinet and found a vial labeled Tdap. Alex reluctantly let go of Mansoor's hand to give the medic room to maneuver. As the medic pressed a needle into his uninjured shoulder, he said, "Take one dose of amoxicillin every twelve hours for ten days. And take these for the pain as needed." He handed Mansoor two pills.

The medic looked Alex over. "What happened to you?"

"Direct exposure to UV rays."

"Hm . . ." He went back to the cabinet and found a white tube. "Spread hydrocortisone on the affected areas. And I imagine a dermatologist would recommend annual skin cancer screenings." Alex accepted the cream, and the medic left the room.

"What happened?" Mansoor asked quietly.

"The soil greenhouse is destroyed, and Riley is dead." She explained briefly what had occurred, trying not to dwell on the details. "I wanted to kill her, for what she'd done to you," Alex said to Mansoor. She returned to his bedside and rearranged his pillow. "But I wouldn't wish that death on anyone."

Mansoor lightly caught her sunburnt hand and gently kissed it. "She invited her fate."

Alex grazed her knuckle against Mansoor's stubbled face. She couldn't stop touching him.

He was alive.

"You need to rest." She turned to Victor and Rashid. "So do you. Go. I'll keep watch here."

"When you said her skin swelled, by what percentage?" Victor asked. "Death on the near vacuum of the lunar surface has only been theoretical until now."

Rashid grabbed Victor's hand and said firmly, "Let's go."

Victor flushed. "Right. We'll talk later, Alex."

279

Mansoor blinked after them. "Are they . . .?"

"Yes," said Alex. She brushed a lock of hair from Mansoor's forehead. "And it's recent, judging from the way they both can't wipe the smiles off their faces."

"Huh. I always thought Victor preferred women."

The corner of Alex's mouth turned up. "I don't think gender is important to Victor in a romantic partner. You aren't surprised about Rashid?"

"No, not surprised. A bit scared for him. Victor's fame keeps growing. I am not sure Rashid wishes to be touched by that spotlight."

"They'll figure it out." Alex kissed his brow. "Close your eyes. Get some sleep. I'm here."

29

VICTOR

VICTOR LAY ON RASHID'S CHEST, LISTENING TO THE STEADY BEAT of his heart. He felt calm, his mind quiet and at peace.

"I can't believe I almost let you die without doing that," Rashid murmured.

"I was never in danger of dying," Victor objected. "You're the one that passed out in the middle of space."

Rashid tilted Victor's face up and kissed him, his thumb lingering on Victor's jaw. "You were very brave today."

"So were you. I'm glad you came."

"For what little I did."

"I needed you," Victor said, looking into Rashid's eyes. His lashes were long and beautiful.

Rashid released Victor, who returned to resting his head against Rashid's chest. "It's strange to be here on the colony after all this time supporting it from afar. And strange to be in this luxury hotel bed with you."

Victor angled his head to look at the floor-to-ceiling windows surrounding them on all sides, showing the open surface of the Moon. "I could get used to this view." His brain did not try to calculate the odds of spotting a falling meteor or the diameter of the nearest crater. His mind stayed on the current moment, with Rashid.

"I'm going to come out to my family," Rashid said softly.

"You may have gotten some practice in today," Victor said, thinking of how Rashid had so confidently taken Victor by the hand in front of his brother.

Victor felt Rashid's shoulder move in a shrug. "Mansoor already knew, even though we've never discussed it. I was afraid to bring it up. He can be awfully traditional when it suits him and rigid in his sense of family duty. The rest of my family won't like it, but I think I've earned their respect this past year. I don't want Malik or anyone else to think they have a hold on me. I don't want to have a secret worthy of blackmail."

"Rashid," Victor said hesitantly. "We can do this thing however you want to play it. I know I'm not exactly low-profile, and I can be oblivious, but I can learn to be discreet. You don't need to upend your relationship with your family for me."

"It's not for you; it's for me. I want to be whole." Rashid blew out his breath. "I know the moment I show up as your date to one of those galas or benefits or film premieres they're always inviting you to, I'll be out to the world. I'd first like to talk with my family on my own terms. Then, I think I'd be ready to be seen in public with you." He hesitated. "Unless *you* want to be discreet?"

Victor snorted. "You know I don't. There's nothing discreet about building rocket ships." He reached over Rashid to where his glasses perched on the bedside table and sat up, putting them on to look properly at Rashid. "When I first started dating Harper, Alex warned me that she was trying to change me. I knew Harper wanted me to be better dressed and better groomed, and I figured the benefits outweighed the hassle. What I didn't see at the time was how she wanted me to come across differently. She wanted me to ignore the tangled thread of ideas that pop into my brain at inconvenient times. She wanted me to fit in. To be normal. And I couldn't do it. I felt her disappointment, and it made me pull away. I worked longer hours. I took on more projects. I never put her first."

Rashid made a noise low in his throat. His right arm was tucked under his head while his left hand made small distracting circles on Victor's bare thigh.

"There are only a few people who have seen me for who I am and liked me for it. And with you, I feel like I can just be. My mind can rest. It's nice."

"Nice," Rashid echoed.

"I'm not going to be good at this. I'm going to ignore your messages and forget to leave work. I'm going to bewilder your friends. I will never, ever remember an anniversary. But I think you know all that, don't you?"

"I do." Rashid sat up and reached one long arm around Victor's back. "And I think you're selling yourself short. I think you're going to be very, very good at this."

30

MANSOOR

WHEN MANSOOR OPENED HIS EYES, ALEX WAS THERE, CURLED ON a chair, dozing with her head pillowed in her sunburnt arms.

"Alex," he croaked.

She gave him a sleepy smile.

Mansoor gingerly sat up and pulled the blanket off with his left hand. He reached for a water bottle on the bedside table and took a long swallow.

"How do you feel?" Alex asked.

Mansoor moved his neck from side to side. His shoulder ached with a dull throbbing pain. "Fine, all things considered." Alex handed him an antibiotic and a painkiller before returning to her seat. He swallowed them and pulled himself up to the side of the bed. "Have you been here all this time?"

Alex shook her head. "Julien sat with you for a while to give me a chance to shower."

Mansoor groaned. "A shower sounds excellent."

"Soon," Alex promised. "The medic plans to check the wound."

"Are you alright?"

MOONRISING

"Yes," Alex said quickly.

Mansoor raised his eyebrows.

"I'm healing." She sighed. "I'm not sure. I've been thinking."

"There is a lot to process."

"Yes." Alex blew out her breath. "I think I figured something out. Something important."

"Oh?"

"When my mother died, my father abandoned me. I think it was too painful for him to be in the same room with me. He was never a warm parent, but Mom's death made him ice cold. He barely spoke to me. He couldn't look at me. It made me—" She rubbed her sunburnt face and then winced. "I was afraid to let myself be loved by anyone. I've never really made friends. I spent time with Victor because he wanted to talk plants, not feelings. I dated, but I never let anyone get close. And then I found Navin, who was perfect because I could never trust him. I could argue with him and sleep with him and never be in danger of falling in love. And then . . ." She spread out her hands. "I came here."

"And then you came here."

"You *saw* me. I could feel it immediately. You liked my opinions and my abruptness. You made me feel like I could be my whole self around you without fear of rejection. And with you by my side, I think I finally figured out how to let people in. I finally felt like I belonged." Her eyes filled with tears. "I'm so, so sorry. I know you'll never forgive me. You shouldn't. What I did—not putting you first when Riley had you at gunpoint . . ." She let out one short sob. "It was unforgivable."

Mansoor held out a hand to her, and she rose to take it. He pulled her next to him on the side of the bed. "What you did was brave and selfless. I have never been more in awe of you. You chose humanity's future, Earth's future, over our lives. I would have you make that choice every time."

285

Her lips parted as if she was going to say something, but then the door opened, interrupting the moment. The Marine medic stepped in with Dr. Naomi Berg. Mansoor's whole body went rigid.

"What the hell is she doing here?" Alex demanded.

The Marine winced. "My experience is in field triage, not end-to-end trauma care. I'm out of my depth."

With impersonal fingers, Naomi removed the bandage and checked the wound. "Your sutures look fine. No sign of infection. This will heal well." Naomi turned and rummaged through the cabinet. She pulled out a handheld X-ray device and directed it to his arm. To the medic, she said, "I see why you asked me to come. The bullet is right there." She tapped on the machine. "It's roughly six centimeters from the brachial artery."

Alex frowned, standing to peer into the X-ray. "The bullet is still in his arm?"

"It is. And under normal circumstances, this would not be an issue." She hesitated, showing the first signs of discomfort in her professional facade. "If the bullet shifts, it could lodge in the artery and cause a stroke."

The medic nodded glumly, as if his theory had just been confirmed.

"Is that likely?" Alex demanded.

"Highly likely, given the velocity of a rocket ship. Especially a launch from Earth. You may be alright getting home considering the lower g-force from a lunar launch, but I wouldn't recommend a return visit."

Alex hissed through her teeth.

"Thank you, Dr. Berg," Mansoor said numbly. "If there is nothing else, I am eager to return to my room to freshen up." He was grateful that in the moment he felt blank. He did not want to give Naomi the satisfaction of a reaction.

MOONRISING

When Naomi and the Marine had departed, Alex turned to him. "Can I help?"

Mansoor shook his head. "I think—" He swallowed. "I think I would like to be alone."

Mansoor looked at himself in his tiny bathroom mirror. His distorted reflection looked back, disheveled and exhausted. His eyes were bloodshot, and he was starting to develop a mangy beard. He looked different than the last time he had beheld himself—and it wasn't just the physical signs of exhaustion. He had faced his own death.

He should shower. He had come into the bathroom to do so. But another thought struck him.

When was the last time he had truly prayed?

He thought of his prayer rug, rolled up in his bedroom closet in Boston. He could picture it in such vivid detail. After all, he had knelt on it enough times. It was burgundy with a pattern of emerald and gold. Scratchy. Threadbare. It had traveled with him to England and later to Boston. It would be dusty now after so long sitting unused.

He took a long time with his ablutions, mindful of his injury. He removed his shoes and socks. His feet were stinking with the sweat of his nightmarish ordeal. The water came out of the faucet in a trickle, brackish and pungent. He washed his hands, beginning with the right, then left, carefully conserving the water. As he followed the steps, ingrained in his mind since youth, a deep sense of calm swept over him. He ended with his feet, washing each one to the ankle three times.

He stepped out of the bathroom and cleared a space in the middle of the bedroom floor. He began to pray, whispering the familiar words of the Quran. He bowed and then prostrated himself, his forehead touching the ground. The floor was hard and cold beneath his knees.

As he moved through the ritual, he thought of what his father had taught him. Prayer was an act of meditation. It was the center of every Muslim's personal relationship with Allah. He thought of the deception he had participated in for years, manipulating, coercing, and bribing his way into a place of influence within the American system of governance. He thought of Aliana and Alex, and how he had done them both a disservice. He thought of the man he tried to be for his father and the man he wanted to be for himself. He thought about the moment of peace he had experienced as he prepared to die.

He arose from *sajda*, rocking back on his heels. He recited the *Tashahhud* on his knees and then turned his face to the right and then to the left, reciting the final greeting of peace.

He rose slowly, his aching knees protesting and his shoulder burning. He felt quiet in his mind, his racing thoughts finally under control. Once again at peace.

He had come to a decision.

31

ALEX

ALEX KNOCKED ON THE DOOR TO HER FATHER'S OFFICE. SAUL ROSE with alacrity and came to her side, sweeping her into a crushing hug.

"Ow," Alex said involuntarily.

"Sorry, sorry." Saul stepped back. "I forgot. They told me you were burned."

Alex sank gingerly into a side chair. "It was worse yesterday. Sleep and medicated cream have worked wonders." She did not mention the possibility of skin cancer. That was a problem for the future.

"I saw the broadcast."

"Oh," Alex managed, instantly sobered.

Saul perched on the edge of his desk. "We've reestablished a connection to Earth. You need to know, Alexandra, your face is everywhere. People are calling you—"

Here it comes.

"—a hero."

"A hero," Alex repeated blankly. That couldn't be right. "Hardly. I was ready to let them kill Mansoor."

"You were ready to die for your ideals. You put the future of the human race over the life of someone you love. Alexandra—it's causing a lot of people to rethink their attitudes toward mutagenetic food."

What?

Alex thought about that terrible moment. Mansoor believed she had made the right choice, but she was not so sure. In her lap, her hands trembled. Alex clasped them together to stop the shaking.

Saul let out a breath. "You should never have been put in such a situation. I take full responsibility. I suspected the ELS of causing the fire, and I did not take appropriate action to protect the station."

"It's not your fault. The ELS took us all by surprise." She blamed her father for many things, but this ordeal was not one of them.

"I want you to know, I'm going to push Anderson to approve an agricultural wing as soon as colony repairs are complete. Rebuilding the greenhouse at its existing size is insufficient. I want you to have your olive grove."

"Thank you." Alex felt tears sting her eyes and blinked them back impatiently. She was done crying.

"I'm glad you're safe. I—" Saul hesitated, his throat working. Nothing else came out.

Alex thought about what she had told Mansoor. She had let this emotionally unavailable man impact her entire approach to relationships. There were things she appreciated about her father. He had imparted to her his sense of duty to country and to fellow humans. She could not have made that impossible choice without those values. But duty was not enough. She was done closing herself off from human connection out of the fear of being let down.

Her father was who he was. She could batter her heart against his walls, wishing he would change. Or she could accept this small, tentative relationship.

She could nurture it like a seedling and see if it could grow.

MOONRISING

"I'm glad you're safe too, Dad," she said, rising. "Thank you, for the olive trees."

"Beluga lentils with caramelized onions." Pierre placed a steaming bowl in front of them on the table. "Massaged kale salad. And a cocktail made with unaged whiskey, muddled strawberries, and basil."

Alex took a sip. It was sweet, strong, and herbal. "*This* is made with the astrophysicists' moonshine?"

Pierre scowled. "That *imbécile* has no finesse. But do not worry. I showed Julien how to refine his technique."

"My thanks, Pierre," Mansoor said, raising his glass in his left hand to the chef. "You did not have to make us dinner after all you have been through."

"Those bullies would not let me properly store my shaved onions before they dragged me away. I had to import the Sweet Vidalias at a considerable weight allowance. They needed to be cooked today. It would have been a crime to let them go to waste."

Across the table from her, Alex watched Rashid hide a smile.

"We will clean up here," Mansoor said firmly. "Get some rest, Pierre."

After Rashid served the four of them, Alex closed her eyes and inhaled the scent of the food. She had forgotten how much she missed onions in her diet. When she opened her eyes, Mansoor was watching her with upturned lips.

"How long will you stay?" Alex asked Victor and Rashid.

They exchanged a glance. "Since I'm here, I want to study the grav boots for a few days," Victor said. "And I think your photocatalytic converter could use refinement, Alex."

"Oh?" Alex said, which was all it took for Victor to launch into a detailed explanation of his many ideas for improvements in the hydroponic greenhouse. Alex tried to listen, but her mind was on the conversation next to her.

"Have you spoken to Father?" Rashid was asking Mansoor.

"I plan to in the morning. And Aliana. I cannot be the person Father wants me to be." Alex heard Mansoor let out a sigh. "I hate to hurt Aliana."

"She seems the resilient sort."

"Yes, I think so. But she will not be considered for another marriage of this caliber. The families will remember this."

"Why should she care about marriage anyway?" Rashid scoffed. "She's going to be an engineer."

Alex saw Mansoor smile at his brother. "You never did play by the rules."

"No." Rashid took Victor's hand, and Victor cut off his lecture to Alex in mid-sentence. "I plan to talk to Father as well. In person, after we go home. And our siblings."

"How will they react?" Alex asked.

"Poorly, I think. But I am done living a lie. If that means I can no longer travel to Abu Dhabi, so be it."

"Give our family time," Mansoor said. "They may surprise you in the end."

"It's worth it," Rashid said, looking at Victor. "No matter what happens."

"All of it was worth it," Victor agreed. "Except maybe that death trap we flew in on."

"There's still one thing I don't understand," Alex said, looking around at the three of them. "What was your involvement in the passage of the Homestead Act?"

Rashid grinned into his cocktail. Mansoor and Victor exchanged a glance. "We wrote it," Mansoor said finally. "And then we shopped it around Washington."

"You wrote it," Alex repeated. "And then you, what? Bribed politicians into passing it?"

MOONRISING

"If only it was so easy," Rashid muttered.

"Nothing illegal," Mansoor said. "But everyone has a price. Senators want Super PAC donations, of course, but they often respond better to something more personal, such as a large donation to the children's hospital that cured their child's brain cancer or an internship in Abu Dhabi for their niece."

Alex raised her eyebrows at Victor. "Or ten years of unrestricted funding to an obscure university lab?"

"Or some really good poetry," Victor added.

"And you believe, you really believe, that there will be a million people living in space in our lifetime?" she said, addressing all three men.

"I do," said Mansoor. "We have the right infrastructure in place. We needed two elements: rapid mass transit to the Moon and political will. In Abu Dhabi, we moved from a nomadic desert tribal people to modern urbanites with global ambitions in a single generation. We will do something similar here."

"So, you looked at Victor, who was an executive in the agricultural industry with a PhD in biological and environmental engineering, and decided he was going to build rocket ships?" Alex asked dubiously.

"Have you met me?" Victor said, indignant. "It was just physics. And our plan is working already. Everyone wants in on my ships: NASA, the European Space Agency, the Indian Space Research Organization. Peary Station is just the beginning. Every country will build their own station before long. Even Abu Dhabi if the ambassador has anything to say about it."

"Malik wants an independent Emirati station?" Mansoor asked in surprise.

Victor's face turned dark. "Malik wants many things."

"He warned me off our lobbying efforts. He didn't want the American colony to be too far ahead of an Emirati colony," Rashid

293

said quietly. "I know I should have told you, but—" Victor took Rashid's hand and squeezed it. "He tried to blackmail me."

"What!" Mansoor's eyebrows drew together.

"Victor handled it. And soon I won't have anything to hide. He won't have any power over me."

"You're turning into quite the dashing rescuer," Alex said to Victor. "How did you know that the ELS was so dangerous? How did you know to take matters into your own hands rather than wait for an official NASA response?"

"They told me." Victor put his fork down. "Riley and Navin and the others came to my factory and they as good as told me they planned to take drastic action to stop the growth of the colony. I didn't listen and I didn't tell anyone. I wish—" He looked at Rashid. "I wish I had done a lot of things differently. Maybe if I had, your colleague Mitch Cooper would still be alive. And, Alex, I'm sorry Navin died."

Alex swallowed a lump in her throat. "He died for me. In his stupid misguided way, he really cared about me. I keep thinking if I had only let him in, shared more of myself with him, he wouldn't have gotten so lost."

"There's blame enough to go around," Mansoor said. "I am immensely grateful to all of you. We protected the colony. This dream. Together."

Alex looked at Mansoor. She knew what it felt like to be betrayed by him. She knew what it felt like to lose him. There was something inside her that wanted to run. To put up those walls again. To protect her heart.

Instead, she reached out a hand for his. *Together.*

32

MANSOOR

HE SPOKE TO HIS FATHER FIRST.

The man looked old, tired, and defeated. "I have always wanted what is best for you, my son. I thought you would find fulfillment in a life of family and faith, at home where you belong."

"I am sorry," Mansoor said, his throat tight. "I wish I could be the man you want me to be. I have tried, Father, for so long."

His father regarded him for a long moment without speaking before saying, "You have done well. I am proud of all you have accomplished. And I am relieved that you and your brother are safe after the attack. I may not agree with this choice you have made, my son, but I must respect it."

"Your respect is of great value to me. Thank you, Father."

Mohammed grunted. "Tell me, this American scientist, Dr. Alex Cole, is she worthy of you?"

Mansoor thought of the fragile trust he and Alex were rebuilding. "The question you should ask, Father, is if I am worthy of her. And the answer is, I will try to be, every day."

While speaking with his father was not as difficult as he feared, the confrontation with Aliana had been excruciating.

"I never expected you to be celibate after our engagement," she said matter-of-factly, looking straight at him with those beautiful brown eyes. "Or faithful after our wedding. You were planning on spending half your time in Boston. Men have needs."

"People have needs," he broke in. "Not just men. You would have discovered that soon enough. A husband halfway around the world would not have been enough for you."

"I would have welcomed the chance to try. I know we had not publicly announced our engagement, but I had told my friends. I was planning the wedding with my mother and my sisters. I was picturing a life with you. And now you are at the center of this public romance with someone else. You have embarrassed me."

He had nothing to say to that. She was right. He had known he was in love with someone else, for all he had tried to ignore his feelings. If he had been honest with himself, perhaps he could have found the courage to be honest with her.

"I'm sorry," he said with humility. "You deserved better."

"I did," she agreed. "Goodbye."

When the conversation ended, Mansoor closed his eyes and rubbed his face. He would bear the guilt. But he felt lighter.

He was ready, at last, to find himself.

"I'm glad we're doing this." Alex's head rested on Mansoor's good shoulder as they lay on a blanket, looking out the hotel restaurant windows. "Do you remember the first time we saw a shooting star together?"

"Mm-hmm," Mansoor said against her hair. "On the ship. It was one of the most memorable experiences of my life. I am glad I got to share it with you."

"I've never spent much time looking at the sky," Alex mused. "You could see stars in Ithaca, but I was too busy with my hands in the dirt."

MOONRISING

"I've been to the desert with my father and brothers many times. The night sky around a campfire is something to behold." He loved camping on the orange-red dunes among the date palm trees. He wondered if he would ever have the chance to see it again. "I believe that's *Ad-Dubb Al-Akbar*. Ursa Major, the Great Bear. The orientation is different here."

"I can't see it."

"Let me show you." Mansoor took her hand and slowly traced the pattern. "That star is *Merak*. My father calls it *Maraqq ad-Dubb al-Akbar*."

"What does that mean?"

"The loins of the greater bear," Mansoor admitted.

Alex let out a giggle and then sobered. "Did you speak with your father?"

"I did. And Aliana. I ended the engagement."

"Was your father very disappointed in you?"

"He was. My father has done nothing but love me and support me my entire life." Mansoor propped himself on his elbow to look at her. "I cannot regret finally being true to myself. I only wish I had found a path to myself that did not hurt so many along the way."

"I know." Alex sat up and reached for her wine cup. "I've been thinking about what I want. For so long, the Institute was all I cared about. I thought if I could just produce the right seeds and develop the right techniques, I could find respect. But here on the colony, I learned how to create real influence. It's not about winning the argument. It's about meeting people where they are. You taught me that. And Sandra. And Carson. And my father. Even Kayla."

Mansoor took a sip of his wine, listening.

"I think the Institute will do fine without me. What happened—" She swallowed. "It was horrible. But—it shifted the narrative. I can't say I'm glad it happened. But I don't know if people's minds would have changed without it. Mansoor—people are starting to see mutagenetic food as safe. Do you know how long I fought for that? It was like beating my fists against a brick wall. And now— I have correspondence going with half a dozen young scientists who are interested in continuing the work of the Institute."

"What are you saying?"

"More progress has happened in the ten months I've been here than the rest of my *life*. I want to be the one who plants fields of wheat on the Moon. I want to figure out how to raise goats ethically in a closed ecosystem. I want to see the apple trees bear fruit. I want to stay."

Mansoor sat up and looked at her. He thought about the prayer he had made, the night he had come to a decision. He was not sure what role faith had in this new, unified life he was building for himself. He had not yet unraveled how he could serve Allah and his country and his family while staying true to himself. The one thing he knew was that he wanted Alex by his side as he figured it out.

"I want to stay, too."

"Good," Alex said with a relieved little laugh. "Even if it means you can never return to Earth?"

"Ah, well, I think I will get a second opinion from a doctor that did not try to have me killed." He pulled her to her feet. Cupping her face, he said, "Yes, I want to stay here with you for as long as you'll have me." He gave her a soft, gentle kiss.

They turned to look up again in time for a shooting star to streak through the black sky.

33

VICTOR

RASHID FINALLY RELENTED TO VICTOR'S PERSISTENT HINTS AND threw himself an art show.

Rashid's paintings were gorgeous, of course. Some were more classic—pristine, archetypal images of the Moon, Earth rise, and the colony dome. Victor's favorites were the messier, more unconventional paintings. Rashid had captured the beautiful, chaotic, and raw reality of the laboratories, robots, hydroponic greenhouse, and kitchen.

The Upper West Side gallery was packed. Some guests Victor knew, like a beaming Sena next to a reserved Malik. Rashid's friends had turned out in abundance. They were a motley collection of artists, actors, and academics. To Victor's surprise, they seemed to like him. Harper's friends had never seemed to enjoy his presence.

The spread of food was lavish, showing off recipes from Chef Pierre's new cookbook featuring mutagenetic produce served at the lunar hotel. The marinated cherry tomato skewers were especially popular that evening. Victor had eaten four of them.

The event had been underway for an hour when the door opened, and a tall woman wearing a headscarf entered. Rashid, laughing with Teru and a group of the Beard Enterprise techs, froze. He grabbed Victor by the hand and threaded his way through the crowd to the door.

"Latifa," Rashid said softly. "You came."

"I apologize for my tardiness, little brother. My flight was delayed." Latifa looked around at the artwork on display. "Did you paint all of these?"

"I did." Rashid cleared his throat. "Latifa, this is Victor. My—my partner."

"It is nice to finally meet the great Victor Beard," Latifa said. "I have heard many stories of what you have done for Abu Dhabi." She turned to Rashid. "Father sends his compliments on the launch of your show. He requests that you call him when you are ready, and he will make an introduction for you to the head curator of the Cultural Foundation."

"He will?" Rashid looked startled.

"He loves you, little brother. Very much."

Rashid squeezed Victor's hand and let it go. "Let me introduce you to Administrator Anderson. He's worked closely with Mansoor on the hotel. And you'll like Senator Jones."

Victor watched them walk away, seeing the way Rashid straightened and grew lighter as he escorted his sister through the gallery.

Later, when the party was in full swing, Rashid grabbed a microphone and stepped up to the low dais. "Good evening. Thank you for coming. Two months ago, I had the opportunity to go to the Moon as part of a clandestine mission to take the colony back from invaders who threatened it. While there, I was able to bear witness to the remarkable resilience of the residents as they weathered a violent invasion of their home and rebuilt from the attack.

"Most of you have not had the opportunity to visit the Moon. I am optimistic that, someday, working or visiting the Moon will be accessible to many more of us; in the meantime, I hope these

MOONRISING

paintings give you a glimpse into the colony as it existed before the boom."

Rashid looked at Victor fondly and raised his champagne glass in his direction. "I'm joined tonight by Victor Beard. Tomorrow, the first homesteaders will be emigrating on the inaugural voyage of a new Beard Enterprise rocket ship. They'll make their home on the colony and start the first families on the Moon. The age of the space revolution has begun."

When all the guests had departed, Rashid bumped his shoulder against Victor's. "You were right. Thank you for bullying me into this."

"I didn't bully. I never bully. I persuaded with my superior logic."

"Threatened," Rashid said, grinning. He kissed Victor, in full view of the window. "What's next, do you think?"

"You mean besides constructing enough rocket ships to keep up with the American demand?"

Rashid waved a hand. "Victor, you have a ship model. You don't need to personally oversee the building of every rocket ship, as much as you'd like to be breathing down your team's necks, terrorizing them into working harder."

There were plenty of options. Helium-3 mining, artificial gravity, a rocket ship built to make the journey to Mars. To Rashid, he said, "What's next is that I'd like to take you home and commission from you a very creative self-portrait with perhaps some hands-on client input. And then, tomorrow, I'd like to make plans to turn this art exhibition into a world-tour to make 'the age of the space revolution' into a household phrase. Can we do that?"

Rashid kissed him again, smiling against his mouth. "Yes, I like the sound of that." He opened the studio door, and they stepped into the Manhattan night.

34

ALEX

"HOW DOES IT FEEL?" FINN ASKED ALEX. "TO BE LEAVING THE university?

Alex pulled up her legs on the phone booth chair. "I didn't expect to resign. I always thought the end of my career in Chicago would come with the university kicking me out and shutting down the lab."

"There's little danger of that now," Finn said. He was taking her call from the Institute greenhouse, and Alex could see the thriving plants around him. "Everyone wants to be eating the food they serve on the famous lunar hotel, grown by the heroic Dr. Alex Cole."

Alex gave an uncomfortable shrug. "How do you like the new director?"

"I miss you. We worked together so long it was like we could read each other's minds." He grinned. "Though she's a lot nicer than you."

"She hasn't made a postdoc cry?"

"Nope. We are tear-free over here."

MOONRISING

"I'll visit, sometime," Alex offered. "But I'm not sure when I'll be able to get away. We're expecting twenty new arrivals per week for the foreseeable future, and there's so much to do. I'm going to need all the help you can give me to build the new agricultural wing."

"I'll be here."

Alex waved and cut the comm. When she stepped out of the booth, the dome was buzzing with activity.

Kayla spotted her and gestured in welcome. "The ship is scheduled to arrive in a few minutes."

Alex joined the other residents hurrying to the hallway near the hangar bay. She found her designated spot against the wall.

Mansoor slipped in beside her, rubbing his shoulder. "Carson seems awfully keen on this plan."

Alex made a face. "I know."

"Places," Carson bellowed in his best football captain voice and found his own spot next to Julien, across from Mansoor and Alex.

The light outside the doors lit green, indicating the hangar bay had repressurized. Two members of the Space Force team opened each door and held them formally. From her place in line, Alex could see the latest Beard Enterprise ship. It was white, with blue and red ribbons wrapped around. *Homestead* was emblazoned on the side.

Saul, with a wink to Alex, gestured Sandra into the hangar bay to greet the new arrivals.

The rest of the one hundred residents waited silently, in long lines stretching down the corridor leading all the way to the central dome. Everyone had come. Kayla had put the mining robots on autopilot for the morning. Herb had torn himself away from his machines. Pierre had arrived grumbling from the hotel kitchen. Natalia had left her research. Carson had abandoned his rocks.

The twenty people arriving from the ship stepped slowly into the hallway, and the residents broke into a cheer. Sandra held her wife's hand in a tight grip and tears streamed down her face. The woman looked wide-eyed and delighted at the warm reception.

"Welcome to the colony," Saul said, his voice raised above the shouting. "Welcome home."

Alex felt a surge of love rise up inside her. For the colony, for her father, for Mansoor. It was terrifying, to feel so much hope. To care so deeply for others. Terrifying, but worth it.

Alex caught Mansoor's eye and smiled. "Welcome home," she echoed.

Outside, the robots toiled away to build the next batch of family quarters. Tomatoes were ripening on the vine. The chickens were clucking around in the hen house. Slowly, oh so slowly, apple trees were creeping up in the park. The Moon was awakening, alive and growing. It was just the beginning.

ACKNOWLEDGMENTS

I first started *Moonrising* over a decade ago, and when I reflect back to my state of mind pre-kids and several jobs ago, I can pinpoint the first ideas for this book to two things: Richard Branson announcing plans to build a spaceport in Abu Dhabi and NASA successfully growing red romaine lettuce on the International Space Station (ISS). Since then, Richard Branson has flown to the edges of space. NASA has cultivated a crop of chili peppers on the ISS. Project Artemis is moving forward to establish a permanent Moon base. The UAE Space Agency (UAESA) attempted to send a lunar rover named Rashid to the Moon.

And a commercial spaceport in Abu Dhabi? In 2025, with Virgin Galactic halting their suborbital spaceflight program, its future is unclear. We may need to wait for Mansoor and Victor to pick the idea back up in 2073.

Moonrising's characters and subject matter contain many things outside my lived experience, none more so than Mansoor and his family's culture and faith. I am grateful to my sensitivity reader, Hagar El Saeed, who helped me ensure the Arabic phrases, references to Islam, and scenes in Abu Dhabi were respectful. I appreciate the many resources the Chicago Public Library has to offer on the UAE, and I spent countless hours at the Harold Washington Library studying this fascinating place. I am also indebted to Omar Saif Ghobash, whose book *Letters to a Young Muslim* helped form my understanding of Mansoor's father's worldview and dreams for

AKNOWLEDGMENTS

his children. I will be following with great interest the progress of the UAESA missions to the Moon and Mars.

After my twins were born in 2019, I put *Moonrising* on hiatus, and I was unsure if I'd ever have the bandwidth to finish it. In the summer of 2023, I was able to take a ten-week paid sabbatical from my job where I finally finished the first draft of *Moonrising*. During my sabbatical, I experienced, for the first time the joy of being a full-time writer. I especially enjoyed my daily writing time at local coffee shops in my neighborhood on the northwest side of Chicago, including the Perkolator and Junebug Cafe. I am grateful to the leaders at the Financial Health Network, Jennifer Tescher and Kelly Emery, for offering a paid sabbatical to employees as a benefit after eight years of service. You gave me the greatest gift of all—time.

I am grateful to so many others who helped me along the way.

To the many educators in my life. Mr. Francis, my fourth and sixth grade teacher, who encouraged my love of writing. Ms. Gerber, my middle school language arts teacher, who taught me how to look critically at my writing. Mr. Marino, my AP Physics teacher, who spent so many hours with me before and after school whiteboarding challenging physics problems. Lonnie Bunch, Marie Scatena, Ray Yang, and Angela Rivers, my mentors through the Chicago History Museum's Teen Chicago program, who pushed my boundaries and helped me to expand my worldview beyond my own cultural lens.

To my agent, Jenna Satterthwaite. You changed my life. I am grateful for your partnership and friendship. Your enthusiasm and honest critique of *Moonrising* has meant everything to me. I wouldn't be here without you. To Team Jenna, the wonderful group of agent siblings I've had the joy of getting to know this past year. And to my editor Toni Kirkpatrick at Diversion Books for your love of these characters and this story. I look forward to our continued partnership.

AKNOWLEDGMENTS

To my friends. To Stacy Huston and Andrew Hamilton, who read the very first version of this story and helped shape it. To Joy Parkhurst for being a valued critique partner and supportive friend. To Bennett Parkhurst for providing a second pair of eyes on *Moonrising*'s science. To Andy Bandyopadhyay for your enthusiasm and mutual love for our favorite author, Lois McMaster Bujold. To my book club, led by Amy Hinsley, who helped me develop a sharper reading lens. To my University of Chicago friends and their partners Harriet Fertik, Isaac Epstein, Jared Sagoff, Paulina Gonzalez-Latapi, James Beatty, Kate Nagle, Andrew Hamilton, Kira Bennett Hamilton, Elliot Hasden, Diana Hasden, and Nikhil Raghuram, for your friendship, love, and support for the last two decades. I hope you enjoyed the glimpse of Jimmy's in 2073.

And finally, most importantly, to my family. To my husband, Rufus Barner, and our three children, Marcus, Miles, and Logan, for cheering me on and supporting my dream even when it's taken away our time together. To my parents, Craig Elderkin and Debby Scheck; my siblings, Grace Elderkin, Luke Elderkin, Nora Elderkin, Lily Elderkin, and Isabelle Elderkin; my brother-in-law Justin Dipietro; and my godmother Virginia Selleck for lovely brainstorming sessions about *Moonrising* over wine, editing and critiquing so many versions of this novel, responding to frantic emergency writing help texts, and for caring about these characters and this story. I appreciate and love all of you, and I would not have been able to accomplish this lifelong dream without you.